THE TEACHER'S NOBLE HEART

A TENDER REGENCY TALE OF LOVE AND DEFIANCE ON THE EDGE OF CORNWALL'S WINDSWEPT MOOR

DOUBLE-DILEMMA ROMANCE
BOOK FIVE

SUSANNE DUNLAP

The Teacher's Noble Heart

First Paperback Print Edition: 2026

Published by Comfortable Prose Publishing
Cover design by 100Covers
ISBN: eBook: 979-8-9938526-7-6; Paperback: 979-8-9938526-8-3

Every word of this book was written by the author. AI tools were used in a supporting role for research, analysis, and marketing.

For Keith on his 80th birthday.
Thanks for being my intrepid partner on long walks in Cornwall so many years ago.

CHAPTER 1

Antonella, Lady Atherleigh, finished reading Friday's copy of the *West Briton* weekly newspaper and laid it on the breakfast table.

"Anything of interest?" Persephone asked, sipping her almost-cold cup of coffee. Although she normally preferred the London papers when she could get them, she reached for the single folded sheet of newsprint and glanced at it.

Before she could peruse it though, Antonella said, "Oh, only the usual nonsense. What will you do today, Persephone?"

Her Christian name on the tongue of her former charge, who for nine years had called her Miss Wilkins, still startled Persephone. "I expect I shall occupy myself much as I did yesterday, unless there's something you would like me to do for you?" She very much wished there was.

"No, nothing. I have my riding lesson this morning, then Malcolm and I will spend some time with Rafiq and the new gyrfalcon. We have been invited to Lord and Lady Abingdon's for dinner this evening, don't forget, so I'm afraid you'll be on your own." She gave a rueful half smile.

"Of course. I shall spend most of my time reading, I imagine. I finally received the first volume of *The Wanderer* from the library in Bodmin. It is quite a departure for Madame D'Arblay. I should like you to read it when I finish." Persephone immediately regretted saying that. She couldn't help slipping back into her role as a teacher, especially since she still lived with her favorite pupil—who happened also to be her niece, although no one beside herself knew it until a few months ago.

Antonella reached across the table and laid her hand on Persephone's arm. "I will if I have time. But you must understand that my life is very different now."

"Of course, silly of me!" Antonella's hint was kind, but it stung nonetheless. Her life *had* changed. And not just Antonella's life, but everything about Persephone's world had been transformed as well. She thought that no longer having to work would bring her freedom and leisure, give her the ability to pursue things that she had to put aside when she was busy managing the education of two spirited young ladies. Instead, it simply made her feel empty and purposeless.

"Heavens! Is that the time? I must leave you, I'm afraid." Antonella jumped up from her chair, ran around the table and planted a quick kiss on Persephone's cheek, then dashed away.

Persephone sighed, poured herself a second cup of coffee, and picked up the newspaper again. It reported the local goings on—visitors of note, the assemblies, local politics, the assizes—things that didn't hold much interest for her. She supposed that was why she skipped over so much of it.

Until, that is, her eye was caught by a small caption separating a paragraph of dense text at the bottom of the "Cornwall Intelligencer" page, right next to an advertisement for a milliner in Bodmin who promised a new selection of hats and bonnets of the latest styles.

Tragic Accident at Delabole

Delabole. She knew of the place, of course. It was an enormous slate quarry about ten miles away. Yet in all her years living in Cornwall, Persephone had never seen it, or even really thought much about it. She knew it as the source of the finest slate in the kingdom, furnishing roofs and flagstones for homes and towns throughout England, but that was all.

Curious, Persephone read the entire piece. It didn't go into much detail about the nature of the accident. A rockfall, apparently. Some error in blasting. It did, however, name the victims and give their ages. Three boys: fourteen, eleven, and nine years old. Children! They should be at their lessons, not laboring in dangerous jobs. Of course, she knew about the children who worked in the Cornish copper mines, mostly above grass, and had long felt dismayed by their plight. But she had never considered that children might work at a slate quarry, and that this practice occurred so close to where she sat in luxurious comfort.

She folded the paper neatly and placed it on the sideboard before rising, coffee cup in hand, her mind still disturbed by what she had read. All her life, although she had not always been in affluent circumstances, she'd been sheltered from such harsh realities. As she glanced around her at the elegant sweep of the grand stair in the central hall, the ornate wainscoting, the polished brass fittings and gleaming floors, she tried to imagine an altogether different world and found she couldn't. Or perhaps, she didn't want to. Yet something at the back of her mind told her she *ought* to.

She headed toward the back stairs, intending to go down to the kitchens and perhaps out to the garden, when the butler came in from the saloon. He cleared his throat and said, "I beg your pardon, Miss Wilkins."

Persephone stopped and turned. "What is it, Penrose?"

"Jenkins just returned from the receiving office and a letter for you was among the letters for Lord and Lady Atherleigh." He held it out to her.

She took it from him. "Thank you."

Persephone hadn't expected any letters that day—only yesterday she received one from Antonella's half-sister Belinda, and Lady Lewiston's had arrived a few days before that. A quick glance at the direction and she was none the wiser. She did not recognize the handwriting. It couldn't be from anyone in her family. Her father—her only living relative—had cut off all communication with her when at the age of twenty-two she chose to become a governess rather than marry a worthy but dull curate.

Instead of continuing to the kitchen, Persephone placed her empty cup on a table in the hall and went upstairs to her bedchamber. Something told her she would want privacy as she read this letter. The unfamiliar handwriting was very neat and elegant, giving it a rather official air. The wafer that sealed it was black.

She took a seat at the deal table that served as her desk, unsealed and unfolded the letter to discover that it came from an attorney's office in Taunton, the closest town to her father's rural parish.

We regret to inform you ...

Her father was dead. Her mother had died years ago, before Persephone came to Amblemere as governess. *I'm an orphan,* she thought. Can one be called an orphan at the age of one and thirty? From somewhere buried deep in her memory a pang of loss rose and pricked her eyes with the threat of tears. That was foolish. Her father had been a stern, uncompromising man who saw everything as either good or evil. That neither of his daughters lived up to his high moral expectations damned them both in his eyes.

Some feeling of parental responsibility must have troubled his conscience toward the end, however, because he left all he had to Persephone, his only living child. The vicarage belonged to the church, of course, but he had a small farm outside of town that he rented out and a modest income from the funds. Altogether it amounted to a few hundred pounds a year. This would now go to her. The attorneys wanted to know if she was content to allow the current tenants of the farm to remain or if she wished to sell it, as well as what her banking arrangements might be so she could receive the income from the estate—small as it was.

Persephone laid the letter down on the desk and looked out the window to her view of the grounds and the woods beyond. This changed nothing. Or perhaps it changed everything. The idea of those children at Delabole still disturbed her. She keenly felt the contrast between her now even greater ease and affluence and the poverty that made it necessary for children to labor at jobs only strong adults ought to perform.

Without another thought, Persephone wrapped her paisley shawl around her and left her bedchamber in such a daze that she didn't even close the door. *I must find Antonella.*

The two startling revelations combined were beginning to answer the unformed question that had been plaguing her for months. She now knew without hesitation that she must be employed in some fashion. Antonella loved her but did not *need* her. Even if she had children soon, they would not be old enough to require a governess for many years.

She was not made for idleness. Yet she felt tied to Atherleigh by affection and dependence. Now, though, one of those ties had loosened. She had an independence and it was up to her what to do with it. Teaching was her passion, it always had been. Why could she not bring her talents to the education of those children who faced little beyond a life of grueling work? It would mean leaving the luxury and comfort of Atherleigh Manor, as well as leaving Antonella. It followed, too, that she would find her status in the world significantly diminished. But had it ever been very high? Most people thought little of governesses even when their pupils were of the loftiest rank.

As to leaving Antonella, she would miss her, but she could bear it. And she was certain that Antonella could as well. She might, in fact, be relieved. After all, Persephone wasn't proposing to move to America or India. Delabole was an easy ride for a visit.

All I need is affordable accommodations—with space for a small schoolroom, of course. Somewhere close to the quarry.

A little thrill bubbled up in Persephone's stomach as her plans began to take shape. She had a purpose again—or she would soon, in any case. She could use her abilities not just to train society hostesses, but to enlighten the minds of those whose horizons were limited by poverty.

Such a decision would mean leaving everything familiar behind. It was frightening. Frightening—and exhilarating. More so even than choosing to become a governess to her late sister's bastard child, who had been adopted as an infant by her lover's family. But even in that case she had gone from one familiar situation of relative ease to another.

Now, she prepared to take a leap into the unknown. She might face disaster. She might find this was the worst decision she'd ever made.

Or she might just discover what it meant to work for the betterment not of spoiled aristocrats, but of children whose lives were sorely limited by circumstance.

I should probably take some time to think it over. That would be the wise course, her ever-sensible mind told her. But she was tired of being wise.

It was time to start living a different life. Those unknown children at Delabole needed her. And if Persephone knew one thing about herself for certain, she needed to be needed.

CHAPTER 2

James Pentarrant took in the sight of the party guests got up in their finery, all smiling and laughing and flirting, and felt sick. They filled the large drawing room at his brother's fine house—built when Eustace married, on a part of the family estate far enough away from Delabole quarry so that not a hint of the noise or dust from the works need remind him of where his prosperity came from. Pentarrent Lodge—the old Tudor manse that had housed the family for generations and where James still lived—was not large enough for his brother's pretensions. Instead, Eustace must live in a structure with more rooms than he would ever need. The thought disgusted James. In fact, almost everyone in that elegant room—with its silk draperies, gilt-framed pictures, and handsome furniture—derived their fortunes from the quarry or some aspect of the business associated with it. And they were equally glad to put as much distance between themselves and it as they could.

"Come James!" Eustace said, breaking free from a group of older men laughing and sharing some story or other. He sauntered over to his younger brother and held out a cut crystal glass filled with expensive champagne. "I won't have you lurking about in the sullens. The Morrison girls are here. And I expect at any moment that Felix Tresillian and his lovely daughter will arrive. That should cheer you up!"

Oh, there was that. The entire extravagant affair had been arranged for the sole purpose of throwing the seventeen-year-old daughter of the wealthiest businessman in Camelford at him. The Pentarrants were to appear as if they were not in need of an alliance that would bring a fortune to their coffers and avoid having to cut workers at the quarry, and so the entertainment must be lavish. Right at that moment, James could imagine nothing less appealing than pretending all was well and courting a girl who was half his age. "I came because you asked me to, and I'll do the pretty. But I'm in no mood to celebrate."

"You mustn't take it so to heart, Jamie! It wasn't your fault after all."

"Was it not? Someone has to take it to heart."

Eustace tsked and wagged a finger at him. "What was good enough for our father is good enough for us. Besides, there are profits enough for all."

James decided there was no point trying to get his indolent older brother to understand that being a principal investor in and manager of the largest slate quarry in the country meant more than just reaping the financial gains. It was a responsibility. Hundreds of families depended on them for their livelihoods. The work was back breaking and often dangerous. Just that morning he had attended the funeral at St. Teath's of the three lads who were killed in the recent rock fall. He could not help noticing that he was the only one of the quarry's investors or managers who had taken the time to attend and bring what comfort they could to the families.

All James wanted to do was go back to his own home

nearer the quarry to pore over the plans and try to figure out what happened, what might have prevented the disaster. He acknowledged, however, that he had a duty to the family name as well. The Pentarrants were not titled, but they were of old Cornish stock and one of the first families of the county. Their grandfather had been a member of Parliament, and they had interests in everything from the quarry to banking to a few copper mines.

All that had once supported them handsomely. But then Eustace married the Honorable Catherine Woodson, daughter of Viscount Fothergill. She brought what seemed an ample dowry, aristocratic connections, beauty, and extravagant habits to the match. The dowry barely covered her demands for carriages, liveried manservants, and jewels.

A burst of feminine laughter made James look across the room to see his sister-in-law, arrayed in costly silks and diamonds—which did nothing to hide her expectant condition—smiling serenely at her guests, all of whom tittered along with her at whatever amusing nothing she had just uttered. Catherine wasn't unintelligent. She simply chose to perform the role she'd been trained for, and did it with grace and elegance.

James gulped down the champagne, vaguely hoping it would go to his head and deaden the sense of guilt and shame he couldn't seem to shake.

At that moment, the aged butler, Tonkin, came to the door of the drawing room and announced, "Mr. Tresillian and Miss Tresillian."

Time to do my duty, James thought. It wasn't the girl's fault he felt such a fraud. What did it matter, after all, who he married? He once thought he was in love, but that had all been a lie. He doubted he was capable of anything warmer than affection. If this young lady was his brother's choice for him, he felt a bit sorry for her. Did she know she was the sacrificial lamb about to be slaughtered on the altar of commerce? And that the marriage everyone wanted to arrange for her would be very little more than a formality?

The delicately pretty blond and blue-eyed young lady stood next to her florid-faced, paunchy father like an orchid that had lost its way to the conservatory and happened to sprout up next to a toadstool. Sophia Tresillian was the acknowledged beauty of the district. James was grateful for that at least. Marrying her would not be distasteful. They would be able to satisfy the usual requirements of breeding. And she was apparently sweet and well mannered. Her ambitious father had taken care to have her well schooled in the ways of the fashionable. But could she do anything that was actually useful, other than bear children?

The smile of amusement at that thought still lingered on his face when Tresillian led his daughter over to him. "Pentarrant! Good to see you, eh? You remember Sophie—I mean, my daughter Miss Tresillian."

"Of course," James said, taking the girl's hand and bowing over it as she blushed a becoming shade of pink and looked down. She was a mere child the last time he'd seen her and he couldn't shake that image. "I gather you are but recently returned from school in Bath. Did they teach you anything?" It slipped out before he could think better of it.

The sarcasm was lost on Tresillian, however, who said, "They deuced well better have! Cost me a pretty penny, that seminary stuffed with honorables and ladies."

"Papa!" Miss Tresillian's blush deepened. "I'm sure Mr. Pentarrant does not wish to hear of my boring school days. He well knows I have emerged accomplished, but barely educated."

He did not expect her self-deprecation. So, she wasn't just a simpering miss after all. If she'd been rubbing elbows with ladies above her on the social ladder, her father's rough heartiness no doubt caused her mortification. The contrast between the rarified atmosphere of privilege at the seminary and the all-too-real world of industry at her family home must be a bit painful. "I'm certain you gained some useful knowledge for your future life, Miss Tresillian. After all, education need not always be culled from books."

Tresillian harrumphed. "So say you, who wasted three years at Cambridge when you could have already started making your fortune as captain of the Delabole works."

Poor Miss Tresillian! However, she appeared to take her father's social ineptitude with equanimity. "Do you find much to entertain yourself with in Camelford?" James asked in a futile attempt to change the subject.

"And speaking of learning," the merchant said, clinging to the topic like a particularly determined dog with a marrow-bone. "I just let a cottage I couldn't get off my hands to a lady who fancies herself a teacher. I told her there's no schools here and all the young ladies of any breeding go off to Bath or Bristol to get their polishing, but she insisted she wanted the house."

Pentarrant thought he knew the dwelling Tresillian spoke of. Better built and larger than the mean hovels most of the laborers' families occupied, it even had a small barn and a garden of sorts. It dated from two centuries or so ago when its situation was not so unfavorable. It was now too close to the works for most people. Yet Tresillian found a tenant who was willing after all. Curious. The tenant must be an oddity.

"I believe the lady, a Miss Wilkins, is very genteel and pleasant," Miss Tresillian said. "I look forward to having her as a neighbor."

"Yes, yes," Tresillian said and glanced around the room. "I say, do you suppose there'll be cards? I want to win that twenty guineas back from your brother."

At that moment, someone at the pianoforte in the music

room started playing a country dance. Another cue for him to do his part. "I don't know about cards, but it appears there will be dancing," James said. He looked down at Miss Tresillian. "Would you do me the honor of standing up with me?"

He would dance with her and then have done his duty. Eustace could not fault him. Did he really think this sweet, innocent schoolgirl could possibly make him a good wife? He did not want someone merely decorative to share his life—even if she'd gained a witty tongue during her schoolgirl years. He'd rather go through life alone than find himself riveted to someone who might turn out to be like his sweet but expensive sister-in-law. Or as faithless as Rowena had proved to be.

James took another glass of champagne from the tray the gaudily dressed footman held out to him, drank it down, then put out his arm to lead Miss Tresillian to the dance floor.

CHAPTER 3

"Well, my dear, what did you think of the fellow?" Felix Tresillian asked his daughter in the carriage on the way home from the party at Tarrant Hall.

"He was very kind and he danced well," she answered, knowing her father was looking for more of a response from her. She wouldn't give him the satisfaction. Not after he informed her as they were leaving to go to the party that he'd found just the man for her and that he expected her to wed him if he offered for her.

"Come now! He's a handsome chap—I'm assured the ladies think so anyway. Not one of your London dandies, mind you. I wouldn't want that for you. And not so high and mighty that he could look down his nose at the likes of us. He knows the value of a day's work. You're as much the lady as he is the gentleman. Both good Cornish stock."

"Yes, Papa." Sophia had long ago learned not to remind her father that their *good Cornish stock* was only a couple of generations deep. Dig much earlier than that and you were likely to turn up a blacksmith or a carpenter, not to mention a brigand or two. She hadn't spent three years in Miss Crandall's Academy without being reminded frequently that her father's wealth did not buy real status.

Sophia sighed and gazed out of the carriage window at the moonlit countryside passing by. She had been looking forward to returning to Cornwall. Her so-called friends in Bath condoled with her over not being destined for a London season. None of them could believe that she had no desire for such a thing. Oh, no doubt in London there would be titled gentlemen in straitened circumstances who would welcome the opportunity to fatten their purses with her father's wealth. She did, however, doubt that any of them would look much past her pretty face and the guineas she would bring to a marriage. She also knew that she would never be allowed to forget her comparatively modest birth. In any such marriage, she would always be inferior.

In herself, she did not feel inferior to any of the ladies she knew. She was at least as pretty as most of them, wealthier than many, and she had more intelligence and good sense than any of her schoolmates at Miss Crandall's. If they used their minds at all, they hid it well. The only subjects of conversation among them seemed to be gowns and jewels and beaus. To a person, the girls who graduated from the seminary would be happy with someone who increased their consequence and gave them a life of luxury and ease. A fine estate in the country and a grand London town house—that was the sum total of their ambitions.

Not Sophia's, though. Sophia wanted more. She wanted more for herself and more in a husband. She wanted someone who took the trouble to look below the surface, beyond her beauty and elegant manners. Someone who would meet her in her mind and soul as well as her body.

Someone who would allow her to keep learning new things all her life, however long it would be, and would recognize her true abilities. Her own mother's life had not been long, but Sophia cherished the memory of not just reading with her, but talking about what they read, taking it apart and examining it for whatever they could derive of benefit to help them understand the world they lived in.

The education her father paid for may have done little to increase her knowledge, but it had also done little to stifle the curiosity the late Mrs. Tresillian awoke in her from her youngest days. To Miss Crandall's dismay, Sophia had been a regular patron of the Bath Subscription Library, a modest establishment that was not as fashionable as Meyer's or Leake's. Instead of furnishing her with the latest volume of poetry or the scandalous novel that had the *ton* in a fever of titillation, the Subscription Library offered books about science and medicine as well as periodicals such as The Edinburgh Review and Philosophical Transactions. Sophia's thirst for knowledge was only limited by her very rudimentary Latin and complete ignorance of Greek. When she asked Miss Crandall if she could engage a tutor for those subjects, the spinster's eyebrows rose almost to her hairline and she said Sophia would be better employed improving her needlework.

In sum, Sophia did not consider herself little better than a prize to be purchased on the marriage market. No, she would not marry without a true meeting of minds, without understanding, and without the deepest love. Who she married would be her decision, not her father's.

However, she knew as soon as she'd returned home that keeping to her resolve would be difficult. That very evening, mere days after she stepped inside the impressive hall of Tresillian Manor, officially released from the schoolroom, she found her father ready to use her as social capital in his business enterprises. She was on parade, under inspection. Certainly, Mr. Pentarrant was civil and attentive to her at the party. He said the right things, had correct manners and address. He was quite obviously the catch of the county. But although he was physically present at Tarrant Hall, Sophia couldn't help thinking he had not brought his entire self there. His craggy, oddly attractive face relaxed into a distracted frown whenever he wasn't actively engaged in talking to someone.

Besides, his sun-browned face and lanky limbs made him seem out of place in a ballroom. She could picture him more easily tramping out on the moors. Of course, he was a quarry captain. He wore gloves, but she wondered if his hands were scarred from handling the sharp stones—or did captains simply sit in the office while everyone else did the manual work? Could she fall in love with him? For the moment she thought not. He was not the kind of gentleman she pictured for herself. Too much the man of physical exertion, not enough the man of intellect.

An amused smile played about her lips when she thought of the Morrison sisters falling over each other to flirt with Pentarrant. They were either too stupid or too naive to recognize his clear rebuffs.

Then there was Philippa Vyvyan. Her old nemesis. She did not flirt as obviously as the Morrison girls, but wherever James Pentarrant went, Miss Vyvyan would somehow contrive to be there.

How many other hopeful daughters lurked in the vicinity of Camelford and Bodmin? Were there more of them than of eligible suitors? Or was Mr. Pentarrant simply the prize?

It was just after midnight when they arrived back at the modern mansion her father built five years ago for his wife and daughter. Grateful it was too late to sit over the tea tray, Sophia retired to her bedchamber after a brief goodnight kiss. She had no wish to answer the questions her father would no doubt put to her eventually, even if her respite only lasted a few hours.

Sophia's maid Adler smiled when she entered the dressing room. "Did ye have a pleasant evening, Miss Sophia?" she asked.

"Not particularly," Sophia answered. "Have all my trunks arrived?" Her clothing and personal items had accompanied her in the chaise from Bath, but she sent her boxes of books and some other items her father would disapprove of through a carrier.

"Yes, Miss. The big trunk is in the stable."

"I hope it's not damp there!" Sophia said, craning to look over her shoulder as Adler unlaced her gown and stays.

"Groom says not."

"It may have to stay there for a few days until I find the best place to put everything." Some of the books could go in empty shelves in the library, but others—she would have to be careful about them. Neither her father nor the servants could read Latin, but one had illustrations enough to render it shocking, especially if one did not understand their context.

Risky as they were, these items failed to represent the limit of her ambitions. She also had plans for a garden. Not roses. Not geraniums or hyacinths or daffodils. No, she brought home seeds she collected on walks around Bath, which she fully intended to supplement with seeds and roots from the woods and moors nearby. Her garden would appear ornamental, she hoped, but it would have a very serious purpose. She hadn't yet decided where this garden would be located or how to prevent the zealous groundsmen from thinking it was nothing but a patch of weeds. That was all to come.

While she was sowing the seeds for a future unlike that of

a wealthy heiress, Sophia was well aware that she would have to play the game expected of her in order to keep her father happy. Like the rest of the world, he saw a good marriage as his daughter's rightful destiny. Indeed, she would ultimately have to marry. But there were several things she simply must do first, and nothing and no one would stop her.

CHAPTER 4

Dr. Nathaniel Rowe put his signature on the letter he'd just finished writing, took the four other sealed letters addressed to an estate in Bedfordshire—each of different lengths that varied between a single lightly covered sheet to two sheets crossed and recrossed with meaningless nothings—and wrapped it around them to create a small parcel. He then directed the whole to Mr. Giles Haverford, Alnwick, Northumberland, laid the bulky letter on his desk, and sighed. This had all been less fraught with danger before Andrew's death, but Rowe knew he could trust Haverford to manage the business. He hoped the steward had enough money left from what he'd given him to cover the ten shillings' postage on receipt in Northumberland.

He would stop at the receiving office on his way out to call on old Mrs. Gorley, who had taken a turn for the worse.

Nathaniel had been in his modest lodgings in Camelford for just two months, having only recently received his licentiate from the Royal College of Physicians. During that time he had come to know many of the villagers—worthy merchants and tradesmen—as well as the important families with grander homes a little outside the town. Principal among these last were the Pentarrants and the Roscarrocks. He had met them in and around Camelford and attended to one of the Roscarrocks's boys who had the croup, but as yet he was not well acquainted with any of them.

His purpose in choosing the area for his practice was not so he could make a handsome living treating the ailments of the wealthy, however. He was more interested in helping those whose situation in life often exposed them to disease and accident and who did not have the means to call in whatever fashionable medical man they wished.

As it happened, on that pleasant early May morning, as he was about to set out to retrieve his serviceable hack from the livery stable, the landlady brought him a note requesting his attendance on one of his well-heeled patients. He could not afford to ignore it for several reasons, not the least of which was the handsome fee he would receive. This was a new experience for him: appearing to care about what he once would have considered a trifling sum. Yet care he must, if his plan were to succeed.

And so he obeyed the summons to the Honorable Catherine, Mrs. Eustace Pentarrant, mother of two healthy boys who was increasing again. A pretty woman despite the ravages of childbirth, when he arrived at Tarrant Hall he found her lying stretched out on a sofa in a comfortable parlor on the first floor. This was not a room he'd ever entered before. The one party he'd attended when he first arrived took place in the more public rooms: a large saloon, a drawing room, and a lofty chamber at the back that served as a modest-sized ballroom.

"Dr. Rowe," Mrs. Pentarrant said, stretching her hand up to take his but not changing her position, her voice weak,

"You find me unable to rise. I feel positively unwell every morning, for hours, sometimes until the day is quite advanced. Surely there is something you can give me to ease my biliousness. I never felt this way with John Eustace or Grayson." After he bowed over her hand she let it drop to the sofa as if she had no control over her muscles.

Nathaniel suppressed the urge to tell her that the quarry women not only rose every day no matter how they felt, but performed their work as bal maidens or even splitters until their pregnancy was too advanced for them to do it any longer. He reminded himself that pointing out the differences between the idle rich and the overburdened quarry workers would serve no useful purpose. So he smiled and felt her pulse, which beat slow and steady, no sign of fever or agitation. If anything, she positively bloomed. "I am sorry you are so troubled, Mrs. Pentarrant. I'm afraid there is little I can offer for your relief other than some ginger tea, and perhaps dry toast. Sometimes it's necessary to eat a little to stave off such symptoms. Perfectly normal for a lady in your condition."

She sighed and wrinkled her brow. "My husband told me you were a more modern doctor than our old Dr. Grinstead. I felt sure you would be able to prescribe something that would alleviate my discomfort."

Rowe acknowledged that the birthing of children was a hazardous business, but it was also natural. In his view, except in the case of danger to mother or child, women should simply make the best of it and be grateful when their infants were born healthy and whole. "If you would like, I shall speak to your cook about the proper preparation of a few different teas that might settle your stomach. But I must get on with my visits to..." He was about to say *to people who actually need me,* but stopped himself just in time. "... old Mrs. Gorley, who has had another bad turn."

Mrs. Pentarrant sniffed. "She isn't dead yet? I cannot imagine what is taking her so very long."

Biting back an acid reply, Nathaniel said, "Perhaps you would find your indisposition less severe if you simply rose and took the fresh air, turned your mind to something other than your discomfort. It's a lovely day. Shall I call your maid?"

"No. I am expecting a visitor this morning. I shall simply rest here and wait for that tea you mentioned." She gave a feeble wave of her hand to dismiss him. He wondered if he'd ever become accustomed to such treatment, and left.

So, she was well enough for social calls. He shook his head, looking down at his feet to hide his disgusted expression from any servants who happened to be passing. When the front door opened, he assumed it was to show him out and quickened his pace.

"I beg your pardon!" A female voice uttered a surprised shriek at the moment the doctor's bag dangling from his left hand connected with whatever it was the lady had in her own left hand. This turned out to be a basket with an unlatched cover, and its contents tipped onto the ornately tiled floor.

Nathaniel found himself standing in the midst of a collection of small glass phials and pots of different colors. One of the phials smashed when it hit the floor and a little puddle of a thick liquid with a pungent odor spread around it. Before he could gather his wits, the lady was scrambling to put the litter of receptacles back into the basket she'd now placed on the floor.

"Please excuse me, Madam," he said as he also crouched down and tried to help her. They both reached for the same pot and his hand closed over hers for an instant before he let it go. She wore mitts rather than gloves, so his own hands—

not yet covered by the riding gloves in his pocket—briefly touched her exposed fingers.

This unexpected human contact sent a spark of heat through Nathaniel's body, and he was still somewhat off balance when he summoned up the courage to look directly at the lady. Her dark blue eyes opened wide and her cheeks flushed a delicate pink. Her lips parted as if to say something and then closed again.

"How very clumsy of me," Nathaniel said, standing as she seemed to have reclaimed all the items that had spilled out of her basket, except the one that broke.

"I believe we were equally culpable, Mr...."

Who is she? he thought before realizing that she was waiting for him to fill in the blank she left. "Rowe. Dr. Rowe." He inclined his head to her, hoping she hadn't noticed that the sight of her bowled him quite over. "And whom do I have the pleasure of addressing?"

The young lady pinched her lips together as though trying to suppress a smile. Her expression brought a teasing light into her very lovely eyes. *She did notice it,* he thought, and that only served to send the heat rushing into his cheeks. She also did not answer his direct question, only saying, "So, Madame summoned you in her all-too-expected distress."

What was she implying? In the time it took for them to exchange these pleasantries, a maid had appeared with a mop to clean up the broken phial and its noxious contents. As she mopped, he breathed the odor in deeply and furrowed his brow. "Rue? What cosmetic purpose would such a dangerous herb serve?" What else, after all, could be the reason for all the preparations an elegant young lady carried in a basket when visiting another lady?

"You assume all this—" she glanced toward her basket— "is for the very feminine purpose of enhancing one's beauty?" Her eyebrows rose and the smile left her eyes.

"Come now, what ought I to think?" He attempted to lighten the tone.

She shook her head. "Precisely that, of course. If you will excuse me, doctor, Mrs. Pentarrant is waiting for me." She stepped sideways so she could walk past him to the stairs, but stopped with her foot on the bottom step and looked over her shoulder at him. "Would you mind awfully telling me what you prescribed for the suffering lady so I do not merely repeat your advice?"

What? Rowe's eyes went down to the floor where the maid had almost finished wiping up the spill, her nose wrinkled in disgust. "Surely you were not intending to give Mrs. Pentarrant a tincture of rue! Are you aware how dangerous such a thing might be to a woman in her condition?"

"I am fully aware that rue, in a certain quantity, can have devastating effects. In very small quantities, however, it will alleviate many feminine complaints. The sort of complaints that doctors generally dismiss as unimportant."

Indignation rose in his chest. All the more so because he had, in fact, dismissed Mrs. Pentarrant's complaint as of no significance. Did this slip of a girl—however beautiful she was—presume to tell him his business? "You are playing with fire if you think old-wives' remedies are more efficacious than modern medical practices."

"Good day, Dr. Rowe," she said, turning away and continuing up the stairs.

He watched her, noting the graceful arch of her neck, her light step, the way she lifted her muslin skirts with the hand that was not clutching the basket.

What was her name? Why had he never seen her before? Judging by her voice and address, she certainly didn't belong to one of the laborers' families. She was most assuredly a lady. So what was she doing bringing a basket full of suspect remedies to one of the first ladies of local society?

He shook his head to clear it. Time to tend to old Mrs. Gorley, who really was very near her end. She'd spent nearly seventy years in her family's cottage close to the brink of the quarry breathing in the ever-present slate dust and her lungs barely functioned anymore. He must put this maddening, impudent, uncommonly pretty girl out of his mind and get on with more important matters.

CHAPTER 5

The landlord of the inn had been somewhat skeptical about the cottage so close to the quarry, owned by the wealthy businessman Felix Tresillian, but Persephone thought it would suit her perfectly. She congratulated herself on finding a dwelling well within her budget and situated precisely as she hoped. It was on the Camelford side of the quarry. The hamlet where the workers lived apparently stood on the other side. Her cottage was sparsely furnished, to be sure, but it had a barn that was large enough to stable a horse or two and it boasted three rooms on the ground floor and three on the floor above—making it likely double the size of a laborer's dwelling.

Now, however, it was time to face the realities of her decision. As she stood on the rutted road outside the rusted gate that opened onto the path leading to the cottage door, she noted the peeling red paint, the overgrown patch of garden, the dirty windows. Persephone had to remind herself that she had chosen this. The stone cottage with its thatched roof—it wasn't grand enough to be roofed with the slate quarried so nearby—was ample to supply her needs. Mr.

Tresillian's housekeeper, Mrs. Thwaite, had found her a maid of all work, Hannah, who could also cook. Their groom's son Bobby was willing to help Miss Wilkins out at odd times for extra wages, the lady also told her, so she had all the help she needed for now. It would, in time, be a small but comfortable household.

After a deep steadying breath, Persephone resolutely opened the gate. The screeching complaint of a rusted hinge sent a mourning dove flapping and cooing away. That would be the first job for young Bobby, she thought, wondering if he could read a list if she made one. She had the iron key out to unlock the door, but one look revealed that said door was too warped for the bolt to slide into the intended housing. She lifted the latch and pushed, finding herself in a small entryway with doorways on either side and a very steep stair directly in front of her. A door at the back of this hall led to another small room and a pantry, she'd been told, which had access to a root cellar beneath it. Without any time to find her handkerchief, she sneezed. Dust, of course.

The room to the right of the entry hall proved to be a cozy and inviting kitchen with a large stone hearth and bake oven, a sturdy oak table with benches, a dresser with a broken drawer, and a settle. The room opposite was a small parlor that could double as a schoolroom—the feature from the description the landlord had given her had made her decide on the house right away. That steep flight of stairs appeared to be the only way to the upper floor. It would be difficult to carry hot water up to her bedroom, so her bathing would have to be accomplished in the kitchen. Despite the fact that Persephone had never been wealthy and had worked for her keep since the age of eighteen, she was unused to such rudimentary living conditions. But what else had she expected? Thank heavens she owned so little clothing! Nothing like the handsome armoire in her elegant bedchamber at Atherleigh could even fit through the door here.

As she made her way slowly through the low-pitched rooms with their exposed timbers, she wondered how many spiders nested in the cracks and crevices while she mentally tallied all the work necessary to make the cottage habitable. Some she would have to do herself, some she could assign to Hannah, and some to Bobby. The list was daunting, and she hadn't even inspected the upper floor closely.

She shook her head and prepared to make the climb when a loud sneeze from the direction of the still-open front door stopped her.

"Pardon me! I'm sorry to disturb you! My papa said you would be moving in today and I wanted to bring you some cheer. Which—judging by what I see at the moment—you are desperately in need of."

Persephone turned to see a beautiful young woman of perhaps eighteen years standing in the little hall, a covered basket dangling from one hand. She was dressed in fine white muslin with blue ribbons at the neckline and the hem, a modest tucker covering her up to her long neck, and a fashionable poke bonnet tied on with satin ribbons atop what appeared to be a mass of dark gold curls. The contrast created by her pristine loveliness made the hall look even more drab than it had initially. At first, Persephone was too taken aback to say a word.

"Oh dear, Papa said I should not disturb you so soon."

The lady—she must be Mr. Tresillian's daughter—placed the covered basket she carried on the floor at her feet and started to leave. Shaking herself out of her stupor, Persephone said, "Miss Tresillian, I collect? I'm so sorry, please come in. You simply took me unawares. And I'm so sorry about the dust!" She walked forward, hand outstretched.

A dazzling smile lit the girl's wide dark blue eyes—or

were they violet? "Please! Call me Sophia. I hate these conventions, don't you?"

"In that case you must call me Persephone. A fire has not yet been lit in the kitchen hearth or I would offer you tea. Perhaps a simple chat would suffice?"

Even as they repaired to the kitchen, Hannah—her gray hair tucked under a plain cap and a pinney covering most of her homespun gown—arrived through the back door and set about kindling a fire in the hearth. She hooked an iron kettle on the crane and swung it into place. By the sound of sloshing water, Persephone guessed the maid had filled it earlier at the pump out back.

"I brought you a few provisions just to tide you over, but my father and I would be delighted if you would come and dine with us this evening. I'm used to being around lots of chattering females, so being alone with my father feels a bit desolate. Not that you'll chatter, of course!"

"I would willingly accept your invitation. As you see, I'm afraid making a meal might be a little beyond Hannah's capabilities right now. I haven't got any food in yet! I don't even know when market day is or where to get the necessities."

At this Hannah, who had clearly been listening to their conversation, said, "Tomorrow, Miss. If ye'll give me some housekeeping, I'll get in what we'll need for the week."

"Thank you, Hannah," Persephone said, already feeling a bit bemused by the extent of the changes she would face.

Miss Tresillian opened the basket and began placing its contents on the table. "In the meantime, I've brought you tea, apples, a wheel of cheese, a side of bacon, and a loaf of bread. There's no hunting at this time of year or I'd bring you a brace of pheasants."

Persephone grinned, recalling Antonella's description of finding the goshawk in a poacher's net. "Pheasants are by no means essential to my happiness!"

Miss Tresillian's musical laugh immediately lightened the atmosphere, and they chatted amiably for a little while about nothing in particular. Persephone learned that the heiress was newly returned from school in Bath, where she had been ever since her mother died three years ago.

"I'm so sorry for your loss," Persephone said. "And now that your education is complete, are you planning to find yourself a husband—as you said your fellow seminarians are all wont to do?" She said it with a smile, hoping to communicate to Sophia that her comment carried no judgment.

But Sophia became serious and looked down at her mittened hands. "That is what everyone expects of me, certainly."

She did not continue and Persephone did not probe further. Clearly a sore point. She changed the subject, asking questions about the nearby towns and the shops and social activities available in them.

"You'll find most basic items in Camelford. If you want London fashions or smarter clothing, you'll have to go to Bodmin."

"Is there a good lending library around? I'm familiar with those in Bodmin. The selection there is uninspiring at best," Persephone said.

At this, Sophia's eyes lit up. "The best one is in Truro, but it's still not very splendid. I have some books of my own that I brought from Bath. Father's library is more like a room with empty shelves at this point!" She gave a rueful little laugh. "He did nothing to enlarge my mother's small collection after she died and I went away to school. Tell me, what kind of books are you looking for?"

"I assume your papa told you I intend to teach here. So I am looking for books that would be useful in teaching reading and writing to children."

She knitted her brow. "But who will you teach? All the gentry send their daughters away to school."

Should she share her plans with this young stranger? It seemed doubtful Sophia could do anything to help her. However, even if she'd been away for three years, the girl had grown up here and would know more of the people and customs than she did. "I have come to establish a school for the quarry children."

This silenced her guest. After a considering pause, Sophia said, "You know they won't like it."

"The children? But if they haven't been taught before how would they know not to like it?"

"The children. Their parents. The quarrymen. The overseers and captain."

She expected a certain amount of opposition to her plan, but this blanket unwelcome was unexpected. "Why is that?"

"Oh, it would take too long to explain right now. We're a closed and crotchety lot here in Delabole. As brittle and flinty as the slate they haul up from the pit. But most are good hearted, once you get past the distrust." She paused and gave Persephone an appraising look. "I know nothing about you, and yet I somehow believe you to be trustworthy. Others will see it too, in time."

The farmers and fishermen near Atherleigh and in Boscastle behaved in quite a friendly and respectful way toward her. Would things be so different only a few miles away? "Well, I shall do my best to earn their good opinion."

Sophia smiled and rose. "I see you have settling in to do and I must get home before Papa thinks I've been abducted by gypsies!" She put out her hand. "But I will see you this evening. I'll send the carriage at four."

"How silly! The walk is not far and the day is fine."

"That may be, but the recent rain has made the walks very muddy. You'll ruin your evening slippers!"

Of course, they must dress for dinner. Persephone was grateful for Sophia's gentle hint and found herself liking the girl. At first, her fresh loveliness led her to expect a tittering debutante with little of substance to offer. But genuine warmth radiated from her expressions and her words, and although nothing in her conversation made it obvious, Persephone suspected that Sophia Tresillian had an inquiring mind.

On first appearance Sophia reminded her of Lady Belinda, with her fair beauty and air of accomplishment. Still, there was something about the way she talked of her past that made Persephone think she hid depths of feeling. This called to mind the more complicated, reserved Antonella. Had Sophia a sweetheart her father didn't approve of? Did she engage in a pursuit that she feared others would censure her for? Whatever it was, discovering more about her surprising neighbor would add interest to her days, no matter what lay ahead.

PERSEPHONE WAS GRATEFUL FOR THE DINNER INVITATION. SHE was more exhausted than she ever recalled being after working nonstop to clean and bring some order to her new abode. The food at Tresillian Hall was simple but delicious, and the conversation lively. She and Sophia were on their way to being fast friends. Their elegant barouche conveyed her home at around sunset.

Home, she thought. Had Atherleigh manor ever felt like home to her? She honestly couldn't say. The contrast between her former residence, the shining, opulent grandeur of the Tresillian mansion, and her humble cottage was laughably extreme. Yet she found the small rooms and low ceilings of her new dwelling perversely comforting. Even though she couldn't fully stretch her arms up in her bedroom without hitting one of the beams, the limited space embraced her; she felt more enveloped than constricted by it. For the first time in her life she could order everything exactly as she liked. So, yes. This was home. She had plans to furbish it up a bit—replace the dimity window curtains whose pattern had faded to indistinguishability; make cushions for the chairs in the kitchen.

The parlor would be her schoolroom, and so would need a table and stools. But until she had students, Persephone wasn't certain how large a table or how many stools.

All this went through her head as she lay in her bed at dawn the next morning listening to the birds—finches and robins mostly, she thought. It was so peaceful.

Until, that is, an ungodly, loud blast shattered the peace, rattling the panes in the window and reverberating through the house. She bolted out of bed, stubbing her toe on the chair at her simple dressing table and hopping around the room. "Blast! The devil!" No one was around to hear her, so Persephone allowed herself to curse until the pain in her big toe eased.

"Are ye whole?" came a rough voice, calling up the stairs.

Of course. Hannah must have risen already. The smell of coffee and bacon wafted up to her, and Persephone smiled through her still throbbing pain.

She quickly donned her unadorned brown round gown, adding her plainest muslin tucker and her stoutest leather boots. The blasts ceased, but she was aware of a constant *tink, tink, tink* sound and the occasional screech as of rope being drawn through pulleys. The noises came and went with the wind, she guessed. Why hadn't she noticed them yesterday? She expected she'd been making enough racket of her own to drown it out, and then the slate works would have been quiet at night.

So, this was to be a constant presence in her life. Perhaps it explained why the cottage had lain vacant for so long.

Persephone made her way carefully down the steep staircase, clinging to the stout rope that acted as a banister, and walked into the kitchen. Hannah was already kneading dough for bread and bacon sizzled in a skillet on the brandreth. A tin pot sat on the table—no doubt it contained the coffee she smelled—next to a chipped cup with no handle.

"Good morning, Hannah."

"Miss," she muttered, not turning to look at Persephone. "Blasting today. Ye'll get used to it."

A moment later a different loud noise—almost like a rumble of thunder except Persephone could see a clear blue sky out the kitchen window—once more rattled the windows and made the floor vibrate. She raised questioning eyes to Hannah.

"Rock face split off," she said, and left it at that.

Persephone sat on the bench at the table and Hannah tossed the cooked bacon on a plate along with a hunk of bread and placed it in front of her.

"I was thinking of walking into Camelford today," Persephone said after she took a bite of the bread and drank half a cup of the surprisingly good coffee.

"Are ye a good walker? It's two mile." Hannah looked up from her work and stared at Persephone. She must have seen the question in her face, because she added, "Better ride. Ye'll have packages and sich."

It wasn't so very far, but Hannah was right. Two miles would be rather a long walk and she might well have packages to carry. She still had the cob she'd borrowed from Atherleigh. Perhaps in Camelford she could find a suitable horse of her own to purchase.

Of course, Hannah had said she would go into Camelford herself to buy the household necessities. She would hardly be riding into town for those. "You surely won't walk to Camelford for the shopping then. How will you manage the provisions, Hannah? You cannot carry them all that way."

"That's the truth. But Kellow's cart'll bring 'em."

For now, Persephone decided not to look too closely into what that entailed. She would no doubt learn soon enough. In any case, she wanted to focus on her teaching needs. She would ride to town that morning and see about getting the supplies on her list. Tomorrow would be Sunday. If she attended the morning service at the local parish church, St. Teath's, she might have an opportunity to meet more of her neighbors. Perhaps the vicar would be able to give her some advice about spreading the news of her school, and others might know where she would be able to procure anything she couldn't immediately find in Camelford itself.

CHAPTER 6

With her basic needs taken care of and Hannah well established in her role as housekeeper and cook, Persephone decided she should not put off going to see the quarry. As she prepared to make the short walk the very next day, she asked herself what made her so nervous about it. She was not a fearful person. At least, she never thought she was. Simply moving to Camelford had certainly tested her courage, and she'd managed it all. Living so alone in unfamiliar country should have made her uneasy, but instead, each morning she awoke brimming with excitement and eagerness.

Except, that is, when she thought about going to see the quarry. What was she afraid of? Just because she'd never seen such a place was no reason to avoid it. She already had something of a sense of it through the distant, brittle sounds of hammering stone, the occasional loud blasts, the squealing winches—sounds she'd grown so accustomed to that already she hardly noticed them, except when they first started up in the morning and when they ceased altogether at night.

None of her small acquaintance in the neighborhood had

given her any insight into what to expect of a slate quarry. She doubted that Sophia had ever been there, her father not having any commercial ties to the business. And her few questions to Hannah about the quarry garnered little response beyond shrugs and *those folks keep to themselves.* When she asked what the works looked like, Hannah stared blankly and said, "like a quarry."

What reason could she give for being there, if challenged? Then she remembered what the stationer had told her—that she could get all the small pieces of slate she needed for he students by asking the splitters at the quarry for the cast off bits.

There was nothing for it but to go. How else could she hope to meet the children who would eventually populate her school? Of course, she must become acquainted with their parents, who—Persephone knew—would represent her true challenge. It was unlikely that any of them had much education and they might not see its value for the next generation.

Perhaps, deep in her heart, she worried that what she had to offer would be deemed unnecessary. Unwelcome. That they would all laugh in her face.

That they didn't, in fact, need her.

Then she would have made this move for no purpose at all. Oh well, better to know that at the outset. Nothing ventured …

Dressed simply, black ribbons and black gloves the only indications that she was in mourning, her stoutest walking boots laced up tight, Persephone set out for the quarry that morning. "I'll be back for nuncheon!" she called over her shoulder to Hannah as she closed the door—which had been swiftly mended by the Tresillian estate carpenter—behind her.

She needed no help to find her way. A path broad enough

for a cart led across the sparsely treed farmland, and she need only follow the increasing noise to know she was headed in the right direction. As she drew closer, the ground rose in front of her in a way that prevented her seeing anything of the site even though she knew she was quite near.

Persephone drew a deep breath and climbed the final rise. When the quarry came gradually into view, step by step Persephone found her eyes widening to take in a vista so extraordinary that she had nothing in her entire life experience with which to compare it. She was accustomed to seeing the great expanse of sea from a high cliff and had once climbed a hill to gain a panorama over farmlands and forests in Somersetshire. But never had such a view exploded before her as this did. It robbed her of breath and quickened her pulse. She found herself gasping and putting her hand over her heart. That such a gigantic gash in the countryside could have been created through the efforts of man was inconceivable. Granted, the pit dated almost from the Conquest. Indeed, it had to have taken centuries to dig so wide and deep, creating a great wound constantly sloughing valuable stone. She soon perceived that the small creatures moving along terraced steps and paths on the inside of the bowl were, in fact, men.

On the north side of the cavity, the great winches turned by work horses squealed and scraped. Persephone watched in fascination as a block of blue-gray stone that looked small from where she stood but must have been larger than a horse made its gradual way from the depths up to the surface, ropes taut and straining as it went.

On the opposite bank of the pit lay a haphazard collection of around fifty cottages, perhaps more over the hill behind them. These were dwarfed by what looked like man-made hills of rubble surrounding them.

Most remarkable of all, though, was that in the very middle, at the deepest point of the pit, was a lake of brilliant blue green. Persephone stared at it, watching as a white gull flew over it and dived down to capture some unperceivable prey.

After a few moments to take everything in, Persephone gathered herself and, spotting the path that would lead her around to the cottages and the rim where most of the activity was taking place, she resolutely put one foot in front of the other and set out. She was here. She must begin to do what she came for.

As Persephone wandered through the scattered huts and skirted the mounds of rubble, the deafening ring of chisels against slate assaulted her ears. A few workers stared openly at her, though most ignored her, too engrossed in their work to heed a stranger.

She was about to turn toward the nearest of the cottages where a thin ribbon of smoke snaked up from a chimney when a very nearby sudden clatter stopped her. Before her, a young boy who couldn't have been much older than seven years, if that, struggled with a sack that was nearly as big as he was. He finally gave up, sending much of the contents of the sack spilling out at Persephone's feet.

Before she could offer the child any assistance, a bowlegged, grizzled man with a pipe hanging out of the corner of his mouth and a birch switch in his hand ran over.

"Ye've done it now! Wasted yer morning. That'll cost ye. And here's so you remember not to do it again." The harsh words were followed by a stinging blow with the switch on the boy's arm.

The boy did not cry. The corners of his mouth pinched downward and he said, "Sorry Mr. Bray. Won't do it again."

The wizened man—who happened to be several inches shorter than Persephone—raised the switch high again to bring it down across the boy's shoulder. But Persephone's hand darted out instinctively and grabbed the man's wrist. "How dare you!" she said.

As if he'd only that minute seen her, the old man—apparently called "Mr. Bray"—turned his fierce eyes to hers. "Mind yer business, Lassie!"

Persephone had never been spoken to like that in her life before, and his words acted like the touch of a squib to a fuse. She took a deep breath and told this evil creature exactly what she thought of his actions, too incensed to notice that their argument had drawn a tall, commanding gentleman over to them.

JAMES HAD JUST FINISHED GOING OVER THE QUARRY ACCOUNTS and was about to step out to do his usual tour of the entire works when an unexpected ruckus stopped him in his tracks. Yelling, emanating from near the rim. *What the deuce?* He instantly identified the harsh, stringent voice of overseer Pasco Bray, saying something about meddling and mischief-making. The other voice, though, was completely unfamiliar.

And female.

Without grabbing his hat from the hook by the door, he raced out in the direction of the disturbance but stopped some feet away. The sight, had it not been so fraught with tension, would have been comical. A small tableau, three participants locked in conflict, unfolded against the backdrop of the pit. Small of stature but fierce and feared, Bray's face had gone purple with rage and spittle gathered at the corners of his mouth. Where normally he could glower down at the young boys who carted the helling stone to the mounds around the pit's edge, here the overseer was forced to look up at a tall, slim woman, not in her first youth but still young, whose lifted chin and flashing eyes did not flinch from his tirade. All this did much to undermine the power of the man's indignation. Further, the lady had lain one calm, gloved hand on the shoulder of the small boy standing between them. The boy—whom James recognized as Jago Penwarden—looked back and forth between the two adults as they traded barbs, his dirty face streaked with the paths of tears.

"Ye think ye're high and mighty, stickin' yer prissy nose in where it don't have no business!" Bray said.

The lady replied with no perceivable trepidation. "And you, sir, have no business beating a child who is trying to perform a task for which he is clearly unfitted."

"No? Well let's ask 'im if he don't want to do it!"

"He is no more than a child! He should not be occupied in this way, he should be in school learning his letters."

At this, Bray opened his nearly toothless mouth and guffawed. "That's rich! An' I s'pose he'll be standin' fer Parliament next year."

At this point, James decided to intervene. "You've done your duty, Bray. I'll resolve this."

With a fierce glower at James and quickly spitting on the ground not quite at the lady's feet, Bray marched away, muttering curses.

"Now, perhaps, Madam—"

Before he could continue, the lady interrupted. "It's criminal! Look at him!" She took Jago's shoulders and pulled him to stand in front of her, then reached down and held up the boy's hands. "Do you see this? How could he be expected to gather these sharp stones, let alone carry what must be a half hundredweight of them the distance of a few feet, much less fifty yards!"

It was true that Jago's hands were scarred and abraded, but so were the hands of all the boys who were too young to do any of the work aside from collecting and transporting the small waste stones—the helling stone. James never saw such damage without a pang and wishing there were some other way. But the older, stronger boys and men were needed for yet harder jobs, and the quarry families needed every penny of the income these children brought to them. He looked into the lady's face. Her hazel-gray eyes glittered with outrage and the threat of angry tears. The conflict had brought intense color into her cheeks. Hers was not a classically beautiful visage, yet the lady's straight, patrician nose and firm, slightly pointed chin, her walnut-colored hair pulled severely back and coiled in a knot at the nape of her neck, and the absurdly girlish straw villager hat tied under her chin with a black satin ribbon, held James's gaze longer than it should have before he could once again speak.

Instead of addressing her concerns, however, he looked down at Jago, whose fearful expression clearly foresaw no good coming from this intervention. "It's Jago, isn't it?" he said. When the boy nodded, he continued. "Are you unhappy to be doing this work at the quarry?"

At that, Jago shook his head vigorously. "No, sir! My 'ands, they don't hurt so much."

"The boy's terrified!" the lady cried, but James held up a hand to stop her without taking his eyes off the lad.

"And what do you do with the money you earn by working here?"

"I gives it to me ma, so's we can mebbe get enough flour for bread."

The lady spoke again. "Surely there are older boys who could do this!"

Again, still looking at Jago, James said, "You have older brothers, don't you Jago." Jago nodded. "What if one of them did this work?"

Jago's forehead creased in perplexity. "Ye mean, give over

workin' in the pit to do what I can do right enough? There bain't no sense in that!"

"Why so?"

"Cause then we'd starve."

James patted the boy on the head and crouched down to help him pile the loose stones back into the sack. He watched Jago hoist the full sack over his shoulder and march away, bent nearly double, but trudging along at a brisk pace.

"You, sir," said the lady between clenched teeth, "are a monster. May I speak to your superior?"

At this, James gave a stiff smile. "In this place, I have no superior. I am the captain of these works. James Pentarrant. And you are ...?"

"I am utterly speechless."

"Well, Miss Speechless," he said, making a feeble attempt to break through her ire, "You clearly know nothing about the workings of a slate quarry, or about the people whose lives depend upon it for their very existence."

"I know how children ought to be treated, however, no matter their situation in life. Their intellectual and spiritual needs are just as important as the physical."

"My primary concern is making sure the quarry thrives so that Jago's family—and several hundred others like them —can survive." James folded his arms across his chest and moved a step closer to her. "I depend upon the church to see to their spiritual needs. And I doubt anyone in Jago's family has even uttered the word *intellectual,* let alone been aware of any unmet need in that regard."

"Oh!" the lady cried, her mouth working as if she wanted to say more, then she shook her head and marched off in the direction of Camelford.

It didn't take long for James to figure out that this must be the schoolteacher tenant of Mr. Tresillian's cottage. She wasn't at all what he expected, judging by what he'd heard here and there. She'd formerly been a governess and he assumed that therefore she would be quite elderly. Apparently the fact that she wasn't old did not prevent her from having very decided opinions. And she had no fear of standing up to him. He didn't remember the last time a lady addressed him with anything other than bashful simpering, and found he much preferred this lady's way of dealing with him—even if it meant they would always be at odds.

Life around Delabole and Camelford appeared to be headed for a very interesting change.

CHAPTER 7

The brisk walk back from the quarry did nothing to calm Persephone's seething temper. Never had she encountered crueler, more heartless men! That horrible Mr. Bray was purely wicked, to beat a child so. As to the other one—Mr. Pentarrant, whose name she had heard at dinner with Sophia and her father—she wasn't entirely certain what to think about him. He appeared to condone the mistreatment of the boy, yet he took pains to talk to him and listen. And he helped him put the stones back into the bag. But still, he hadn't found anything to criticize in the practice of forcing so small a boy to carry a weight that she herself could never lift. The fact that picking up the jagged slate rubble led to cuts and scrapes only added to the injustice of it. No, she could not like Mr. Pentarrant.

She wished she'd stayed longer and stood her ground with the man. If he was truly in charge there she worried that she might have an even more uphill battle to persuade the parents to allow their children to come to school. No doubt the quarry captain would have to be in favor of such a change, and his attitude with regard to the little boy wasn't very promising. In a rather roundabout way, he made the obvious point that Jago's work added to his family's subsistence, and the boy seemed distressed at the idea of losing that income. But how much did lads like Jago earn? Surely it was only pennies. Would that be enough to make a difference? Perhaps she should go back to the quarry the next day and seek out the captain so she could explain to him why she was there and what she wanted to do. She had such a strong conviction that some learning could only be good for the children, although she hadn't formulated all her arguments yet. That would be necessary in the face of opposition, so perhaps she should think it all through more carefully first.

Yet even if she had all the cogent reasoning at her command, Persephone couldn't be certain Mr. Pentarrant would listen to her. How could it matter to him whether the children who worked in the quarry could read and write? And why did she think he might be persuaded by her that it was important? She found herself trying to remember what it was about his looks that had made her think it possible. His eyes were not hard. His expression, though not friendly, was far from hostile. If anything, he seemed puzzled by her. And frankly, he puzzled her in turn. Mr. Pentarrant's strong-featured face spoke of a man accustomed to hard work in the open air. Yet his speech was that of a well educated gentleman. And his serious blue eyes—could eyes be serious? She remembered him crouching in front of Jago, the muscles of his thighs straining against his buckskins. This was no indolent lounger. His hands as he helped Jago pick up the stones were clean and manicured but strong, as if he were capable of putting them to good, practical use and yet took a certain pride in his appearance. The man was full of contradictions.

But oh! That revolting Mr. Bray! No contradictions there. Persephone feared after she left that her intervention might have resulted in Jago's receiving more of the birch switch.

Her breast heaved with impotent fury. She thought she was prepared to face this new life, this project she had set herself to put her inheritance and her gifts to good use. Perhaps she was being naive. To be honest with herself, she was more overset by what she saw at the quarry than she thought she would be. The harsh sounds of industry faded as she hurried home. Yet Persephone would now be able to hear them with a clear image of what they represented and have difficulty shaking off the memory of that poor little boy struggling under such a weight for mere pennies.

The welcome smell of bread baking and the sight of the cheerful fire in the kitchen hearth greeted her, but it did little to lighten her mood. Hannah wisely placed a cup of milky tea in front of her then muttered something about pulling potatoes as she hastened out the back door of the cottage. Apparently someone had sown them there, and despite the fact that the patch of vegetation was nearly wild, it did in fact yield potatoes.

Still mulling over all she saw and heard at the quarry, it took Persephone a minute to register the knock on the front door. She called out to Hannah to answer it, forgetting that the housekeeper had gone out to the garden. So she smoothed down her hair and her skirt and walked with what dignity she could muster to greet this unexpected visitor.

"Miss Wilkins!" said Sophia Tresillian, looking as lovely as ever in a pale green muslin gown and darker green spencer, her blond curls tucked becomingly under a fetching feathered bonnet.

"I thought we'd got beyond that! It's Persephone, remember?" Persephone gestured for her to come in, struck by the stark contrast between the pristine loveliness of her new friend and the gritty reality of the nearby quarry. "Would you like tea? I can be much more hospitable now that my kitchen is in order and Hannah has taken me in hand!"

Sophia remained in the open doorway. "I'm afraid I cannot. In point of fact, nor can you. I should like you to accompany me on an important errand, and we haven't a moment to lose. I have the gig." She gestured behind her to a small open carriage with one compact, sturdy horse—hardly bigger than a pony—harnessed to it. "I'm afraid I must climb back in quickly or Galahad will wander off, mischievous beast that he is." She tripped back to the gig, where the pony had indeed started nosing around in search of grass to munch. In one quick, graceful movement, she sprang back in and took the reins.

"Where are we going?" Persephone asked, marveling at this young lady's confident command of her circumstances.

"To Bodmin. Hurry! Time's wasting."

Persephone laughed out loud at Sophia's command. "I see! And what are we to do in Bodmin?"

"Oh!" Sophia reached into her reticule and drew out a pasteboard card, which she waved in Persephone's direction. "We must be ready by Monday."

It wasn't an explanation, but Persephone was happy to be distracted from her disturbing thoughts and decided she might as well go along, whatever it was that Sophia deemed so important. She quickly tied her hat back on, wrapped her shawl around her shoulders, and picked up her reticule, checking to be sure her purse was within it. Hannah had come around from behind the cottage with a basket of potatoes, doubtless drawn by the voices. "I'm off to Bodmin with Miss Tresillian," Persephone told her.

"She won't be back in time for dinner, but I daresay she'll want supper later," Sophia added, as if she were addressing a servant of her own.

Persephone shook her head, smiled, and climbed into the gig, taking the card from Sophia. Thick pasteboard covered in elegant copperplate script informed her that she was invited to a ball at the home of Mr. and Mrs. Edward Roscarrock, at their manor house near St. Endelion on Monday—a few days away. A less formal note on the other side of the card said that she and Miss Tresillian would of course be welcome to stay the night. "But I don't know these Roscarrocks," Persephone said, thinking what an absurd contrast dancing at a ball would make to the way she had just spent her morning.

"I happened to mention you to them when they came to dinner the other day and they are most eager to meet you. They sent the invitation to me because they didn't know how to direct it to you. Besides, the Roscarrock Ball is the event of the season hereabouts. You'll meet everyone of importance there."

Everyone of importance. Among them might be those with influence in the area who would support her in her endeavor to set up a school. Would that include Mr. Pentarrant? Perhaps it wasn't such a frivolous idea after all. "I see."

"I'm glad you do. Are you quite settled? You might want to tuck that rug around you. The sun is warm but the wind is sharp." Sophia gave the reins a twitch to set the pony in motion, then said, "Forgive me for making an assumption. Well, I made several assumptions, really. First, I did not think you would have any evening gowns—nothing suitable for a ball at any rate—having come here not for the purpose of making a mark in society but in order to work. Believe me when I say it will benefit you to appear to advantage among those who hold the reins of power around here, such as they are."

Persephone smiled. "Your assumptions were correct, and I have no objection to making myself a suitable ball gown."

"Oh that won't do!" Sophia said. "The Misses Martin will whip something up in a day or two, as long as we can find the right silk. I think something blue would suit you best. Do you really have to wear black gloves?"

Persephone mentally added up the potential cost of this excursion. Fabric, a seamstress, dinner… She didn't want to demur and risk alienating her only friend in Delabole, though.

"Of course, you dress so plainly I was a little afraid you would read me a sermon about the sinfulness of women's adornments when I suggested this. You're not a Methodist, are you?"

"No!" Although not a scrupulous churchgoer, Persephone did intend to go to morning service at St. Teath's in Camelford on the following Sunday. Perhaps her absence on her first Sunday, when she was not yet truly settled, had been remarked. As Sophia maneuvered the turn to get back onto the county road, Persephone said, "I haven't been to Bodmin since the last time I went to the subscription library there, some weeks ago."

"Then you'll already know that the shops there are not up to London or even Bath standards, but there's more variety to be had there than in our own dear little Camelford."

Sophia was too occupied to talk for a moment as they went over a very rutted stretch of the Camelford Road, and the unsprung gig jolted them mercilessly, forcing Persephone to cling to the seat. Once they passed through the village and reached the turnpike road to Bodmin, the way smoothed considerably and the little horse responded to Sophia's urging to a brisk trot. *She's a creditable whip,* Persephone thought.

"So, we have a little time and no one to overhear us," Sophia said. "It will take us some time to get to Bodmin."

Persephone was tempted to ask why they'd only started out at noon, and whether Mr. Tresillian knew his daughter would not be at dinner that day, but decided against it.

As if she read her mind, Sophia said, "You think me rash to start out so late, I wager. But don't worry. We'll take a private parlor at the Royal Hotel and dine there before we return. I told my father not to expect me before six."

Persephone wished she'd known of this plan before they set out. She wasn't certain the funds she'd brought with her would stretch to both a couple of ells of silk and a decent ordinary dinner.

"Don't look so worried, Persephone! The silk will go on account, you needn't pay the dressmaker until she delivers your gown, and the hotel is very modestly priced. But that's not what I wanted to talk to you about. I need your advice."

"My advice?" Persephone wondered what possible help she could give this educated, accomplished young lady who seemed to know so much of practical use in that country. "Unless it has to do with Italian or philosophy or playing the pianoforte, I'm not certain how I can be of help."

Sophia laughed. "Well, it doesn't directly. It has to do with life, and with what we, as women, are permitted to hope for. You, for instance, seem like a gently bred lady, yet you've never married. And you are certainly handsome enough to attract a gentleman."

Persephone sighed. Apparently she was to act as surrogate governess. So be it. "I thank you, but my circumstances were not conducive to marriage."

"You mean you had no portion, I imagine. Forgive me for being so bold as to say such things on so short an acquaintance with you, but I cannot consult my father on this matter because he has very fixed ideas about what my future holds." Sophia edged the gig over to the side of the road to allow a smart chaise and four to fly past them.

Once it was safely beyond them Persephone said, "Your candor makes me bold to ask, what exactly are your father's aspirations for you?"

Sophia wrinkled her nose and glanced sideways at Persephone. "Of course I'm to marry. And he has his eye on the younger son of the most eminent family in Camelford. I mentioned them the other evening. He says I'm to marry James Pentarrant."

The color rushed into Persephone's cheeks. The quarry captain. Why did it surprise her? More, why did his name make her blush? She was grateful for the breeze that would explain it if Sophia happened to look over. "Why does he wish for that?"

Sophia heaved a deep sigh. "It's all to do with business, naturally. For the Pentarrants, I mean. And I suppose for Papa as well. We're not a very old family, just a very rich one. Marrying me into the Pentarrants would elevate us to a more respectable level. But there's more to it than that."

Persephone was astonished at how coolly Sophia talked about machinations that could determine the direction of her life. She was fully aware of the fact that in noble families like the Ambletons and the Tennants such alliances were often a matter of course. She hadn't expected to find similar motives here, where as far as she knew there were no titled families in the vicinity. "What other considerations are there?" she asked.

"They want Papa to become an investor. What they call an *adventurer.* Makes it sound quite romantic, don't you think?"

Persephone could hardly imagine the financial complexities of running a business on the scale of Delabole.

"I suppose the gain would all be on their side, in one sense," Sophia said. "They get the money and me. And I get—what exactly? That's what I can't quite fathom."

An image of Mr. Pentarrant's hard, handsome face refused to stay out of Persephone's mind. He was a gentleman, to be sure, but he hardly seemed the kind of person who would appeal to a girl just out of the schoolroom, more interested in entertainments than in holding household. Her immediate thought, on the admittedly slight acquaintance she had with both of them, was that they wouldn't suit at all. "I suppose they assume you will acquire standing, and having your own establishment is certainly something. And there would be children, too."

Sophia appeared to be entirely focused on the road ahead, and the two of them lapsed into silence. "Yes," Sophia said after a while, as if their conversation hadn't been suspended at all. "Children. Do you know how often women die giving birth? I don't just mean poor women who don't have a doctor to attend them. I mean even those who have supposedly received every care. My own mother… I mean, doctors don't know what to do when things go awry. A skilled midwife is a much better choice."

Persephone gazed in wonder at Sophia's profile. What she had said was so wholly unlike anything she would have expected a young lady who had been at a select seminary in Bath to say. Childbirth was taboo as a topic of conversation in such settings. Her words brought up a flood of painful memories. All she could think of was her own sister, who had perished giving birth to Antonella, the illegitimate child of the married Marquess of Lewison. After taking a moment to consider how to respond, Persephone said, "And yet, many women become mothers many times over and are content to devote their lives to their families. How else would the generations go on?"

Sophia flashed a quick, apologetic smile at her. "You no doubt think me mad to say such things, or even think them at this juncture! Ladies are supposed to remain in blissful ignorance of anything that happens beyond the wedding day. Yet our bodies warn us ahead of time, every month in fact, that great struggles await us." She gave her head a little shake.

"But that isn't what I intended to say to you. I have no real objection to marrying Mr. Pentarrant, except that he is twice my age. And he may be a member of one of the foremost families in Cornwall, but I'm told he lives hardly better than a parson or tradesman."

"Are you worried that he will not keep you in the manner to which you are accustomed?" Persephone asked. She wouldn't have thought it of Sophia, but what did she know?

Sophia pursed her lips into a pout that made her look her age in contrast to the almost world-weary sentiments she had just shared. "It's not that exactly. I met him briefly, at his elder brother's dinner. He was very much the gentleman."

"So what has you in a worry?"

"I'm not certain. I just think that we are two such very different creatures, as though an unnavigable ocean lies between us. If I married him and became that woman my father thinks I should, I would lose myself."

They had reached the edge of Bodmin and were starting down cobbled streets. Sophia slowed the horse and paid closer attention to the traffic, letting their conversation die away.

Yes, Persephone thought, Sophia Tresillian and James Pentarrant inhabited different worlds. And yet they might be forced into an alliance that, however advantageous in a practical sense, would force a profound change upon both of them. But what power, if any, did an eighteen-year-old girl have to determine the direction her life would take? So many simply accepted the decrees of their parents and circumstance. What gave Sophia the courage to even think about the possibility of making a different choice? Clearly that had been where their conversation was tending, even though it never reached that point.

At the Royal Hotel, an ostler took the gig and the now quite tired Galahad around to the stables. Sophia threaded her arm through Persephone's. "Now let's forget all that is serious and enjoy ourselves in a way that no one will question. After all, gowns and fripperies are the only things ladies care about, aren't they?"

Sophia's eyes danced with mischief, but Persephone couldn't help sensing a shadow of something else in their depths. She squeezed Sophia's arm. "Yes. Let us put all our effort into making ourselves beautiful on the outside. Not that you need any improvement in that regard."

Sophia tilted her chin up and laughed, a rich, silvery sound that drew numerous admiring glances to her as they walked down Fore Street to the linen draper's.

Until, that was, Sophia stopped walking and pinned Persephone's arm to her side. Ahead of them, a young man had just stepped out of the apothecary's shop, a wrapped paper parcel tucked under his arm. "What is it?" Persephone whispered.

"Dr. Rowe," Sophia said, not to Persephone, but aloud so that the gentleman heard it and turned his head toward them.

CHAPTER 8

Apart from when he was practicing medicine, Nathaniel tried to avoid notice as much as possible. He was under the illusion that he managed to do this because his mind was normally so occupied with some vexing problem of diagnosis, or pondering a new treatment he'd read about in one of his medical journals, and he was blissfully unaware of the admiring eyes aimed in his direction as he went about his business in Bodmin. But this particular lady commanded his attention instantly. He had tried, but simply could not forget her from having bumped into her at Tarrant Hall after attending on the lady of the house. They'd spent less than a minute in each other's company. Still, every detail of her features was etched on his memory. With a supreme effort at suppressing a start, he said "Madam," in answer to her greeting and bowed. All the nuances of her expressions and how they'd wrought on him, causing everything from delight to embarrassment to consternation, flitted through his mind. How could she—who was, after all, hardly more than a schoolgirl—have such an effect upon him?

"Dr. Rowe," the lady said, "we weren't properly introduced the other day when we passed each other at Tarrant Hall. I am Miss Tresillian. This is my friend, Miss Wilkins."

He bowed to the other lady, whom he had hardly noticed until Miss Tresillian pointed her out. "Nathaniel Rowe. Your servant, Madam. What brings you to Bodmin?" he asked, feeling quite foolish and madly trying to match the name Tresillian with those of the affluent families he knew of in the Delabole region. In any case, it wasn't any of his business what two ladies would be about in a bustling market town. They would hardly be going to the butchers or the chandlers. And the linen draper's was only a few doors down from the apothecary shop so he might have guessed their destination.

Miss Tresillian apparently recognized his faux pas. Her smile was so broad he might almost have called it a grin, and she couldn't keep the tone of amusement out of her voice. "Why, we are here to furnish ourselves with the finery and fripperies we need in order to make a decent showing at the Roscarrock ball, of course! Why else would ladies wander around Bodmin on a day when there was to be no public assembly?"

How had he managed to step into her conversational trap? Miss Tresillian knocked him off balance. Yet she herself seemed perfectly poised.

Before he could say anything else, she added, with a wicked little gleam in her eye, "I might, however, visit the apothecary myself when my other errands have been accomplished. I am well equipped with the salves and tinctures ladies use for the preservation of their complexions, but I also have an interest in serving my fellow creatures in more important ways."

She was testing him. He had taken her to task on the day of their original meeting, and quite rightly in his view. The significance of that broken phial was not lost on him, and his reaction to it had most definitely not been lost on her. However, the middle of the street was hardly a place to have a conversation about the unsuitability of naive young ladies pretending to physic people when they had no training of any kind. But he couldn't simply let it go. "And where, might I ask, do you come by your knowledge of how to, as you say, serve your fellow creatures in more important ways?" He tried to keep his voice light, but he had a firm conviction that Miss Tresillian was playing with fire and should be discouraged from any more medical interfering.

"That, dear sir, is something I cannot explain to you in a brief conversation. Tell me, Dr. Rowe, where did *you* acquire all your knowledge?"

He squared his shoulders and glanced quickly up and down the street. Did she really want to enter into such a subject there and then? Well then. "I am a licentiate of the Royal College of Physicians." Why did he feel it necessary to puff off his credentials to this slip of a girl? Especially when that information did not seem to impress her very much.

"I see," she said. "And how many women were admitted to this college so they could benefit from that excellent training?"

None of course! What was she playing at? "You know, I suspect, that there were no women at all."

He was about to touch the curly brim of his beaver hat and bid them good day when her features softened, and all he could think was how surpassingly lovely she was. He let his hand drop back to his side.

"You are right, Dr. Rowe. Ladies are not permitted to engage in such activities. They are not expected to deliberate, discuss, and dissect. They are only expected to dance, dally, marry, and suffer the consequences."

Before he could stop himself, Nathaniel put out his hand to take Miss Tresillian's and bowed over it, saying, "Those amusements are a great deal more pleasant than attending upon the sick, or even discussing such things. Permit me, Miss Tresillian, to engage you for the first two sets at the Roscarrock ball, so that we may sample such amusing pastimes together."

The two ladies exchanged quick, surprised glances before Miss Tresillian said, "of course, Dr. Rowe," and curtsied prettily, the faintest blush stealing into her cheeks.

They murmured parting words and the two friends passed on toward the linen draper's. Nathaniel watched their trim figures retreat from him, Miss Tresillian stepping lightly and turning to her friend every now and again as if to share a confidence. Yet he was certain her eyes flicked in his direction more than once.

But he must move on and get back to his business. He had come into Bodmin to restock his medical supplies and to see about purchasing a simple gig. His long-suffering hack was not happy being loaded up with bags of instruments and tinctures, nor did the trusty old fellow take well to being saddled at all hours to attend the sick. The gig and a horse to pull it were expenses he would have preferred to avoid, but there was no helping it. He was not in a position to apply to his father for funds. He could not do so without revealing more about his whereabouts than he wished.

Nathaniel turned his steps down the Shambles toward the livery stable to see if they could put him in the way of something that would not stretch his resources too far. Fortunately, he already had some well-paying patients. That was one benefit of being the nearest doctor to the quarry. His proximity gave him the almost exclusive care of the gentry whose business interests centered on the quarry and who were willing to pay handsomely for his services. What he'd amassed in the short time he'd been in residence wasn't much, but it was enough to make it possible for him to contemplate his coming purchase and to enable him to tend to the poor quarry workers and their families without any expectation of payment.

He wondered what he would do if he were ever called upon to treat Miss Tresillian. It should make no difference. He should be no more disturbed by that thought than the thought of attending someone like Mrs. Pentarrant. But there was no denying he was. What had emboldened him to ask her for those dances? He was quite certain he'd been invited to the ball more out of curiosity than anything else. Aside from the fact that single young men were always welcome at such affairs, he was new, moderately good looking, and though he took pains to distance himself from his family, he spoke and acted like a gentleman.

However, none of that would serve to make anyone perceive him as an eligible match for the likes of Miss Tresillian. In the time it took him to reach the livery stable he recalled what he knew of the family. Mr. Tresillian was one of the wealthiest residents of Camelford and Delabole. Nathaniel hadn't been there long enough to have gained the knowledge that he happened to have a beautiful daughter.

A daughter who, though a diamond, had somehow acquired some rather unorthodox ideas, it seemed. He told himself he should come to know her better so he could advise her, perhaps prevent her from using her mistaken knowledge in a way that could have disastrous consequences. He knew himself well enough, though, to recognize that he had other motives. Foolish ones, to be sure. For all anyone knew, he was only a physician with modest means and no certain prospects. He could have no pretensions to recommend himself to an heiress.

In some sense that made it safe for him to get to know her better. If nothing else, he would have the pleasure of two country dances with her at the ball. In that, at least, he could show himself to be bred a gentleman without having to reveal anything else about his background.

WHAT WERE THE ODDS OF MEETING DR. ROWE IN SUCH A WAY? Sophia supposed they were high enough, since Bodmin was the closest town equipped with both a linen draper's and an apothecary. What would she tell Persephone? How much could she trust her? That was as yet uncertain. Her somewhat older friend no doubt still saw her as a spoiled child capable of little more than social niceties and interested only in making a creditable match now that she was no longer in school.

Perhaps not, though. Persephone was a great deal more perceptive than most of the people she knew. She had an air of circumspection about her. Not reserve, not exactly. And not caution either. To be cautious she would not have uprooted herself and moved to a community where she had no family, no friends, no connections. The marvel of it was that she didn't seem fearful or lonely.

Sophia liked Persephone. She was enough older that there would be no element of competition between them. Not that Persephone was beyond marriageable age at all. She just wasn't in that feverish, heady, ripe for love stage that seemed to make all Sophia's contemporaries foolish beyond permission. She supposed Persephone's solidity and thoughtfulness came of being a governess. And yet, she did not have that pinched, spinster-like aspect of most ex-governesses. She was, in fact, quite beautiful in her way. Not pretty—not classically pretty at all—but her well-proportioned features and wide, hazel eyes rimmed by long dark lashes, her slender, graceful figure and melodious voice, could easily command a man's attention if she allowed them to. The question was whether she wanted any such thing.

"What do you think of this lilac crepe?" Persephone asked, jolting Sophia back to the matter at hand.

They hadn't spoken after the encounter with Dr. Rowe—a necessity as the flagway ended in filthy and uneven cobbles—until they entered the linen draper's.

"Now, Miss Sophia," Persephone said in a low voice, pretending to focus entirely on the selection of silks. "I demand you tell me about Dr. Rowe."

"Not here," Sophia murmured and took the bolt of material Persephone had pulled from the shelf out of her hands. "Why do you choose a matron's color? If, as you say, you are not in full mourning, there is no need to keep to grays and violets. Those colors don't suit your complexion. You are not a pale, fragile bloom. Your face has vibrancy and vigor. Something with more life, something braver I think!" If Sophia could help it, Persephone would not be permitted to fade into the background as she clearly wished to. Hardly surprising for someone who had missed all her first youth educating someone else's daughters.

Persephone shook her head at the pomona green satin Sophia held up for her inspection.

"Why not?" Sophia asked.

She shrugged. "It's too—conspicuous, perhaps. I'm sure my sole purpose in attending this ball is to act as your chaperone! Why else would I have been invited? Be honest."

Sophia hung her head a little shamefacedly. "I will confess that I was able to persuade my papa that he needn't accompany me if you were to be my companion. But I don't intend you to act the chaperone! I fully expect you to dance and enjoy yourself."

"Won't the Roscarrocks be shocked if I do so? I'm certain they must assume me to be some old matron who will drive away the gazetted fortune hunters—oh no, that won't do at all!" Persephone was responding to another length of silk Sophia held up for her inspection from the small selection available. It was a rich gold color that shimmered and appeared to alter subtly when the light hit it from different angles.

"Nonsense! I am persuaded, in fact, that this would be much better than the green. It will bring out the gold glints in your eyes."

Hearing her cue to support a decision to purchase, the proprietress walked over to them. "Yes, Madam, I was like to say summat the same, begging yer pardon." It wasn't often that two fashionable young women not only entered her shop but also prepared to buy her most costly merchandise.

"Mrs. Hendon," Sophia said, "Do you not think this shade becomes my friend very well? And that a gown with a Russian bodice and a little thin gold braid around the sleeves and along the decolletage would answer the purpose? Perhaps some pearl buttons on the diagonal cross. The longer waist will suit you," she said.

"Sophia!" Persephone said. "I could never—"

Cutting her off, Sophia addressed the dressmaker. "We'll take three ells of the gold, and that braid over there—how many yards do you think?" She was not going to give Persephone a chance to demur.

"What about your gown?" Persephone asked.

"Oh, I have so many I may wear. None have been seen hereabouts so everyone will assume they're new. I shall purchase a new fan and stockings, and perhaps some new ribbons for my hair. Shall we go to the milliner?"

With a look, Sophia indicated to Mrs. Hendon that she should package up the material for Persephone's dress and put it on Mr. Tresillian's account. Sophia would deal with her friend's objections later.

When they were once more outside on the now cloudy spring afternoon, Persephone said, "I fear that silk is a little beyond my touch. I must go back and tell the modiste there has been a mistake."

"Nonsense! I mean to make you a present of it."

Persephone's eyes widened. "Sophia! You mustn't. It's too much. And I assure you, I'm capable of purchasing my own gowns."

Was she offended? "Oh, I have no doubt. It was the only way I could persuade you to take the silk that will truly become you. If we're to be seen together you must present a worthy picture!"

Persephone smiled, shook her head, and took her arm. "Just this once I will permit you to indulge your fancy. But I expect a fair exchange."

"Oh?"

"I expect you to tell me everything about that Dr. Rowe. It's clear he admires you."

If only she knew! Dr. Rowe most certainly did not admire her. He saw her as a potential nuisance, that was all. "After I purchase my fan." Sophia turned a merry smile on her friend. "You'll have to get used to my ways, Miss Persephone Wilkins! Besides, I didn't purchase something I knew you wanted. I purchased what I wanted for you."

Persephone was a little embarrassed by Sophia's generosity. It really was a great presumption for her to make a gift of such a thing. How could she decline it though? How could she do so without either insulting or embarrassing Sophia in turn? It was simply that Sophia was possessed of such easy address that her actions and words could not be displeasing.

In point of fact, Sophia Tresillian had poise, manners,

address, and countenance. She was a little younger than Antonella and Belinda, yet she seemed years older. Perhaps her maturity arose from the fact that she'd been away to school, not educated and sheltered at home. But from what Persephone knew of ladies' seminaries in Bath, the students were very closely watched and hardly learned more than the rules of etiquette and how to embroider cushions. Sophia knew a great deal more than that. The difficulty was how to discover what exactly that was, and why she took such pains to hide it.

"Where shall we go after the milliner's? It's still too early to return to the Royal for dinner," Sophia asked.

"After furnishing you with your fan and gloves, I should like to see if the bookseller has *The Child's New Spelling Book.* If not that, at a minimum some copy books and pencils. As yet I have no pupils, but I'd like to be ready for them when they come," she said. "In any case, I need a few quires of paper and some quills and ink. I've already written so many letters to Atherleigh and London that I've quite decimated what I brought with me."

"Of course!" Sophia said as they walked into the milliner's. "I must also stop at the apothecary."

"Oh?" Persephone said. What could Sophia need there?

Without looking at her Sophia said, "I choose to make up my own rouge and face creams. I got into the habit of it at school. Such things amuse me."

Persephone couldn't help thinking there must be more to it than that. She would not, however, force a confidence. Her experience with her two charges at Amblemere taught her that patience often produced a much more candid and thorough revelation. And something told her that Sophia wanted to tell her more, but simply didn't trust her enough as yet.

Something also told her that being in Sophia's confidence might end by involving her in affairs she'd rather avoid.

CHAPTER 9

Eustace had urged James to build a larger house in a better location as befit the dignity of the Pentarrant family. James took a certain amount of perverse pleasure in choosing instead to live in the well-built but modest dwelling his family had abandoned a generation ago. He kept only three servants: a cook, a groom, and a manservant. The manservant, Glynn, served as footman and steward as well as valet on the occasions James needed one. Which wasn't often. By far the best paid servant was the groom, a crusty Cornishman named Digory.

The well-paid groom was a necessity because of his one other extravagance. He rode a handsome thoroughbred gray gelding and owned a matched pair of bays—bought at Tattersall's at great expense—to pull his smart sporting curricle. The irony was that he rarely drove the curricle. The local roads were not well kept and at some times of year became nearly impassable. He could walk to the quarry office and easily ride to Eustace's house or into Camelford. Still, he took great pride in his cattle, and would drive to

Bodmin or Truro if the occasion arose—sometimes even if it didn't—and the weather cooperated.

Aside from the condition of the roads, James's habitation suited him. He was near enough to the quarry that the noise of its works was a constant presence within the house from dawn to dusk, always reminding him of the industry that had been bred into him and that formed the entire focus of his life and energy. The quarry office itself was less than a quarter of a mile's walk away, and he could get there in just a few minutes in an emergency. He spent a few hours of every day in that office reviewing the accounts, meeting with the overseers, addressing any workers' grievances, arranging carting and transport, making plans for expansion, and seeing that the orders from all over the kingdom were fulfilled.

Those tasks finished, James would then go out and visit every part of the works. He had taken over the captaincy at the age of one and twenty after coming down from Cambridge, and he worked tirelessly to ensure the safest possible conditions for the workers. It was not uncommon for him to navigate the steep terraced paths to help a team having difficulty winching up a slab, or to advise on the placement of gunpowder for blasting. He would also assist when necessary in coaxing a recalcitrant donkey to cart the finished slate tiles to the port of St. Isaac, where they were loaded onto ships to be delivered around the kingdom. And he not only watched, fascinated, as the splitters found those precise fault lines in the large stones that would sheer off the sheets a tenth of an inch thick for roof tiles—thicker for pavers—but had a go himself on some of the scrap slate not deemed large enough to produce tiles of the appropriate size.

James knew the quarry operations so well that he could read the noises that filtered to his house. His keen ear detected everything from blasting to winching to splitting to dressing and so on, and he often recognized voices almost too far away to hear. He was also able to perceive any slight changes in the sounds that might indicate that something was likely to go wrong.

Except, of course, when he wasn't. When his ability failed him. As in the recent rock fall.

Everyone knew that although the quarry still yielded excellent stone, the existing terraces would soon be mined out. With hundreds of families depending on the quarry for their merest subsistence, it was time to undertake the dangerous job of excavating a new terrace and removing the overburden. Recent explorations gave every indication that such would yield a rich additional source of good quality stone and make new setts available for contracting to the local men. And this prospect caused everyone to overreach and take shortcuts to speed up the process.

Worst of all, he had allowed it.

"Cheer up, James! You look as though you're going to your execution, not to a ball where you will dance with the prettiest young ladies for at least thirty miles around, possibly others who have come from yet farther away," said Eustace, who was seated next to James in the barouche as they traveled the ten miles to Roscarrock Manor.

James had been surprised when Eustace arrived alone to collect him from the lodge. "Catherine is unwell?" he asked. He'd never known his sister-in-law to decline attending a party if it was at all possible for her to go. She seemed formed only for such entertainments.

"Yes. Or so she claims. Never was with the previous two. I expect she's simply playing on my sympathy, perhaps hoping to get a diamond pendant out of it."

Unable to understand from his personal experience what women endured when they were increasing, James suspected his brother was not as sympathetic as he might be. "And she didn't mind that you would attend without her?"

Eustace raised an eyebrow. "She has nothing to say to that. I expect she knows it's important that I put in an appearance among the local gentry, whatever she might otherwise feel."

Eustace's suppressed smile told James everything he needed to know. Despite having married a diamond of the first water who dutifully presented him with an heir and a spare within less than three years of marriage, Eustace devoured every attractive woman with greedy eyes. Although his brother never owned it directly, James was tolerably certain Eustace kept at least one mistress in Bodmin, and had dallied with numerous maids and farm girls before he married—perhaps still did. It was his own business, to be sure, except that mistresses were expensive, and Eustace's habits had been a drain on the quarry's profits for some time.

James did not endeavor to converse with Eustace after that, but subsided into his own thoughts. These ranged over the quarry, his brother's quirks, and who might be at the ball. The usuals, he supposed, would attend, including the determined Miss Vyvyan. Eustace's insistence on his going made him more than suspect that Miss Tresillian would also be present.

At that moment the carriage rocked and James gripped the strap to prevent himself falling to the floor. The poor horses—bred more to strut around Hyde Park than negotiate rough country lanes—strained on the steep inclines to St. Endelion and their erratic pace reflected the condition of the roads, which were narrow, winding, and rutted.

After over an hour of uncomfortable travel they arrived. Before they stepped down from the carriage, James put his hand on his brother's arm and said, "I shouldn't have come. I won't be good company."

"You can be good company if you simply choose to be. Leave the quarry behind, man!" Eustace punched him jokingly on the arm before they mounted the broad slate steps up to the imposing entrance of Roscarrock Hall.

After the formality of being announced and greeting their hosts, passing through the grand entrance hall and into one of the large, fashionably decorated saloons, James girded himself to face the guests. He wondered if Miss Tresillian was already there. Eustace's efforts to pair them were very unsubtle, James thought with a rueful smile. She was another reason for all the haste at the quarry. Eustace was pushing for a spectacular win to entice Tresillian to invest. The wealthy businessman had wanted to become one of the adventurers twenty years ago, before he married and while he was still making his fortune. At the time, James's father didn't consider Tresillian gentleman enough to welcome him into the syndicate. Now Tresillian had made his fortune and could choose his investments with impunity.

A footman paused before him with a tray bearing glasses of wine. He took one and sipped it. Eustace had already abandoned him to flirt with the widow Horsley, who was young, pretty, and wealthy enough to attract suitors. When he tired of that, no doubt Eustace would go to the card room and lose a small fortune. James had no appetite for either activity.

"Mr. Pentarrant! I'm so pleased to see you here."

James turned to see Miss Philippa Vyvyan's apple-round face and eager eyes peering up at him. "Miss Vyvyan, delighted." As he expected. And so soon.

"I am so pleased you have decided to attend this ball. I had hoped to see you at the Welson's picnic, but, alas, I was disappointed." She smiled. Miss Vyvyan's features, despite their setting in what might have been a jovial face, tended to relax into an expression that suggested she'd just tasted something sour. James suspected that was the reason she made an effort to smile almost continually. Unfortunately, the smile turned her already fairly small, pale blue eyes into little more than slits. It was unfortunate, because she wasn't otherwise a complete antidote.

"I cannot easily attend entertainments during the daytime. The quarry keeps me constantly busy," James said, trying not to make it obvious that he was trying to catch someone's eye to relieve him of the burden of conversation with Miss Vyvyan. She was not yet old enough to be considered a spinster, but she hadn't *taken* in the two London seasons her father, Sir Waldo Vyvyan, had franked her for and was now reduced to combing through the local gentlemen for appropriate suitors. No doubt her position was unenviable and she could be excused for using all the arts and stratagems at her command.

Regrettably, no one joined them to introduce a topic of conversation that would drive her away, and Miss Vyvyan fingered her dance card in feigned absence of mind. James gave into the inevitable and said, "Do you have any room on your dance card for me, Miss Vyvyan?"

"Let me see…" She scanned the scattered names that had already filled a few of the slots as though searching for an empty space. "It appears I have not been claimed for the first waltz or the supper dance—a quadrille, apparently." She dipped her chin down and simpered up at him through her lashes.

"I'm afraid I never learned either the waltz or the quadrille," James said, which was a small untruth. He knew the steps but felt very uncertain about them. "Might I not stand up with you for a country dance?"

The mischievous light in her eyes dimmed a little and her

smile seemed a bit forced. "I believe I have the fourth dance free." She offered him her card and pencil, taking care to obscure everything after the sixth dance, and he wrote down his name in the vacant slot.

Had it been cruel of him not to give her the answer she truly wanted? James was gentleman enough to know he should have offered to sit out either the waltz or the supper dance with Miss Vyvyan. But it was more than he could bear. At such a large ball, there were likely to be twenty or more couples in a set, which would mean long repetitions until everyone had gone down the center of the long-ways dances and completed all the figures of the quadrille. What could he possibly think of to fill a half hour of conversation with Miss Vyvyan? Left to herself, she would likely stray into gossip about their neighbors' foibles—a topic that held no interest for him at all. He supposed he should be more understanding. It must be difficult for a lady who was only moderately pretty and who had little wit to make up for it.

The guests were still arriving, and after an awkward moment or two, Miss Vyvyan excused herself to go and talk to a friend on the other side of the room. James spotted Thomas Carminow in a group of men he recognized from other such gatherings and was about to join them when a stir at the door announced the entrance of Miss Tresillian. Instantly, every male head swiveled in her direction, many pairs of eyes openly scanning her from top to toe. James, on the other hand, found himself distracted by the sight of the woman who had walked in with Miss Tresillian. Hanging back behind her—not as if she was shy or diffident, more as if she wanted to take the measure of the company before entering—was the very woman who had argued with Bray at the quarry a few days ago. James didn't know her name. He'd called her Miss Speechless as a joke and cringed to remember it. Here she was no longer clad in a serviceable hare-brown pelisse with her hair severely confined in a knot at the nape of her neck, but rather in a gold silk gown, modestly adorned, that set off her straight, slender figure. Nut-brown curls that fell from the knot on top of her head framed her serene face. In the ballroom as at the quarry, her confidence showed in her carriage, her graceful strength, and most of all, her wide, intelligent eyes.

Who was this lady to Miss Tresillian? Apparently he was about to find out. Eustace had moved to join him and took hold of his elbow to draw him toward the two new arrivals.

"Remember, we're all counting on you," Eustace murmured to James hardly altering his bland smile.

When they reached the ladies James said, "Miss Tresillian," and executed a decent but perfunctory bow.

She turned her smiling blue eyes up to him and curtsied. Was she aware how thoroughly she represented the ideal in most men's minds, James wondered? He also wondered why her charms left him appreciative but unmoved, as though he were gazing at a portrait painted by a master artist rather than a living creature capable of bestowing affection.

"Gentlemen," Miss Tresillian said, encompassing them both in her polite nod. Her greeting acknowledged, she said, "Persephone Wilkins, allow me to introduce Mr. Eustace and Mr. James Pentarrant. We are neighbors in Camelford. Mr. James, as I gather you already know, is the impressive captain of the works at the Delabole quarry. He lives not far from your cottage, I might add. As to Mr. Eustace—I'm certainly well acquainted with the magnificent Tarrant Hall, but I'm afraid I lack the knowledge to explain what you have to do with the quarry." She bestowed a dazzling but somehow impudent smile on Eustace.

James bit his tongue to stop himself saying *nothing. He does nothing.* Perhaps Miss Tresillian possessed more wit and intelligence than he had originally assumed.

"We have not been not properly introduced, but, as you percieve, I have encountered Mr. Pentarrant before." Miss Wilkins curtsied gracefully and betrayed no emotion. "And I must concur that he is most impressive, especially when exerting his will on someone a fraction of his size."

"What can you mean Persephone?" Miss Tresillian asked in an amused tone, unaware, James thought, of the scene that had passed between himself and Miss Wilkins at their previous meeting.

James was about to acknowledge the introduction when they were surrounded by men who wanted to claim Miss Tresillian for a dance. Eustace elbowed James, who exerted himself to ask her for the first two sets.

"I am afraid I have already promised those to someone else," Miss Tresillian said. She did not offer him a different set but instead presented her dance card to the three or four other gentlemen who vied for a chance to stand up with her.

This suited James, but Eustace again nudged him. His brother could be insufferable. It must be patently obvious to the heiress that he was being thrown at her, and so James turned to Miss Wilkins and said, "Are you already engaged for the first two dances, Miss Wilkins?"

"You want to dance with *me*?" she said.

She was surprised! Did she not believe anyone would ask her with Miss Tresillian around, or had she assumed *he* would not, after their rancorous first encounter? James was a little ashamed to admit he was enjoying her discomfiture. "Dancing is the usual activity at a ball."

Miss Wilkins's somewhat olive complexion did not flush rosily, it simply deepened a shade, throwing her luminous eyes into greater relief. "I am afraid, sir, I am a little out of practice at attending balls."

"Odd that you should appear so admirably suited to the activity," James said, indicating her elegant attire with a gesture. "It would surely be a waste not to use such a lovely gown and those dainty slippers for their intended purpose."

A spark of amusement lit her eyes. That was fortunate, James thought. He half expected her to bristle at his teasing, knowing how capable she was of being roused to anger.

"You make a strong case, Mr. Pentarrant," she said with a slight lift of one arched eyebrow. She presented him with her dance card, which was as yet entirely unfilled.

James wrote his name in the first two spaces. She held her hand out to receive the card back, but he did not relinquish it. Instead, with a sly glance into her eyes he turned the card over and penciled his name in for the supper dance.

She lowered her voice and said, "Sir, you cannot claim me for more than two dances. It isn't done. At least, not where I used to be."

"Are you a debutante? A come-out?" he asked, knowing full well she couldn't be. He could not guess her exact age, yet something about her spoke of experience in the world.

She pressed her lips together and said, "No, Mr. Pentarrant. I was never a debutante before and never will be."

"Good," he said, and smiled at her. "Then we need not be so over particular about you being labeled fast because you danced with me more than twice at one ball."

This brought the smile back into her eyes. "You are right. How good of you to remind me that I am past my days of courtship."

He hadn't meant to imply that at all! Now he was blushing. "Not in the least," he managed to say. "I merely—

Before he could redeem himself, Miss Tresillian turned back to them and said, "Come, Persephone, I'd like to introduce you to some of my old acquaintances," She dismissed her cluster of supplicants with a flick of her fan and slipped her hand under Miss Wilkins's elbow.

James's eyes followed them. From the back, he got a

perfect view of Miss Wilkins's long neck and the tendrils of hair that teased at it. His fingers twitched with the urge to unpin the restraining top knot and let her hair tumble down her back. That would unsettle her serene countenance. A serene countenance below which lurked disruption and turmoil, he was certain.

The question was whether that disruption would be limited to her interference at the quarry, or extend to her interference in his peaceful, ordered world.

CHAPTER 10

Of all the people to meet on first entering a ball where she did not know anyone other than Sophia! Mr. Pentarrant certainly appeared a different man in this setting, but she couldn't fail to recognize him instantly. Of course, all men looked better in evening dress, even those pinks who prided themselves on their yellow pantaloons and shiny hessians as they strolled down Bond Street. But the only other time Persephone had seen Mr. Pentarrant he'd worn buckskins and top boots—not very highly polished ones either—his shirt was wrinkled, and a veneer of stone dust clung to his coat.

Not a speck of dirt sullied his attire now. She owned herself a bit taken aback by his formality in contrast with an appearance that made it quite clear he spent most of his time out in the open doing real work. Skin-tight satin breeches did nothing to hide powerful thighs, and his tanned face contrasted with those of the other men among the guests, most of whom likely spent their lives in drawing rooms and carriages.

Of course he was there. She shouldn't have been

surprised. The society in that part of Cornwall was limited, and the Pentarrants were one of the first families of the county. She was the unexpected one. Despite her maturity and the many assemblies and parties she'd gone to with Antonella and Belinda, Persephone found herself at sea in her current situation. Without charges to keep under her watchful eye or to revel in observing them as they tripped daintily through the country dances, she didn't know what to do with herself. Sophia had made it clear that she wasn't to act as her chaperone. But that was the role that suited her. This elegant creature she'd become at the hands of Sophia's skillful abigail was a stranger.

Persephone smiled involuntarily remembering how Antonella had felt so much the opposite, going one moment from being the privileged daughter of a marquess—from Lady Antonella—to a mere Miss Ambleton when the dowager revealed the truth of her relation to the family.

This was different, though. *I am in essence the same as I always was.* The modest legacy from her father merely conferred a degree of independence and freed her to use her talents in a different way.

"So lovely to see you, Miss Vyvyan."

Sophia's voice recalled Persephone to the present even before she felt the subtle nudge of her friend's elbow. Standing before them was a small young lady of undistinguished but pleasant enough features. Her nondescript dark hair hung in lank curls around her face and her gown was in the first stare of fashion. Sadly, pink did not suit her ruddy complexion and her rather pale blue eyes seemed to repel intimacy rather than invite it, which immediately put Persephone on her guard.

"Why, Miss Tresillian! All polished up and returned from Bath, I see. Perhaps we Camelford and St. Endelion folk are too insignificant for you now." She tried to make light of her words with a brittle little laugh, but the pinch was perceptible. Smiling blandly, Sophia did not respond, and Miss Vyvyan addressed Persephone. "I'm afraid I have not the pleasure of your acquaintance."

"This is Miss Wilkins," Sophia said. "Persephone, Miss Philippa Vyvyan. A neighbor."

The introduction was not merely brief, it was dismissive. Sophia was almost rude, which surprised Persephone. "A pleasure, Miss Vyvyan," she said. "I am but newly arrived in Delabole and welcome all the acquaintance I can find." She made an effort to gaze kindly into Miss Vyvyan's inscrutable eyes in an effort to smooth over the slight and was rewarded with a broad smile.

"Ah! I believe you are the new resident in Mr. Tresillian's cottage!" Miss Vyvyan said.

"Yes, indeed." How did she know this?

"Are you here in the role of chaperone for Miss Tresillian? I believe she is not yet out."

"Nor do I have any plans to make my come-out," Sophia said, interrupting their conversation. "I am not fond of such barbarous institutions. You, I believe Miss Vyvyan, have subjected yourself to the awful scrutiny of the *ton*—what is it, twice? How did you fare?"

Persephone felt not a little sorry for Miss Vyvyan, who clearly lacked the address to parry Sophia's blistering assessment. With a nervous little smile before she curtsied and wandered off again.

"Sophia!" Persephone hissed. "What did she do to you to deserve such Turkish treatment?"

"Don't scold! She tormented me as a child, before I went away to Bath. We were for several years taught together in her father's house by a governess who valued only accomplishments, not actual learning."

"I gather you were not a model pupil."

Before she could say anything more, the ensemble struck up the introduction to the first country dance.

"Here comes Dr. Rowe to claim me as his partner. I must leave you for the moment, " Sophia said.

Sophia had told her the story of their first meeting on their way home from Bodmin the other day, and Persephone had some inkling of what might now be going through her friend's mind. Sophia, it appeared, would face her own struggles against prevailing opinions, just as she herself would—even given the very modest ambitions she had shared with Persephone. A ballroom, however, was not the place to make such a stand.

Persephone sighed. Once again, she found herself alone in a crowd of strangers. How many times in her life had she been in such a situation? If not alone, certainly not regarded. She always took a place out of the way, in the background. Why should she behave any differently that night? She'd much rather sit quietly and think and plan than exert herself to be entertaining. She glanced around for somewhere to sit. Seeing a row of delicate gilt chairs placed discreetly along the wall for ladies without partners, she walked to them and sat.

CHAPTER 11

Nathaniel marveled at the ease and grace with which Sophia Tresellian moved through the company. Such had no doubt been the purpose of her education, the sum total of what she was taught at whatever ladies' seminary she had just emerged from. Nothing unusual in that. Nathaniel was acquainted with many similar damsels, all polished up and flung onto the marriage market to try for the best match they could manage. He thanked whatever better angel helped him discover a way out of that particular fray at the same time as giving him a worthwhile occupation.

"He's a butcher, is Buonaparte!" said Reverend Ballard to general agreement. "They say he's marching his army toward Belgium. The question is, can Wellington defeat him?"

Nathaniel listened with half an ear to a conversation that was no doubt occurring in ballrooms and drawing rooms all across the country. These Cornish gentry could add nothing new to it so he barely attended, instead continuing to observe Miss Tresillian's elegant progress through the room.

"Will you join us for whist in the card room?" Sir Timothy said to him, forcing his attention.

"I beg your pardon? No, thank you, I'm engaged for these first two sets."

"Ah, I see how it is. You're a young blade yet! Plenty of pretty girls here. Who takes yer fancy?" The elderly baronet's eyes gleamed with wry amusement.

The ensemble struck up the introductory measures of the first country dance. "If you will excuse me," Nathaniel said and bowed politely.

Eager to reach Miss Tresillian before the set was fully made up, Nathaniel crossed the room, careful not to appear hurried. He paused to let couples stream toward the ballroom, then joined her where she stood with Miss Wilkins, the lady who had accompanied her to Bodmin. A duenna of sorts, he guessed. Strangely, Miss Wilkins did not act like a chaperone and Miss Tresillian didn't treat her like one either. Despite the clear difference in their ages, they appeared to be on terms of intimate friendship. Miss Wilkins was attractive and assured, graceful and gracious. If Miss Tresillian had not been present, she might even have found herself the most sought-after lady in attendance. But Miss Tresillian *was* there. He couldn't have identified exactly how or why Sophia Tresillian drew all eyes to her, absorbing the attention of every man in the room. She was dazzling. She was dangerous.

His mind fully occupied with those disturbing thoughts, Nathaniel hardly knew how they came to be in the ballroom where they joined the set in third position. Miss Tresillian leveled a serious gaze at him. No coquetry, no games. No doubt she well knew how to play such roles and simply chose not to. What would they speak about? Not the weather, he guessed, and smiled.

"How long have you been in Camelford, Dr. Rowe?" Miss Tresillian asked the first time the movement of the dance brought them together.

Safe ground. A trifle more interesting than the weather, at least. "About two months."

"And where did you practice before?"

"I came to Camelford directly after I was licensed by the Royal College of Physicians."

A pause before Miss Tresillian spoke again. "So you have not practiced before on actual patients."

"We worked with patients at the University of Edinburgh Medical School, where I assure you we were exposed to a vast variety of conditions and complaints." Nathaniel mentally kicked himself for sounding defensive. Who was she to judge him in that way?

"Tell me, Dr. Rowe, what do you do when you are not practicing medicine?"

And so we move on to other pleasantries. "I have little time for leisure, but I enjoy riding to hounds."

"Do you have hunters here?" she asked, one eyebrow raised.

She might well wonder. He thought about the stable of high-bred hunters he left behind in Bedfordshire. His sturdy hack was no kind of jumper, and the horse he'd recently purchased to draw his gig was suited for nothing else. Why had he mentioned hunting? "Unfortunately, no. I assumed I would not have the time to indulge in that sport and so I sold my one hunter before embarking on my studies." It was an innocent enough falsehood.

She smiled knowingly at him as they circled around each other, arms crossed to hold both hands. "Have you brothers and sisters?"

How much did he want to tell her about his family? His past? He had no desire for his background to become known. Not so soon in any event. He had counted on having a little more time to gain experience practicing medicine as nothing more than a humble doctor. In any case, he need tell her little at a ball. Or afterwards. The likelihood was that the unfortunate animosity of their first encounter would keep them at arm's length from each other for the foreseeable future, whether or not that was as he wished.

The set ended and so did their conversation. He opened his mouth to ask her if she would like a glass of lemonade, but before he could say the words another gentleman came to claim her for the quadrille.

So be it, Nathaniel thought. He had the supper dance with her, a waltz. He'd claimed it instead of the second country dance. He had to admit she was a puzzle. A puzzle, he thought with a rueful smile, that it would be a pleasure to tease out.

CHAPTER 12

Not long after Persephone had taken her seat by the wall, Miss Vyvyan bustled over to sit next to her. "Such a squeeze!" she said, fanning herself vigorously.

Persephone thought the room rather empty, most guests having decamped for the ballroom.

Before she could say as much, she became aware of a presence between herself and the chandelier in the center of the room. "Miss Wilkins."

She looked up. It was James Pentarrant. He held his hand out to her. "Surely you haven't forgotten?" he said.

In truth, at that point she had assumed for some unknown reason that he wouldn't come to claim her, that his show of setting his name down on her dance card had been purely to disconcert her. The fact that he had been in earnest about dancing with her sent her into a flutter of confusion, which she hoped she managed to cover with a polite smile. She let him help her up and placed her hand on his arm so he could lead her to the set that was just forming. Persephone did not look back, but she had the distinct impression that Miss Vyvyan's eyes were fixed upon them.

They were the last to join their lines, and so took their place at the end, facing each other. Sophia and Dr. Rowe occupied the third position near the top. The lead couple was, of course, Mrs. Roscarrock and a gentleman Persephone assumed must be a guest of rank or distinction.

She looked into Pentarrant's unsmiling face, which stared directly at hers with his intent, dark blue eyes. She did not know him well enough to read his expression. It wasn't precisely hostile, but at the same time not inviting. Questioning, she thought. What did he wonder about her?

At that moment, the movement of the dance brought them together to circle one another, heads turned, eyes still locked. All around them, couples took advantage of the excuse to exchange pleasantries and laugh. But they two remained silent.

So, perhaps he wasn't disposed to think well of her after all. Disappointing. But what did it matter? They didn't have to be more than distant acquaintances. Yet she realized she would have to gain his sympathy for her project with regard to the quarry children if she were to have a chance of success. It would not be as easy as she'd hoped it would, apparently.

They separated and then came together again, Persephone deciding to smile encouragingly.

Pentarrant did not return her smile, but said, "Why were you at the quarry the other day?"

No pleasantries. No polite inquiries. So that was why he had asked her to dance. "I wanted to see for myself how the children are accommodated there."

"They live with their parents in the quarry cottages," Pentarrant said just in time before the dance parted them again.

Persephone suspected he well knew that was not what she meant, and it vexed her. At the next opportunity, with a defiant spark in her eyes, she said, "I see there is no school for the children. Are they all unlettered?"

Pentarrant would have had time to answer, yet he said nothing until the next time the dance brought them together, which happened to be when they reached the top of the set. "You would do well not to interfere in a system that has been in place and working adequately for centuries. The quarry children are well cared for."

He had just thrown down the gauntlet. So that was his attitude. Would they have to be enemies? Or if not actual enemies, on opposite sides of this issue?

Just as she was deciding whether to answer him in the same provocative tone, Pentarrant said, "Tell me, do you ride?"

She supposed as conversations went, that was as good a way to change the subject as any. "I do. And you?"

"Horses are one of my chiefest pleasures in life. What do you ride?"

They were separated by the dance, and Persephone had time to decide exactly what to say regarding her current lack of personal transportation. "Right at the moment, I have a borrowed cob that is more suited to drawing a cart than riding. My niece is letting me use him until such time as I purchase my own mount."

For the first time since they started dancing—for the first time that evening, in fact—Pentarrant smiled. His angular, stern face transformed in an instant. The corners of his eyes lifted just slightly and the hint of a dimple showed in one cheek, making him appear almost boyish. "It would be my pleasure to help you choose a beast that will suit you."

Ah, she thought. He wants to show me that he knows best about everything! "I thank you for your kind offer, but I believe I am capable of judging a horse for myself."

One eyebrow lifted, but his smile remained. "No doubt.

But do you know the best place to procure one here? And which trader you can trust not to cheat you?"

"I think after nine years as a governess I am a fair judge of character." She was annoyed with herself for sounding rude. His offer was kind.

"So your charges were hardened horse traders, then?"

Despite herself, Persephone laughed. "No, but you wouldn't believe the subterfuges two gently bred young ladies resort to when it's in their own interest to do so."

This broadened Pentarrant's smile into a grin. "Nonetheless, I would take care if I were you. Seth Carrowmore would try to swindle his own mother if he thought he could profit by it."

"Then it's fortunate I am not his mother," Persephone said.

The set ended and they bowed to each other.

"I know I'm supposed to ask you if you would like a glass of lemonade after the exertions of the dance. But as you are a grown woman, would you prefer a glass of wine?"

Did he mean to remind her of her age? How ungenerous! "Even grown women might prefer lemonade, sir," she said.

"As you wish," he said and went to procure the refreshment.

PERSEPHONE DANCED OFTEN THAT EVENING, MORE THAN SHE had since she was quite a young girl, still at home and attending local assemblies. She had forgotten the feeling of moving to the beat of the music, the sheer pleasure of the intricate steps of the quadrille and the cotillion. Teaching them was a far cry from actually doing them with an attentive partner, from being swept away in the moment and forgetting everything around her.

By the time of the supper dance, a waltz, Persephone felt

as if her whole body was smiling. Nothing, she thought, could dim her ebullient mood. She caught occasional glimpses of Sophia, but not because she wasn't dancing. In fact, her friend hadn't sat out once. Did she imagine it, or did Sophia glitter more brightly during the set she danced with Dr. Rowe? And now, on the other side of the room, she and the doctor faced each other for the waltz. Persephone could almost feel the sparks that connected them across the regulation twelve-inch separation.

As to Mr. Pentarrant, she had seen him dancing occasionally with a variety of partners, some of them girls sitting disconsolately on the gilt chairs by the walls. How kind, she thought. And what a contradiction. How could someone so considerate in a ballroom leave the management of the quarry boys to a brute like Bray?

"I believe this next dance is ours."

Persephone turned toward the now familiar voice of James Pentarrant, her face warming in a blush. "Why yes, I believe so," she said, relieved that he could not know what she'd been thinking moments before. She put her hand in his and he led her out to the floor as the ensemble played the opening strains of a waltz.

Mr. Pentarrant was taller than she was, but not by a great deal. Yet he somehow gave the impression of height. Did his upright, solid exterior reflect what was within him? He appeared to be well liked, moving quietly through the room with a kind word for everyone, leaving a trail of smiles in his wake.

"I have not danced the waltz often, Miss Wilkins, so I hope you will forgive any missteps," he said as they took their positions.

She smiled up at him. "You cannot have danced it less than I have, sir. The last time I heard music like this was when I was teaching the steps to my charges in the schoolroom some years ago. So it is you who may have to be careful of your toes."

"Shall we make a pact?" Pentarrant said.

It was not what she expected him to say just then. "A pact?"

"Let us not talk about the quarry or the education of children for the duration of this dance."

Persephone ruefully realized that their first conversation that evening had been inappropriate for such a setting. He started it, but she should not have engaged in the subject. "Agreed," she said.

He pressed his hand to her waist. It had no effect upon her, she told herself. Further, the comfort of his strong shoulder beneath her hand did not send a little thrill of something down her arm and into her middle. No. Such reactions were positively girlish, and she was by no means a girl. Nor was he a green youth. They were simply two acquaintances dancing politely in a room full of strangers, some of whom undoubtedly had their eyes trained upon them. The quarry captain and the spinster governess. Such an unlikely pair—but they were not, of course, a pair.

Most of the time Persephone kept her gaze resolutely upon Pentarrant's face as they danced. Once she glanced to the side and caught Miss Philippa Vyvyan staring at them, her lips in a pucker of distaste. A moment later Miss Vyvyan turned to talk to a dowager clad in heavy violet silks.

When the waltz ended, Pentarrant put out his hand to take hers and guide her to the supper room. He should have clasped it lightly and transferred it to his arm, but to Persephone's surprise, he held it in a strong grip, not relinquishing it until he had found her a chair at one of the long tables in a saloon on the floor below.

She and Sophia would have so much to talk over in their shared room at Roscarrock. She smiled, feeling as if the years had fallen away, and she was once again going to share secrets with her beloved sister in the attic of the parsonage in Somerset.

CHAPTER 13

Against her better judgment, Sophia had allowed Rowe to relinquish one of the country dances for the supper dance. To make matters more shocking, it was a waltz. So why did she look forward to that dance with such a sense of delicious anticipation? And now, here they were, standing across from each other, not yet touching.

The music started and Rowe reached his right hand out to encircle her waist.

Before she could place her left hand on his shoulder, a footman approached him with a note.

"Excuse me," he said, removing his hand and stepping a little away as he unfolded the paper and read. Scratched on it in pencil were two words. Sophia inched forward to where she could see the writing. The note said, *Missus porly.* It must have come from someone in Delabole.

"I am afraid I must take my leave," Nathaniel said. "My apologies for abandoning you at this juncture. A patient needs me."

"Which patient? I would guess someone from the quarry."

Miss Tresillian made no attempt to pretend she hadn't stolen a glimpse at a private communication.

An icy chill came into his eyes as he looked down at her. "Of what possible interest can that be to you?"

"I imagine there is no time to waste in such cases, Dr. Rowe." Sophia ignored his impertinence, hoping he would simply accept her participation in whatever crisis was transpiring. She followed him out to the hall where she commanded a footman, "Our cloaks, please." Before Dr. Rowe could protest, she asked him, "Did you arrive in your gig, or shall I summon my coach?"

His eyes opened wide. "I came in my gig, and you shall remain here at the ball. This is no errand for a lady." He took hold of her hand and gripped it. When she glanced down at their joined hands he let hers go, leaving a tingling sensation still in her palm.

"What are you afraid of?" she said to him, her voice gentle.

His unyielding expression softened for a moment, until the footman arrived bearing their evening cloaks. "The lady will not be requiring hers," he said, taking his own and swirling it quickly around him. "Afraid? Madam?" he said over his shoulder as he strode to the door. "I am only afraid that I must leave you now to attend to one of my patients. I am certain you will not lack for partners for the remainder of the evening."

Sophia had a feeling, based on the scrawled note she'd seen, that one of the quarry women was having trouble birthing a child. While physicians certainly knew how to bring babies into the world, she was afraid men were sometimes more concerned with the mechanics of the process rather than the comfort or ease of the mother. It could be a brutal business. By rights, she shouldn't know anything about it at her age and in her station in life. But she had been at home when a breach birth took her mother's and her infant brother's lives. *I could do nothing*, the doctor had said.

How those words haunted her. And when she was sent to school in Bath soon after, she did what she could—despite all efforts to channel her zeal for learning into more ladylike pursuits—to discover what she could about women's ailments and the hazards that attended them in childbed. It wasn't easy. She had to bribe one of the footmen at the academy to procure books for her. That was how she acquired her copy of *Culpeper's Herbal*.

But it was through listening to the maids whenever they spoke of their female relatives' experiences that she discovered the name of a midwife who lived in the countryside just outside Bath. The first time she stole away to visit her, the old woman—Mattie Davy—thought she'd come because she was in the family way and wanted to rid herself of the embarrassment. That had marked the beginning of Sophia's true education.

The Roscarrock ball was a world away from Mattie's thatched cottage. That evening was hardly the right time to attempt to persuade Dr. Rowe that she could in any way help him.

Sophia went back toward the ballroom, her mind anywhere but on the party. Couples whirled happily in the waltz. To her delighted interest, Persephone was in the arms of the younger Mr. Pentarrant. A handsome gentleman, but reserved. The Pentarrants were almost as important as the Roscarrocks in that part of the county. If there were a Roscarrock son of the right age, no doubt her father would be pushing that alliance. As it was, Sophia had no interest in any marriage just then. Especially not with James Pentarrant, despite what her father told her the other night, that he wanted to know she was safely and creditably married before he died.

Before he died! Her father was in his fifties, and he seemed hale and hardy enough, aside from becoming tired and breathless at times. He was a little too active, had a hearty appetite and drank his fill of fine wines. That notwithstanding, surely he had many years ahead of him yet.

Whatever her father wished didn't alter the fact that James Pentarrant was too old for her. And besides, she could tell he wasn't really interested. She had seen it in his attitude at the Pentarrant party—only half there, his mind on other matters entirely, and no flicker came into his eyes when he looked at her, as so often happened with other gentlemen.

He behaved altogether differently with Persephone that evening, though. Even from across the room, Sophia detected interest in his expression. Not just interest: complete focus. His mind was not on the quarry. He was entirely there, and attending to Persephone. As to Persephone, her attitude was harder to ascertain. Long habits of masking their feelings made women adept at concealing emotion.

"Miss Tresillian, you appear to have lost your partner. Did he abandon you?"

Eustace Pentarrant appeared at Sophia's elbow. Sophia hadn't been in Cornwall above a week before she became aware that Mr. Eustace also had an interest in promoting a match between herself and his brother James. She quizzed her father about it and discovered that his desire had something to do with the need for an injection of cash to the quarry. Such matters often drove marriage alliances, so she wasn't shocked. She smiled pleasantly up at him. "I'm afraid Dr. Rowe was called away by the demands of his profession."

"How tiresome that must be. If I were in his shoes, I wouldn't give up such a charming partner so willingly."

Sophia was fully aware of Eustace's wandering eye. Everyone knew of it. Without altering her expression, she said, "Then it is fortunate you are not—fortunate for the lady who might require your urgent attention, I mean to say."

Without the faintest appearance of having recognized Sophia's words for the cut they were intended to be, Eustace said, "Perhaps I—or my brother—would be an adequate substitute for the good doctor in the next dance?"

The waltz ended and couples made their leisurely way in to supper. "I am afraid, Mr. Pentarrant, that my dance card is already full, except for the cotillion, which I intend to sit out so that I may rest my feet. New slippers, you understand."

Eustace signaled to his brother who was leading Persephone toward the supper room.

"I was just saying to Miss Tresillian that it is a pity she is unable to take the floor with you. As she has lost her supper companion, perhaps she may join you and Miss Wilkins."

The younger Mr. Pentarrant appeared mildly vexed at this idea, but Persephone said, "Oh yes! Do join us, Sophia."

"I believe I have the cotillion with you, Miss Wilkins, after supper," Eustace said. "Miss Tresillian does not intend to dance that time. Perhaps you might sit with her while she rests, James."

A line of annoyance appeared between James Pentarrant's eyebrows. "I must speak with Roscarrock about a matter to do with the quarry, and we arranged to meet in the card room after supper."

Eustace said nothing, but stared fixedly at his brother.

James shrugged and said, "This is a ball, however, and I daresay I can speak with Roscarrock another time. I would be delighted to sit with you, Miss Tresillian."

"Piqued and re-piqued," Sophia said. "It appears you have no choice, Mr. Pentarrant. I promise you my conversation is not so vacuous. I should like to know what you do at the quarry. I understand that, unlike most gentlemen here, you actually work." She gave Eustace a polite but dismissive smile.

After that, the evening couldn't end soon enough for Sophia, despite the fact that James Pentarrant proved an amiable companion and the remainder of her time was taken up afterwards dancing every set.

Sophia kept half an eye on the door to the ballroom, hoping that Dr. Rowe would return. He did not. Her heart sank. She hoped the poor woman he'd gone to attend had survived her ordeal.

CHAPTER 14

Nathaniel had an uncomfortable feeling that he had left Miss Tresillian rather rudely at the ball. In the moment, he had allowed his annoyance over her nosiness about the patient he had been summoned to see to interfere with his good manners. Even if he was a country doctor now, he was born and bred a gentleman, and one did not treat well-born ladies that way—or any ladies, really. The practice of medicine among such varied classes and kinds of people had had a leveling effect. Each person he saw, after all, was human—the same body that worked in the same way and was subject to the same ills. He sometimes thought members of the upper class forgot that simple fact, if they ever considered it at all.

So it was as a gentleman and not a physician that he rode his hack to Tresillian Manor late in the afternoon the day after the ball. He knew it was likely that the ladies from Camelford had been invited to stay that night at Roscarrock, so they would hardly have returned and be ready to receive visitors in the morning.

The elderly butler, Hosking, led Nathaniel up the stairs to

a drawing room. Lively voices tumbled out the open door before he reached the top of the stairs that branched off in two directions to galleries on either side. *It seems others had the same idea,* he thought, partly relieved, partly vexed.

Hosking announced him and the four other gentlemen visitors stood as he entered, but took their places again almost immediately. He found himself amid the totality of the single young hopefuls in that part of Cornwall who might have pretensions to Miss Tresillian's hand. He'd learned a great deal at the ball, before he was called away. All of those present were eldest sons, most of landed gentry rather than nobility; one he'd been told was distantly related to a baron and was that baron's presumptive heir.

The heiress surveyed them all with polite interest, not distinguishing any one of them particularly. But when her eyes met his, something danced in them—amusement, perhaps? What was funny about his coming to see her?

Then he remembered. Here he was not a prize catch for an ambitious lady. Here he was simply the local physician, perhaps given credit for being gentlemanly, but hardly of the same class.

He stepped forward between the two swains standing closest to Miss Tresillian and vying for her attention, put out his hand to take hers, and bowed over it. "Miss Tresillian, your servant," he said, casting his haughtiest look at the slender youth with hardly a whisker on his chin standing to his right. The lad went crimson and moved away.

"What brings you here today, Dr. Rowe?" Miss Tresillian said, a challenge in her eyes.

"I have come to apologize, Miss Tresillian."

"Apologize for what? Is it not enough to simply pay your respects?"

"I fear I left you rather rudely when I was called away last night."

"The hazards of being a working cove, what?" said one of the gentlemen. The others snickered their agreement.

Without directly answering her guest or treating his remark as if she had heard it, Miss Tresillian said, "I am grateful that you have taken time out of your busy schedule to visit, doctor. As a guest you have an advantage over many others, however." She paused and swept her gaze around at the callers in the room, then continued, "The advantage is that because you work, you are able to contribute to a conversation with something more than the idlest pleasantries. How did you find your patient last night, Dr. Rowe?"

"I say! That's hardly fit conversation for a lady!" said another of the young gentlemen who had squeezed his rather ample self into a very tight-fitting coat of green superfine.

Miss Tresillian glanced pointedly at the clock on the mantlepiece. These visits of ceremony were supposed to last no more than a polite ten minutes, and it seemed clear to Rowe that one or two of the guests had outstayed their welcome. Apparently that same thought occurred to them. A flurry of hasty farewells were uttered. Miss Tresillian rose and allowed her hand to be kissed by all of them without uttering a single protest against their leaving.

To Nathaniel's surprise, that left the two of them alone in her drawing room but for the maid who sat quietly stitching in a corner. The abigail looked up and exchanged a quick smile with her mistress before once more concentrating on her work.

"Please sit, Dr. Rowe," Miss Tresillian said, indicating a wing chair opposite her own seat. "Might I offer you a glass of wine?"

"Only if you will join me," he said as he sat.

She glanced toward the maid, who rose. "Summon Hosking and ask him to bring some sherry, Adler."

Miss Tresillian was very young, clearly just out of the

schoolroom. But she did not act young. His experience of girls of her ilk was of ready blushes and giggles behind fans, and hardly more than a *yes sir,* or *no sir,* to say in answer to any question. Miss Tresillian had a mature command of her situation and in the few instances of their meeting had said things that surprised him. Add to that the fact that he had rarely seen even the most formidable of society matrons clear a drawing room with such dispatch as this young miss had that very afternoon.

"You say you want to apologize," Miss Tresillian said. "You did indeed behave rather badly, but I understood why, and I daresay it couldn't be helped. You may atone by telling me something about the lady you attended last night. What was her complaint, and what did you do for her?"

"How did you know it was a female? Not a lady, of course."

She shrugged prettily. "An educated guess. And I peeked. Was she in difficulty with her labor?"

"Miss Tresillian, this really is hardly suitable conversation for a lady such as yourself."

"And what sort of a lady do you think I am exactly, Dr. Rowe?" Her eyes flashed and her normally pouty lips compressed into a hard line. "Do you think I am one of those genteel misses who know nothing more than the manners and accomplishments they've been taught by their governesses or, in my case, at their exclusive ladies' seminary? I thought better of you. But if that is in fact your way of thinking, you will not want to waste your time talking to me. I have no accomplishments. I hate small talk. And I'm quite capable of being as ill mannered as you were last night."

Nathaniel couldn't help smiling at this. "You are right, of course. It's a foolish convention that ladies must not discuss or even know anything about the body."

"Especially since it is the women who have been taking

care of other women's health for centuries. I think it's rather the men who become tongue-tied when faced with having to think about women and disease. This is most notably true when it comes to those uniquely female complaints."

Nathaniel didn't quite know what to say. What had happened to give Miss Tresillian such a jaded view of medicine? And what had she done to educate herself about the human body, when the word "body" wasn't even supposed to be uttered in her presence?

"But I have transgressed one of the cardinal rules of polite society," she said, as if having heard his thoughts. "We should not discuss anything more controversial than the weather."

By that time Hosking had come in with the tray and poured each of them a glass of excellent sherry.

Time for him to steer the conversation onto safer ground. "You said you were in school. Where was that?"

She wrinkled her nose in distaste. "Bath. I think my father spent a small fortune to send me there, and all I learned from my teachers was how to curtsy and embroider useless ornaments. Oh, and they taught me how to walk and dance."

"I can assure you the dancing lessons were not a waste of time," Nathaniel said with a smile, conscious that he had uttered a flirtatious nothing.

But Miss Tresillian appeared not to have heard him and continued her own thread. "It was my good fortune to discover another source of education in Bath. I say good fortune, but it was really a necessity."

"What was that? I know there are several good lending libraries there. I expect you could get just about any book if you wanted it." Was she learning about medicine from romance novels? He hardly imagined she could have laid her hands on any medical textbooks or *Culpeper's Herbal*.

She cocked her head to the side and examined him, a curious half smile playing on her lips. "No. I don't think I know you quite well enough yet to divulge my scandalous secrets."

How could so young a lady have had time to acquire scandalous secrets? "If that be so, Miss Tresillian, perhaps you will give me an opportunity to further our acquaintance. I have been told there are some lovely rides hereabouts, even if the country is not ideal for hunting. That is irrelevant at this time of year anyway, but I'm sure you know what I mean."

"You have not been misinformed," she said.

"In that case, would you do me the honor of riding out with me one day? Since you spent your youth here I imagine you must be well acquainted with the best places. Of course your groom will accompany us." Where did all that come from? He hadn't really meant to invite her out. His intention was only to beg her pardon for being so stern with her the night before and then resume a polite, distant acquaintance with her.

Her eyes widened. "Are you certain you want to do that, Dr. Rowe? I warn you, I'm not a timid rider. I grew up throwing my leg over a horse without a saddle and galloping off astride. Of course, I don't do that any longer. And I have a very fetching habit made in London that I have been eager to put through its paces. So, if you are indeed in earnest, the answer is yes. I would be delighted to ride with you. Would tomorrow be agreeable?"

The plan made, Nathaniel took his leave. He had expected to be somewhat disappointed by Miss Tresillian in the light of an ordinary afternoon, free of the entrancing effects of crystal chandeliers and music and the magic of dancing. But the opposite occurred. She surprised him—again. Each time he encountered her, she said or did something wholly unexpected that revealed another side of what he was coming to believe was a character of depth and subtlety.

The groom led his horse around from the stable. Nathaniel shook his head to clear it and swung himself up into the saddle. Don't be a fool, he thought. To strike up a flirtation with an eligible female had not been his intention when he settled in Camelford. If he allowed it to continue it would complicate his already rather precarious life.

He couldn't back out now, though, and what was one ride, after all? He spurred his hack on and cantered back toward his Camelford lodgings, attempting to ignore the persistent feeling that he was in serious danger of being much more than friendly with Sophia Tresillian.

CHAPTER 15

A few miles down the road from Tresillian Manor, James Pentarrant approached Miss Wilkins's cottage with a now rather bedraggled bunch of wildflowers in his hand. He'd picked them earlier that morning, but had had to spend a few hours at the quarry going over plans for the coming excavation to dig a new terrace—plans that he and his brother had been arguing over for months. All the time he was there, he kept thinking of the visit he planned afterwards. It was very unlike him—both his distraction and the deed itself. He'd never before called upon a lady the day after a ball. He rarely danced with anyone at assemblies and parties even when he deigned to attend them. He never saw the point when he had no plans to marry. Why lead anyone on, or engender false hopes? Besides, his heart had been broken into a thousand pieces years ago, and he had no desire to risk it happening again.

But Eustace persuaded him that the Roscarrock ball was too important to miss, and that Miss Tresillian would be there and he should improve his acquaintance with her. What Eustace could not have known was that with Miss

Tresillian came Miss Wilkins. The annoying, interfering, naive Miss Wilkins, who was of an age that she should have known better than to try to put her nose into the man's world of slate quarrying—where it certainly didn't belong.

So why, then, did he dance with her three times, including the supper dance? And now, why did he feel he should call on her, like a wet-behind-the-ears lovesick swain? He most certainly was not lovesick.

He was, however, intrigued. Miss Wilkins was an odd combination of assurance and reticence, as if she knew her own mind but not her place in the world. All that business about buying a horse! She would be cheated for sure.

The garden at the front of the modest cottage where she lived showed signs of recent cultivation, although James could see there was as yet much to do before its wildness would be tamed. He mentally weeded a bed and chopped down an overgrown hedge before he reached the newly painted front door and knocked.

A middle-aged serving woman answered, appearing surprised by his presence. "Mr. Pentarrant?" she said, as though not entirely certain of his identity.

"Is your mistress at home?"

Unlike a well-trained butler, who would have made him wait while he ascertained whether the lady was at home to visitors, the woman led him into the small hall and on to a room that led off it to the right. He found himself in a comfortable, spacious farmhouse kitchen where Miss Wilkins was engaged in poring over what appeared to be a ledger at a sturdy oak table. She stood so fast that the quill she was holding flew out of her fingers and landed at his feet.

James bent down and picked it up. "If you want to repel invaders I'm afraid you'll have to choose a more effective weapon."

A ready smile came to her lips and amusement livened

her eyes. "It is said that words can cut more deeply than a surgeon's blade, so perhaps it's not so unsuitable after all. How do you do, Mr. Pentarrant." She came around the table with her hand out to shake his.

James wasn't sure whether to put the flowers or the pen into her outstretched hand, since both of his were occupied with these impediments.

They laughed. Miss Wilkins took first the pen, then the now very wilted flowers, which she handed to the servant. "Perhaps these will revive in a little water, Hannah," she said, then gestured gracefully to two chairs on either side of a small table near the hearth. "Won't you sit and take some refreshment?"

Now what? James thought. He suddenly felt utterly foolish. What purpose could he claim in coming to see her? "I wanted to say how much I enjoyed dancing with you at the ball last night."

To his surprise, his remark appeared to disconcert her. "Did you also enjoy my impertinent arguments? I must apologize for being so ungracious."

Was she ungracious? Not exactly. "And you must forgive me for rising so swiftly to your fly. I'm not accustomed to talking to ladies about the concerns of the quarry and those who work there."

Their conversation paused while the maid, Hannah, brought them a pot of tea, a jug of milk, and two somewhat chipped porcelain cups. Miss Wilkins grimaced as she examined them. "I have never had a home of my own before and I'm afraid I am ill equipped to entertain visitors as yet."

"I think you said you came from not very far away to settle here," James said, hoping it wasn't impertinent of him to try to get her to reveal something of her background—and hoping that it had been she who gave him that information and not Eustace.

"No indeed. For nine years I was first governess and then companion to the late Lord Lewiston's two daughters. The estate is not much above ten miles away." She poured out the tea and lifted the jug of milk with a questioning look. He shook his head and she laced her own cup with a splash, then took some time to stir it and sip.

This gave James an opportunity to study her a little, and to realize that although she had given him information, she hadn't really told him anything that would shed any light on her past. "A governess. Of course. And now a teacher. I imagine you will be disappointed in the caliber of pupils you may attract hereabouts. None of them are likely to require instruction in embroidery or the Italian language."

Her pleasant smile froze on her face, and James was immediately sorry he'd said something so presumptive and belittling.

"I didn't mean—" he began, but Miss Wilkins cut him off.

"I confess, I am at a loss to account for your taking the trouble to come and visit me. It appears that you hold me in low esteem."

She made as if to rise, but James put his hand out and touched her arm. "That was clumsy and insensitive of me. I'm not accustomed to making small talk with ladies. I know so little about you that I'm afraid I just grasped at the only straw I could find. I do not, indeed, hold you in low esteem. Quite the opposite."

Miss Wilkins settled back into her chair and the hardness drained from her expression. There was something about that face. Her eyes—hazel, or gray, not a vibrant color. Their uniqueness was rather in the shape. They turned down slightly at the outer corners giving her a questioning, inquisitive expression when her face was at rest. Her eyebrows were set quite far apart, which added to the effect.

"You are forgiven," she said with a mock-serious inclination of the head.

"What I meant to do, somewhere in all this, was to ask why you have chosen to settle in Camelford, and so near to a noisy, dusty slate quarry in a house that—frankly—is barely adequate for a lady."

"As I said, I am not a lady. Not really. I have lived in luxurious surroundings, but I have always worked. The Ambletons were kind and generous employers, but I took on a great deal of the work of running the household as well as charge of the twins."

"Did they at last give you a handsome pension so you could escape from your drudgery?" he said, this time taking care to smile when he said it so she would understand it to be partly in jest.

Her answering smile assured him that she had. "No, not exactly. I could have lived out my days in idle luxury at Atherleigh Manor after Antonella married the baron. But I am not accustomed to idleness, and I wanted to do something. I wanted to put my abilities to use where they might be needed, not where I would be merely polishing up elegant females who would be treated as breeding commodities in the marriage market." She paused and looked out the window. "Perhaps that sounds irreverent to you. But education is a privilege. Those who are educated have more power than those who are not. I don't mean in the manner of power over the government or even over their livelihoods. I mean power to make more of their innate gifts, to contribute more fully to the betterment of society."

When she once again focused her eyes on him, they shone with zeal. "I am no revolutionary, I assure you. Perhaps I might best be described as an individualist." She shook her head. "When I received a modest legacy from my late father, I seized the opportunity to put some of my theories to work. And here I am."

Here she was. Even if he disagreed about the wisdom of teaching the quarry children to read and write and figure, he understood her. "You have a reformer's spirit. I fear that you have perhaps set yourself an impossible task, however. The quarry folk are leery of strangers and resistant to change."

She stared directly at him. "Are you?" She took the edge off her words with a smile. "I'm challenging you, and that is not polite." She glanced at the clock on the mantel above the hearth.

"I've stayed too long, Miss Wilkins." James said, not really wanting to leave but unable to think of any reason to remain.

Miss Wilkins rose as well and put out her hand. "After berating you with my unrealistic dreams, I hardly expect you to darken my door again. You have discharged your duty to a grateful dance partner, and we may now meet in company with relative ease and greater familiarity."

Even her dismissal displayed a certain elegance of mind, he thought. James took her hand and lifted it to his lips. She gave an almost inaudible gasp, and her cheeks went a slightly darker shade than the light olive that some people called a brown complexion, but that James found much more attractive than the pale peaches so prized by fashion.

"I'll see myself out," James said, and went on his way, wondering if he should have made some appointment to call on her again, or to take her out in his curricle. He simply wasn't well versed in the niceties of courtship.

Was this courtship, though? As James made his way back to his house about a mile away, he puzzled over that question, barely noticing which way he went, only discovering after a quarter of an hour that he had somehow arrived home.

CHAPTER 16

Sophia was not vain, but she knew she looked her best in a smart, tailored riding habit. This one was in the very latest military style, having been designed and fashioned by Madame Pauline's in London—the only modiste who also had expert tailors specifically for such pieces as outer garments and riding habits. The dark blue twill set off her pale complexion and deepened the color of her eyes, and the epaulets and braided frog closures gave a cheeky masculine note to her otherwise very feminine appearance.

As she pinned the little top hat to the knot on the top of her head, its jaunty ostrich feather curling over her cheek on one side and a veil that swirled down and attached to her shoulder on the other, she wondered that she should care so much for her appearance. It was just a ride through countryside she knew well with a gentleman who was only a doctor. Besides, her groom would be in discreet attendance.

Yet there was something about Dr. Rowe that aroused her fighting spirit in a rather tantalizing way. Perhaps the scene had been set by their first encounter in the vestibule of

Tarrant Hall when they clashed subtly about the efficacy of certain remedies. The subsequent times they'd met when he'd made it clear that he disdained her *lady's* knowledge of medicines and cures should have given her a distaste of him. But somehow, each time she encountered the doctor, she became more and more interested in him. Of course, she'd allow him to believe his initial judgement, that she really knew nothing. She preferred to keep the extent of her medical library and the hours she spent formulating tinctures and salves to herself. Her unusual occupation was all in the service of finding better, more effective ways to treat the ills unique to women, and she knew such things didn't interest most medical men.

So far she'd confessed her zeal to no one. Her father assumed she was concocting cosmetics in her dressing room, which she'd taken over as a sort of formulary. To humor him, every once in a while she would make a new pot of rouge. She had, in fact, made a decent amount of additional pin money at school by selling cosmetics to her fellow students.

Sophia wore no rouge that day, though. She needed nothing to heighten her color. Somewhere in her middle a little thrill of anticipation was keeping her spirits elevated more than usual.

Her bedchamber on the second floor looked out over the wide sweep of the drive that led to the front door of the manor, and so when the sound of a horse trotting over the fine gravel sailed clearly up to her ear she scurried over and peeked out of her window.

Dr. Rowe sat a horse extremely well, she thought with approval. His clothes had not been made by a country tailor, his hands were quiet, and he had an overall air of confident command. And the hack—a thoroughbred, if she wasn't mistaken, its coat brushed to a glossy sheen—would have been at home in any nobleman's stable. It must have cost upwards of three-hundred guineas. Sophia had no clear idea of how much a doctor earned, but she was tolerably certain no physician she'd ever known could have afforded a mount like that. The exception was perhaps Sir William Knighton and a few others like him, whose London society fees were reckoned to climb into the thousands. But she knew for a fact that no doctor in Camelford would ever earn enough to set himself up in style. Dr. Rowe's family must have money. In that case, why would he choose to pursue such a humble profession? It was a mystery.

At that moment, Birch led two horses out to the yard from the Tresillian stable—her own feisty roan and the Welsh cob Birch rode when called upon to accompany her on a ride.

Without waiting for Adler to come and fetch her, Sophia snatched her whip and riding gloves from the table, skipped down the stairs and out through the door that Hosking held open for her. "You are exactly on time, Dr. Rowe!" she said.

He swung his leg over his horse's back and jumped gracefully down. The footman who had followed Sophia out hurried to take the bridle from him while he approached, sweeping his hat off and giving her a beautiful bow. And that. Where did he learn such elegant manners?

"Doctors learn punctuality quickly, since arriving on time can sometimes mean the difference between life and death," he said, his smile lightening the tone of his words.

Without asking, he took Sophia's hand and led her to her horse, checked the girth to make sure it was secure, then tossed her up into the saddle. He was much stronger than she expected him to be, although she had sensed his wiry strength in those few moments of the waltz they danced at the ball before he was called away. She settled her leg and skirts around the pommel and took the reins. As soon as the frisky mare, Penny, felt Sophia's light hands, she sidled and pranced. Rowe did not step away, but took hold of the reins near the bit.

"Stand away, doctor," Sophia said. "She'll shake out her fidgets soon enough."

He did as she said with a glance at the groom, who had seated himself on the cob. "Don't you be worryin' about Miss Sophia. She's got the best seat and the lightest hands in all Cornwall, I b'la."

Dr. Rowe smiled up at her and remounted his own horse. "I see that I must be on my mettle!"

"I hope you're prepared for a real ride. We'll have to go where we can have a gallop first of all," Sophia said. "You left yourself wide open by suggesting that I knew the best rides." She started down the drive at a brisk pace. A quick glance behind assured her that Rowe had settled himself into his saddle and was cantering up to join her.

They didn't speak at first while Sophia led them over fields, jumping hedges easily and splashing through small streams until they reached a wide dirt road where they could have a good gallop. "Race you to the cliff!" she called. She squeezed her thigh and calf against Penny's side and tickled her rump with the whip. It was enough to set the lively beast at a solid hand gallop over a road she knew well. Sophia loved the feeling of the wind whipping her cheeks into flames and the ground racing by beneath her. The sheer power of her horse and the heady sensation that even her lightest gesture could control her was positively intoxicating. *This is what flying must feel like,* she thought.

Sophia had hardly reached the end of the gallop when Dr. Rowe pulled his bay up to an impressive sudden halt right next to her.

"Almost, but not quite!" Sophia said. "I won! What should my prize be?" Her eyes were alight with mirth.

Rowe's answering smile brought a dimple into one of his

cheeks, and Sophia had a sudden overwhelming urge to put her finger on it. She laughed.

"I don't see that your victory was so very impressive. You started before me!"

Sophia gave a saucy toss of her head. "You're right of course. Next time we'll do it properly. You still haven't offered me a prize."

By that time, Birch had cantered up and stopped discreetly several yards behind them.

"I have nothing to give you, except my company. I hereby declare myself ready to ride with you whenever you desire it." Then he added as an afterthought, "provided my work allows."

"I shall hold you to it. For now, let's go on. It's a rare day, is it not?" Sophia filled her lungs with the fresh, salty air, thinking how wonderful it would be to ride like this every day with such a handsome, accomplished rider by her side.

"This is indeed a beautiful part of the country, in its wild way," Dr. Rowe said.

"Did you know Cornwall before you came here?"

He looked down at his hands as if to settle them on the reins better, but there was really no need. "No, never."

"Where are you from? Where is your family?"

"Northumberland," he said quickly.

"That's very far away. I'm surprised you decided to practice here. Do you have brothers and sisters?"

"I had a brother. What about you? Have you lived in Cornwall all your life?"

Had she imagined that he deliberately directed the conversation away from his own family? She wanted to ask about his brother, about where he went to school that he learned the ways of a gentleman so thoroughly. But perhaps now was not the time. She'd let him keep his secrets.

"Yes. I was born here. I only went away to Bath for school."

"And do you have brothers or sisters?"

She paused before answering. "I, too, had a brother. But only for a few hours. He and my mother both died the day he was born."

"I'm sorry," Dr. Rowe said, and they both fell silent.

They walked their mounts side by side along the narrower cliff path. Dr. Rowe stayed on Sophia's right, nearer the cliff edge, which was still a few yards away. Sophia gazed out beyond Rowe to the unimpeded view over the sea, rolling waves dotted with sailing vessels of all sizes, from fishing scows to schooners. "I wonder where they are all going," she said, pointing with her whip handle.

"Have you traveled much, Miss Tresillian?" Rowe asked.

She shook her head and smiled. "Only to London a few times. Bath doesn't really count. Somersetshire is still the West Country. My father's businesses keep him here, and I would not go anywhere without him. I once thought I should like to see Paris. Some of my friends from school planned to go to Belgium with their parents. But is it still safe? From what I read, Napoleon is preparing to attack near Brussels." She sighed. "Wars."

"He won't succeed. How can he?"

Sophia shrugged. "I imagine he'll have a hard time getting the better of Wellington." She narrowed her eyes at him. "You're not one of those Whigs who think the duke a terrible general, are you?"

This made Rowe laugh more heartily than her question warranted, she thought, as if her comment brought some private joke to mind.

Once his laughter subsided, Sophia said, "Have you been outside of England?"

"Once. As a boy. But first my medical studies and now my

practice have taken up all my time and I expect I'll never have reason to go abroad again."

"Who would want to leave when we have such beauty here?" Sophia shifted her gaze toward him, intending to say something light and change the subject, but the expression in his eyes stopped her, and she swallowed.

He gave his head a little shake and the expression vanished. "What do you call your horse, Miss Tresillian? I thought I heard you say something like Penny."

"Yes, that's right. Penny," she said with an impish smile. "Short for Pennyroyal. Which reminds me, a little farther along here is a patch of samphire among the rocks just over the edge of the cliff. I wanted to collect some of the buds and leaves, but the last time I was here it was rainy and wet, and I didn't dare attempt it."

Gathering the herb from its treacherous rocky bed would be dangerous. But so would spending any more time looking into Dr. Rowe's expressive eyes, Sophia thought. She urged Penny to a trot and stopped at a place where a declivity split the cliff to form a steep, rocky path toward the beach that ended in a sheer rock face too high to leap from safely.

Sophia slid down from the saddle before Rowe had a chance to dismount and help her. He tossed his horse's reins over a stump nearby and strode to stand next to her to look down at the break in the rocks.

"See, it's just there." Sophia pointed to a clump of plump, bluish-green leaves like fingers with tiny pale yellow buds at their ends about six feet down from where they stood. "If I can just get a handful that will be enough."

"You aren't really going to try to reach that!" Rowe said. "It's madness."

Sophia lifted her chin. "Of course I am! I have you here to help if I come to grief—but I won't." She scooped up the long tail of her riding habit and tucked it into the belt that ran just beneath her ribs before starting gingerly down the slippery rocks. She had to admit that she wasn't as unafraid as she pretended as the loose pebbles shifted under her boots.

"Miss Tresillian!"

Dr. Rowe's sharp voice made her lose her footing. She reached for a stubby shrub growing between the rocks to steady herself, but Rowe had already climbed down to her and grabbed her, clutching her to him. "I-I thank you, but I was all right. It was just a small slip, and it isn't even steep right here." She placed her hands against his chest, feeling it rise and fall with his breath. They were so close she could see the tiny shards of darker brown in his light brown eyes. "I am well now, sir," she said, a little unsteadily. She had never been so close to a gentleman before, even while dancing.

He moved his hands to grip her shoulders and held her a little away from him, as though he had read her thoughts. "Of course. Forgive me."

They were only about halfway to the patch of samphire. "It's not far. Perhaps if you held my hand to brace me I could make my way to it."

"No." Rowe spoke with a tone of command that caught Sophia by surprise. People didn't generally say no to her. "You shall return to the top, and I will get your specimen." His face was stern and set.

"I'll wait for you right here," Sophia said, deciding that arguing about who would accomplish the herbal theft would not be dignified, and frankly thankful that he said he would do it.

She bit her lower lip as Rowe scrambled, half climbing, down to the clump of greenery. His straining muscles showed even through the wool of his driving coat. Sophia felt the heat of a blush stealing up into her cheeks and focused on the samphire instead. "Be careful. Don't pull out the roots! Break the stems." Suddenly Sophia was wracked with guilt. What if he fell? She saw that his feet were solidly wedged between fixed rocks, and gave a silent sigh of relief.

"Do you have any other instructions, My Lady?" Rowe said with an acid tone. But he did as instructed and soon had negotiated the rocks back up to where Sophia waited for him.

Rowe had removed his riding glove so that he could more easily pinch off the stems of the samphire and when he transferred the sprigs to Sophia their fingers touched. Sophia was conscious of a warm current of something between them, as if the shared act of gathering the samphire had somehow connected them in a more intimate way. Their acquaintance had started with their fingertips touching, but that had been followed by a disagreement. This time, they were in harmony with each other having shared a task and meted out equal portions of their pasts.

"Perhaps it's time we rode back," Sophia said, her voice low and quiet.

Rowe gestured for her to lead the way back up to their horses. By this time, having seen them start to climb down into the little ravine, Birch had ridden up and held the reins of all three of their mounts. He gave Sophia a disapproving look and shook his head. She hoped he wouldn't say anything to her father.

They did not gallop on the way back, but conversation between them became a little strained. Sophia stole a few glances at Rowe's profile as he rode next to her, noticing his straight nose with delicately chiseled nostrils and his sculpted lips.

What would it be like to feel those lips on hers? She inhaled sharply.

"Is something the matter, Miss Tresillian?" Rowe said as they turned down the drive to the manor.

"Not at all, Dr. Rowe. I had a lovely time. When we ride

together again you must choose where we'll go—remember, another ride is my prize for winning the race!"

Once they were in front of the house Rowe jumped down from his horse, tossed the reins to the waiting stable boy, grasped Sophia by the waist and lifted her out of the saddle. He held her for a beat longer than necessary and Sophia met his eyes. "What?" she whispered.

As if recalled to himself, he let go of her suddenly. The absence of his warm, strong hands made Sophia shiver. Then she remembered her manners. "May I offer you some refreshment? You must be parched after our ride."

"I thank you, no. I have absented myself from my work long enough for one day. I must go back to Camelford."

She put out her hand to shake his. Instead of doing so, he lifted it to his lips and dropped a soft kiss on her gloved knuckles. Then, saluting her with his riding crop, leapt back into his saddle and rode away without looking behind him.

Oh Sophia! she thought as she went inside to change out of her habit. Papa would never approve of a doctor. What am I thinking! Perhaps it doesn't matter. It was just a ride, after all.

But she knew that it had been much more than that. In some material way, her world had shifted in the space of an afternoon. She was not the same person as she had been that morning. She was no longer someone who needed no one to make her feel whole. Now she had become someone who felt as if her world would never be complete without one particular person.

A person who was in no way eligible.

CHAPTER 17

Now that she knew her way to Bodmin, Persephone felt confident riding Angus there alone on the next market day. There would be enough others on the well-worn road from Camelford so that she needn't be anxious about being set upon by highwaymen. This thought made her lips twitch into a smile. Of course, she had brought a significant amount of money with her, but who would ever suspect it? And it was a lot for her, but possibly not enough to tempt a thief.

Bobby, who acted as her stable boy, told her where the horse auction was likely to be and recommended she stable the cob and then go on foot to the auction paddock. As he said, "Becoz no cull seein' that poor old cob wouldna be tempted to sell ee a bone shaker and say he's a high bred 'un." It made sense, Persephone thought with a laugh. Poor old Angus wasn't really a riding horse, but he was sweet and strong, and the only horse Antonella could do without for a few weeks.

Persephone had drawn forty guineas from her bank in Camelford and tucked it safely in her reticule, which she kept inside the large pocket of her riding habit. It felt almost indecent to have that much money on her person. She hoped it would be enough, but she didn't dare spend more. If she could purchase only one animal for that amount a cart horse would be more practical, much as she would have liked to have a spirited hack. The thought of a gallop along the cliffs made her sigh. Soon, she hoped, she would be too busy to notice the lack of some of her more enjoyable former pursuits.

Atherleigh Manor seemed a world away from Delabole, even though the distance was less than ten miles. She wondered sometimes what everyone there was doing. Would they have a ball in the summer, when the season in London was over? Or would this year be different because of Napoleon? So much of the talk at the Roscarrock ball had been about his escape from Elba and the army he'd managed to raise. How did Lord Atherleigh feel, not being able to rejoin his regiment because of his injury? Antonella must be grateful, Persephone thought, but also sensitive to her husband's frustration at not being able to rejoin his regiment.

And then, Persephone thought, if there was to be a battle, how many of the young men at the Roscarrock ball would be sent to the continent? There had been a sizable contingent of officers in attendance. None of them had danced with her, but as many as half of Sophia's partners wore scarlet coats and gold braid and carried ornamental smallswords.

Such matters made her own concerns feel petty. And yet, they were important to her, and she hoped that if she could bring them to fruition, they would be important to the children she taught. So why hadn't she made a start yet? She told herself it was because she wanted to make sure everything was prepared in her schoolroom, that there were enough copy books, slates, and horn books, one abacus, and storybooks of moral character.

But no. To be honest with herself, the biggest reason for her lack of action was her dread of facing Mr. Pentarrant. She could not picture him without experiencing a welter of confused and disturbing feelings. Such a contradiction! He was unlike anyone she'd ever met before. Her father's sleepy parish had boasted mostly farmers and tradesmen, plus a few superannuated landed gentry and professionals in the nearby town. At Amblemere, whatever members of the *ton* made it to Cornwall brought their genteel manners and address—along with their snobbery—and cordially ignored her. None of the men she'd met before had prepared her for the likes of Mr. Pentarrant. He was gentry, but he worked hard and seemed unafraid to own it. He was educated and well-mannered, but he put on no airs. He was well spoken, but he wasn't afraid to be straight with her and did not soften his opinions to spare her feelings.

She was forced to admit that she found him intriguing—and very appealing. Yet whenever they spoke, they rubbed against each other. They couldn't help it. They held opposite opinions about nearly everything, and neither of them was willing to give in. It was maddening! What did that make him think of her? And why should she care at all?

Her ruminative ride ended all too quickly. In the hour it took to get to Bodmin, the morning's clear sky had clouded over and the distinct threat of rain hung in the air. Persephone stabled the cob and walked the half mile to the auctioneer's on the edge of town, glancing now and again at the sky and wishing she had thought to bring an umbrella. It would have been difficult mounted on a horse. All the more reason to focus on acquiring a cart horse and a serviceable cart.

She had hoped her presence at the auction would appear no more than a matter of course to anyone else there. Her riding habit was not stylish—brown serge with very little adornment, and a simple helmet cap. But as soon as she reached the auction grounds, it became clear to her that nothing she wore would have helped her avoid notice. She was the only female present among the considerable crowd clustered by the fence around the auction yard, and thus drew every gaze.

Men of all conditions gathered there. Most of them—likely farmers and tradesmen—eyed her up and down and then returned their attention to the horses being led around the enclosed ring. *I might as well be on the block,* she thought, and couldn't avoid comparing this coming parade of horse-flesh to the assemblies at Almack's. One or two smartly dressed gentlemen leaned negligently against the white fence and continued to stare at her in frank amazement. Her cheeks heated. She hoped the fresh breeze might account for the change in color, and kept her eyes steadfastly focused on the middle distance.

The first animal to go under the hammer was a very spirited black stallion. The stable hand could barely keep him standing in one place as the auctioneer enumerated his qualities: high bred, sixteen hands, only three years old, a real gentleman's hunter. Two of the smartly dressed men touched the brims of their hats alternately, bidding against each other until one finally shook his head. The horse sold for more than three-hundred guineas. Persephone gulped. She had no idea such fine horses would find their way to a provincial auction. Was it possible, at these prices, she would leave without achieving her aim?

She stood very still and watched as four more animals were sold at prices ranging from seventy to one-hundred-twenty guineas. These horses were all much too fine for her use. She prepared herself to pay little attention until more common beasts appeared.

But then a boy led the most beautiful chestnut mare out

of the barn and into the ring. The mare's soft brown eyes and black lashes calmly regarded the assembled crowd as if she fully expected to be appreciated by all. She had a perfectly formed head—no Roman nose there—and a slight arch to her neck. Someone had brushed her coat to a coppery sheen. She passed near enough that Persephone could reach out and run her gloved hand lightly down her neck. The mare gave a soft, answering nicker.

"She'd suit you."

The voice came from right behind Persephone's shoulder. She recognized it in an instant and resisted the impulse to turn around. "She is above my touch, Mr. Pentarrant."

"Purchasing an inferior beast is a false economy, Miss Wilkins."

"Nonetheless."

The bidding started for the lovely creature. Persephone found herself at first hopeful when the amounts began at thirty guineas. Bids soon rose, though, and the horse—an ideal lady's hack if ever there was one—eventually sold for ninety guineas. At least, Persephone thought, it was too much more than she could afford to tempt her to overspend. She sighed. Lord Atherleigh would have purchased such a horse for her in a trice if she had wished it. But she was now independent and must live within her means. This life had been her choice.

Half the buyers left as the stock dwindled and only more common specimens remained. Persephone identified one she thought on first glance would do well enough to pull a cart. If she could get it for under twenty-five guineas she would be able to purchase the cart and all the tack she needed as well. As the gelding was led out to the center of the yard, she leaned in more closely.

"That horse won't do," Pentarrant said.

Persephone looked over her shoulder at him this time. "I

thought you'd gone. These creatures are well beneath your interest, I should imagine."

He smiled. That same disarming smile she'd first seen the night of the ball. Bidding started, and she almost missed it.

"Ten guineas! Any advance on ten? Come now! This fellow ain't a day over eight years and good for ten more of useful work I b'la!" The auctioneer scanned the crowd, his eyes stopping on Persephone. "As right a beast to pull a sweet cart as ever I see'd."

Persephone was about to raise her hand when Pentarrant's shot out and caught it, forcing it down. She struggled a moment but stopped when he called out to the auctioneer, "Come man! You tried to sell that broken-down tit last month! He's fifteen if he's a day."

The crowd erupted in laughter, and the auctioneer good naturedly shrugged and they passed on to the next horse.

Persephone wanted to sink into the ground. She'd insisted when they were dancing that she could judge a horse well enough on her own, that she didn't need Pentarrant's help. And here she was, humiliated. With luck, no one else saw her nearly fall for the auctioneer's salesmanship.

"This one, Miss Wilkins," Pentarrant whispered in her ear, raising gooseflesh on her neck. "She's not pretty, but her hocks are well formed, she isn't short of bone, and you can tell by the condition of her hooves that someone has cared for her. A good Cornish cob."

Another ten-guinea bid was raised for this one, a stocky bay of less than fifteen hands. Persephone took a deep breath. It would be contrary and foolish to ignore Pentarrant's excellent advice. Still, it rankled.

"Any advance on ten? Come now! This is no bone setter! I'm sellin 'er for ten. Ten guineas, going once—"

"Fifteen!" Persephone called out the amount in a voice that was louder and more emphatic than it needed to be. She heard a soft chuckle behind her and felt the tops of her ears burn.

"The lady says fifteen guineas! Anyone going against her? Fifteen it is to the lady.

Somewhat abashed, Persephone turned, preparing to thank Mr. Pentarrant for his advice and part company with him.

He smiled down at her. "I'm persuaded you've made a good choice, Miss Wilkins. Would you permit me to act as your agent for the transaction? I assure you, in this part of Cornwall, ladies do not handle such things by themselves."

In truth, Persephone had hardly thought much beyond the moment of agreeing to buy a horse. She had never made such a large purchase in her life before—not in hard currency. Normally everything went on account to be settled monthly. She swallowed her pride. "That would be very kind of you, Mr. Pentarrant. Perhaps you could also direct me to where I might acquire a small cart and harness."

"So you admit that I might have some knowledge that would be of use to you after all." He tucked her hand into the crook of his elbow and led her away from the auction yard toward the attached stables.

She didn't answer, only smiled ruefully at him. When they reached the stable she gave her bank notes into Mr. Pentarrant's hands and waited outside for him. He was gone for what seemed a long time, and Persephone began to wonder if he hadn't decided just to leave her standing there, embarrassed, as punishment for not having taken his advice in the first place.

Finally he emerged. Persephone held out her hand to receive any currency that remained from the transaction—Pentarrant had assured her that he could arrange for the cart at the same time.

At that moment, the clouds that had continued to thicken

all day began to let loose fat rain drops. Pentarrant took her hand and once more tucked it beneath his elbow. "We must seek some shelter. In any event, it would not be seemly for currency to change hands between a gentleman and a lady on a public street."

They hurried down Fore Street and stepped inside the White Hart just as the true deluge began. "We may as well sit in comfort, Miss Wilkins. Shall we go to the coffee room?"

She assented—how could she not?

They sat in awkward silence at first. Persephone had never felt so awkward in all her life. Yet it must be said that Mr. Pentarrant was doing his best to smooth over the events of the morning by not mentioning them.

The waiter brought them coffee and cakes. Persephone busied herself with pouring, trying to think of how to initiate a conversation that would allow her to thank Pentarrant for his help without completely debasing herself. At last she said, "Mr. Pentarrant, I am aware that I am greatly in your debt for your help this morning."

"Please do not mention it. I could not have borne to see you cheated."

She gave a soft laugh. "You warned me about that fellow. I should have listened. I am truly sorry that I seem to have so thoroughly misjudged you." She paused to sip her coffee. "But I don't understand why you are in Bodmin today. Should you not be at the quarry?"

"I had a mind to purchase a new hack for myself. It's my weakness, you know. I enjoy nothing so much as riding or driving through the country hereabouts."

Persephone wasn't sure she quite believed him. Why would he have chosen that particular day? And aside from the one unruly stallion at the beginning of the auction, she hadn't seen any other really exceptional horses. "If you are such an enthusiast I imagine you would prefer to go to Tattersall's to find a mount."

"Alas, my work at the quarry seldom affords me enough time to go to London for any other purpose than business." He kept his eyes on his coffee cup for a moment as if searching for something there. Persephone couldn't help admiring the symmetry of his face, the set of his square jaw. "How are you settling into your cottage?" he said. "You have not visited the quarry of late."

He'd deftly changed the subject. But the last thing Persephone wanted to do was reignite their dispute over educating the quarry children. Not right there, when they seemed to have found a measure of equanimity in each other's presence. "I find I have many details to arrange at the moment and no time to satisfy my curiosity about the inhabitants of Delabole."

"The next time you come, I would ask that you let me take you around. You'll find me in the quarry office most times. If I am not there, one of the clerks will come and fetch me."

So, he wanted to keep her under his eye when she visited the quarry. "I would not want to put you to any trouble, sir."

"It's no trouble. And a slate quarry can be a dangerous place. I should be grieved if you were to suffer an accident there and would feel easier if you allowed me to be your guide."

She did not relish the thought of his company when she went to talk to the quarry workers' families in the village that straggled nearby. They would likely only say what they thought he wanted to hear. Sophia might be able to help her think of a way out of it.

After that they spoke of commonplaces—the weather, which had started to clear; the likelihood of a good harvest; a forthcoming ladies' picnic being organized by Miss Vyvyan.

Half an hour later, they'd finished their refreshments and Pentarrant reached into his pocket to remove a folded paper, which he placed on the table and pushed toward Persephone. She cast him a puzzled frown.

"Your money, Miss Wilkins. There was a little left after paying for your cob and the cart and delivery to your house tomorrow." He nudged it toward her.

She reached for it and their fingers touched. Persephone drew in a quick breath. All at once she was back in the Roscarrock ballroom with him, whirling in a dance, gazing at him as if no one else existed. She quickly pulled the paper toward her and tucked it in her reticule. "I thank you for your kind help in this matter," she said. "Excuse me."

Before he had a chance to say anything more, she hurried away to reclaim Angus from the stable at the Royal Hotel, nearly going the wrong way in her utter confusion.

CHAPTER 18

"What will you call her?" Sophia asked when Persephone showed her the Cornish cob she'd purchased the day before.

"I had thought I would call her Humble Pie, after I was so dismissive of Mr. Pentarrant's offer to help when we were at the ball. He said nothing about going to the horse auction when he came to visit the day after. If he hadn't been at the auction, I might have ended up with a completely unsuitable horse. But I decided against that name, and have settled on Miss Pie."

"Quite fortunate that he was there, then," Sophia said. "And I think Miss Pie is a splendid name." She pursed her lips to suppress the wicked smile she was so tempted to flash at Persephone. "So, James Pentarrant called on you the day after the ball. Which other of your partners did so?" It was perhaps wrong of her to tease, but her new friend appeared to have so little idea of her own power to attract despite her air of confident assurance.

Persephone stared at her blankly for a moment, then said, "Why, no others. Most of my partners were old gentlemen who were simply being kind to me so that I would not be sitting out for the entire ball."

"That was not what I saw! In any case, I'm sure that James Pentarrant did not dance with you out of kindness." Did Persephone not see that he took an interest in her? He was hardly the kind of person to make calls of ceremony after dancing with someone. And to attend a horse auction simply because he wanted to help her choose well and not be swindled—that was a gesture that went beyond common courtesy. "To be serious for a moment, though," Sophia said, "This horse and cart of yours couldn't have come at a better time. There is something I would very much like to do. It will require the use of a carriage or a gig of some kind, but I don't want to use any of ours."

"Why?" Persephone asked. They left Miss Pie quietly munching the tough grass in the small yard behind her barn and went into her cottage through the back door.

Once they were seated at the table in Persephone's kitchen, Sophia said, "I envy you, in a way. You have mastered the trick of passing quietly through the world."

"You mean, I'm beneath most people's notice!" Persephone's musical laugh took the self-deprecatory sting out of her words.

"Of course, you know that's not what I mean, wretched woman! Only that here, in such unvarying company, I feel as if my every move is watched. I suppose having been away the better part of three years is partly to blame."

"You think people are spying on you?"

"Not spying exactly, but if I set one foot in someone's house the fact that I've done so is sure to be a topic of conversation all over the county. Not to mention that everyone is trying to marry me off."

"Am I to presume that you had callers after the ball as well?"

"Yes," Sophia said, suddenly examining a bit of lint on her skirt with great attention. Much as she liked Persephone, she really didn't want to talk to her about Dr. Rowe.

Thankfully, Persephone did not question her further on the matter. She simply rose and poured the boiling water into the teapot. "As it happens, I was hoping for an opportunity to return to the quarry, so taking you there tomorrow would suit me."

"Wonderful! We should leave here relatively early. We ought to have some things to give the people in the village, hampers with fruit and cheese or bread."

"Hannah will manage it. She is a marvel. I'm sure I don't know why she takes such good care of me. When she heard you were coming to see me today, she made sure everything was ready and baked these saffron buns. Perhaps I could persuade her to make some more for tomorrow." Persephone took a cloth off the top of a platter loaded with the golden treats.

Sophia had smelled them from the door when she first arrived. The aroma took her back to childhood, before her mother died. "I used to love these." She helped herself, placing a bun on the small plate in front of her on the table. "Our cook considers himself too elevated to make such common delicacies. You wouldn't think it possible for someone with a French chef in the kitchen to feel deprived."

Persephone laughed again. "Yet I don't think it's so much to bear, living in affluence with fine horses to ride and elegant meals, and all the new gowns you could possibly want."

"Do you miss it?" Sophia asked.

Persephone had recounted her history to her, so Sophia knew that as a governess in a *ton* family, she was accustomed to live in a degree of luxury, even if she remained out of sight in the schoolroom much of the time. "I'd be lying if I said I didn't miss some things about my former life. But it's the price I decided to pay for my independence, for doing what matters to me."

"And what matters is teaching, not marriage." Sophia reached across the table and took Persephone's hand. "You're so brave. You live here all alone. You go to Bodmin alone to buy a horse—even if you ended up having some help. You order your cottage just as you wish, and don't seem to worry about fripperies and furnishings."

"Next you'll point out that I take little care over my dress and my hair, and then I shall feel a right peasant!" Again, Persephone laughed. She soon grew serious, though. "What has you thinking these things, dear Sophia? I'm accustomed to you always seeing the bright side of everything."

"Oh, nothing. I'm just being silly." Her thoughts were so tangled that she doubted she could explain them to herself, let alone to Persephone. Instead, she seized on the one thing that might plausibly explain her mood. "I just found out that my father isn't at all well. I thought he was simply bilious, but it seems it's more serious than that."

"Has Dr. Rowe seen him? What does he say?"

"Papa refuses to tell me what Dr. Rowe said. He came when I was out." Dr. Rowe. She most certainly would not tell Persephone—not yet—how the handsome young physician had a way not only of calling her competence into question, but of intruding into her thoughts at the most inopportune moments.

Persephone's expression softened, and she said, "I'm sorry, my dear. But let's not dwell on that. Perhaps things are not so bad as you fear. So tell me. How are Miss Pie and my humble cart going to help you break out of the gilded cage you find yourself confined in at present?"

Sophia wished she could tell Persephone more—most of all how grateful she was for her ready acceptance of her exactly as she found her, without judging or criticizing. "Oh, I don't have any plans! Not yet anyway. Not beyond visiting the quarry families together, bringing them some provisions as I said, and seeing if there are other ways we could help."

"Ah yes, play the lady bountiful—no one would question that about you. Why do you not want to take one of your elegant carriages with your matched team?" Persephone rose and poked the kitchen fire back to life. The day was mild, but the sun had moved behind a cloud and a chill crept into the small cottage.

"That's it precisely. I want to be helpful, but not in a way that announces it to the world. Besides—" she stopped just in time to avoid saying *I don't want our coachman to know what I'm doing.* After a little laugh, she said, "I have a fancy to see how well you drive a rustic cart!"

Persephone tipped her head on the side and fastened her searching gaze on Sophia. When Sophia said nothing more, she looked down into her cup of tea and said, "You don't have to tell me anything if you don't want to. I am more than willing for us to go together—behind sturdy little Miss Pie in my humble cart. I confess, having your company will make me feel much braver than going alone."

"You? Cowardly?" Sophia laughed. "Never! I honestly believe you have enough strength of spirit to tackle anything."

"Even a picnic with Miss Vyvyan?"

Sophia groaned. "Don't remind me! I'd forgotten that it's the day after tomorrow. Oh well. I know I must go. She does this every year. Always waiting until I'm back from school so I can't get out of it. And every year it rains and we are forced to take refuge under the hoods of the carriages."

Persephone laughed. "Speaking of which, do you have room in your gig for me?"

That was a question. She did have room, but she also had

plans that made it unwise for Persephone to depend on her for transportation back and forth to the picnic spot. "I would, except I have an errand on the way home, and I fear it would not be comfortable for you."

A questioning light flitted into Persephone's eyes. "So be it. I was hoping to use you as an excuse to refuse Miss Vyvyan's invitation to travel with her. She says she will collect me at noon Wednesday."

"Keep your enemies close," Sophia murmured.

"I beg your pardon?"

"It was nothing! I daresay you'll be entertained enough. But mind you don't let her monopolize you at the picnic. She is most definitely not to be trusted." Persephone was doubtless not yet aware that she had a target on her back simply by virtue of having gained James Pentarrant's regard at the Roscarrock ball. Philippa had considered him her property for years.

"Where do we go? Is there a famous view hereabouts? I can't imagine what would justify putting a party of ladies to such trouble for anything else," Persephone said.

"I believe this year our destination is Rough Tor on Bodmin Moor. Miss Vyvyan is of a very romantical disposition and likes to fancy a ghostly presence there. I confess, it is a rather unearthly place." This aspect was partly why Sophia had agreed to go at all.

"Well, that is something. Should I bring my sketchbook and pencils?"

"By all means! You should most definitely have something to do to relieve yourself of the tedium of listening to Camelford gossip."

Sophia helped herself to a second saffron bun and Persephone smiled. "I'll be certain to tell Hannah how much you appreciated her baking!"

"I don't suppose we'll have anything as nice for the picnic.

Philippa's cook is mediocre at best, but she won't hear of anyone else supplying the viands. It's her pride and joy, this outing."

Her pride and joy, and her web of intrigue. Sophia wondered if Persephone would perceive it, and made a vow to herself to keep an eye on her friend to make sure she didn't get ensnared in Philippa's sugary trap.

~

I MUST BE OUT OF MY SENSES, JAMES THOUGHT, AS HE WALKED along with the groom to lead the chestnut mare around to his stables.

"Beggin' yer pardon, yer honor, but this lass int quite up to yer weight, I b'la."

Digory didn't look at him, but James knew him well enough to imagine his expression and did not dignify his comment with a response.

"She's right pretty. A lady's mount. On'y tha's not got a lady to ride 'er."

He couldn't argue with that. But as soon as he had seen how Miss Wilkins reacted when she caught sight of the spirited chestnut the day before, he couldn't imagine anyone else riding the mare. Foolish. What did he imagine he could do with the creature? He couldn't make a present of her to Miss Wilkins. That would be improper in the extreme. He might invite her to come riding with him and offer the chestnut as a mount. But what would she think? She would recognize the mare as soon as she laid eyes on her, he had no doubt, and wonder why he hadn't mentioned his purchase at the auction. Despite her near disaster with that broken down old nag Carrowmore tried to trick her into buying, she clearly appreciated a fine riding horse—if not a serviceable workhorse.

Digory looked up at him with a question in his perceptive eyes.

"I thought to make a present of her to my sister-in-law," James told him. It didn't matter whether the groom believed it or not.

"Mistress Pentarrant won't be ridin' anytime soon, if I hear'd right."

The horse went docilely into the loose box and directly to the bucket of oats Digory had put within as a welcome treat.

"What did you hear?"

"She's by way of bein' poorly with her confinement, so Sal in the great house kitchen tells us."

Catherine was very close to her time. If she had been his wife, no matter how many other children she'd had, he would have spared no expense to get her the best care. He certainly wouldn't go off all day to carouse with young Roscarrock. Sometimes James wondered how he and Eustace could have come from the same parents.

He leaned his arms on the top of the stall door and watched the mare eat and accustom herself to her new home. A whinny behind him told him that Arrow was a little jealous. James went to the bay gelding, whose head peeked over the door of his box. "She's no threat to you, my boy," he said and fished the lump of sugar out of his pocket, letting Arrow lip it off his palm. "You might well think me a fool. Why does that woman disturb me so? I think she could be trouble. But her heart—and her eyes, and her waist, and her smile, oh yes, her smile—I find I cannot forget. Of course, Eustace wants me to marry the Tresillian heiress."

At this, Arrow shook his head and nickered. "You say no?" James laughed. "I know that's not it. You just want more sugar. But that's enough. We'll ride later." James rubbed behind Arrow's ear and down his neck and then left the stable.

It struck him as he walked away to go to the house and take a light nuncheon before returning to the quarry for the afternoon that he housed his cattle in more luxury than himself. Some might think him mad for this, but horses couldn't take care of themselves, not so that they'd be up to the work he asked of them. And they were loyal. They would not turn on a fellow if he treated them well.

He stopped. A lead weight lodged in his chest. Rowena would have loved that mare, and she had the seat and the courage to ride her. How he had been fooled by her! They were playmates as children. He went away to school and Cambridge, and when he returned home at the age of one and twenty, she had blossomed into a beauty with spirit and courage. They fell hard. They were going to run away—they couldn't marry in the open because neither his family nor hers wanted the match. His because she was just a splitter's daughter. Hers because he was not a Methodist. None of that mattered to either of them, he thought then.

Until something happened. Something changed Rowena. The last time they met, she was evasive, nervous. *Yes, yes, I'll meet you, but I must go!* were her parting words. The next day she sent him a letter saying she was going to marry Hubert Rowse, that it was what her parents wanted and she wouldn't disobey them. No other explanation. The blotchy ink told a tale of tears. Rowse was a decent man, but Rowena had no more than a vague liking for him, James was certain. It didn't change the facts, though. She was gone. Lost to him forever. Her family would not even tell him where she and her husband had settled.

James had no doubt that his father had played a part in that farce, and for that he never forgave him. From that moment on, he refused to fulfill the expectations placed upon him. He would not play the gentleman. Only hard, physical labor that made him so tired he would sometimes fall asleep over his dinner served to distract him from bitter thoughts of what might have been.

Perhaps that was part of what made him so dedicated to his work. It had been a dozen years since Rowena, and she came to mind rarely now. Yet something about Miss Wilkins brought his former love up to the surface from the deep lake of his memory. What was it? Her spirit in standing up to him at the quarry? Her refusal to make polite, insignificant conversation at the ball? The glow in her eyes on seeing the chestnut mare? He shook his head. He would not fall in love. He could not. Women were not to be trusted. Those of his class only wanted one thing, and it wasn't love.

He chuckled. Perhaps it was what Miss Wilkins *didn't* want that appealed to him. She didn't appear to want what all the other county ladies wanted. She took no pains to flirt or to appear helpless and in need of guidance—the kind of behavior which, when it was aimed at him, only made him want to run away. Miss Wilkins had apparently not come to seek a husband.

So why was she here? What drove her to this precise place? They did not speak of her past when they met in Bodmin. All he really knew of her was that she was educated and had been a genteel governess. A teacher. He inferred rather than knew that she wanted to set up a school for the quarry children. What else could explain her comments at the quarry and at the ball?

And that fact would keep them at odds in all likelihood. It wasn't so much that he saw no value in teaching the quarry children to read. It was more that any such change to the delicately balanced pattern of existence at the edge of the quarry might have unforeseen repercussions—the misplaced blast that weakened a seam on the other rock face and caused chaos.

Miss Wilkins threw him into confusion without lifting a

finger. She was a self-contained, intelligent woman who didn't need his help—except perhaps in choosing a cart horse—and all he wanted to do was lift her burdens off her shoulders.

The problem was that she probably wouldn't let him do it. He smiled.

CHAPTER 19

Persephone was unaccountably nervous about venturing into the hamlet of cottages where the quarry families lived. She almost wished she'd made herself do it right away, before she had time to become acquainted with the possible negative sentiments she might encounter. Before she had met James Pentarrant, in fact. He'd asked her to allow him to escort her when she came to the quarry, but she really didn't want him to. She thought his presence would inhibit conversation with the families.

She drove the cart to Tresillian Manor to be greeted on the front steps by Sophia herself. Dressed in plain cambric with a scarf tied around her head, Sophia still managed to be stunning. That was because her beauty, Persephone had come to realize, wasn't just a function of her perfect features, her trim figure, or her mane of golden curls. She had a glow from within. She radiated charm and grace without condescension. A rare quality indeed.

"So, are you prepared?" Sophia said as a footman handed her up to the bench seat of the cart.

"The question is, are you?" Persephone said with a lift of one eyebrow. "This is the meanest conveyance possible! If it rains we'll be in a difficult case."

Sophia laughed. "It makes me feel free. As if no one expected anything of me. And your Miss Pie is full of gig! Look at her, with her ears pricked up and picking up her hooves like that!"

Miss Pie was, indeed, an exceptional little goer. One more reason to feel grateful to Mr. Pentarrant and guilty that she had no intention of doing as he requested with regard to visiting the quarry village.

Collecting Sophia from Tresillian Manor added about a mile to the one-mile trip she'd otherwise have taken on foot, as before. In addition, today she had a hamper of food and Sophia also brought a basket, but Persephone had no idea what it contained.

An advantage to driving was that she had a different perspective on the countryside. What she hadn't noticed on her previous walk to quarry was what lay beyond the stone walls and hedgerows that marked the road. She had to keep a sharp eye out for bumps and holes, nonetheless Persephone stole some glances over into the fields and meadows they passed, trying to figure out which land belonged to which family. The ground was not very rich hereabouts, so it wasn't uncommon to see a field given over to hay or simply left to grass for a season. One such lay not immediately next to the wall but farther off, separated by another fence. She was about to turn her attention away from it when a beautiful horse galloped, tail flying, into view. It stopped and bucked, shaking its head and prancing as if simply enjoying the fine spring day. Persephone smiled. Just like us, she thought.

Then she looked again. A copper chestnut. And if she wasn't mistaken, a mare. On the small side, but beautiful points. Could it be? "Whose field is over there? The one with the horse in it?" she asked Sophia.

Sophia craned her neck to see, but by that time, they'd gone around a bend in the road and the chestnut was no longer visible. "I don't know which one you mean. Some of them are ours, although most of the arable land is to the east of Tresillian Manor. I think there's Pentarrant land here too." She put her finger to her lips and thought for a moment. "Oh! The squire has some acres out this way I believe."

"The squire?" Persephone thought she'd met all the people of consequence in the vicinity of her cottage, but she hadn't met a squire. Nor was there such a person at the Roscarrock ball.

Sophia must have seen the confused look on her face. "You won't have met him yet. He's been off in Bedfordshire. His daughter was widowed, and he had to go and help her settle things, so my papa said. I think they returned only a few days ago. She's to keep house for him, at least for now."

Persephone pictured quite an elderly man, if he had a daughter old enough to be a widow. "I gather his family is rooted here."

"Yes. You may perhaps have heard the name Carlyon here and there. He's Squire Edmund Carlyon, and I think they've farmed this land since before the Conquest. Old Saxon stock."

"Do you know him well?"

"Not well, no. I think he sees my father as a bit of an interloper! His lot don't think much of anyone who has made their fortune in trade, even if it was generations ago. And ours is new enough to smell the press of the mint on the coins.

Persephone laughed. But she knew too well the kind of snobbery that would consider someone with a brilliant mind for business and the ambition to put it to use to be beneath reproach. It was another of those injustices she was entirely powerless to correct. How odd it would be if somehow it had been the squire who purchased the beautiful chestnut mare from the auction. Perhaps he bought it for his daughter.

"I daresay Philippa has invited the widow to the picnic, if she'll come. I don't know when her husband died, but she might be out of her blacks by now."

If she met her, Persephone decided she would ask about the chestnut.

By then, they'd made the final turn to the road around the rim of the quarry, a road that led past the offices. These were in a squat, stone building with small windows, all of them facing the works. *I hope he's inside and doesn't see us,* she thought.

"Let's start at that end of the village. Those houses seem a little bigger than the others, and I see some women carrying baskets of laundry," Sophia said.

At that moment, Persephone's ear picked up a change in Miss Pie's rhythmic clopping, and her gait shortened. She pulled her up. "What is it, girl? Sophia, will you take the reins for a moment?" Without waiting for an answer she handed them to Sophia and climbed down from the cart, walking to Miss Pie's left front hoof.

"What is it?" Sophia asked.

Persephone huffed out an exasperated sigh. "She's thrown a shoe. It's still there, but only partly attached to her hoof, poor thing!"

"Oh dear. However, there happens to be a smithy, as I recall, on the other side of the village. He cares for the horses in the whims, so I'm told," Sophia said.

"How fortunate! I'll see if I can get the shoe off and walk her there." Persephone faced toward the cart and leaned her left shoulder against Miss Pie's leg so she could get her weight off it and lift up the hoof. That was all it took to make the shoe fall to the ground. Persephone managed to pull two nails out that were left behind. "No wonder! Well, I'm relieved there's not too much damage to her hoof." She bent to pick up the horseshoe then let the cob's leg go and stroked down from her poll to her nose. "You be all right, lady? It's not far. I'll lead you." Instead of climbing back into the cart, Persephone took hold of the reins just behind the bit and drew Miss Pie forward. She resisted at first, but soon started to move.

"Wait!" Sophia called.

Persephone halted Miss Pie and looked back.

"If you think I'm going to sit up here like the Queen of Sheba and let the poor creature struggle, you don't know me very well." Sophia looped the reins around the rail on the side of the bench seat and hopped down in one graceful movement before coming to walk beside Persephone.

Thus they entered the hamlet of Delabole, drawing gazes from the women busy with their household chores and a few toddlers playing in the dirt.

"Tha's s'posed to let the horse pull you, not t'other way around," said one old woman to the amusement of several others clustered around a well.

Persephone smiled. "My poor girl has thrown a shoe. Are we in the right direction to reach the smithy?"

Most of the women simply stared at them, but one—a little younger and obviously with a child on the way—said, "Jes keep on and ye'll come to 'un. Might not be there, though."

"Thank you. Might we know his name? And yours, so we may thank you for your help," Persephone said.

"He's Old Bart. Me, I'm just Maudie Bray."

"Well, just Maudie, I'm grateful for the information."

Persephone immediately regretted her pleasantry, worried that the girl might misinterpret her intent to be kind.

But a broad smile brightened Maudie's face. "I'm by way of going that direction mysel', so I'll show you," and she fell into step beside them.

Deciding to risk being thought too inquisitive, Persephone said, "Is your father an overseer here? I may have met him."

The girl's smile faded. "My father by law. My Burt is no wise like his da."

So, Bray wasn't much liked among his own either.

"And ye are?" Maudie asked, looking back and forth between the two of them.

"Of course! I am Persephone Wilkins, and this is Sophia Tresillian."

When she heard Sophia's name, the girl's grey eyes widened and she made a shallow, awkward curtsy. "Miss Tresillian! What's the likes of you doin' here?"

Sophia laughed. "I live a mile away, and I've never been here before. I have some things the women in the village might find useful. You especially," she said, nodding toward Maudie's distended belly.

"Beggin' yer pardon, Miss," she said to Persephone, as if she suddenly realized she'd been remiss. "I dunno any Wilkins."

"I've only lived in Delabole for a few weeks. I moved into a cottage I rent from Mr. Tresillian."

At that, Maudie stopped walking abruptly and put her hands on her hips, disbelief in her eyes. "You mean, ye've *chose* to come here and live?"

On reflection, Persephone thought it might seem a bit mad, so she decided she may as well explain herself a little. "I'm a teacher. I've come to set up a school."

This silenced Maudie. The three ladies continued along

without speaking past the neat rows of two-room cottages until they reached the end of the road. They heard the ringing of iron hitting iron before they saw the blacksmith. He looked to be hammering a tool of some sort into shape for a man standing nearby. "Thank you, Maudie Bray," Persephone said and put out her hand.

Maudie stared at it for a moment before taking it briefly. "There's the smithy," she said, unnecessarily.

Sophia said, "Which cottage is yours, Mrs. Bray?"

"It's the one we passed five back, the small one with the door that's broken." She looked down at her feet, as if a little ashamed.

"I'll come and visit you while Miss Pie here gets her shoe mended," Sophia said, giving the girl her warmest smile.

"Oh no Miss! You mustn't! It in't proper."

"Nonsense!" Sophia took her hand. "Will I find you there if I come in a few minutes?"

Maudie dipped an uncertain curtsy and walked away.

"Why will you do that?" Persephone asked.

"She interests me," was Sophia's only reply, and she walked to the cart and removed her basket.

By this time, Old Bart had seen them and hobbled bow-leggedly over. Persephone explained her predicament, and he freed Miss Pie from the traces before leading her over to his workshop.

Sophia had gone off in the direction of Maudie Bray's house, and Persephone stayed behind, completely at a loss. Why exactly was she here? She'd never traveled abroad, but this place, with its unfamiliar landscape, massive wound in the ground, and people who looked at her with suspicion in their eyes suddenly felt as foreign to her as if she had sailed to the Americas.

"A thrown shoe is no reason to be so Friday faced," said a deep voice behind her.

She whirled around to confront the man she'd seen with the blacksmith. He stood before her with an expression of faint amusement, feet planted sturdily apart, holding a newly trued spade in his hands. But this was no tenant farmer, she saw. He wore fine buckskins and top boots, a coat of expert tailoring, and a curly brimmed beaver hat of the latest style. His face was somewhat lined and threads of gray wove through his brown hair, but his brown eyes crinkled into a smile at the corners.

He immediately removed his hat and bowed. "Edmund Carlyon at your service, ma'am."

Persephone curtsied. "Squire Carlyon!"

He looked puzzled. "Have we met before?"

"No, sir," she said a bit ruefully. "My friend just happened to mention your name to me on our way here."

"I see my reputation precedes me." His smile broadened, revealing straight white teeth and a decided twinkle in his eyes. "And who would this friend be who bandied my name about?"

Persephone suddenly remembered her manners. "She is Miss Sophia Tresillian. I am Persephone Wilkins. And very pleased to make your acquaintance."

"I know Miss Tresillian's name well enough. We are neighbors, although we don't have so very much to do with one another. I'm a farmer, not a businessman. But your name is unfamiliar to me. Are you visiting Miss Tresillian?"

"No, I moved here from near Boscastle a few weeks ago. I rent a cottage from Mr. Tresillian."

"Not the little place that's so close to the quarry he couldn't get anyone to take it!"

Persephone blushed. "It's not so close. And I've become accustomed to the noise." Recalling what Sophia had said to her about Carlyon's ancient lineage and disdain for those who made their fortunes in trade, Persephone changed the subject. "I wonder, sir, do you happen to possess a fine chestnut mare?"

He opened his eyes wide in surprise. "Not that I'm aware of. If you're wanting such an animal you might well find one at the auction in Bodmin."

"No, I was just curious. I saw a horse answering that description in a field on the way here." She thought of telling him that she had indeed seen a horse like that in Bodmin, but changed her mind. So the mare did not belong to him. In any case, if he'd been away until a few days ago he would be unlikely to have attended the auction. Besides, Pentarrant no doubt knew him and would have greeted him if he'd been there.

"What brings you to Delabole?" the squire asked.

"Today Sophia and I have come to see if we may be of any service to the families here. We have brought some things." She decided to keep it vague and hope he wouldn't inquire further.

"I meant more generally. It's odd for a gentlewoman to take up residence in such a place, and on her own."

She supposed it was. How to explain it without having to tell him the whole story? She shrugged. "I am not so gently bred as you might think. Until a year or so ago I was a governess in a noble family. I received a legacy that has granted me the freedom to live life as I choose."

He scoffed. "And you chose to come here? Well, I'm sure Miss Tresillian has been introducing you to the gentry hereabouts. Such as it is. The old families have mostly moved to estates away from the sound and sight of the quarry."

"Yet you remain," Persephone said, then realized she had been a bit impertinent.

"So we do." He shifted his sight up and slightly past Persephone's shoulder, but quickly looked back at her and settled his hat on his head. "I have brought my widowed daughter to live with me. I shall take the liberty of telling her I met you, and she may call upon you. Lydia has not been herself since her husband's death last year and I think some society might cheer her up."

"I'd be delighted to make the acquaintance of Mrs…"

"Tresize. You will likely be asked to call her Lydia. We don't stand on such ceremony as the Pentarrants do."

This subtle dig was not lost on Persephone, but she simply smiled and put out her hand to the squire. He took it and bowed over it briefly. "Goodbye Miss Wilkins." He walked off just as Sophia came forward to join Persephone.

He'd seen Sophia and did not acknowledge her. Was there such bad blood between the two families? If so, why hadn't Sophia mentioned anything?

Before she could question her friend, Old Bart led Miss Pie back out and harnessed her to the cart. "That'll be one and six, Missus," the smith said. "The old shoe weren't any use."

"Yes, of course." Persephone suspected that Miss Pie's shoe, which appeared hardly worn to her, might have served, but she wasn't about to argue with the fellow. She took her purse out of her reticule and gave him the coins. He tugged his forelock and walked away without a word.

Sophia said, "Was that Squire Carlyon?"

"Yes, it was."

"What did he say?"

"He said that his daughter, Mrs. Tresize, might call on me."

"And yet, he gave me the cut direct."

Persephone took Sophia's arm. "I expect he didn't see you. Shall we leave Miss Pie and the cart here and walk through the village? Was your time with Mrs. Bray of use to you?"

Sophia shrugged. "She's young and slight. I fear she'll have a bad time when her baby comes. I've given her some ointments to rub on her belly. She said the infant is pressing hard under her ribs. I hope if it's breach now it will turn before her time."

Persephone stopped suddenly, mouth open. "Do you have an interest in midwifery?" It was a singularly ungenteel occupation. Persephone couldn't imagine how Sophia had come to acquire such knowledge.

"No, not precisely. I'm interested in all the conditions—not just illnesses—that only women experience. They aren't talked about, even by doctors. I had a friend…" She stopped speaking.

Persephone didn't inquire further, assuming Sophia would tell her about it sometime.

"Come!" Sophia said. "Maudie said she'd introduce us to a few of the women who have children working at the quarry. Only the ones with very young children or infants to mind are actually here. Everyone else is employed in some fashion or other in the slate business."

How like Sophia to befriend someone in a place where she was a stranger! Persephone thought she never could do it, not so quickly.

Arm in arm they walked back along the narrow village street, attracting notice but now with more curiosity than hostility in the eyes turned to them. *This wouldn't have happened if Pentarrant had been here,* Persephone thought. She gave Sophia's arm a little squeeze and they smiled at each other.

"Well," Persephone said, "I can't tell which families would have children ready for school, clearly, but I'm not sorry we came. I won't be afraid the next time. Did Maudie happen to say when might be a good time to find more people around?"

"After the workday ends, which is at six in the evening at this time of year."

Persephone said, "I doubt evening would be the best time

to disturb them, after the fatigue of a long working day. Perhaps I'll come by myself tomorrow morning. Philippa won't come for me until noon, and I don't want to put it off any longer than necessary."

"I wonder which event will prove the more enjoyable." They laughed and climbed back into the cart. Miss Pie, having had a good rest, was ready to head back to her barn.

CHAPTER 20

A messenger arrived at Nathaniel's lodgings in the middle of the day with a note summoning him to Tresillian manor. *So soon?* he thought. It had only been a couple of days since he had attended Mr. Tresillian for a bilious complaint. On that visit, Nathaniel had given him a dose of calomel to purge his system. His pallor at the time worried him, and he put his ear to the man's chest so he could listen to his heart and noted its slightly irregular beat. But he found nothing of immediate concern and merely prescribed laudanum to soothe his abdominal pain.

This time, he found the gentleman in his bedchamber—dressed, but lying on a sofa in an uncharacteristically listless attitude. His face was pale and he was sweating a little. Nathaniel marched over and took hold of his wrist. The pulse was very erratic and weak. "When did you start feeling unwell?" he asked.

With some difficulty, Mr. Tresillian said, "Just after breakfast this morning."

"Why didn't you send for me right away?" Nathaniel tried to keep the irritation out of his voice. He suspected that

Tresillian had suffered a mild heart seizure, or strong palpitations. Whatever it was, his heart was most definitely affected.

"I didn't want Sophie to know! Don't want to worry her. I waited 'til she went off with that Miss Wilkins to send for you today." He paused and took several breaths, wincing as though it pained him a little to do so.

"I think, sir, that this is more serious than a simple attack of biliousness. Are you able to climb stairs?"

Tresillian glowered up at Nathaniel, his gray eyes hard. "If I move a little slower these days, what of it?"

Nathaniel had seen this kind of reaction before in strong, proud men whose bodies began to betray them after a life of hard living, rich food, and copious amounts of wine. Usually it was gout that felled them. But it seemed that Tresillian had a weakness of the heart instead. "You aren't going to like what I have to say to you, sir," he said, taking a phial of syrup of poppies out of his bag. "You must rest and not overtax yourself. A light diet and no wine, at least for a while." He had little hope that this final instruction would be followed. Many patients, he found, assumed that because drink made them numb to whatever was ailing them that it must somehow be efficacious. Other medical professionals did not share his views, except in the case of gout, but his observations convinced him that wine was no remedy for most ailments.

Tresillian let his eyelids droop as if holding them up cost him great effort. After a moment he looked up at the doctor. "I don't want Sophie to know I'm a bit ill. I'm sure I'll soon be right again, and I wouldn't want to worry her. She's so young, and her mama left us just a few years ago."

"I understand. All the same, I think it would be better if Miss Tresillian did know so that she could help you." What he really meant was that she could keep an eye on him and make sure he wasn't overtaxing himself or overindulging. "When do you expect her to return? I would feel more confident about your prospects if I were able to instruct her concerning the medications I should like to prescribe for you." A vision of Miss Tresillian at her father's side, her soft eyes bent on him in concern, her golden curls tumbling around her shoulders momentarily distracted him. Don't be foolish, he thought. What was it about the idea of seeing her, of meeting her lively, intelligent eyes and possibly crossing swords with her that had the power to affect him so?

Tresillian chuckled. "More likely she'll tell *you* what she thinks I should physic myself with and tell *me* I should take more walks in the country air."

Nathaniel suspected this was true, and it brought a smile to his lips. He pictured the defiant light in her eyes when he had refused to let her come with him to attend Mrs. Judd the night of the Roscarrock ball. "Do you honestly believe, sir, that she would want to be kept in ignorance of the state of your health?"

The old man closed his eyes again and said, "Very well," on a long sigh. "But don't you say anything to her. I will."

Nathaniel wasn't sure he trusted him to be honest with his daughter about the seriousness of his condition. On the other hand, she was observant enough, surely, to see for herself that all was not well with him. "When you have spoken with her, I would be grateful if you would grant me the opportunity to share my professional opinion with Miss Tresillian."

At that, Tresillian's eyes flew open and he made an effort to sit up straighter. "You'll do nothing of the kind! It's my health, and I'll decide who's to know what. I don't want Sophie to hide herself away at home caring for me—which is what she'll do if she thinks I've had notice to quit." He started to cough and pressed his hand over his heart.

"I suggest you take a draft of this now and try to rest," Nathaniel said, taking the stopper out of the bottle and pouring a measure of the thick syrup into a small glass.

When Tresillian caught his breath, he took the glass and downed its contents in one gulp.

"I want you to leave me before Sophie gets back home. I don't want her to know you've been here," Tresillian said, not taking his eyes off Nathaniel.

Although he would vastly have preferred to remain and see Miss Tresillian, Nathaniel had to accede to her father's wishes. "Of course. Don't hesitate to send for me if your symptoms worsen. And especially don't hesitate to do so even if your daughter is at home. I am persuaded she would not want you to postpone receiving medical help out of a mistaken sense of delicacy or pride."

"You think you know my daughter? Eh, well. You're young, so perhaps you know more than I do. Are your parents yet alive, Rowe?"

An inquiry of this nature risked getting into dangerous territory. "Yes," he said, hoping his short answer would depress any temptation on Tresillian's part to ask anything more, and he wrote out a note which he gave him. "Have your man take this to the apothecary to make up. For the next week, take it twice a day."

Mr. Tresillian grudgingly agreed to follow Nathaniel's instructions. Nathaniel was not sanguine about Tresillian's prospects for recovery, and was very troubled that Sophia would not know her father was so ill. It wasn't that the merchant was elderly. He couldn't be beyond his fifties. Perhaps he had some underlying weakness, some tendency in his family. He only hoped that Miss Tresillian wouldn't encourage her father to do anything that would exacerbate his condition—or dose him with any remedies that would do more harm than good out of mistaken notions. Miss Tresillian was intelligent and obviously had a degree of practical knowledge, but she wasn't a physician.

She was, however, a darling, he thought with a start. And all things considered, Nathaniel was sorry she hadn't been there.

SOPHIA'S MIND WAS FULL OF ALL SHE'D HEARD FROM MAUDIE Bray that day when Persephone left her at the door of Tresillian Manor. Her friend had declined the offer of staying to dinner, saying she had much to do at her cottage. Sophia did not press her, although she would have welcomed the opportunity to share her insights about Maddie's life as evident in her home. The cottage was as clean as Maudie could make it, but it had a dirt floor and the hearth was situated so that it didn't adequately heat either the combined parlor/kitchen or the small bedroom—if it could have been called that. This was not so important at this time of year, but come winter, with an infant not yet out of the cradle, it could leave the way open for all manner of diseases.

These thoughts absorbed so much of her attention that on entering the house she didn't ask where her father was, assuming he had gone out to see to something on the home farm—an activity that made him feel like a true gentleman and not someone who had become wealthy through clever investments in steam power.

In any event, it was close to dinner time so she went directly up to her room to change into evening clothes. As she was on her way down the second pair of stairs, she encountered Hosking on his way up with a glass and decanter on a tray. "Where are you going with that, Hosking?"

"The master asked for it in his room, ma'am," he said.

"In his room? But surely he will come down to dinner at any moment. Hadn't you better bring it to the saloon?"

The butler stopped with his feet on two different steps, looking up toward the bedroom floor, and then down toward the floor where the saloons and the drawing room were located. "Begging your pardon, ma'am, but he asked me only a few minutes ago to bring him up a glass of Madeira."

This was puzzling. "Thank you, Hosking. I shall take it to him." He relinquished the small tray to her rather reluctantly. "Don't worry, I'll ensure he knows that I bore you down and insisted."

This behavior was so unlike her father that Sophia instantly became concerned. She tapped on his door but entered without waiting for him to bid her to come in, thus he didn't have time to straighten himself up from his lounging position on the sofa. "Papa!" Sophia said and, nearly forgetting her burden, hurried over to him. She placed the tray on the small table next to the sofa.

"Hello my dear, you've spilled half my Madeira!" he said with an effort at levity.

"That's neither here nor there, Father. Are you ill? Have you had an accident? Why are you not dressed for dinner?" She took his hand in hers and pressed it to her cheek as she knelt down by him.

"Oh, just a little bilious my dear. You know, the old complaint."

"But surely you've never had it this badly before, not that I recall. Have you seen the doctor?" Sophia did not attempt to treat her father's illnesses, other than suggesting the most benign remedies for the headache. She knew the limits of her knowledge, even if she thought some of her treatments might be quite effective for certain common complaints. Her training could never match Dr. Rowe's in its breadth or depth, to her abiding annoyance. But she knew nonetheless that her father was indeed quite unwell. She thought she'd exaggerated the trouble when speaking with Persephone yesterday, but apparently not!

"Yes, Rowe was here. He's given me a tonic and some very disagreeable instructions about what I cannot eat or drink. But I think it's not as bad as all that." He smiled at her and tried to hoist himself up a little higher.

She gently pressed him back down. It didn't take much for her to figure out that he was sicker than he wanted to let on. She could see it in the grayish undertone of his skin and his bloodless lips. She pointed toward the half-empty glass of Madeira. "Did Dr. Rowe say you should drink wine? Perhaps it's not a bad thing that I've brought you only half!"

He shrugged and didn't meet her eyes. "He didn't tell me not to drink Madeira."

She raised an eyebrow and pursed her lips. "Oh, and what else didn't he tell you not to drink?"

"One little glass can't hurt. I've a powerful thirst." He shifted slightly and winced.

"What hurts, Papa?" Sophia asked. She would get to the bottom of this. He could be so damnably stubborn! She took his wrist to feel his pulse, but he shook her away.

"Don't fuss, girl! A quiet evening and I'll be right as rain in the morning."

"What about dinner? You need to eat."

"I've asked for a tray," he said.

This was something he never did. Although he enjoyed the status he had earned as a wealthy man capable of affording the elegancies of life, he never forgot that his servants were people, and consequently avoided whenever possible putting them to unwonted trouble. "Then I shall take my dinner with you here." She pulled the bell rope by the fireplace and when Hosking came in told him that both of them would have their dinner on trays in that room.

Sophia knew that nothing she could say would convince her father that he might not be miraculously better the next day. Nor was he likely to confide to her what Dr. Rowe had said to him. She would have to take matters into her own hands. After dinner she would ride into Camelford and see Dr. Rowe. The slip of paper he'd left on the dresser had an address. Would he tell her what he thought was wrong with her father? Doctors were supposed to treat patients confidentially. But surely, even though he was newly come to the neighborhood, he had been there long enough to understand how important it was that she remain informed of her father's health.

THE DAYS WERE LONG AT THAT TIME OF YEAR, AND SO SOPHIA had Penny saddled and rode the short distance into Camelford in the early evening, cantering when the road allowed. The distance was not great, nonetheless she had time to consider what she would ask Dr. Rowe—assuming he was to be found at his lodgings—and how best to ask him in a way that wouldn't provoke one of their fraught confrontations about medicine. Why was it they couldn't seem to see each other without setting off such sparks of disagreement?

This vexed her, and not simply because she would so much have preferred to have his respect both for her not inconsiderable knowledge as well as the extent of her serious —albeit unofficial—study. It vexed her because something about him attracted her despite their antipathy. They had made a connection the day they rode together. She didn't think it was his warm brown eyes, or the way his curly golden locks refused to be quite tamed, or the furrow in his brow when he concentrated on something. Perhaps it was partly the memory of the sinewy, subtle strength she felt when he held her briefly in his arms at the ball and saw when he climbed down to gather the samphire. Although not as obviously muscled as Pentarrant, Rowe's upright bearing and the way he jumped easily into a saddle or up to the seat on his gig spoke of the athlete. An athlete with an intellect. For, disagree with him over some things though she might, she knew enough of doctors and their popular treatments to recognize the practical and theoretical knowledge that underpinned Rowe's dictums.

The nearer she drew to her destination the more anxious she became. She had never called on a gentleman of any description in his lodgings before, and would never have dared were it not for her deep concern about her father. But Rowe was a doctor. Surely that made everything acceptable.

After delivering Penny into the hands of a lad standing on the street, promising him six pence if he would walk her sweating horse up and down, Sophia draped the long skirt of her riding habit over her arm and took a deep breath. *It's perfectly natural for you to be here,* she said to herself. She stood as straight as she could, lifting her chin in a suggestion of haughtiness, then knocked briskly on the painted door.

One or two men passed by and inspected her insolently. She glared at them and lowered their eyes, but she could hear them whispering to each other as they wandered off. The door opened suddenly after that and a woman—a housekeeper or a landlady, she thought—stared at her in some surprise.

"May I help you, madam?" she said in a way that was hardly less insolent than the men who had passed by.

"I am here to consult with Dr. Rowe. I believe these are his lodgings and his surgery?" She clipped her words, attempting a tone of businesslike inquiry.

The lady opened the door wider. "I s'pose. Please wait in here, ma'am," she said, gesturing for her to come into the rather cramped hall, and then asked with exaggerated politeness, "Whom shall I say is calling?"

"Tell the doctor that Miss Tresillian is here to consult with him about her father."

The familiar name made the woman stand a little straighter. "I'll fetch the doctor for you." She went away toward the back of the house and passed through a door.

By now, Sophia was beginning to think this had been a terrible mistake. She could have sent a boy with a note and asked Rowe to attend her at the manor. It was too late to back out now, so she forced herself to maintain an icy calm while her mind raced trying to think of how to extricate herself from this situation as quickly and smoothly as possible.

After what felt like a long time, the woman returned. "Dr. Rowe says you're to come back to his office." The way she said it with a slight purse of her lips disturbed Sophia. She followed her nonetheless.

The housekeeper led her to a small room where Dr. Rowe was standing behind a desk littered with a mess of papers. Every available wall held bookshelves crowded with volumes, some upright, some lying flat, many stuffed with yet more papers. Added to that, a few crates of even more books lay open on the floor, leaving very little space to walk around. The room was illuminated by a single candle—necessary at that time of day because its one small window faced the outer wall of the next building only a few feet away. Under that window was a small table with several knives and probes lined up on it. Among all this was a single chair pushed up to the desk at a slight angle, as though Dr. Rowe had just stood up from it. The loose knot of his neckcloth and the disorder of his hair clearly showed that he was not expecting any visitors.

"I am so sorry to disturb you, Dr. Rowe," Sophia said,

feeling a blush steal up from her neck and into her cheeks. "I would not have come except that I am most concerned about my father, and I know you attended him today."

"Please don't be anxious on my account, Miss Tresillian," he said and bowed, as if he remembered his manners belatedly. "I am glad you have come, because I wanted to speak with you about your father's condition. I had suggested I call on you in the morning. Did he not say?"

Sophia gave a short laugh. "Of course not. And he would have made certain I was nowhere to be found when you arrived. I know he doesn't want to worry me, but I think I could be of help to him if I knew what was wrong."

Rowe raised an eyebrow and screwed his mouth into an ironic smile. "Why, Miss Tresillian! I felt certain you would examine him and make your own diagnosis."

A spark of anger surged inside of her. "However little you think of me, Dr. Rowe, I wish you would set that aside for now. I am too aware of my own limitations, and too concerned about my father's health, to attempt anything of the kind."

The skeptical look on his face vanished, and his eyes softened. "Please forgive me. Won't you sit down?" He gestured toward the one chair, which would have been difficult for Sophia to get to in that small room without brushing past him.

"And have you standing over me like a cross schoolmaster?"

This made him laugh. "Yes, that would not do. As you see, I am not accustomed to seeing patients here. I have yet to set up a proper surgery, although I have found the space and am negotiating with the landlord."

This brought the blush back into Sophia's face. "Y-you don't see patients here?" She was suddenly conscious of the impropriety of being there, alone with him in what were clearly simply one room of his lodgings.

"I don't. But I'm certainly happy to see you here." At that, Rowe also blushed.

"Well, perhaps you could tell me what I must do to ensure my father regains his health." She turned her gaze to the window, not trusting herself to meet Dr. Rowe's eyes.

He stepped out from behind the desk, dragging the chair with him and placing it beside her. Then he picked up one of the crates and moved it to reveal a wooden stool. "Let us both be seated," he said, "and I will tell you what I can without violating my patient's confidentiality."

She was afraid he would say something like that. She took the seat, sitting primly straight with her hands folded in her lap. "I appreciate that my father no doubt told you not to worry me. But sir, I beg you to let me have the truth with no bark on it. How ill is my father?"

Dr. Rowe had seated himself on the stool facing her. The crowded space meant that his knees were only inches away from hers. *He could reach out and touch me,* Sophia thought, some part of her wishing he would do exactly that.

Perhaps sensing her thoughts, Rowe leaned slightly forward. His hands twitched as if he wanted to take hold of hers, but instead he curled them into fists, which he pressed resolutely against his thighs. "Your father, I fear, is quite unwell. It is—you must understand—difficult to know exactly how much so. I have known men with his heart condition live on for many years."

She nodded. "I suspected it was his heart. I have no direct experience with such complaints, but I feared it was not the biliousness he blames for every indisposition. What can I do?" Until that point, Sophia had kept her eyes focused on her own folded hands. But on her last beseeching words she lifted them to meet his.

Dr. Rowe swallowed audibly and cleared his throat. "I'm afraid the only thing you can do is encourage him to follow my directions and advice."

She shook her head. "In order to do that, I must needs know what those are. Won't you please tell me?"

He opened his mouth to speak, then shut it again. Finally, he said, "I mustn't act so directly counter to his wishes by telling you. However, we could discuss in theory how I might treat such a patient as your father if he were suffering a heart disorder."

Sophia smiled and let her shoulders relax. Dr. Rowe had scruples, but he also had a conscience. He would tell her what she needed to know.

For the next half hour, Rowe explained everything he knew about treating heart ailments to Sophia. Most of it was merely what Sophia expected, based upon her own common sense. But she was nonetheless glad to have her instincts corroborated by someone properly trained.

At the end of their interview, Sophia said, "I cannot thank you enough for telling me all this. Now I shall know what to watch for, what to encourage him to do or not do. It may not seem much to you, but it makes me feel a great deal less helpless." She put out her hand to shake his.

He took it, his grasp warm and firm. Sophia allowed him to hold her hand longer than was strictly proper, and when she tried to pull hers away, he put his other hand over it. "You must feel you can call on me for anything at all. At any hour of the day or night. Simply send a message to me and I will come."

His expressive eyes bereft her of the power of speech. He seemed to see inside her to the very depths of her soul and his mind reached out to hers in comfort and companionship. She reluctantly drew her hand out of his grasp. "Goodbye,

Dr. Rowe. Don't forget that you owe me another ride together."

"Ah yes, your winnings. But you could have commanded that from me even if you'd lost."

Sophia's pulse quickened and her breaths became shallow. "Why, thank you, sir."

"Your most obedient, Miss Tresillian," Rowe said, perhaps taking refuge in formality to dispel the intimacy that had suddenly encroached on them. He opened the door and gestured for her to pass through it ahead of him. In the confined space of what was more a study than an office, their arms brushed. Sophia heard his sharp intake of breath. It was almost more than she could bear, and she rushed away as quickly as she could without actually running.

Oh Sophia! she said to herself. The boy walking Penny met her out front and made a step of his interlaced fingers so she could climb back into the saddle. She had not been with Dr. Rowe long, but it was enough for the shadows to have lengthened and a chill tinge the air. By the time she returned to the manor, it would be twilight. She would go up and sit with her father and then excuse herself to retire for the night so she could ponder everything that had happened that day and sort out her unruly feelings.

CHAPTER 21

Persephone walked to the quarry village on her own the very next morning, before the picnic. She decided not to go in the evening. To encroach on the time when families would be having their supper and likely be exhausted from a long day of work either in the quarry or around the home would not dispose them to look upon her with favor. She would sacrifice thoroughness for willingness.

As it was, she was able to talk to several mothers of children too young to work in the quarry, mothers who also had older children engaged in various aspects of quarry work. Everyone listened to her politely, but no one seemed enthusiastic about the idea of education for all—despite the fact that there wasn't even a Methodist Sunday school available to them. Apparently the preacher was only an itinerant whose flock encompassed several small villages.

At first, Persephone couldn't figure out why they were apparently so uninterested in the opportunity she was offering them. Then, finally, a young woman with an infant on her hip and two toddlers clinging to her legs told her that the true sticking point was time. "Every day is already full as it can hold. The wee ones start with the helling stones when they're five or six. My Jenny—she's my eldest—she ain't here as she's gone down the quarry to take a bit of bread and cheese to her da. When she comes up there's the laundry and mending to be getting on with."

It all did sound utterly exhausting. How would she be able to persuade any of them that it was worthwhile to add to their children's overburdened schedules with a half-mile walk to her cottage for the luxury of being educated? While all their other tasks had tangible, immediate benefits it was hard to persuade them that an investment of time now would pay dividends in the future.

By the time she had visited half the workers' dwellings, she had significantly altered her original plan. Her vision of a classroom full of students who would come every morning vanished. The best she could do would be to offer a Sunday school after the Methodist preacher had released the congregation from prayers. Would they be willing? It seemed likely the preacher would have to endorse it, and also that he would insist on a degree of religious education. Well, she would do what she must. And she might as well start that Sunday.

For a full hour, she navigated the dusty village paths, spreading the word about the forthcoming Sunday school at her home. Everyone seemed acquainted with the cottage, as it was the nearest dwelling outside the village other than Penterrent Lodge where James Pentarrant lived. It wasn't, perhaps, precisely what she'd hoped for, but it was a start.

So why did she feel so hollow? Surely she'd expected nothing more. Or had she? Deep in her heart she had thought that Pentarrant was sure to appear. This gave her a curious mixture of dread and pleasurable anticipation. In truth she little relished the idea of having to justify her actions to the man, still something about his presence on the previous times she had encountered him reassured her. If he added his voice to hers to emphasize the importance of education, no doubt all of these reserved, hard-working people would do what they could to comply.

But he would not add his voice. Everything he'd said to her before seemed to indicate that he did not favor her project.

The fact was that the inhabitants of the quarry village were not her people. She was not gentry, but her upbringing, her life, had been so fundamentally different from theirs that she couldn't help but be aware of the vast gulf in understanding that lay between them. It was odd, though, that somehow, even though he was even farther above them in rank and situation than she was, they *were* Pentarrant's people. His association with the quarry was generations deep, certainly, but little though she knew him, she understood that this sense of belonging stemmed from more than that. Several of the women she talked to spoke of him not just with respect, but with affection.

"Miss Wilkins!"

Maudie's voice called her out of her distracted meanderings. "Mrs. Bray! How lovely to meet with you again."

"Where's yer friend?" Maudie was struggling under the weight of a basket full of wet clothes.

"Let me help you with that!" Persephone said and went to her with her hands out.

Maudie shook her head. "I'll just get these on the line so they dry before my husband gets home."

Persephone followed her around the side of her cottage to a small yard behind it. "Miss Tresillian had other things to attend to this morning. I wonder, Maudie, if I could speak with you a little."

"If you can talk while I do me chores. I've this and then I have to see to the vegetables." She jerked her head in the direction of a weedy patch of haphazardly sown produce, including a pea vine trailing up a rusted rake as well as what looked like carrot tops.

"I'm relieved to see you're not working in the quarry," Persephone said and—ignoring the girl's protests—handed her dripping garments from the basket at her feet so she wouldn't have to keep bending over. When that task was finished and Maudie knelt down to begin yanking the weeds out of the little kitchen garden, Persephone knelt beside her. "Don't, Miss!" Maudie said. "Ye'll mucky yer frock and yer hands."

Persephone smiled at her and shrugged. "There's nothing I love better than getting my hands dirty in this fashion. I've just started trying to reclaim my small garden from the weeds that must have been growing there for years! I was used to do a lot of gardening in my previous situation."

For a short while, the two of them worked side-by-side in charged silence, rendering the incessant sounds of industry from the quarry suddenly noticeable: the squeaking pulleys, the ring of stone being hammered and split, and the occasional dull boom of a huge boulder being deposited on the grass. Persephone stole a sidelong glance at Maudie, who was biting her lower lip. "What will you call your baby when it is born?" Persephone said, hoping this might encourage her to ask her question.

"Old Bray says it's bad luck to think of names before ye know the wee babe will survive." Persephone perceived a tightening at the corner of Maudie's mouth, as if she hadn't yet said what she truly wanted to say.

"Childbirth can be a frightening prospect, so I'm told. But let's assume your baby will thrive. Would you want him or her to be able to read and write?"

A long pause ensued. "I don't see as there's much call for that. They'll just be sent down the quarry one way or t'other."

"What if they had enough learning so they could do a job in the office instead? Or even get a position as a footman or lady's maid at a fine house?"

"We're nobody's servants here!" Maudie said and struggled to her feet. "I thank 'ee for yer help, but I can manage from here."

Persephone sat back on her heels and looked up, her hand shielding her eyes from the sun. Maudie's lips were pressed in a fierce line and her eyes flashed. What had she said? "There are other jobs that require reading and writing and sums. I think here, too, you must sign contracts for your setts. Is that not so? Does no one read what those papers say before putting their mark on them?"

Before Maudie could answer, a gruff voice from a few yards away said, "See! I told you she was up to no good. Puttin' radical ideas in them as has no need of 'em."

At that, Maudie's face went completely white and she said, "I didna ask her to come. She weren't sayin' nothin' I regarded."

Bray. Persephone took her time standing and brushing the soil off her skirt and hands. She wondered where Bray came from, how he knew she was there, and how much of their conversation he had heard. "I believe Mrs. Bray is capable of listening and coming to her own conclusions."

Persephone finally looked at the man, ready to unleash her unvarnished view of ignorant bullies on this tyrant, but the words froze in her throat. At that moment, Pentarrant walked forward from where he stood a few feet behind the overseer.

"Good morning, Miss Wilkins," he said, touching the brim of his cap. "I am chagrined that you did not allow me the pleasure of showing you around the quarry and village myself, as I offered to do."

Was he angry? Or amused? He smiled, but she could not read the gaze that pinned her to her spot.

After a moment Pentarrant said, "Thank you, Bray, for letting me know about our visitor. I expect your work in the quarry is not quite at an end for today."

Bray, doubtless feeling cheated of seeing an uppity woman set down, wheeled around and stalked off.

"Mr. Pentarrant," Persephone said and met his eyes.

"I see you've met Maudie."

The girl's attitude of hostility melted as soon as Bray disappeared. She blushed and hid her dirty hands behind her back.

"Yes. We met yesterday, when I came with Miss Tresillian," Persephone said. "We were just talking about the benefits of educating children. I have spoken to a number of mothers today, and they seem well disposed to having their children learn. It is finding a good time that is the challenge. It's one I believe I may have solved, however."

He cocked his head on the side and looked at her in a considering way. "One of the reasons I wanted you to allow me to guide you around the quarry was to help you gain a better understanding of these people's lives."

"I would welcome such an opportunity. I'm not certain what it has to do with learning to read, however."

Instead of responding, he put out his arm to her and said to Maudie, "Excuse us. I have business with Miss Wilkins."

Maudie bobbed an awkward curtsy. "Yes sir. Miss."

Persephone had no choice but to take Pentarrant's arm. It would have been pointedly rude not to. As they walked in silence out of the village proper and toward the horse whims, the feel of his well-muscled arm under her hand called to mind their dances in the ballroom, and she felt a blush steal into her cheeks. Blushing! Like a schoolgirl. Foolish, she thought.

As soon as Persephone judged no one in the village could hear them, she said, "What exactly is it that offends you, Mr. Pentarrant? My design of teaching the quarry children, or my failure to seek you out as my guide today?"

"Offends me? I am most certainly not offended. A little disappointed. But here you are now, and I will gladly acquaint you with the workings of the quarry."

His exaggerated formality hid some other emotion, she was sure. Had it been resentment at being pulled away from his work by Bray? The better understanding they seemed to have reached in Bodmin had vanished.

"I shan't take you down into the pit," he said, leading her to where a path started its treacherous descent to the lower levels. "You can see from here, though, how the large rocks are dug out before the winches lift them up to the level of the grass."

She watched, fascinated, as a small group of men on the opposite side of the quarry worked with picks to loosen a huge slab of the gray slate from its place in the quarry wall. Once it was free they laid it on the iron bed suspended by chains from the winches above. The pulleys screeched as the horses started their circuits of the whims and, inch by inch, hauled the massive rock up the face of the quarry. "It must be dangerous," she said, noting how men down in the pit scrambled out of the way as the boulder swayed in its cradle.

"It is. But the men are well trained and exercise the greatest caution. Once the big pieces are brought to the surface, cutters knock away manageable slabs for the splitters. It's a skilled job, to find just the right point to make it so the splitters can find the fault lines that will become the slates that roof great houses all over the kingdom. Smaller ones become flagstones or are used for other ornamental purposes."

As Pentarrant spoke, Persephone had the impression he

was delivering a lecture he had memorized, perhaps having repeated it many times for potential investors or visiting dignitaries, and she began to feel a bit irritated. After he took her to watch the splitters at their highly skilled work and then the dressers finishing the stone to get it ready to be transported to the ships that would take the prized Delabole slate to the buyers, she said, "This is fascinating. But I don't quite understand why you are telling me all this just now." They had reached the building that housed the offices, and Persephone prepared to take her leave of Pentarrant and return to her own cottage.

"Let me answer you by asking you a question," Pentarrant said. "When you watched the operations just now, what did you see?"

"What did I see?" She thought for a moment. "I saw men, women, and children working in concert, one process leading to another."

"Did anyone appear ill-used to you?"

"No. But I have never suggested that the workers here were mistreated."

He cocked an eyebrow at her. All at once she recalled her run-in with Bray the first time she was there, and blushed. "I did not see any very young children today, or any who appeared unsuited for or unable to do the work that was asked of them. I am, however not at all convinced that Mr. Bray isn't capable of abusing his position of authority over the young workers."

Pentarrant rubbed his chin and sighed. "Bray has spent his entire life here and worked his way up from helling stone collector through all the operations to quarry overseer. There isn't a single part of the operation that he doesn't know inside out."

"We didn't start on the right foot, Mr. Bray and I," Persephone said. "That doesn't change the fact that when he passes by I see fear in the eyes not only of the lads like young Jago but in his own daughter-in-law."

"It is no bad thing for an overseer to be feared. This is a dangerous place. Strict discipline is essential to prevent accidents." He drew his brows together and looked down.

Of course, the rock fall. Persephone wondered what had happened, and what Pentarrant had had to do with it, if anything. But she would not ask. "Discipline and cruelty are two separate things. He clearly resents the idea of my bringing education to the quarry children, perhaps because they will be in a position to question his actions when they have learned something about the wider world."

"I thought you were purely interested in teaching them their letters."

"So that they may read, and learn, and be better able to thrive in the world. That includes gaining broader knowledge. Would you deny them the smallest crumb in comparison to the education you had?" Did he really not see how important this was?

"You are right. And I have no objection to your efforts. Whatever you end up doing must in no way interfere with the works, however—for the sake of the quarry and the families who depend on it for their livelihoods."

Nothing must change. That was his message. Yet change would come, resist it or not. "It is not my wish to be disruptive."

He smiled at her with an expression of something beyond kindness in his eyes, and it caught her by surprise. "I am afraid, Miss Wilkins, that you are by definition disruptive."

They had stopped by a small building that appeared to be empty and have no obvious purpose. "What goes on here?" Persephone asked.

He examined the structure briefly, then said, "It was for something I thought we might do, but nothing came of it."

It seemed he didn't care to say anything more so Persephone did not press him. After they said their adieus Persephone turned her steps back toward her own cottage—which in comparison to those of the quarry folk seemed palatial. She made a mental note that in addition to a diet of letters and sums, she must provide her students more practical nourishment in the form of rolls and buns. Perhaps that, if nothing else, would bring them to her on a Sunday afternoon.

CHAPTER 22

Philippa Vyvyan called for Persephone in her landaulet for the picnic excursion to Rough Tor an hour after she got back to her cottage, when her mind was still distracted by all she had seen and learned at the quarry. The idea of a pleasure jaunt that would take nearly a full day seemed the height of self-indulgence compared to the constant work of the quarry folk. She had to remind herself that this, too, was her world. She must engage in such activities if she was to retain the support and good opinions of the local gentry—support she might find herself in need of once her school was up and running.

They spoke of meaningless nothings as they drove around to several other homes to assemble the party that would join the excursion. By the time they reached the center of Camelford, the Landaulet was at the head of a train of about ten carriages and gigs drawn by one or two horses, each one carrying two or three ladies aged sixteen to about fifty.

After a glance behind with an expression of smug satisfaction, Miss Vyvyan turned to Persephone. "I'm so delighted to have this opportunity to get to know you better, Miss Wilkins."

"The pleasure is mine, I assure you," Persephone said disingenuously. They soon left the cobbled streets of the town and joined the packed dirt pike road that led toward the moor. Persephone said, "I don't see Sophia here."

"I expect she felt she should remain at home with her father. He isn't well, you know."

She knew. But not that it was bad enough to make Sophia feel she must remain at home. Something must have occurred the day before. "I hope he will soon be in better frame," Persephone said, disappointed that she wouldn't have the leaven of Sophia's lively presence to relieve the tedium of Philippa's insipid chatter. *It's only one day,* she thought, and pasted a complacent smile on her face.

It didn't take them long to leave the tamer countryside behind and start across the almost treeless expanse of Bodmin moor, its contours subtly colored by flowering heather and gorse on the upper elevations. Grazing sheep had denuded it of much of the vegetation in the lowlands, but somehow the landscape did not feel uninhabited or barren. For thousands of years, communities came and went, leaving echoes of their presence behind. From the ancient Britons to the Druids and early saints, mysterious stone circles and barrows, and remnants of medieval settlements, the moor had accrued an eerie spirit of its own. Not far from where they were going was the stone circle said to be the remains of King Arthur's round table, and many places showed evidence of people from times before history. Their dwellings and other structures had not been covered over by modern buildings or dug up to make way for agriculture. The soil was too poor, suited only to rough grazing for sheep and ponies, and bogs made traveling across the moor hazardous for those who didn't know the terrain intimately. Persephone shivered, but not in an unpleasant way. The wildness, the freedom, was exhilarating. She could almost believe in ghosts in a place like that. One felt isolated on the moor, but never alone.

Such thoughts were never far from Persephone's mind when she ventured onto Bodmin moor, but on that May day, she was more concerned with keeping her hat from blowing away in the stiff east wind. She pressed one hand on top of her head to supplement the efforts of the ribbon tied under her chin. A glance at the other open carriages revealed that this expedient had been adopted by many. Those who knew better—or were perhaps not quite so adventurous—chose to travel in closed chaises.

Miss Vyvyan inched closer to Persephone on the forward-facing seat they shared. "I hope you will forgive me for crowding you into the carriage with some of the picnic fare," she said, gesturing toward the opposite seat piled high with hampers and baskets.

"Not at all," Persephone said. Noting that what lay on the seat opposite hardly seemed sufficient for such a large group, she suspected that it had been put there so that no one else would fit in the carriage. "I understand you host a picnic every summer, Miss Vyvyan."

She laughed with a high, bubbling titter that reminded Persephone of a trained monkey she had once seen at a fair. "It has become somewhat of a tradition. But you must call me Philippa, my dear. We needn't stand on ceremony! I can tell we will be great friends."

Persephone thought that very unlikely, but said, "And I am Persephone, as I believe you know."

"I understand you were a governess to the Ambleton family, to the Marquess of Lewiston's sisters in fact. I was in London for the marchioness's come-out—the honorable

Olivia Ambrose that was. Were you at Amblemere Court during the scandal?"

"What scandal do you speak of?"

"Why, the daughter who wasn't a daughter after all. Imagine perpetrating such a deception. I'm sure I don't know how Miss Ambleton managed to win Lord Atherleigh." She pursed her lips in a disapproving moue. "But perhaps you were not there at that time and so were untouched by it."

Persephone had the distinct impression that Philippa knew full well that she had been deeply involved in the entire affair. "I was indeed with the family. Lady Lewiston did me the honor of asking me to remain in the role of companion to Antonella and Belinda after they left the schoolroom."

"Weren't you shocked?" Philippa said, her eyes open wide in a pretense of scandalized morality.

"My only care was to help the family weather the revelation, especially Antonella, Lady Atherleigh. She is a woman of great spirit and a keen intellect, with a heart to match." She hoped that reminding Philippa of Antonella's now unassailable status would silence her on that subject.

"Well, I suppose you have been constrained to make the best of it. It is not as if we have no scandals of our own in Delabole and Camelford. Of course, you've doubtless heard the one involving Mr. James Pentarrant." She lowered her eyes and flicked an invisible speck of dust off her muslin skirt.

What? Persephone could not imagine the stolid, honorable Pentarrant embroiled in scandal. As far as she knew, he did nothing but work—and turn up unexpectedly at horse auctions in Bodmin, or disturb her tranquility by surprising her when she was visiting Delabole village. "I try not to pay attention to talk that concerns people I don't know well. I'd rather make my own judgments, and I find it best to err on the side of acceptance."

"Of course! It was so long ago. But they say he never got over it. It's why he's never married, you see." Her voice trailed off.

She wants me to be curious. I won't give her the satisfaction. Of course, the damnable creature said something that made her burn to know more. Best to change the subject. "Tell me about where we're going. It's been years since I've been to Bodmin Moor, and I have never seen Rough Tor."

Persephone listened to Philippa's rambling and largely inaccurate account of the history of the tor, the Cornish piskies said to inhabit the moor, ghostly sightings—nothing Persephone hadn't heard many times before. She thought they would never reach the picnic grounds and was relieved when Philippa called to the coachman, "I see them ahead, Jennings!"

To Persephone's surprise, they drew up and climbed down from the carriage before a rather elegant spread of linen-covered tables and silver-domed dishes huddled in the shade of an oddly stunted hawthorn tree. Decades of westerly winds had made the tree grow in a manner that suggested a windswept coiffure, all in one direction. She was glad she had brought her sketching things. She had forgotten how surprising the moor could be, opening vistas one would never see in any other kind of landscape.

Something about it made her think of James Pentarrant, too. He was a little like the moor. Rocky, hard, unyielding, yet with a living core, a beating heart.

"There you are, Persephone!"

Sophia! She must have joined the group late. At the pace they took, she would hardly have had to urge Galahad to a canter to catch up.

Sophia took her arm and drew her away from Miss Vyvyan, who had gone to inspect the picnic arrangements while everyone descended from carriages with the help of various footmen. "How did you stand your tête-à-tête with Philippa? What poison did she spew into your ear?"

"Mostly she was inquisitive about me and about the Lewiston scandal. She tried unsuccessfully to get me interested in hearing about something in James Pentarrant's past. She mentioned your father, too. Is he very ill?"

Sophia sighed. "In Pentarrant's past I know of nothing important. As to my father... I knew he wasn't himself. He had some kind of mild heart seizure the day we went to Delabole together. But he was much better today and insisted I go with you all. In any case, I want to gather some herbs and flowers I can only find on the moor."

"Has Dr. Rowe seen him?"

"Yes," Sophia said, without elaborating, but with a suspiciously pink tinge staining her cheeks.

I'll ask her about it later, Persephone thought, idly watching the coachmen unharness horses and lead them to where they could be secured to rocks and allowed to graze lazily. Their services not required until it was time to leave, the coachmen then wandered off to find somewhere to sit and doze in the shade of a carriage or leaning against a wheel. Not so leisurely was the fate of Miss Vyvyan's poor footmen, though. They stood at attention behind the tables like lead soldiers in their green and gray livery, the relentless wind ruffling their cravats and threatening to send their powdered wigs flying into the air like miniature clouds.

"I fear we'll be in Miss Vyvyan's orbit for quite a while, although I intend to go for a walk of my own before the picnic is over." Sophia rubbed her hands together. "Will you be able to come with me? Or has Philippa made you promise to hew close to her side all day?"

Persephone laughed. "She has extracted no such promise. I intend to find a view to sketch, if nothing more."

"Ladies! May I have your attention!" Philippa's strident

voice made Persephone jump. Their hostess had climbed a little way up the rocky hill behind the picnic tables and gestured toward a young man in a peasant's smock carrying a stout walking stick, who had sauntered over from behind the hawthorn tree. "This is Alfred Polkinghorne, a shepherd who grazes his flock on the moor. I have hired him for the rest of the morning to guide us up to the tor and show us any other sights of interest before we have our picnic. Bring your sketching materials, if you have them!"

Persephone caught Sophia's eye and flared her nostrils. So they were going to be managed. "Did you bring a book and pencils?" Persephone asked.

"I don't draw, much to Miss Crandall's dismay. I think I was her biggest failure."

"How will you occupy your time then?"

"Oh, I'll climb up to the Tor. It will provide an excellent view." Sophia came closer to Persephone and hooked her hand under her elbow. "You see that patch of gorse up on that hill not far distant?" she said.

At first Persephone didn't see it. "Where? I just see the mauve and blue of the heather."

"You're not looking far enough. The next hill beyond that one."

"Ah, yes. But it's quite a distance from here I think. Things are often farther away on the moor than they appear." Would Sophia really stray alone from everyone else at the picnic?

"I shall slip away after we eat, when everyone is drowsy and stupid with the elderberry wine Miss Vyvyan brings to her picnics. No one will notice, and I'll be back in plenty of time. You didn't really think I would spend an entire day like this and not make some use of it."

Persephone laughed. "I did not. How long have I known you? But a couple of weeks, and already I see that you are not to be prevented from pursuing whatever it is you have in your active mind." She fetched her sketchbook and pencil case from Philippa's landaulet. Sophia retrieved a basket from her gig, and together they followed the rest of the picnickers up to the crest of Rough Tor.

THE WALK TO THE TOR WAS NOT STRENUOUS, BUT IT INVOLVED a bit of a climb, and more than one of the ladies decided to admire the strange rock formations from below rather than tax themselves. Sophia managed it easily, however. In addition to gaining a superior view of the surrounding landscape, she wanted to examine the vegetation at that higher elevation with the idea of gathering some seeds, flowers, and leaves to augment her supplies. There were no moors around Bath, and therefore she had had little chance of procuring such treasures as rowan berries, useful for stomach ailments. She thought the berries might possibly also be effective in treating the nausea that often comes with pregnancy, perhaps more so than mere ginger tea. She had the idea that combining some of the natural herbs whose qualities she knew about could produce a beneficial effect, but was also aware that she would have to know a great deal more before trying such combinations on people other than herself. How she wished she knew of something that would work on her father's heart ailment!

Tansy was another moorland plant Sophia was eager to locate. It didn't flower at this time of year, but she hoped to discover where some grew so she could return later in the summer. She also thought she might find some red raspberry leaves to pick for a tea that helped women with their monthly complaints. The canes needn't be in flower for that.

Alas, the area immediately around the Tor yielded

nothing of interest. Willow and Alder—whose barks had a variety of efficacious uses to treat many different complaints—did not grow so high up and so far away from a water source. She guessed that the exposure to harsh winds and cold temperatures created an inhospitable environment for vegetation. Thus, for an hour or so, as about half a dozen of the ladies found places to sit and sketch the Tor or the vista out over the moor while others—having seen the view—wandered back to the picnic spot, Sophia simply sat and gazed at the horizon.

What was she doing? Why couldn't she just be happy settling down to a conventional life in a fine house with a brood of children to raise? It was her father's wish for her, and now he was unwell. Would she lose him as she had lost her mother? And what then? He had marked James Pentarrant as her ideal suitor. But it would never have done. Pentarrant was a kind man. He would likely have given her a measure of freedom to pursue her interests, especially because he spent so much of his time working at the quarry.

However, two unexpected things had happened since she returned home a finished lady. These were not so dramatic—or even, perhaps, of any moment to the world. But they decided her absolutely against acquiescence to the marital machinations of her father.

The first had to do with herself only. That was her meeting with the intriguing, maddening Dr. Rowe. In one flight of fancy, Sophia imagined a life where they worked together to heal people in Delabole, a man and a woman as a team: he with his modern methods, she with all the knowledge she'd learned from Mattie Davy. So much good could be done thus.

Yet she could not fool herself that the desire to work together fully explained her inability to banish the doctor from her mind. She found it all too easy to recall the way his light brown eyes gazed into hers when they partnered in a country dance, and how the candlelight brought out the glints of gold in his hair. He had not James Pentarrant's obvious physical power, yet his lean frame was certainly strong enough. Altogether he was handsome, yes, but it was more than that.

Sophia stood up and stretched as several of the ladies grew tired of their sketching and packed up their books and pencils. She stole a glance at Persephone, who appeared wholly absorbed in her drawing. Did she see what Sophia saw in the young doctor? Did any of the other women see it? What exactly was that? She couldn't quite grasp it, but whatever it was went beyond his attractive appearance. He had a quality, an essence within him. She'd had a glimpse of it at their very first meeting, and then it showed itself more powerfully when the footman brought him the note at the Roscarrock ball. His entire demeanor altered. It was as if he suddenly shed his pleasantly sociable mask and revealed the core beneath it. What had passed through his mind in those moments? Did he mentally comb through all the weighty tomes he'd had at his disposal in medical school? Did he conjure up a picture of the patient and figure out what would be best to do for him—or her, in this case—before he even reached the bedside? Sophia envied him so deeply for his access to all that learning, the hours and years he had been allowed to spend acquiring knowledge, that her envy at times almost overwhelmed the softer feelings that had been encroaching on her inexorably, day by day.

Dr. Rowe disturbed her equanimity in a way that maddened her—and thrilled her. She had no idea where any of it might lead. She knew little of his background, and he seemed oddly unwilling to enlighten her—or anyone—about it. He was undoubtedly educated and well-spoken and possessed of good manners and correct address. Yet he might not suit her father's idea of an appropriate suitor for her. Dr. Rowe could be a tradesman's son, or a member of a professional family. Sophia would not make any inquiries, although surely someone in Camelford knew. How ironic! The Tresillian's position in society did not bear scrutiny by a high stickler. Despite that, her father wanted more than anything for her to marry a gentleman born and bred.

The other reason she decided to abandon any thought of acquiescing to a match with James Pentarrant also revealed itself to her on that same evening of the ball. Pentarrant held no real affection for her, Sophia well knew, and if they married, it would have been a contractual arrangement, nothing more. Part of her wasn't even certain the man was capable of tender feelings for a woman, he so rarely looked upon the world with anything other than a measuring, stern gaze. So it had surprised her to see a completely different expression in his eyes when he danced with Persephone. Did Persephone know it? Nothing she said indicated her awareness of Pentarrant's regard for her, yet something came over her when she spoke of him. When she told Sophia about their verbal sparring at the ball and about his intervention over the boy at the quarry, she sparkled not just with annoyance, but with deep interest. Were her friend's views too opposed to Pentarrant's for a match between them to be desirable? Surely not.

In any case, she herself would not marry Pentarrant no matter how much pressure her father and Eustace Pentarrant exerted to bring it about. She might persuade herself to face a loveless marriage under certain conditions, but she could never marry in a way that would deny love to someone she cared about. Or that would deny her own chance of happiness.

. . .

Persephone immersed herself so deeply in her sketching—an activity that had always given her imagination free rein—that she didn't stop until a very brisk gust of wind curled the paper up so that she couldn't continue. By that time, all the other ladies who made the climb up to the Tor had gone back down. From the general chatter that floated up to her from below—along with the clinking of plates and glasses—they were already partaking of the picnic fare, and had been for some time.

She quickly gathered up her materials. Glancing at the drawing she made before shutting her sketchbook, she gasped. While the distinctive outline of the rocky promontory was definitely there, as well as the hard shadows she'd captured when the clear spring sun laid everything bare for a few minutes, her wayward hand had superimposed a man's profile over the whole. A profile she recognized. Heat flooded her cheeks and she slammed the sketchbook shut, tucking it under her arm as she scrambled back down to join the others and eat a little something.

"Where have you been?" Sophia asked, bustling up to her and taking hold of her free hand. "And I don't mean physically!"

Did this perceptive young lady know her so well already? "I stayed to sketch," Persephone said, not inviting any more comment.

"So I saw. You thought nothing of leaving me to the tiresome prattle of Miss Vyvyan. I suppose it's only fair, since you had to suffer her all the way here and will be subjected to more of her poisonous observations on the way back to Delabole."

"I had hoped you would take me up in your gig instead." Persephone had no desire to hear more gossip about Mr. Pentarrant, which she did not doubt would furnish the material for their hour-long homeward journey.

Sophia looked over her shoulder as if checking to make sure no one was near enough to hear and said, "I'm not going back the same way you are. I have something to do, as I told you before. I couldn't find a good moment to slip off, so I'll have to accomplish my task another way."

Just as Persephone was about to scold Sophia for deviating from the planned excursion and risking the uncertain terrain of the moor, she clapped her hand over the crown of her hat to prevent it being carried away by a sudden fierce gust. She scanned the sky and said, "I think it will rain soon. Surely you will not go off on your own! It's not safe. There are bogs and rabbit holes everywhere."

"I used to come here as a girl and roam far and wide—unbeknownst to my governess or my mother, who thought I was visiting at the home of one of my friends. I know my way. And I refuse to leave without gathering some Pennyroyal."

"What will you say to Philippa?"

"Simply that I had promised to stop in at my aunt's house in Highertown to deliver a message from my father." She smiled and dashed away before Persephone could scold her any more.

By that time, the grooms, coachmen, and footmen had leapt into action and were rapidly clearing away the elaborate picnic things, dumping plates with a clatter into baskets and rolling fine linen tablecloths into balls. The ladies, who had taken such pains over their attire for this bucolic entertainment, now lifted their skirts with no thought of decorum and hurried back to their carriages. When it was possible, the coachmen raised the hoods, and those who had chosen to come in closed chaises from the start were now doubtless congratulating themselves on their foresight.

Persephone was quite concerned about Sophia going off on her own and hoped that the sturdy Galahad would be able to avoid hazards underfoot. What worried her more immediately was how to prevent Philippa from demanding to see the sketch she had labored over with such concentration. As to finding out anything more about a scandal buried deep in James Pentarrant's past—she had no appetite for that either.

Just then, the heavens opened, and Persephone clambered unwillingly into Philippa's landaulet, whose hood had been raised, and braced herself for an unpleasant hour of spiteful comments and insinuations.

That is, if the dreadful weather didn't make the track deteriorate to the point where they were either trapped in mud or toppled over. And what, Persephone couldn't help thinking as she tried to see behind them through the side windows of the carriage, would Sophia do all alone in such weather? Foolhardy girl! She had said she would come directly to Persephone's cottage after she'd finished her business.

How long should I wait before I raise the alarm? were the words that kept circling through Persephone's head as Philippa chatted away.

CHAPTER 23

The sky and wind threatened a storm and rain showered down in fits, but at first the cloud cover was not unbroken. Here and there a dagger of sunlight broke through. *No more than a passing shower,* Sophia thought. She'd spotted a drover's track that led deeper into the moor in the direction she wanted to go and headed down it, hoping for the squall to blow itself out quickly.

She managed to drive about halfway to the promising patch of vegetation she'd spotted from atop the tor before she realized her hopes had been rather unfounded. The capricious winds of the moor swept in darker and darker clouds, and within minutes, a violent storm was upon her. *Perhaps I should go back,* she thought, craning her neck around to see behind her. No sign of carriages. Even the track she'd been following had become difficult to make out.

Of course, Sophia's gig had no hood, and she was soon drenched, the brim of her bonnet drooping and impeding her view so that she tore it off and tucked it under her seat. That was when the first lightning bolt ripped across the sky to strike a tree about a mile away. The cob shied and whinnied at the leaves and twigs the wind swept across their path. Every subsequent rumble of thunder made him start and look wildly around. "Come along, Galahad. At least try to live up to your name!" Sophia said, not amused just at that moment by the horse's rather comical misnomer.

As she urged the frightened horse on, the rain continued to bucket down, the wind driving it nearly sideways at times. She clung to her belief that all would be well, that the storm would blow itself out, and all that she would suffer would be a good drenching. The bright patch of yellow gorse she'd been heading toward was no longer visible through the driving rain. Did she really know where she was going? *I should seek some shelter,* she thought. But the moor in that place was uncooperatively featureless, with only gentle undulations varying the landscape. The irregularly spaced boulders that marked the track were too small to be of any use.

It had been a wet spring, and in places the ground became little more than muddy puddles. Poor Galahad would need more than a good brushing when they returned home, she thought, seeing the dirt caked all the way up his hocks!

Home. The idea of a crackling fire and a blanket tucked around her knees had never sounded so alluring. Sophia shivered and her teeth chattered. She was wet all the way to her skin and her hair clung limply to her shoulders, all semblance of curl eradicated. What had possessed her to undertake such a hazardous errand? Even if she reached the patch of vegetation, likely it would be too wet to gather leaves or seeds.

It's time to turn around, she thought at last. Pushing on would accomplish nothing. She hadn't gone so very far from Rough Tor, where she would be able to pick up the slightly better-worn track to the edge of the moor. However, accomplishing the turn on the narrow path she now traversed would be a feat even in dry weather. Still she must try. "Come, Galahad! There's a good fellow. You'll have to leave the path to do this, but I know you're capable." She was talking to herself as much as to the horse.

But Galahad stubbornly refused to pay attention to her signals. The thunder distracted him. All he did was dance back and forth. She had only one choice. Gathering her skirts up in one hand, Sophia climbed down from the gig and went to Galahad's head, sinking up to her ankles in mud with every step. No wonder Galahad didn't want to move. It must be hard for him to lift his hooves. She would have to lead him around.

Another flash of lightning made Galahad pull away from Sophia, lifting his head high and backing off, teeth bared and eyes wild. Sophia removed the shawl that lay across her elbows and wrapped it around his head to cover his eyes. This calmed him enough that he responded to her pull on the bridle to turn. "Easy boy. That's it." She murmured reassurances to the nervous beast, wondering how she would ever be able to persuade him to walk on without his head covered once she'd succeeded in turning the gig.

Sophia was paying such close attention to Galahad and to the path ahead that she completely missed what was happening behind her. It wasn't until the horse couldn't move any farther, that straining against the traces accomplished absolutely nothing, that she looked back to see one of the gig's wheels sunk six inches in mud and the entire equipage tilting ominously.

"Blast!" she screamed. After all, no one was there to hear her. She could do nothing at that moment, not on her own. She had no choice but to wait there and hope the rain would stop, and that some shepherd or cowman would pass by and help her. It was late in the afternoon, but the days were long at that time of year. She desperately hoped that she would be able to find her way off the moor before sunset.

At first, she thought she only imagined it because she wished it to be so, but the rain lessened quickly and the thunder moved off to the west. It would still be too wet to free the wheel for a good while. She could always unharness Galahad and ride him home. As a girl, she'd often thrown herself astride a pony's bare back for a gallop on the beach. She hadn't done anything so brazen for years, though. But if no one came by soon, it might be her only hope for returning home.

Except that she hadn't bargained on one thing. The rain was stopping, and the wind dying down to barely a whisper. But the mist rose and soon became a fog so dense that she could hardly see the length of Galahad's back. She wasn't so naive as to think she could have any hope of finding her way out in those conditions. She would just have to wait. Would anyone come to find her? She'd told a clanker to Philippa, so she would likely raise no alarm.

Persephone, though, might figure out something had happened. How long would that take? And if she realized something was seriously amiss, who would she go to? Sophia hoped not her father. The last thing she wanted was to worry him if there was any way at all to avoid it. She had told Persephone about his heart seizure, and Persephone was intelligent enough to understand that alarming him when he was still in a weakened state would not be advisable.

What was she thinking? At this point, it hardly mattered how she managed to get home. All that mattered was that she do so before night fell. And all she could do in that fog was sit and wait, and hope either the fog blew away, or someone was able to find her anyway.

With that object in mind, Sophia tried to think of a way to make some noise that might bring someone to her aid. *I may as well sing,* she thought. Her voice was passable and strong enough to be heard. She took a deep breath and began,

Far o'er the misty moor I roam,
The heather wet beneath my tread;

Except, she thought, it's only mud that's wet beneath my tread!

I call thee home, my love, my own,
But answer none my calling sped.

She couldn't remember all the rest of the words, and so invented some to suit her predicament. *I'm stuck here on the misty moor, my wheel lodged fast within the mud; I call thee, whoever, wherever you are, but you don't seem to hear me.*

Making up the verses helped her pass the time and after a while, a light wind sprang up and began to drive the fog away. She still couldn't see very far, but her hopes rose that perhaps someone would soon find her and take her home.

How would she ever explain what she was doing in such a place, alone and unprotected? Aargh! she thought. Being female was so vexing at times. Yet one more proof that she must do whatever she could to seize control of her own destiny, before it was too late.

~

JAMES WENT OVER HIS DISPUTE WITH BRAY AGAIN AND AGAIN IN his mind. The man simply couldn't see beyond the potential profits of creating a new terrace. He remained blind to risks of not taking every precaution, no matter how much such measures delayed the work. Bray was ready to start blasting before all the tests could be completed, all the investigations that would not only reveal whether the slate lode would be significant enough to prolong the life of the quarry and to determine whether it was safe to undertake this project. In this, Eustace backed the overseer. This was unsurprising. Because Eustace was in a higher position than James was, his words held more sway. Ironic, since he knew little about the actual operations of the quarry.

James was haunted by his memories of the rock fall that took the lives of three boys. It could have been prevented. It hadn't resulted immediately from blasting, but poor preparation had undermined the structure of the rock. All it took was a heavy rain. Rushing this new operation, digging down too soon through the overburden, could put so many at risk. Even if it proved possible, there would still be all the work to widen and shore up the upper terraces—essential work. He did not want more deaths on his hands.

He trudged to the gate that led to his house that afternoon, a deep frown etched on his brow. Miss Wilkins was the last person he expected to encounter just then, so it took him a moment to register her voice and look up from his distracted contemplation. What was she saying? Whatever it was, he had never before heard her speak in so agitated a manner.

"Mr. Pentarrant! You must help. I don't know who else to ask." She laid a hand on his arm, heedless of the dust and dirt on his coat. She, he noted, hadn't even put a hat or gloves on before leaving her cottage to find him.

He straightened his hunched shoulders, his concern for

Miss Wilkins driving thoughts of the quarry out of his mind. "Miss Wilkins! How can I help you? What's happened? Come inside, let me get you a glass of wine. You are in distress."

"Not me, sir. I am well. But I have grave fears for Miss Tresillian."

The two of them arrived at the front door of his house, which his one manservant, Baldock, opened to them. They went into the hall, but Miss Wilkins would not be led into a parlor to sit down. "Calm yourself," James said, taking hold of her shoulders and steadying her, his eyes searching hers.

It seemed that his touch, rather than reassuring her, caused tears to spring into her eyes. "Oh! I'm being so silly, only I'm terribly afraid for Sophia. You see, she did not return with us from our picnic on the moor, and there was a storm, and she still isn't back."

"I don't understand. Surely you all traveled together."

"We did so on the way there. But Sophia wanted to go somewhere without everyone else afterwards."

He shook his head. "Alone? Foolish girl! Does she not know how dangerous it can be?"

"How well do you know Miss Tresillian?" Persephone asked, a wry twist to her mouth.

He understood. He did not know her well, but even he could see that the young lady was not to be dictated to. "I presume she is in her gig," he said. Miss Tresillian drove her modest gig and Welsh cob with skill. Under normal conditions, she would be well able to navigate the rough tracks on the moor.

"Yes, and I would have expected her to return perhaps an hour after we did. You see, she was going to come to my house before going home, to—well, never mind that, it's not important. Only it's been three hours and there is no sign of her. A sudden storm blew up, but it soon passed, so I wasn't very worried at first." She angrily wiped away a tear that had found its way down her cheek and wrung her hands.

The storm had swept over Delabole earlier as well, but after about twenty minutes scudded on its way leaving a clear, cleansed, sunny afternoon behind. Perhaps it had done the same on the moor? "Do you know where she was going?" The moor in a storm, whether or not it passes quickly, can be dangerous. Even those who knew the moor well could become lost or trapped in a bog.

"Yes. She went off the track we took to Rough Tor and headed east from there just as the rain was starting."

"East you say. Further into the center of the moor." Which meant away from the edges, where some signs of habitation were to be found. "Have you informed Mr. Tresillian?"

"No. Sophia asked me not to. She told him that upon returning from the picnic she was to spend the remainder of the day with me and dine with me as well so that he wouldn't worry. He's not well, apparently. A heart complaint."

James had never heard of Mr. Tresillian having such a weakness. Was it true? "What is it you wish me to do?"

"You have horses. A curricle, you said. You would be able to find her more swiftly than almost anyone. You do know the moor, don't you?"

The eyes that met his were vivid, searching with a kind of desperation.

"No one ever truly knows the moor. But I believe I have an idea of where she might have gone. There are a few drover's tracks on that part of the moor that lead to some uplands."

"Then you must go! And quickly! It will soon be dark, and then…"

Yes. It would not be safe for Miss Tresillian to be out on the moor alone after dark. Miss Wilkins was right to be so worried. "I'll start right away," he said. The relieved gratitude in her eyes made him want to wrap his arms around her and reassure her. IT unsettled him to discover that he was more disturbed by Miss Wilkins's distress than by Miss Tresillian's likely danger. He quickly turned to go back outside.

"I'll come with you! I may be able to direct you, from what I remember."

"No!" He said it with more heat than he intended. They could not go off alone together on such an errand. Even if it made sense that there be two of them. "Best you remain at home, in case Miss Tresillian arrives after all."

"Then what will you do? You cannot stay on the moor once the sun is gone in any case."

She was right. However, there was no question of leaving Miss Tresillian to rescue herself, whatever had befallen her, whether she was lost or had suffered an accident. "I will bring her back. Try not to worry."

She gave a short laugh. "I'm not sure that's possible. But I will endeavor not to have an attack of the vapors!" A smile trembled on her lips, not reaching her eyes.

"I would see you home, but I think there isn't a moment to lose, if you will forgive me." Of course, he would far rather escort Miss Wilkins to her door than race off without her, but that wouldn't do at all.

"Yes. You are very good. I'm sorry I'm in such a state. When you find Sophia bring her to my cottage, not to Tresillian Manor, if you would be so kind."

She was still protecting some secret or other. What could possibly be so important? No time to worry about that now.

Miss Wilkins gave him her hand and he gripped it in both of his. Her eyes widened in surprise, and he let go. "I'll be on my way then."

She did not immediately hurry away, but followed him out to the stables and watched Digory harness the bays. In the chaos of the moment, Pentarrant forgot that he'd let the chestnut mare graze in the near field. When he caught sight of the beautiful horse, gleaming like a copper coin in the afternoon sun, he flushed deeply.

"Are you quite well, Mr. Pentarrant?" Miss Wilkins said.

"What? Yes, of course. You should go home. That path over there is a quicker way." He pointed to the muddy track that led between the stable and the small dairy—a route that might prevent her catching sight of the chestnut.

"As you wish," she said, a slight edge to her voice.

Was she offended? He stole a glance at her. Fortunately, she wasn't looking over at the field, but eyeing the team Digory harnessed to the curricle with dispatch. "I would be honored, Miss Wilkins, if—when Miss Tresillian is safely returned from her adventure—you might allow me to drive you out one day. There are some very fine views not too far afield."

He had no time to wait for her answer. Digory led the curricle up and he jumped in, gathered the reins and cracked the whip. His responsive horses snorted and set forth eagerly at a brisk trot.

James resisted the urge to look over his shoulder at Miss Wilkins, reminding himself that his goal was to find a young lady who was stranded on Bodmin Moor and return her to Delabole before dark, not to reassure a lady whose distress ate at his heart.

CHAPTER 24

Sophia's voice was giving out and she was chilled to her marrow. Not a soul had passed anywhere near her—unless, she thought with a bitter laugh, my singing repelled rather than attracted them. She had unhooked Galahad from the gig and let him forage some scraps of grass nearby, still considering clambering up onto his back and riding home. She could see the path now a few yards ahead. The mist was intermittently less heavy, although she didn't trust it not to summon all its strength and blanket the world once again.

"Oh Galahad! Why did you let me do this? Why could you not have whispered sense into my ear and told me we should follow the others and find an excuse to return another day? I know, you just wanted to—" She stopped speaking abruptly and listened. Nothing. Her ears were playing tricks on her. Fog had a way of distorting sound. She thought she heard hoofbeats, but no.

And then, there they were again, a little louder, and definitely approaching. Her heart pounded. "Hallooo! I'm over here and I need some help! Please come!" she shouted with all her might, sincerely hoping she wasn't encouraging a highwayman to find her and rob and murder her. She was so desperate to be rescued, though, that even that remote possibility did not have the power to stop her calling out continually and waving her arms over her head.

The snort of horses joined the sound of hoofbeats. "Over here! Keep coming! I'm on the track!"

"Is that you Miss Tresillian?" came an answering voice.

Thank God! It sounded like Pentarrant, but it didn't matter who it was at that moment. She could just see the indistinct form of a pair of horses pulling a curricle, and in her excitement, ran forward—and a moment later found herself sprawled on the ground, a searing pain in her right ankle. A rabbit hole. Stupid!

"Miss Tresillian!"

The voice was quite close. The horses broke clear of the fog. If she weren't in such pain she would have cried out with joy. Instead she moaned softly and struggled not to cry. Pentarrant pulled the horses to an abrupt halt and they snorted and stamped, mouths foaming. Had he sprung them in all this fog? Was he a fool? Who was she to talk of foolish actions!

Pentarrant looped the reins around the seat rail of the curricle and jumped down. A few seconds later he was crouched down by her. "You are injured. Let me help you."

"No, I can manage." She tried to stand, but a sharp stab of pain in her ankle made her nearly crumple to the ground.

"Don't be ridiculous," Pentarrant said in a harsh voice, and without another word scooped her up and carried her to the curricle, gently placing her on the seat. "You'll be all right here while I see what's to be done about your horse and gig."

All business. As she would have expected. For a fleeting

moment, Sophia wondered if he would have been so dispassionate if it had been Persephone out on the moor alone, injured.

As if she had been holding herself together out of necessity and through sheer force of will, once she was seated safely in the curricle, Sophia's self-command deserted her. She shivered so violently her teeth chattered, and to her shame, her breath came out in hoarse sobs.

Pentarrant, who had stepped away to bring Galahad to the curricle, dropped the cob's reins and rushed to Sophia's side. "Miss Tresillian! Please calm yourself. We shall be out of here soon. The fog is lifting and you are not far from the edge of the moor."

"P-please don't trouble y-yourself about m-me," she gasped out between sobs. "I d-don't know what's come over me. See to G-galahad."

Pentarrant took hold of her hand and stripped off her glove, then pressed her bare fingers between his hands. "You are like ice. We must get you back and into the warmth as quickly as possible." He reached beneath the seat and drew out a blanket, which he unfolded with a snap and then tucked around her shoulders and over her lap. Sophia knew it was because she was so very cold, but the heat of his hands made her wish that he would fold her into his arms, as he had when he carried her to the curricle.

"I'll tie the cob to the back and he'll follow us home. I'm afraid there's nothing else to do but leave your gig to be retrieved tomorrow—if it's still here."

She didn't much mind about the gig. "M-my basket," she managed to say between her chattering teeth.

"I'll fetch it," he said.

A few moments later, the basket was at her feet and Pentarrant on the seat next to her. She found herself pushing as close to him as she could without impropriety. “I'm so sorry,” she said as he turned his team and they set off first at a walk through the swirling—but clearing—mist, and then quickened to a trot. “It's just, I'm so very, very cold.”

“And still soaked through,” he said, moving the reins into his right hand and reaching his left arm around her to pin her next to him.

This is not proper, Sophia thought, but his body was warm and solid, and at that moment she didn't care. She thought she'd never be warm enough again.

What in the name of the Almighty had Miss Tresillian been thinking? It was bad enough that she was cold and wet and risked developing an inflammation of the lungs. When she fell right in front of him and did something to her foot he didn't know whether to feel sorry for her or to scold her for her foolishness.

Now the poor girl trembled so violently that he could barely hold her next to him. Miss Wilkins had said he should bring Miss Tresillian to her rather than to her father, but he doubted the humble cottage could be made comfortable enough. And the doctor must be summoned immediately. No, this was no time for coy games.

Within minutes the remaining mist had dissipated and he urged the bays to a canter, reaching all the way around Miss Tresillian to take the reins in both hands. She leaned her head against his chest. He felt her damp curls tucked just beneath his chin. She was as slight as a child and barely older than one. James couldn't help wondering how different this might have felt with Miss Wilkins in her place. He might not be able to reach right around her. She was taller and a little bigger than Miss Tresillian. But he would enjoy trying. The thought of it was enough to distract him from his awkward situation.

Before long, they were on the streets of Camelford. They had to slow and attracted more than one curious stare. No use worrying about that now, James thought. All that mattered was getting Miss Tresillian somewhere warm and seen by Dr. Rowe.

He took the turn for Tresillian Manor and Miss Tresillian sat up suddenly. "Where are you going? Don't take me home! Persephone will be worried. I said I would go to her cottage."

"Who do you think fetched me?" he said. "I'll ensure she knows that you are returned and safe."

"But my father! He mustn't be alarmed." Her voice tightened.

Did she really think she could keep her father in ignorance of what had happened that day? "Your father will know you've had an accident in any case. It's your business how you choose to explain it, but I am persuaded you must return home."

By that time, they'd turned onto the winding drive that led to the manor, and before long James pulled his horses up at the grand entrance. Two footmen ran out and down the steps. One held up a hand to take Miss Tresillian's. "I'll get her down," James said. "She's hurt her ankle."

He lifted her out as easily as he'd put her in the curricle and carried her up the shallow slate steps, through the hall and into a saloon. The housekeeper swept in, frowning with worry, and immediately took over from James, directing him to put Miss Tresillian on a sofa as close to the fire as possible. "Will you send a lad to fetch Dr. Rowe?" James asked her.

"Right away, Mr. James," she answered, bobbing a shallow curtsy without taking her eyes off her young mistress.

"I shall take my leave of you now, Miss Tresillian," James said, bowing.

She reached out her hand. Her cheeks had lost some of their pallor and she had stopped shivering violently. "I can't find words to thank you enough, Mr. Pentarrant. You will go to Persephone now?"

"Yes," he said, and left.

~

"YE'LL WEAR A HOLE THROUGH THE FLOORBOARDS, MA'AM," said Hannah as Persephone paced back and forth in front of the kitchen hearth.

"Oh Hannah! I'm so worried about Sophia! It's been hours."

"I'm sure Mr. James will find her. He knows the moor as well as anyone."

Persephone didn't bother to point out that if by chance a thick fog had rolled in, it wouldn't make the slightest bit of difference how well he knew it.

When she was halfway across for the thousandth time at least, a knock on the front door stopped her. Not giving Hannah a chance to answer it, Persephone ran to the door and threw it open, relief and gratitude on her face.

Except it wasn't Sophia Tresillian standing on her doorstep. It was Philippa Vyvyan.

"Philippa!" Persephone said, barely disguising her vexation.

Philippa smiled and said, "I bring you good news! Miss Tresillian has returned."

How did she know when I didn't? "It was good of you to guess that I would be anxious for her when the storm blew up on the moor. I'm very happy she is safe."

"Well, we have Mr. James Pentarrant to thank for her rescue. He seemed to be taking very great care of Sophia when I saw him drive her through Camelford in his curricle."

What an odd comment to make. What could she mean? "Of course he would take care. She must have been chilled through." So, he took her back to Tresillian Manor instead of bringing her to the cottage. A wise choice, Persephone thought, not able to imagine how he prevailed upon Sophia to allow him to take her home. "Won't you come in? I'm afraid I have few comforts in my humble dwelling, but you are welcome to sit for a while."

Philippa entered the small hall, drawing off her gloves and trying not to make it obvious she was examining the modest furnishings. "I imagine this is quite a change for you —from Atherleigh Manor, I mean. But how can you bear the noise?"

"It doesn't bother me. Honestly, I hardly hear it." At that moment, a distant explosion rattled the windows, and she smiled. "As to the cottage, it suits my needs nicely. And I enjoy being mistress of my own modest establishment." What a nerve Philippa had! Then she checked herself. Her concern for Sophia had made her testy. Perhaps Philippa meant it kindly.

Persephone led her guest into the kitchen, which had come to double as her parlor.

Without a thought, Philippa took off her hat and pelisse and held them out to Hannah, who lifted her eyebrows at Persephone before taking them, dipping an ironic curtsy to Philippa, and simply placing them on the stand by the back door that was only two steps away.

Instead of settling back into the armchair Persephone gestured toward, Philippa perched, sitting straight-backed, hands folded primly in her lap like a schoolgirl trying to prove she had done nothing wrong. "My, I wouldn't have thought of sitting in a kitchen, but you've made it quite welcoming."

She watched Hannah prepare tea, as if waiting for the

servant to leave the room before she said anything else. When the tea was ready, Hannah curtsied and went out to her own small room at the back of the house. No doubt Persephone would hear her opinion of the presumptuous Miss Vyvyan later.

"As I said, I—along with several others—happened to see Mr. Pentarrant and Miss Tresillian driving through Camelford in that smart curricle of his. I must confess, I was a trifle shocked at the way he was holding her. It was almost an embrace! Honestly, I wonder at what young girls do nowadays to trap a man."

It took Persephone a moment to register what Philippa had just said. "I'm afraid I don't know what you mean. I don't believe Sophia wishes to entrap anyone. She has no need to." Nor did she believe James Pentarrant would embrace the heiress in public. She didn't think he would embrace her at all, in fact. He never appeared bowled out by Sophia as all the young men in the neighborhood did.

Philippa pursed her lips and gave Persephone a knowing look. "Well, really. Such a tale, to say she had to go visit her aunt rather than follow the rest of us safely back. We both know that was just an excuse."

Of course, Persephone did know that. But what Sophia wished to hide had nothing to do with James Pentarrant, of that Persephone was certain. "Surely you can't be saying Sophia planned for the weather to turn foul so she could lose herself on the moor, and then have a particular gentleman happen to come out to rescue her." She laughed.

"I suppose not. Unfortunately, the circumstances have compromised her. And him."

Persephone's heart started to race. What could Philippa mean? How could they be compromised? Pentarrant had performed a gallant act of rescue. "I dare say the exigencies of the situation will excuse any impropriety."

Philippa gave a long, deep, melodramatic sigh. "Well, you know, with Mr. Pentarrant's past, he'll have no other choice but to offer for the young lady."

Persephone warred with herself. She didn't want to hear anything else from Philippa. Yet now she burned to know about Pentarrant's supposed scandalous past. She could have changed the subject, could have insisted that she had no desire to hear any ill of a gentleman who had carried out such a kind, unselfish deed. But she remained silent.

Leaning forward just a little, Philippa said, "It was the talk of the county. *She* thought they were going to elope. Nothing more than a common quarry wench."

Persephone was disgusted by the snobbery laced through Philippa's every word. Surely this was just malicious gossip.

Philippa lowered her voice to just above a whisper and said, "It would have been a terrible misalliance, of course. Really, the orders should not mix in that way, don't you agree?"

Persephone didn't, but judged that it would be a mistake to enter into an argument about it. She simply smiled and sipped her tea.

"Of course," Philippa said, spreading her fingers out on the surface of the table, "The rumors were that she was—you know—that he felt compelled to marry her. Old Mr. Pentarrant put a stop to it just in time, and the chit went away."

This made Persephone catch her breath. But why should something in Pentarrant's past matter to her at all? If he had been willing to act honorably, surely that spoke well of him. Nonetheless, a tiny spark of something inside her flickered out in that moment. "When was this?" Persephone asked, her voice dry as paper.

"Oh, I was very young, so I suppose it must have been ten years ago or more. But you know, in the country, people don't forget. Now if this were London, I daresay another scandal would have come along in a matter of months to push this one right out of everyone's mind."

Persephone didn't know quite how to think about this. Had Pentarrant loved the girl? Or had he taken advantage of an innocent not of his own class? She wasn't quite sure which thought was more disturbing. And that in itself disturbed her. "Do you know where he found Sophia?" she asked, now desperate to direct the conversation elsewhere.

"Oh, no. I didn't actually speak to him, only saw them pass by. As, so I said, did everyone who happened to be in Camelford this afternoon, including the vicar. Mark my words, the banns will be read on Sunday! Mr. Tresillian won't stand for having his daughter's reputation damaged."

No, this was all wrong! How could it be? Persephone was certain Sophia was in love with Dr. Rowe, or at least had a very strong *tendre* for him. And what about Pentarrant? Surely he could not be in love with Sophia. *The way he looks at me*—she knew it—despite their differences, his desires seemingly in conflict with hers. It was all so confusing! She wanted Philippa to go away so she could think about everything in the privacy of her own bedchamber.

At that moment Hannah came in and said, "Beggin' yer pardon, ma'am, but if you want yer dinner at a decent hour, I'll have to cook it."

Fortunately, Philippa took this as her signal to go.

"Don't you listen to that one, miss," Hannah said as she began chopping up vegetables after Philippa's departure. "Everyone knows she wished Mr. Pentarrant would give her the time of day, thinking her fortune might be enough to tempt such a fine gentleman. Only that sort of thing don't weigh with him."

Why would Hannah feel that she had to reassure her like that? *Did I say something that has led her to believe I have a* tendre *for Pentarrant?* "I think I'll fetch a warmer shawl from my room," Persephone said, when really she just needed an excuse to get away to a measure of solitude. She climbed up to her bedchamber, her mind whirling. If what Hannah said were really the case, that Philippa thought of Pentarrant as rightly belonging to her, why would she promote the idea that he and Sophia must wed? Why had Miss Vyvyan chosen to come and tell her all this? What purpose would it serve? Unless she had seen something else, something that made her think Persephone had a warm interest in James Pentarrant, just as it seemed that Hannah had. Philippa had seen her dance with him at the ball. But it was just a dance.

No, Persephone had to admit it was more than a dance.

That was completely beside the point, though. Still... Pentarrant embraced Sophia, so Philippa said. That image made something twist inside her. She closed her eyes and imagined his strong arms wrapped around her, her senses filled with his indefinable scent of stone dust and sea air.

She was jolted out of her imagination by another knock on the front door, this one loud and definite. She was in no mood to talk to anyone else, so she let Hannah do her job and greet whoever it was.

"Is Miss Wilkins here? I wanted to speak to her on a personal matter."

"I'll just see if she's at home."

Pentarrant! Why was he here? He hadn't come to bring Sophia, that she knew. Persephone stole a quick glance in the small mirror over her dressing table and patted her hair into place. She mustn't let him see how shaken she was. Hannah tapped on her door. "Yes, I'll be right down. Would you show Mr. Pentarrant into the parlor."

Somehow she needed to face him in the less personal surroundings of her as-yet-unoccupied schoolroom.

She found him standing in front of the bookshelf, looking at the spines of her small collection of volumes for teaching.

He turned at the sound of the door closing behind her. "Miss Wilkins, I wanted to assure you that Miss Tresillian is home and safe. She has apparently injured her ankle. I believe Nathaniel—Dr. Rowe—is with her now."

Straight to the point. Mr. Pentarrant did not waste his breath on pleasantries. "I thank you, but you have made an unnecessary call. Miss Vyvyan has just informed me that you brought Sophia back in your curricle."

"Miss Vyvyan? How on earth would she have known so quickly?"

"I believe you drove through Camelford, did you not?"

"Yes, but—" He stopped speaking abruptly, comprehension dawning in his eyes. "I suppose people must have seen us. I did not notice. I was too concerned with Miss Tresillian's welfare."

Too concerned with holding her near you? Persephone didn't want to think it, but his clear confusion gave unwelcome weight to Philippa's insinuations. "Understandable, I'm certain. How has she fared?"

Before answering, he glanced around the room, his hat in his hand. She couldn't keep him standing there. "Won't you be seated? I'm afraid the chairs in here are not very comfortable." She sat at the table on the opposite side of the room from where he stood.

He strode over and, instead of sitting across from her took a seat next to her. "I believe she will be all right. She hurt her ankle, but I don't think it is broken. Mostly she was just wet and chilled. I hope she does not develop a fever. I did my best to keep her warm until she could be restored to the comfort of her own home."

Philippa's words kept nipping at her thoughts. He kept her warm. Of course, that would only be natural.

"Miss Wilkins, is something amiss?"

She had to lift her eyes to his. There it was. His intelligent, probing gaze that somehow managed to be smiling and serious at the same time. "I'm glad you were able to warm her." It was all she could say when faced with that look.

He took a deep breath and shook his head. "Her gig was stuck in the mud, she was chilled through, and then she stepped in a rabbit hole. I felt it was important that she be seen by a doctor right away, and that her own home would be the most comfortable place for her, which is why I didn't bring her here, as she wanted."

A practical man, she thought. Practical and thoughtful. Surely his actions meant nothing more. "You are right, of course. But you should be aware that Philippa—Miss Vyvyan—saw you driving Sophia through Camelford and seemed to be scandalized by what she saw."

"Scandalized?" He sat up straighter and knitted his brow.

He truly didn't see it! "Well, she intimated to me that you and Sophia were very close together in the curricle. As you say, you sought to keep her warm. Others may attribute a different motive to your actions." She paused, not sure of how open to be with this man she hardly knew and yet found herself strangely drawn to. No sense in being coy, she finally thought, and continued. "She used the word *embrace.*"

He laughed. "I certainly would not choose to embrace Miss Tresillian—nor would she welcome such an attention from me, I am sure. If I were to embrace anyone it would be—I mean, I wouldn't, especially not in public." His cheeks darkened in embarrassment.

Persephone rose to her feet, making Pentarrant stand as well. "I am afraid, Mr. Pentarrant, that your gallant actions may have placed you and Sophia in a rather compromised position."

He paced away and drove his fingers into his hair, shaking his head. "Ridiculous. Why, you and I—we—are in a more compromising position here, alone in this room, than

Miss Tresillian and I were in an open carriage in view of everyone."

"Ah, but I am an undesirable old spinster. Sophia is a beautiful young heiress."

This brought Pentarrant over to her in two quick strides. "Only one half of what you just said is true."

They stood in charged silence for a moment before he broke it by casting his gaze around the room. "This is a schoolroom." His voice held a note of surprise.

"Yes." Persephone's pulse had quickened at his previous words, but his sudden shift to the prosaic slowed it again. What did he not want to say? "Surely you know I have come here for that purpose, to establish a school—to create an environment conducive to teaching the quarry children their letters and sums."

He raised one eyebrow. "I wasn't aware you intended to teach them here. You have gone to a lot of trouble, and as I think I said, I believe your efforts will not meet with success, or be welcome."

"By whom? I can't see that the children will mind."

"That's as may be, but the quarry folk do not take kindly to changes. You must have got some idea of that on your visit this morning."

"Is it the quarry folk, or the quarry management who are afraid of change?"

How did they get into this contentious territory? It seemed Mr. Pentarrant was more comfortable being at odds with her than approaching anything like friendship. He had done the same thing when they were in Bodmin, at the White Hart. "Well, we shall see, won't we? To begin with, I will have a Sunday school. There is none here, and the quarry does not work on a Sunday."

"I cannot stop you, of course. But do you really know what may result from your actions?"

This man was infuriating! "I would hope the result would be that children whose futures have hitherto been narrowly circumscribed the education might gain opportunities to better themselves."

Pentarrant said, "I have no objection to educating quarry children. I'm not certain that an outsider who does not understand their lives, their daily struggles, is best placed to make any difference."

Persephone drew herself up. He had touched a raw nerve. Her status as stranger—foreigner—was the one aspect of her plan that she kept stumbling over. "I shall simply have to give them a chance to become better acquainted with me. I tried to do so earlier." And had met with little success, she thought. She was entirely uncertain what else she could do to accomplish this.

Silence descended again. The late afternoon sun did not penetrate her small parlor and the darkening space began to feel chilly. She hugged her arms to herself.

"I didn't come here to question your intentions, Miss Wilkins. I'm sorry," Pentarrant said.

"Why exactly did you come? You could have sent a message."

He took a step closer to her and looked into her eyes. "I suppose I wanted to assure myself that you were not still in distress over your friend. When you came to me earlier you were beside yourself. I wanted nothing more than to help you—I mean, help Miss Tresillian. She is such a friend to you."

He was talking himself around in a circle, and her cheeks warmed. "I thank you for your consideration. It really was very kind of you." She put out her hand for him to shake, a signal of dismissal.

He took it between both of his and lifted it to his lips to press a gentle kiss on her knuckles. In a quiet voice he said, "I have stayed too long. I simply wanted you to know that your friend is safely home."

He let go of her hand and bowed, then left the schoolroom. She didn't move but stood rooted to her spot, listening to his steps as he walked down the hallway and click of the door latch as he let himself out of her cottage.

CHAPTER 25

Dr. Rowe was deeply engrossed in his study of the most recent issue of *Medical Transactions* early in the evening when Mrs. Dunmore, the housekeeper, knocked on his study door and called out, "Dr. Rowe! Urgent message fer ye."

He put his letter opener between the pages, sighed, and skirted the stacks of books and papers to walk the few feet from his desk to his door. When he opened it, Mrs. Dunmore stared at him for a moment before she handed him the sealed note without walking away. "Thank you, ma'am" Nathaniel said.

"Boy come from Tresillian Manor. I 'spect it's the old man."

Mrs. Dunmore was a generally placid woman but also incurably curious—even more so ever since Miss Tresillian's unexpected visit the other evening. She clearly enjoyed having the local doctor living in her lodging house for the glimpse it gave her into the lives of many of her neighbors. She had tried her hardest to wheedle information about Miss Tresillian, but all he said was that she had been to seek his advice about her father's condition. Even that was more than she was entitled to, but Nathaniel didn't want her to start spreading gossip about the heiress.

He smiled and closed the door before she could say anything else and took the sealed note to his desk. Without hurrying, he picked up the letter opener and slid it under the wafer, expecting that perhaps Mr. Tresillian had had a relapse.

To his surprise, though, he wasn't being summoned to attend upon the old man. Apparently Miss Tresillian had suffered some kind of accident.

All Nathaniel's incipient languor fled, and he grabbed his coat and hat from the hooks by the door, snatched up his doctor's bag, and raced out, taking the steps down to the street two at a time. He didn't want to wait to order his gig to be brought around from the stable, so he ran there himself, holding his hat on his head. When he arrived at the livery stable he breathlessly told the lad to harness up Juno, and in a matter of minutes he was driving the two miles to Tresillian Manor, his willing mare moving along at a brisk pace.

The door opened as soon as he drew up. Clearly Hosking was watching for him and led him immediately up to the bedroom floor and into an elegantly furnished lady's boudoir. At first Nathaniel didn't see her. Mr. Tresillian sat in a chair by the bed blocking his view, so his initial impression was only of a quantity of blue velvet bed drapes trimmed with silk tassels. The frivolous luxury seemed so out of keeping with what he knew of Sophia Tresillian that he had a momentary impression that he'd come to the wrong place.

But on hearing the door open behind him, Mr. Tresillian stood and approached Nathaniel, his hand outstretched. "Not me this time, good doctor! I'm feeling a deal heartier just now. But my girl, my Sophia, had a bit of an adventure today. She's got a terrible chill. We've bundled her up and there's a hot brick at her feet. And then, there's her ankle."

He led Nathaniel over to the bed. Sophia was all but buried in blankets, her golden hair splayed out carelessly on the pillow, curls in an unruly tumble. She wasn't shivering, but her normally rosy lips were white and her lids drooped over her cornflower blue eyes.

She smiled weakly at him. "You see me a poor creature, Dr. Rowe. I'm sorry I can't greet you properly."

"Good evening Miss Tresillian. Let's see if we can't put you back in frame." He took the chair Tresillian had relinquished and placed his hand on her forehead. Burning up. What had the girl done? "Any sore throat?" he asked.

She shook her head. "I just ache all over and I'm so tired. I've instructed Adler to brew me a tea with some willow bark and a little rue, and she's bringing a basin of vinegar and lavender oil along with some cloths to wrap my ankle."

There she was. The Miss Tresillian he had come to know. Even in fever and pain she had her wits about her—misguided though they were. "The most skillful medical professionals understand that it is dangerous to diagnose oneself. Your home remedies could do you more harm than good, Miss Tresillian."

A spark of defiance lit her eyes and brought a hint of color into her cheeks.

"That's what I've told her again and again, Rowe!" Mr. Tresillian said. He'd moved to the foot of the bed and surveyed his daughter with concern etched on his brow, his face still a little pasty.

Dr. Rowe, not wanting to have two patients to attend to at that moment, said, "Perhaps you might take a seat on that settee over there, Mr. Tresillian. It will take me some time to examine your daughter and you're looking a bit unsteady yourself." He softened his command with a smile. "It must have been upsetting to find her in such a state."

Tresillian did as he was bid and sank gratefully onto the small sofa against the wall. "When Pentarrant brought her, I thought she was dead. That would've killed *me* as well. No more Tresillians."

"Pentarrant?" Nathaniel, who had started gently probing Sophia's neck to see if there were any swellings and trying not to be distracted by the soft whiteness of her skin, said, "What did Pentarrant have to do with Miss Tresillian's accident?" He pictured the two of them riding together, and her coming to grief trying to jump over a hedge. Unaccountable rage at this imagined carelessness on the part of Pentarrant caused him to inhale sharply.

"She lost herself on Bodmin Moor. Silly puss. She was separated from her party in a storm and the gig stuck in the mud. Got soaked through, out there for hours, and with an injured ankle by the time Pentarrant found her."

It made no sense. What a mad thing to do, to venture anywhere on the moor alone! He wasn't a native of these parts, but he'd heard the lore. "What did you hope to achieve by yourself out on Bodmin, Miss Tresillian?" he said. He couldn't keep the edge of censure out of his voice.

"That," she said, "is no concern of yours."

Except, he thought with sudden self-knowledge, he very much wished it was his concern. Impossible woman. Why should he want anything to do with her? She thought she knew so much, but she was as green as the greenest girl. A good deal more intelligent than most, he had to admit in spite of himself. But his professional conscience quickly took over, stopping this fruitless train of thought, and he lifted her wrist to feel her pulse. It was fast, but not erratic. "I need to examine your ankle, Miss Tresillian, if you will give me permission."

"Of course. Although I doubt you can tell me anything I don't already know. It's not broken. I simply caught it in a rabbit hole and twisted it. I expect the ligaments and tendons are a trifle injured, but not very badly."

"Sophie!" Tresillian cried. "You didn't spend all that time at the seminary learning to be rude to someone who is only trying to help you!"

She turned back to Nathaniel, chastened. "He's right. I'm sorry."

As apologies went, it was not abject. But her earnest gaze melted him a little.

Nathaniel went to the foot of the bed and lifted the blankets to reveal Sophia's feet. One ankle—the uninjured one—was so slender and perfectly formed that the other looked grotesque beside it, even though it clearly was not broken. The foot was at the correct angle to the leg, and nothing protruded where it shouldn't. He gently took hold of both legs just above the ankles and ran his hands down them, feeling for their differences. He looked up when he heard a slight gasp come from the head of the bed. "Does this hurt you?" he said, certain he'd not put any pressure on the swollen ankle.

She shook her head and closed her eyes.

He finished his examination and put the blankets back down over Miss Tresillian's feet. "You are feverish, but I don't think it's anything to cause alarm. No doubt the chill has brought it on. I won't bleed you, but I will give you a paregoric draft to help you sleep. You must stay warm. I shall also bind your ankle—and I forbid you to put any weight on it for at least a week."

"You forbid me?" Sophia said, lifting her eyebrows, her voice sharp.

He smiled. "Just making sure you were listening to me."

A gleam of amusement lit her eyes. "Why would I not? You are a licentiate of the Royal College of Physicians."

How could she merely state that fact and load it with meanings no one else in the room could possibly guess? It took all Nathaniel's strength not to rise to her verbal fly. Instead, he said, "I understand we have James Pentarrant to thank for your safe recovery."

"Yes," she said, then paused when her abigail returned with the tea, liniment, and bandages. The maid hovered nearby, a worried frown on her face. "It's all right, Adler! I'm not at death's door, as I have assured everyone long since." She found herself unable to take her eyes off Nathaniel, who had started measuring out lengths of lint in order to bind her ankle.

SOPHIA'S INTEREST IN DR. ROWE'S MINISTRATIONS WASN'T simply clinical. Yes, she wanted to see exactly how he prepared the bandages and wrapped her swollen ankle without squeezing it too tightly. She was so tired, but she made an effort to prop herself up on her elbows so she could watch.

At first, he seemed unaware of her scrutiny, but when he was nearly done securing the bandages, he met her eyes. His were full of unexpected tenderness and she felt herself blush. He turned away almost immediately and said, addressing her father, "The wrapping should remain on for three days before it is changed. You must do your best to keep your daughter from putting any weight on that foot. I shall return tomorrow to check on her fever and possibly tighten the bandages if the swelling has decreased."

Whatever she thought of his attitude toward her own medical ambitions, his confidence, his conviction that he knew just what to do and could fix her, was curiously comforting. Was it the tone of his voice? Or his precise movements?

Or perhaps it was his hands. The gentle touch of his fingertips first on her forehead, then her neck, and then on her calves and ankles sent arrows of longing through her middle. That was the only way she could think of describing it, as if the sensation was transmitted from his hands through her nerves and directly into her heart.

Oh dear, she thought. It must be her weakened state. The feeling of Pentarrant's arms had been comforting, and once she was safely in the curricle, she was glad to be held to his side. Dr. Rowe's touch, on the other hand, was decidedly not comforting. Far from it. She had felt it first at the Roscarrock ball when they danced. They had a connection that cut across the bounds of propriety and their lack of acquaintance. She realized with a start that she would have welcomed an embrace from him even then. Now, she would not simply welcome it. She yearned for it.

Soon, however, exhaustion overwhelmed her. Dr. Rowe brought her the paregoric draught, but she pushed it away. "I don't need it. I'm not in pain. Just sleepy." She absently took his hand, too tired to think of propriety, and fell asleep with a faint smile on her face.

CHAPTER 26

Persephone tossed and turned all night after the picnic. She couldn't stop imagining what might have happened out on the moor and in Pentarrant's curricle. The unwelcome shrill of Phillipa's spiteful words kept circling through her mind. Surely the situation hadn't been as shocking as the catty Miss Vyvyan made it sound. Still, she wouldn't be easy until she heard the whole story of her friend's misadventure from her own lips. She wanted to see Sophia as early as politeness dictated the day after the picnic, but that wouldn't be until late morning.

Too restless to read, after breakfast Persephone went out to her patch of garden to work off some of her agitation pulling weeds. She was engaged in this homely occupation when Hannah came out to her holding a pasteboard card between her thumb and first finger to keep her flour-covered hands from dirtying it. "This just come fer you, Miss," she said.

Persephone rose, brushed the dirt off her work apron, and took the card. Elegantly etched across the top of it was *Lydia Tresize, Carlyon Grange,* with a handwritten note below it that said, *My father and I would be delighted if you would do us the honor of dining with us today. We shall send the carriage for you at four. If this is not convenient, please send word and we will arrange another day.*

The assumption that she would be free to go on such short notice struck Persephone as rather insulting. She was tempted to decline on principle, but that would be petty. Besides, she in fact had no other engagements. The squire was well aware that she was new to the district and so would be justified in assuming she had few demands on her social life as yet. Her plan for that day consisted only of the visit to Sophia, and afterwards an afternoon spent planning a lesson for that Sunday. In two days' time it could be that perhaps a couple of children would come to her to begin their education. But she had to own that seemed an unlikely eventuality at this point. She had not been given much hope when she spoke to the quarry villagers.

Another reason she wouldn't decline the invitation was that she had to own she was curious about Squire Carlyon and his daughter. Her meeting with the squire had been brief, but he made a good impression. She liked him. He seemed a man of sense and education. It could never hurt to have such an ally among the local gentry. His daughter was a widow who might be close in age to her, perhaps a little older. And without the pressure to find a suitor Mrs. Tresize might prove to be less ambitious of moving in polite society. Persephone laughed at that thought. She herself was certainly not in pursuit of a husband. So why was everyone treating her as though she must be? She was well past the age of falling in love, certainly—which made it all the more mystifying as to why the thought of Sophia possibly marrying James Pentarrant disturbed her so.

Persephone shook her head. It was all nonsense. Once she

saw Sophia and discovered what really happened yesterday everything would be clear.

It was now close to eleven, which she judged to be a decent hour for visiting. After she changed into a sprig muslin day dress and a twill spencer jacket and tied the ribbons of her villager straw hat in a neat bow under her chin, she told young Bobby to harness Miss Pie to the cart. "I'll be back in an hour or so," she called to Hannah on her way past the open kitchen door. "Do you need anything from Camelford? I could easily stop at the market on my way home."

"No miss," Hannah said.

"Oh, and I shan't be at home for dinner."

At that, Hannah peeked out of the kitchen and said, "So yer goin' to't squire's then"

Of course, Hannah must have read the card. "Yes, I am." Persephone said nothing more before leaving the house and climbing up to the driver's seat of the cart.

As she drove away toward the manor, she tried to enjoy the mild, sunny weather and rid her thoughts of the unease Philippa had planted there. This was easier to do in the open cart with the gentle breeze caressing her cheeks. Driving herself in her own modest vehicle had become an unexpected pleasure. The sense of freedom this simple action gave her lifted her spirits. To be fully her own mistress and go wherever she wished—so long as there was a road that could accommodate the cart—was still a novelty. She sighed. The only thing better would have been if she could have afforded to purchase the chestnut mare. She longed for a gallop over fields and perhaps even on the nearest beach. But such activities belonged to a life of leisure. She had come to Delabole to work and must put those frivolous pastimes behind her.

The drive to Tresillian manor was soon accomplished.

The groom took her horse and cart around to the stables and Hosking led her up to the drawing room. "Miss Tresillian is not still confined to her bed?" Persephone asked on the way up the grand stair.

Hosking said, in a voice that could hardly disguise his admiration, "No, Miss. Nothing could keep the mistress in her room. But she's on the sofa, and not supposed to walk around, so the master would take it kindly if you would discourage her from attempting it."

She thanked him and entered the pleasant chamber, thinking that the Ambleton's butler would never dream of saying so much to a guest. She rather liked the informality of the Tresillian household, though. For all their wealth, Sophia and her father did not put on airs.

Sophia sat on a divan between two long windows. She was a bit pale, but otherwise as freshly pretty as ever. "Persephone! I'm so very glad you are here. For a time yesterday I thought I might never see anyone I knew ever again." Sophia's suppressed smile told Persephone that she was likely never seriously worried about such a thing.

"I expected to find you sipping hartshorn and water and being waited on hand and foot," Persephone said, taking the seat near her. "And look at you! Shouldn't you at least have your feet up?" The only evidence of her injury was her bandaged foot propped on a low stool. A heavy book lay open on Sophia's lap. She placed a sheet of paper in it to mark her place and moved it to the table by her elbow. Persephone glanced quickly at the title. *Culpeper's Herbal.* She had heard of it, of course, but never seen a copy herself. She wondered how a genteel young lady like Miss Tresillian had managed to procure one.

But that was none of her business, Persephone decided, and gestured toward Sophia's swollen ankle. "Are you in pain? Will you be long off your feet?"

"Of course not. It's nothing. A slight sprain. I shall be walking around tomorrow, if I have anything to say to it." She masked her obvious strain in a brave smile at Persephone.

Persephone said, "I have no doubt you will be up and making mischief soon enough! But first I want to know everything. What happened yesterday? How did you come to be found?" As she said the words Persephone briefly wondered whether she spoke the truth. Did she want to know all? There was a part of the story she rather dreaded hearing. But that was cowardly. Pentarrant did not have a *tendre* for Sophia, nor she for him. Of that Persephone was certain. He seemed genuinely surprised that anyone could have mistaken the intent of his holding Sophia so close.

As she might have predicted, her friend made light of the very real danger she had been in. Persephone was relieved, too, that in her telling there was no hint of anything improper between her and Pentarrant. "I am sorry to have worried you," she said when her narrative ended. "Mr. Pentarrant told me it was you who raised the alarm when I did not come to you at the time you expected me. I wanted him to take me to your cottage so I wouldn't worry Papa as well, but, as you know, he didn't. When did you find out I had returned?

"I heard of your successful rescue from Philippa," Persephone said.

Sophia's brow creased in confusion. "From Philippa? How on earth did she come to be possessed of that knowledge?"

"She happened to be in Camelford when you passed through on your way to the manor." Persephone waited for the servant who entered the drawing room with a tea tray to set it down and leave, then rose and poured out two cups of tea. "It's one sugar, yes?" she asked, delaying the moment when she would tell Sophia of Philippa's suspicions.

"Yes! Now I know we are friends!" Sophia said. "Soon I expect we'll know all of each other's preferences—although I confess I didn't remark how you drank your tea the last time I visited you."

Once they'd settled again, Persephone told herself she was hen hearted not to come right out and tell Sophia what Philippa said. She stirred her tea, placed the spoon in the saucer, and said, "Sophia, about Philippa."

"What about Philippa?"

"She told me she saw something, which she interpreted in a certain way."

"You're being mysterious, Persephone! What did she see?"

Oh dear. How to say it? "She saw you and James Pentarrant in his curricle driving through Camelford."

Sophia drew herself up and stiffened. "Yes, of course I was in his curricle. How else would I have been able to come home?" She stared into the middle of the room and absently sipped her tea.

"It wasn't the fact that you were in the curricle. It was the way you were...arranged." Persephone wanted so to avoid using Philippa's word, *embracing.* She was so certain that it was inaccurate. When Sophia said nothing, only gazed at her with uncharacteristically troubled eyes, Persephone said, "He had his arms around you, so she said."

Sophia let loose a crack of laughter. "Is that all? He was doing his best to keep me warm. Had he not I might have ended with an inflammation of the lungs. Really, Persephone, how can you place any trust in what that viper would say?"

Persephone wished she could just dismiss Persephone's words, but she feared that Sophia would have to face the fact that she had been in a somewhat compromising position with Pentarrant. "I think you underestimate Philippa's capacity for seeing exactly what will serve her purpose."

"All right," Sophia said, the tinge of amusement absent from her voice. "What does she say she saw? Tell me exactly."

After a calming breath, Persephone said, "She used the word *embrace.*"

Sophia shook her head. "Because of course a gentleman must not so much as touch a lady unless he intends to marry her."

Sadly, Persephone thought, that was precisely what society would say. "It's nonsense, of course. Naturally, I don't believe there was anything amiss. But Philippa will no doubt spread rumors all around Camelford for some mischievous reason of her own. And that might well put Mr. Pentarrant in a very difficult position."

Sophia kept her eyes focused on her hands, which were now engaged in twisting and untwisting a lace-edged handkerchief. In barely more than a whisper, she said, "You have no idea how cold I was. No one does, except possibly James. Mr. Pentarrant I mean, of course."

Persephone's heart sank. She believed that Pentarrant had only been trying to keep Sophia from becoming chilled, but that didn't change the fact that he was seen by several people alone in a carriage with his arms around her. "I just thought you should be prepared."

Before she could say anything else, Hosking entered and said, "Dr. Rowe is here, Miss Sophia."

The change that came over Sophia's face was so sudden and so dramatic that Persephone had to suppress a smile. Her furrowed brow smoothed and in an instant her pale cheeks took on more color than they had the entire time Persephone was there. The smile that trembled on her lips was so expressive of tenderness that Persephone felt a little like an interloper when the young doctor came in and bowed to his beautiful patient.

"Miss Tresillian, I'm very happy to see you out of your bed, but only as long as you allowed someone to carry you here." He took her wrist in a gentle grasp and held it still while he felt her pulse, never taking his eyes off hers.

Well, whatever appearances had been, Sophia was not in love with Pentarrant, despite any feelings of gratitude she may have had for his unexceptionable kindness to her. It was obvious. And Dr. Rowe returned Sophia's feelings. They just seemed right somehow. "I should leave you to the ministrations of the good doctor," Persephone said and prepared to leave.

Before she could say her goodbyes, Mr. Tresillian entered the drawing room leaning on a footman's arm. Persephone had not seen him above three times since she arrived in Delabole, but he looked years older than he had just a few short weeks ago. When Sophia said her father was ill, Persephone thought perhaps he had dyspepsia or gout. Whatever ailed him, it was far worse than that.

"Mr. Tresillian, I just came to visit the invalid," Persephone said, with an effort at cheeriness.

He bowed slightly before the footman led him to a large wing chair near the fire.

Sophia said, "Papa! Have you had a turn? It was not necessary for you to get out of bed. I would have come to see you soon."

"I've stayed too long. I shall leave you in peace," Persephone said, sensing that father and daughter had something to say to each other that her presence would not facilitate. Why she thought that, she wasn't quite sure. Something troubling lurked in Mr. Tresillian's eyes.

But Sophia put her hand out to her and said, "No! Stay a

little longer. I haven't had a chance to talk to you and find out all the *on dits* of Delabole."

Before Persephone could protest and take her leave, Mr. Tresillian spoke. "I'm sorry to say that I can enlighten you about that." He reached into his coat pocket and removed a folded paper. He held it out to Dr. Rowe. "Would you kindly give this to my daughter."

Rowe dutifully took it and passed it into Sophia's hands. She frowned as she unfolded and opened it, scanning what looked like a brief letter. When she finished, her lips parted and her eyebrows rose. "What nonsense! Nothing of the sort happened, Papa. You must believe me."

Persephone felt a lump of dread in her stomach. No doubt some "well-meaning" neighbor had written to tell Mr. Tresillian that his daughter had been compromised. Could it have been Philippa? Persephone thought she would be more than capable of such a spiteful gesture.

"True or not, my girl, your reputation has been damaged. I have already written to Pentarrant to ask him what he intends to do about it."

Persephone's and Sophia's eyes met and held for a brief moment. It was enough time for Persephone to register the helpless fury, disappointment, and resignation that must have been going through Sophia's head. How utterly absurd it was! Anyone with the least amount of sense must have understood what was really happening in that open curricle.

Something made Persephone turn to look at Rowe. He stood utterly still, staring down at Sophia, his face white. "I think, Dr. Rowe, we had better leave Sophia and her father to their personal matters," she said.

The doctor reluctantly tore his gaze away from Sophia and addressed Mr. Tresillian. "Yes. I shall come back to see you later, sir, and see if I need prescribe you a different tonic. Miss Tresillian appears to be going along well. She must stay off her feet for a few days, give the ligaments time to heal." His words sounded rehearsed, as though he were reading them out of a medical textbook.

Persephone picked her hat up off the table where she'd tossed it when she came in and walked out of the drawing room, followed by Dr. Rowe. When they were both out on the wide gravel drive, waiting for the stable boys to bring their carts around, Rowe said to Persephone, "You know what this is about, don't you."

"Yes," she said, "I fear I do." She told him about Philippa's visit the day before. After she had done her best to be tactful when relating the circumstances to the obviously disturbed doctor, she said "I feel certain that Miss Tresillian feels no tenderness for James Pentarrant. The whole affair will no doubt blow over in a few days."

"I have not been here long," Rowe said, "but in that time I have learned that memories endure, that neighbors nurture grudges over supposed slights for much longer than seems necessary, and that there are people in Camelford and Delabole who will make mischief for those they envy or despise without any thought to the consequences. I thought I had left all that behind. Apparently not. Good day, Miss Wilkins."

He touched the brim of his hat, handed Persephone onto the seat of her cart and climbed up into his gig. He cracked his whip sharply over the horse's ears and the creature started forward at a trot. Persephone followed at a slower pace. She wanted to give herself as much time as possible to think about things before she had to greet Hannah and pretend that everything was just as it should be.

CHAPTER 27

With every shallow step up to the door of Tresillian Manor James felt as though he were climbing a mountain. Before he received Mr. Tresillian's letter, he had nearly persuaded himself that what Miss Wilkins had told him the previous day about Miss Vyvyan's observation would have no consequences. Surely everyone knew that Sophia Tresillian was stranded on the moor in a storm and was like to catch her death of a chill if she wasn't bundled up and warmed until she could make it home. Surely.

And then the letter arrived. It didn't exactly spell out what the man expected of him. Despite that, the message was clear enough. And now, he found himself in the position of having to make an offer of marriage to a lady who—although he liked and respected her—he did not love. Perhaps at one time he thought the two of them might make a go of it to please both their families, but everything had changed in three weeks. Before, he assumed that he would never have tender feelings for a woman again, and after all, marriages for his sort were often more business arrangements than anything else. But now—things had changed.

"The master is waiting for you," Hosking said after taking James's hat from him. "This way, sir."

He did not call him Mr. James, which most of the long-standing servants in Delabole took the liberty of doing. Clearly the butler knew that something serious was afoot. James followed him into a library sparsely populated with books. The massive desk was covered in ledgers and papers, all neatly stacked and organized. Mr. Tresillian was not seated behind it, though. Instead, he occupied a chair near the fire.

Warm afternoon light streamed in through the windows, but Tresillian's face was pale and sickly. James had fleetingly thought he would refuse to do the honorable thing, certain that Miss Tresillian did not want to marry him either, but would such a course push Tresillian to his deathbed?

"I believe you must know why I've asked you here. I cannot dismiss the gossip that said you had behaved most improperly with my daughter. She is just out of the schoolroom and too easily taken advantage of. I won't have it." At this, he began to cough. Weak, dry coughs, and he pressed his hand to his chest.

Pentarrant drew himself up to his full height. He had not been offered a seat. "Sir, I have no wish to disrespect your daughter—or you. I believe the actions I took merely to protect her from further injury or illness have been grossly misinterpreted."

"That's not relevant. The fact is you must make it right. It's your responsibility. Damn it, man! What were you thinking?"

Clearly there would be no use simply restating that he thought only of Miss Tresillian's health and safety, that he had no designs on her. "I thought only of Miss Tresillian's safety. But there is no need to tell me what I must do, sir. I am a man of honor. Miss Tresillian does not deserve to have her reputation ruined." He drew in a deep breath, steeling himself. "Therefore I intend to ask for her hand."

At this, Tresillian sank back against the soft cushions behind him and closed his eyes. "You know it's what Eustace and I both want. I would not have pushed you into it, but these events have changed the complexion of things, as you must see."

James merely nodded. Tresillian and Eustace would not have pushed him into it, but circumstances managed it nicely for them. Best to get the deed over with. Time would not make having to commit himself to Miss Tresillian any more palatable. "Is your daughter at home to visitors?"

"She is in the back parlor. I told her you were coming and asked her to wait there. We needn't settle the business side of this now. She's handsomely dowered, of course. And I will ensure that my investment in the quarry goes through."

"Sir, I would never marry for such considerations!"

"Don't fly into the boughs!" Tresillian said, again coughing. "I know you are not hanging out for a rich wife, but you've got one, and you may as well reap the benefits. You will live in the Manor, of course. It's what she's used to."

James was beginning to feel as if he'd stepped through a mysterious portal into someone else's life. As if the legends of the moor followed them out, keeping them caught in an inescapable magical web. None of this seemed real. Just days ago, he had realized that he might well have met his match in Persephone Wilkins. That, in itself, had surprised him. She wasn't a beauty. She wasn't young. They rubbed against each other frequently. Her dream of opening a school—naïve, yes, but he couldn't help admiring her for it. Perhaps because she challenged him she filled his thoughts at quiet times, those moments when the demands of the quarry did not force everything else out of his mind. When they'd last seen each other he was certain there had been something between them. A kind of sympathy. Perhaps more than that. Even if nothing happened to deepen their connection, he would have welcomed a friendship with her. He would have enjoyed continuing to argue and discuss things with her for the rest of his life. What was he thinking? To be honest he wanted more. Much more. But it wasn't to be.

Moments later he found himself in a parlor decorated in feminine floral prints of pinks and violets. Miss Tresillian, just as her father had been, was seated, her injured foot wrapped and propped on a stool. James bowed to her, trying to read her expression. Her face was pale, her eyes a bit hollow, her lips tightly pressed together. "Miss Tresillian," he said and walked toward her.

"Before you say another word," she said, "I want you to know that I tried to persuade my father that this drastic step was unnecessary. I don't care what anyone says about me!"

"But you should care," James said, taking a seat near her without being asked. "You don't want scandal hanging over your life, surely."

She gave one short laugh. "We are not so lofty, as you know. And we have enough money to erase a scandal if the will were there. But is it? I know well that this is what my father hoped for. I can only feel that your kindness to me is being repaid with punishment."

He shook his head. "How can you speak of punishment? I want you to know, in turn, that although it was not among my intentions, this marriage is by no means repugnant to me. How could it be? I would be a fool not to be happy to have such a prize as you." And yet, he thought, he was a fool.

She shook her head slowly. "You are a good man. But you don't love me, and I don't love you. I love—" She cut herself off. "Well, never mind that."

"Many marriages are founded on nothing more than mutual respect and are quite successful." His own parents had had such a marriage. They were content. But were they happy?

"That is not the kind of marriage I have always aspired to. I want more than bland acceptance. And you—you have remained a bachelor. I imagine you, too, have been hoping for more than the convenient match. I can see it in you. Forgive me for being so bold, but I believe you're in love with Persephone. Are you?"

The heat rose into his face. Love? He hadn't even spoken the word to himself. If Miss Tresillian guessed it, others might as well. He thought he was better than that at keeping his feelings hidden. "Whether or not I am is of no account. But Miss Tresillian…" He paused and looked away from her, scanning the room, afraid of revealing the turmoil of his heart to her. He collected himself and said, "Your candor does you credit. It makes me bold to be equally honest. You must know that you have it in your power to prevent this marriage, should you wish to. I must offer for you, but you are not obliged to accept me."

She heaved a sigh that seemed drawn from deep within her. "What we *have* to do… That is the question. I've thought and thought and I keep arriving back at the same place. I am afraid, Mr. Pentarrant, that I have no other choice but to accept your offer. I don't doubt that you saw how ill my father is. I think it would quite likely kill him to be engulfed in scandal. That it would be short-lived may be the case. Yet I think it would last long enough to do him real harm. However little I relish being forced into a marriage in this way, my father is of more importance to me than any consideration of my own feelings."

Silence engulfed the two of them for what seemed like many minutes. The clock on the mantel ticked gently. The light breeze stirring the leaves of the trees outside the window was the only other sound that penetrated that ridiculously feminine room.

With a start, James realized he hadn't actually made Miss Tresillian the promised offer. He had not uttered the words —words he would far rather be saying to someone he had met only two short weeks before. There was no putting it off any longer though. If she had been Miss Wilkins would he have gone down on his knee? Such an action seemed inappropriate in these circumstances, so he remained upright, cleared his throat, and said, "Miss Tresillian—Sophia—will you do me the honor of becoming my wife?"

Before she said a word, a tear dropped onto her lap. She swiftly dashed it away and lifted her chin. "Yes, Mr. Pentarrant. I will marry you."

It was surely the most sorrowful proposal ever made, James thought. He took Sophia's hand and lightly kissed it. She pulled it away quickly. Did Mr. Tresillian really want his daughter to be unhappy? Because she was, at least right now. *I must do my best to fix that, whatever it costs me,* James thought as he bowed to her and left, taking his hat from Hosking and walking out of the Manor in a daze.

THE SQUIRE'S CARRIAGE WAS COMFORTABLE BUT NOT OPULENT. It spoke of quality rather than luxury. Persephone was not surprised, therefore, to find herself set down before a rambling, two-story stone house of great antiquity—much older than either the Manor or even Roscarrock Hall—but of comparatively modest proportions. Although the Carlyon family had never been elevated to nobility, they had clearly been landowners for centuries. She wondered if the dynasty predated the Conquest, if they were of Saxon stock. Often these venerable squires with their many acres and lengthy pedigrees were holdouts who had kept their noses out of the shifting sands of politics and simply carried on farming their land, thus becoming prosperous without attracting the notice—good or bad—of the reigning monarch.

Once inside, her impression was strengthened. Oak paneled walls predominated. The hall, despite its large size, was not grand, and the stair that led to the first floor made no pretensions to elegance. The uncarpeted steps gleamed with polish, while the wear at their centers indicated that none of the Carlyon squires felt any need to update a feature that adequately performed its job in the dwelling.

The wizened servant—a butler in function if not in appearance—led her to a large drawing room on the ground floor with a low-pitched ceiling, traced across with age-darkened beams.

A lady who had been standing quite immobile in a shadowed area between the hearth and a window so that Persephone hadn't noticed her upon entering the room walked forward. "Miss Wilkins. I am Mrs. Lydia Tresize. I am so glad you were able to join us this evening." She was a petite woman engulfed in a black silk dress trimmed with a quantity of Brussels lace. Her eyes—light brown with a faint gold ring around the outside—held Persephone's in a steady gaze. "My father was delayed helping bring in a calf and will be with us when he has finished dressing for dinner."

Persephone responded with a polite greeting and her thanks, and they sat opposite each other in wing chairs that flanked the massive hearth. The carpets were clearly a newer addition, handsome creations from the Axminster workshops, to cover the slate-flagged floors—no doubt to make the room warmer in the wintertime. Mrs. Tresize folded her hands in her lap and, rather than initiate conversation as a hostess would, continued simply to look at Persephone.

"I am sorry for your loss," Persephone said.

Mrs. Tresize closed her eyes briefly and left the thread of the conversation hanging.

"I expect this house has quite a history," Persephone said, longing for this lady to unbend and chatter a bit. She judged the widow to be younger than she was by perhaps five years. Too young to have suffered such a loss.

Mrs. Tresize said, "Yes. Carlyons have lived here as far back as anyone knows. It takes a great deal of determination to farm successfully in a land with such poor soil."

She did not offer any further comments, and Persephone was about to ask her outright if she would like her to go away when the drawing room door opened to admit Carlyon.

"Miss Wilkins! Please forgive me for my tardy appearance. I trust Lydia has been keeping you entertained?"

He took the hand Persephone held out to him and raised it to his lips. The gesture caught Persephone by surprise and she could feel the heat of a blush steal into her cheeks. "I just asked about the history of this house," she said.

"Ah, poor Lydia! That is something she has heard me drone on and on about so often that I daresay she fairly blanched when you asked her."

Was that his way of saying he wouldn't take up that subject in conversation? Persephone couldn't decide whether that was a polite or an impudent response. She gave him the benefit of the doubt.

"You came from Bedfordshire, I understand?" Persephone said to Mrs. Tresize.

"Yes. My husband was Cornish, but inherited an uncle's estate in that county."

Another conversation ender. Persephone wanted to know, why had she returned? Was she a poor widow? Why hadn't her husband's family taken her in? But clearly, those questions would remain unanswered.

"And you, Miss Wilkins, have moved here from not very far away. Wilkins is not a Cornish name, though." The squire's slight country accent betrayed his local origins.

"No, my family is from Somerset. My father was a clergyman there." Persephone detected in this oblique question an attempt to place her in the appropriate rank of society. She hoped that her answer would provide enough information to allow her to be gently bred but with no pretensions to wealth or station.

"Wilkins from Somerset…" the squire mused, casting his eyes thoughtfully upward. "No, can't bring anyone to mind. But that's of no consequence. You found yourself in Boscastle, you say. After your father died?"

It was before, but she decided that was information she would keep to herself for now. They needn't know that it was her father's death that had provided her with the income to set herself up in Delabole. "I was fortunate enough to be employed as a governess to the Marquess of Lewiston's daughters," she said, wondering how Mrs. Tresize would react to this. Did she know of the scandal? If she did, she gave no sign of it.

The squire said, "Ah yes! I knew Lewiston a little. His son's inherited now. Good lad. But he stays in London with that granddaughter of a cit he's married rather than taking care of his estate in Cornwall."

Persephone's instinct was to rise to his defense and say that the estate was in the very capable hands of a steward, and that Lord and Lady Lewiston lived there during the summer—in the same manner as most members of the nobility. But she merely smiled.

At that moment, the same fellow who had led her to the drawing room entered, cleared his throat, and said, "Dinner."

The squire put out both his elbows, indicating that Persephone should take his right arm and his daughter his left.

DINNER WAS PLAIN BUT DELICIOUS, AS PERSEPHONE WOULD have expected based on what little she knew of the squire. However, Mrs. Tresize only picked at the food. Was she being delicate and discerning or did she have some indisposition? Perhaps she was still grief stricken. Her bright, probing eyes—somewhat catlike, Persephone decided—relieved the pallor of her complexion. She focused these intent eyes on her father mostly. Perhaps she imagined it, but Persephone could swear they narrowed slightly on those few occasions when she turned them on Persephone.

The squire took the burden of conversation and deftly steered them through several safe topics. He successfully drew Persephone out on the subject of teaching, and mentioned that Mrs. Tresize had been educated at an exclusive ladies' seminary in Bristol. "Not sure what she learned, though. Enough to get her a husband, although he turned out—"

"Papa, Miss Wilkins is not interested in the education of ladies, but of the common folk." A pointed glare accompanied this comment.

"So she is, so she is," said the squire. "But do you really think it can be done? And who will benefit?"

These were questions that had plagued Persephone. Yet no one else had asked them of her so directly. "I don't know if it can be done effectively, sir. But I believe both the children and the quarry management will benefit."

The squire cast a skeptical look at Persephone. "I don't see how educating the workers can do anything but make them dissatisfied."

"On the contrary," Persephone said, warming to her

subject, "greater knowledge and ability on their part will make them more capable of learning new things, embracing more advanced techniques. Steam, for instance. Surely those who work the machines must have an understanding of them that the ability to read will only enhance."

Squire Carlyon tipped his head back and laughed. "I could just see my cowmen learning to read so they could spout poetry to the herd."

It was a funny image, but Persephone couldn't help being a little offended. "I daresay there are advances in farming and husbandry coming that might be more acceptable to your workers if they could read about them before they were introduced."

Carlyon stopped laughing and cocked his head on the side. "There is sense in that, I have to say."

They continued to debate this issue until it was time for the ladies to retire to the drawing room and leave the squire in splendid solitude to enjoy his port. Such an odd custom, Persephone thought. Why not simply serve the port in the drawing room when there was only one gentleman?

Mrs. Tresize was a little more talkative after dinner than before, but Persephone couldn't help feeling she was keeping her at a distance, that the lady regarded her as through a pane of glass. It was the oddest sensation. She smiled to herself when she compared the widow's behavior toward her with Sophia's.

The squire soon joined them, and after tea Persephone rose and said it was time for her to leave, that she had enjoyed their hospitality and thanked them for inviting a newcomer to the district into their home.

"It is we who must thank you. We are poor entertainment, I am sure. You have livened up our solitude," Carlyon said, rising. "Pull the bell for Jory and have him bring the carriage round, Lydia."

After shaking the widow's hand, Persephone took Carlyon's arm as he escorted her out to the carriage. "I hope you will not be a stranger to us," he said. "My dear girl has had a time of it. She needs friends. I could tell when I met you, so fearless and open at the quarry, that you might perhaps be able to coax her out of her doldrums."

"She is young to be left a widow. I would be honored to count her my friend."

"Not her alone, I hope. I've enjoyed our conversation this evening. Perhaps you will do me the honor of coming again soon?"

He had taken her hand firmly between both of his large and slightly callused mitts. They were the hands of someone who did manual labor in spite of his status as a gentleman. Something to be admired. Persephone tugged gently and he released her quickly. "You are most kind, sir," she said, unwarranted heat flooding her cheeks.

Carlyon handed her into the carriage and watched it drive away until it turned onto the lane. It wasn't altogether dark yet. A glow of orange lit the western sky so the coachman could see the way clearly and in very little time she was back at her cottage.

When she walked in, Hannah was awaiting her in the kitchen. "So, the squire himself deigned to entertain you! What's 'e like? They say he's a bit stiff and superior. And that daughter of his has come back a widder. He married her off right out of school to a wealthy good for nothing, so they say."

"Good evening, Hannah," Persephone said, removing her hat and gloves and sinking into a chair by the hearth. "They were polite. The dinner was good. I think Mrs. Tresize hates me, however, but I can't imagine why."

"Can't ye?" Hannah pursed her lips and flared her nostrils.

"Oh it's nothing like that! The squire is just being kind."

She sniffed. Then said, "A letter come fer ye this evening." She stuck her hand in her pocket and drew out a somewhat crushed but still sealed note.

"Thank you, Hannah." Persephone took it from her but did not open it, clearly disappointing the housekeeper.

"I'll make some tea, Miss," Hannah said and creaked to her feet.

"No, I'm tired. I'll go up to my room and see you in the morning."

She was tired. But that wasn't why Persephone wanted to go upstairs. She recognized Sophia's handwriting, uncharacteristically messy though it was. What could she want? They'd been in each other's company only the day before. A heavy dread settled in Persephone's stomach. For the hours she had been at the Grange, she had put the episode of Sophia's injury and Philippa's gossip out of her mind. Something told her that those events were about to be forced upon her notice, and she felt the bile rise in her throat. She was tempted not to open the letter, at least not until morning.

That would not make its communication any the easier to bear, if it had anything to do with what Persephone suspected. With trembling hands, she slid her finger under the edge to break the seal, and read.

I'm so sorry. I will explain all to you when I next see you. Please come to me as soon as you can.

Sophia

She stared down at the few, devastating words inked on the page. The letters danced and rearranged themselves into nonsense. Sophia hadn't said it outright, but Persephone guessed that she could only mean that Pentarrant had been forced to offer for her. And that she had accepted him.

It's as I imagined it would be, Persephone thought. Why should it make any difference to me to know it for a fact? He doesn't even like me. She shook her head. All we do is come to cuffs whenever we meet.

And yet, what had he meant, that time in the schoolroom? He seemed about to say something to her, something she thought no one would ever say. Surely she imagined it. She was nothing to him. How could she be? She was neither an heiress nor titled. Her breeding was respectable but not genteel. She was nothing.

It took a long moment for Persephone to realize the words on the page were now hardly legible. They had been obscured by her own tears, dripping silently down her cheeks and onto the paper.

CHAPTER 28

James wanted to wipe the satisfied smirk off his brother's face. He'd had that urge many times during the course of their lives, but never so strongly as at that moment. He clutched his hands together in his lap after their solitary dinner at Tarrant Hall. They sat in the library over brandy—something James never remembered doing with Eustace before. He knew what his brother wanted to discuss, but he'd managed to forestall the conversation until that moment. The last thing he wanted to talk about was his betrothal, so in a final effort at deflection he said, "How is Catherine? Will she join us when the tea tray comes in?"

Eustace grimaced. "Of course not. She's still claiming to be indisposed after Jillian's birth. That was weeks ago!"

"It was less than two weeks ago, and if she's still unwell something may be wrong. Perhaps she's ill. Have you sent for Rowe?" Whatever James's preoccupation with his own concerns, he was genuinely concerned about his sister-in-law. It wasn't like Catherine to hide herself away like that.

Normally the mere mention of a party would have her buzzing merrily about making plans.

"Believe me, there's no need for that. She's just using it all as an excuse to keep me out of her bed."

From what James knew of Catherine, he didn't think she'd have the steel to make up something in order to avoid Eustace's attentions. She generally did everything he asked of her and never questioned his actions. "All the same…"

"You know nothing. Although you soon will. I can't wait to see how you manage under the yoke of marriage!" Eustace poured more brandy into his glass.

His brother's words disgusted James. Even if it was just the two of them for dinner, it was Catherine's home. Indeed, her fortune had paid for significant improvements to it, not to mention the purchase of fine hunters and the spanking Pentarrant barouche. But of course, marriage rendered a wife's fortune her husband's.

After replacing the decanter on the tray, Eustace said, "That was clever of Miss Tresillian to catch you like that, granted it's worked out for the best."

Did Eustace really say what James thought he said? "What are you implying?"

"Admit it, she caught you!"

Through gritted teeth James said, "Miss Tresillian did not set a snare for me. She would not have needed to do that for any man."

"Are you in love with her? I must say, I didn't dare hope for so much." Eustace's smile said, *You've been had, brother.*

James clamped his lips together and took a deep breath before saying, "You know that is not the case. This absurd gossip put her in a compromised position."

"As I understand it, you were the one who accomplished that."

He could not deny the truth of it. How would anyone

ever believe he had no thought of seduction in his head at the time? "I simply sought to get her home. She was chilled right through, trembling so that I worried she might break a tooth. But what do you know of concern for others?"

Eustace cocked an eyebrow. "I know you think me a heartless wretch, but I swear this is the best thing that could happen to you. She's a perfect match. She brings money and beauty to the family. Can't do anything about her breeding, but in another generation that will all be forgot. Besides, she's not hard to swallow as a bedfellow."

"That will do!" James roared, perilously close to leaping out of his seat and drawing his brother's cork. "She does not deserve to be subjected to comments like that. I am not in love with her, but as a lady she is to be respected."

"All right Jamie. Take a damper." Eustace dismissed James's ire with a wave. "I didn't bring you here to talk about love in any case."

"What did you bring me here for, then?"

"To plan the celebration, of course. The neighbors will demand it. I think a dress party, don't you? That will bestir Catherine to get out of her mopes, I'm sure, and she knows how to do the thing."

The idea of a betrothal party filled James with dread. What a mockery. He was fairly sure Sophia wouldn't want it either. Her father, however, probably expected it. "Shouldn't that be up to Tresillian to organize?" He was clutching at straws.

"He's not in very good frame. I've already talked to him about it. Went this morning. Didn't look well at all, despite his high spirits. I hope he isn't about to stick his spoon in the wall. Better get her dowry nailed down soon—and his investment in the quarry as well."

Was this really all Eustace cared about? When they were boys, Eustace didn't seem heartless or obsessed with money.

What had happened to change him so? "Did I just hear you say that the money is more important than a man's life? The quarry is in profit! Perhaps not as much as it once was, but it would be plenty if—" He caught himself before launching into a critique of Eustace's spending habits. There was no point. Instead he said, "Even without Tresillian's cash we're on track to outperform last year, albeit modestly."

Eustace didn't answer right away. "There are other expenses. You don't understand because you live in such a quiet way. We—I—am expected to be *someone* in the county, to cut a dash, and that costs money."

"You know what I think about that." James could have pointed out that cutting a dash needn't involve wagering large sums at piquet and whist with the Roscarrock crowd, among many other examples of Eustace's profligacy. The Pentarrants would never be of that ilk, no matter how free Eustace was with his wealth. Marrying the daughter of a viscount had gone to his brother's head, almost as if he expected her nobility to be passed down to their children and for himself to be treated as nobility because of it. "I draw the line at a party. And I refuse to have a big wedding. The quieter the whole affair the better."

No matter how quiet, though, James's mind would scream with frustration. He could not banish the thought of Persephone Wilkins from his mind. A sharp pain somewhere in his middle stabbed him whenever he remembered their conversations—her courage in going to Bodmin alone to the horse auction; her passion for education; her warm, intelligent eyes; her unconscious grace. Yet nothing had actually passed between them beyond words and conversation. He'd hardly touched her. Nonetheless, being near her lit a spark that animated his soul. And somehow all these jollifications proposed by Eustace would feel like an insult to her. Bad enough that Sophia was her friend.

"I've spoken to Reverend Williams already," Eustace said. "He'll read the banns for the first time tomorrow."

So soon? No doubt news of the betrothal was all over the county by now anyway. Somehow, though, the idea of that official step knocked him off balance. When he recovered himself he said, "Why the haste? Miss Tresillian still isn't able to walk. She won't be in church." But, he thought, Persephone would be. She had been the previous Sunday. She sat near the back, as if placing herself where she could observe, staying a little aloof, an outsider waiting to be invited in. If she only knew—but now she never would know that he had welcomed her into his heart almost at the moment they met. If only he had realized it sooner.

"I thought Thursday for the party." Eustace had continued talking about the event while James listened with only half an ear. "Catherine can write the invitations tomorrow. We'll have everyone important."

James gave a travesty of a laugh. "Tresillian is too ill to go out, and Sophia might not be able to walk yet, let alone dance. A betrothal party with neither the bride nor her father there would be odd, to say the least."

"Tresillian isn't essential. Rowe assures me that your affianced is not so injured that she won't be back on her feet in a couple of days."

"No. I insist we wait for—" What did he want to wait for? Nothing would change the future. Still, James felt an overwhelming need to buy time. "For Tresillian to recover his health a bit. And the affair should not be scheduled without talking to Sophia."

Eustace smiled without genuine cheer and said, "I'll leave it to you then, shall I? Oh, wait. You don't want this match, do you? Well, putting it off isn't going to change anything."

"Nonetheless, we will wait. A week or two at least."

"Very well. Do you trust me to make up the guest list?"

"I doubt you'd listen to my suggestions, so by all means." Since James had no particular friends outside of the men at the quarry, he cared little who would attend. Would Eustace invite Persephone Wilkins? Sophia would probably insist. But she might not come. Perhaps it would be better if she didn't.

All James wanted to do was leave, get away from his brother's plotting and planning, from the thought that his life had been so thoroughly mapped out for him in a direction he had not foreseen. Poor Sophia deserved more than being used as currency in a mercenary exchange.

Yet if that future were truly distasteful to her she could cry off. She could have said no to begin with. But she did not. It was because of her father, she said. Having never had any great affection for his own father, James had a hard time understanding her consideration. If only Tresillian wasn't ill!

Enough. James stood. "I'll leave you now. I won't stay for the tea tray. I have to be at the quarry early. We're doing some exploratory digging and I want to make sure it's safely handled."

After perfunctory goodbyes, James emerged from Tarrant Hall into a long, mild May twilight. He breathed in the air, fragrant from the just blooming rose gardens near the house. The ever-present odor of stone dust didn't penetrate this far away from the quarry—a fact that made James give a crack of ironic laughter. The groom brought his curricle out from the stables. James jumped up into it and soon set his beautiful pair off at a brisk pace.

He wished, in a way, he had a longer journey ahead of him. And then he had a thought: why not make it longer? No one and nothing awaited him at home. It would be an hour before the dusk made it more difficult to see any hazards on the road. He could take the longer route home. It was the way they used to run as boys.

The way that would take him near Miss Wilkins' cottage.

James feather-edged the sharp corner that led in that direction before he had time to remind himself that it was a terrible idea. He justified his decision by believing that he wouldn't stop. He would simply drive by. Perhaps she wouldn't even be there.

But when he arrived at the gate leading to the cottage he pulled up his horses. Rather than being dark and lifeless, the window into the kitchen was brightly lit—bright enough that he could see inside to Miss Wilkins, seated at the table writing. Beyond her, the servant—Hannah, if he remembered correctly—bustled at her work, scrubbing out pots while a kettle simmered over the fire.

How he wanted to be in there too! But he must not. This was madness.

Just as he had decided to urge his horses forward, Miss Wilkins looked up from her writing and saw him. The expression on her face was impossible to read. He simply stared back at her. She rose and turned away, and he thought she had probably decided to remove herself from his contemplation. A sensible idea.

Then, a moment later, the front door of the cottage opened and there she stood. "Mr. Pentarrant. Is there something I can do for you?"

Now it would be patently rude for him to drive off. He lifted his hat and bowed slightly. "I-I was simply passing by."

"Hannah was just making tea. Would you care to join me?"

He couldn't say no. Or rather, he could, but he wouldn't. "If it's no trouble."

She stepped aside and gestured into the vestibule. James climbed down from the curricle and tossed the reins over the post, entering Miss Wilkins's cozy cottage for the second time in a week.

. . .

WHY WAS HE HERE? WHAT COULD HAVE POSSESSED Pentarrant to come, to invade her serene home, to stir up feelings that she spent every moment working to suppress? He had no right. He was a married man in the eyes of society. She was a spinster of unimpeachable morals.

All this went through Persephone's mind as she led James into the kitchen to sit where he'd sat when he called on her after the ball.

He passed the brim of his hat through his hands like a schoolboy who didn't know what to do with it. Hannah stepped forward and held her hands out. He relinquished it absentmindedly and said, "I was on my way home from dining with my brother and I had to come this way to… to…"

Persephone didn't force him to explain further. "Please sit. As you see, Hannah has the tea all ready. I hope you like yours strong. I've come to appreciate its bracing effect." She was rambling and she knew it, but she continued speaking in a voice that was so brittle she thought it might shatter on the air. "We're having such delightful weather. I daresay you wanted to drive through the countryside on such a beautiful evening." *Please let him leave!* Persephone thought, not certain how long she could sustain her light tone.

"I wish—"

No, she thought. It seemed she would be forced to talk about the matter that hung between them like a corpse on a gibbet. "What you or I wish is of no consequence. Matters stand as they stand. We must all live with them." Persephone avoided busied herself pouring tea and offering milk and sugar, both of which he declined.

"Look at me, Persephone," he said.

She gasped at the sound of her given name on his lips and finally met his eyes. They were dark and deep and drenched with sadness, and her throat tightened with the threat of tears.

"I had to do it. You must know that. And Miss Tresillian—Sophia—she is sacrificing her own happiness as well."

Persephone lifted her chin and forced herself to harden her eyes against his implied plea for understanding. "Nonetheless, it is a fact. You must not make her regret it. She is my friend. She deserves consideration and kindness."

"She deserves more than that! She deserves love—love that I am unable to give her because—" He stopped and rubbed his face hard.

Persephone rose and walked away so she did not have to face him. "That is enough. You must not say anything more. If you have finished your tea, I would be grateful if you would leave. Indeed, it was wrong of you to come here." She heard herself saying these harsh words as if she had stepped out of her own body to do it.

She heard the chair he was sitting in scrape on the slate floor as he pushed it back. He walked toward her and stopped. His body could be no more than six inches away from her, she thought. But she did not turn, did not flinch.

"Good bye, Miss Wilkins."

The words were spoken in such a soft whisper that Persephone could barely hear them. She closed her eyes and remained rigidly upright until Pentarrant's steps faded away out the door of her cottage.

He was gone. He'd said goodbye. They could not continue their association, except as common and indifferent acquaintances. She must relinquish the hopes she had allowed to blossom in her heart. Her life would be filled with other things.

Hannah entered the kitchen and stood just inside the door, her expression as dejected as Persephone's. "Don't," Persephone said, and ran past her and up to her bedroom.

CHAPTER 29

Persephone let Miss Pie choose her own pace home from St. Teath's that Sunday. She was so numb she could hardly bestir herself to lift the reins, let alone appreciate the fine weather. At any other time she would have been eager to return so she could change into a plain frock and go for a walk through the spinney or to the cliffs—on the assumption that this Sunday would be no different from the previous three, and not result in visits by any of the quarry children coming to learn their letters. But that day Reverend Williams's sonorous voice still rang in her ear like a death knell. Even after James's visit to her the evening before she had not truly relinquished hope that things might end differently. That hope had now vanished, no more than a dreamlike memory. The betrothal was a fact. The banns had been called.

She drove the cart directly to the little barn at the side of her cottage and sat in it, unmoving, for how long she did not know.

"Miss?"

A small voice called her out of her distraction. She looked

around. At first, she didn't see anyone, but then a child crept around the corner of the barn and swiped his soft cap off his head, offering her a clumsy bow.

"Jago!" she said. Good heavens, she thought. Had he actually come to learn? "Help me unharness Miss Pie and turn her out in the field, will you? Then you may come inside and have some cakes."

Jago's eyes grew round and he froze for a moment before a wide smile lit his face and he set to work quickly unharnessing the cob.

Their task accomplished, Persephone led Jago Penwarden to the back door of her cottage. She glanced down at his feet to see if his shoes were covered in mud. They were quite clean, as if he'd brushed them to a dull shine before going to the Methodist meeting, and he wore what Persephone assumed were his best clothes—a brown wool jacket that was almost too small for him, a clean homespun shirt with the collar buttoned at the top, and worn but clean brown corduroy breeches.

"Tell me, Jago," she said, "Do your parents know you've come here?"

His eyes shifted away guiltily and he said, "No Miss."

"Won't they be worried?" she asked.

"No Miss. I says I'm gone with t'other boys down the beach."

She wasn't happy that he'd lied. But if he told his parents where he intended to go they would perhaps have stopped him, very likely disapproving. "Why did you come?" she asked, ushering him into the parlor schoolroom, noticing how small he looked among the so far unused tables and chairs. A schoolroom should have chairs whose legs have been kicked by restless boots, she thought, and ink stains on the tables.

"I come for book learnin', Miss," Jago said, taking in every bit of of the room, his eyes lingering on the shelf that held a tidy row of volumes.

"You want to learn to read, then. But first you have to know your letters. I can teach you, but you must come back every week. One day won't be enough. Do you understand that?"

Jago wandered over to where one of the spelling books Persephone had bought at the bookseller's in Bodmin lay on a table and traced the letters on the cover with one tentative finger.

"Why don't you sit here," Persephone said, pulling a chair out from the nearest table, "And I can teach you some letters today."

She placed her hand on Jago's back to guide him to the chair. As soon as she touched him he flinched away from her. "Did I hurt you?" she asked. Her touch had been very light.

He shook his head vigorously.

Something gave him pain. "Did you have an accident?"

"No Miss," he said. "Only Mister Bray, he said I must pay for dropping the stones."

Bray, Persephone thought, an angry knot forming in her stomach. As she had feared, the overseer had wreaked his retribution on Jago once she and Pentarrant were out of sight on that first day she went to the quarry. Did he do such things often? How badly was Jago hurt? Was it the same for all the boys?

Much as she wished to know the answers to these questions there was nothing to be gained at that moment by pushing the boy more, so she brought the spelling book over and fetched one of the slates and chalk. She then sat down next to him and wrote out the first few letters of the alphabet. "Now you see if you can draw them the same. Each letter has a sound and words are made up of letters put together. Let me show you."

She reached over to his slate wrote out J A G O in large, clear strokes. "The first one is J, and it sounds like what it is. The second is A and it sounds like—"

"Jay!" he said. "Like my name starts."

"That's right. Then the G is hard, *guh,* and the O altogether make—"

"Ja-go," he said in hushed wonder.

How fortunate his name was so simple and phonetic, Persephone thought. She showed him the whole alphabet on a chart that she unrolled on the table. "There are twenty-six letters in all. And every word in the English language is made up of just these letters. But you don't have to learn them all at once."

He seemed to grasp the principle fairly quickly but appeared a bit overwhelmed. A bright boy, she thought. Nonetheless, she couldn't shake the image of him straining under that heavy sack of stones, and the abject fear in his eyes at sight of Bray. His body had been strained and punished so much for one so young. She guessed him to be about eight years old, revising her initial estimate of six or seven upward when she saw his alacrity with the letters. If she could help him develop his mind, then perhaps he would one day have the wherewithal to better himself. She knew that was a bit of a fantasy, but there would certainly be no harm in his learning to read.

They'd been sitting there for half an hour, and in the joy of teaching Persephone found she was able to put the morning's distressing revelations out of her mind. But the signs that Jago was tiring and losing interest were clear, so she said, "Let's go see if Hannah has those cakes I mentioned, and a glass of milk."

Hannah, no doubt understanding as any woman would that a boy of Jago's age is hungry all the time, had put a slice of seed cake on a plate at the table in the kitchen along with a cup of milk. Jago glanced uncertainly at Persephone. "It's for you! Sit down and enjoy it."

She didn't have to say it twice. Persephone had never seen something edible disappear so quickly. She was tempted to give the boy more, but didn't want to make him sick with unaccustomed rich food.

When he finished, Jago got up from the bench and said, "Thank you, Miss," and squashed the hat he'd stuffed into his back pocket onto his head again.

"It was my pleasure, Jago. Will I see you next Sunday?"

"Yes Miss," he said. "If I can."

She couldn't ask for anything more from him, so she smiled her acknowledgment and led him out through the front door.

As she watched him lope off across the neighboring field, she heard the rhythmic clop of trotting hooves and the scraping crunch of carriage wheels approaching from the lane that led toward Tresillian Manor. For an instant, she thought it might be James Pentarrant and her heart leapt. But of course it wouldn't be, not coming from that direction. It also couldn't be Sophia. Last she heard, she was still unable to get around very well.

But the vehicle that rounded the curve toward her cottage was driven by a man. A gentleman.

Dr. Rowe! What could he be doing here?

He pulled up his horse and jumped down from the carriage before looping the reins over the post. "Miss Wilkins. Forgive me for calling on you unexpectedly." He said this as he walked, stopping in front of Persephone with his hand out to shake hers. "I wonder if I could speak with you for a moment. You perhaps have some idea why I'm here."

She had seen him in church that morning, sitting stone-faced at the back on the other side of the aisle from her. "I'm afraid you have me at a disadvantage. Neither I nor Hannah is unwell."

"Not all ills are physical, Miss Wilkins. May I be so bold as to assert that you are, indeed, suffering, as I am?"

"You'd better come inside," Persephone said and led him into the cottage to the kitchen. She cast a significant glance at Hannah, who was not slow to comprehend and quietly left the room. "Tea? Or perhaps something stronger?"

"Tea, yes. No. I don't know."

Deciding for him, Persephone went to the cupboard and brought out a decanter of Madeira and two glasses, which she placed on the small table between the two comfortable chairs near the hearth. She poured them each a measure of the wine and then sat, waiting for Rowe to speak. What could he possibly have to say to her? Why come that day?

Rowe sat in silence for a while. Emotions played across his features and he took a sip of the Madeira. After a deep breath he said as if continuing a conversation with himself, "She is infuriating in so many ways." He smiled. "She has wit and a degree of knowledge uncommon in young ladies. Strength of character, too." He swirled the ruby liquid in his glass contemplatively. "I don't understand it. Why didn't she have the strength to say no?"

Persephone had known ever since the day after the picnic that Dr. Rowe was in love with Sophia, and she had suspected for longer than that. Her heart ached for him. "You refer to the banns read at church this morning, I see. It's a wretched business," she said. "But I don't quite understand why you have come to me."

Deep sadness darkened his warm brown eyes. *A handsome man,* Persephone thought, but in a different way from Pentarrant. Rowe had an air of refinement about him that James lacked. She wondered about his background. Doctors were certainly often educated men, but there was more in Rowe's air than education.

After a moment he spoke. "I've seen the way Pentarrant looks at you. And I've seen how you respond to him."

Persephone turned away in confusion. She was so certain she had not betrayed feelings. "I don't know what you mean."

"I think you do. Come, Miss Wilkins, what have we to gain by being coy with one another? I think you must admit that both our hopes were dealt a death blow today. The irony is that I think Sophia's and Pentarrant's hopes also died."

All four of them. Miserable. For what? "You must know that Sophia returns your affection. I've seen it in her eyes. But what can be done now?"

He leant his elbows on his knees and took his head between both his hands, gripping his dark blonde hair as though he would pull it out. "There must be a way to put a stop to it!"

"There is," Persephone said, and then regretted when she saw the burning hope in Dr. Rowe's eyes. "Sophia can cry off. She could have refused Pentarrant's offer in the first place. Why did she not?" It made no sense to her. Honor was satisfied simply by James offering for Sophia.

"It's her father. He is very unwell, and he told her this marriage with Pentarrant was his dearest wish. His heart could not stand anything that agitates him just now, and Sophia—Miss Tresillian—does not want to upset him in any way. She is mortally afraid of being the cause of his death."

"Is he really so ill? I had no idea." Persephone envied Sophia her affectionate relationship with her father. To put his wishes above her own happiness—that was love indeed. But need she have done it in such a case, when her decision would affect the rest of her life and determine her happiness?

"Yes, his heart is very weak. Even so, I can't help feeling

that if he truly knew how she felt—how we felt—he would not make her go through with this charade." On these last words he stood abruptly and strode around the small room, filling it with the force of his anger and frustration. "He wants her to make a good match, marry into a good family. An old family."

"And a doctor, perhaps, does not suit his idea of someone deserving of his daughter?" Doctors—even those with the most prestigious training and impressive licentiates—still bore the stigma of being considered little more than a sawbones, the butchers of old who augmented their incomes attending to the injured.

Rowe's laugh held not a trace of humor. "That is the most ironic thing of all. The Pentarrants are a fine old family, but they are trade. Whereas I—" He stopped abruptly and clamped his lips shut.

"You?" Persephone asked in genuine curiosity.

Rowe rubbed his face again, as if he was struggling with himself. "I misspoke. It's of no consequence."

"What is it you wanted to tell me, Dr. Rowe?"

He took a deep breath and expelled it in a loud sigh. "As I said, it was nothing. Please don't regard it." He paced around the room again then stopped directly in front of Persephone. "Oh, what is the use! It matters little now, I suppose. I wanted to make my own way, to do what I was passionate about and help others. My family would not have permitted me that freedom, had they known. And truly, I had no desire for my name to be the golden key that would open my world." He shook his head and rose, adopting an almost haughty expression. "Allow me to introduce myself properly. I was the honorable Nathaniel Rowe-Wisbeach, second son of the earl of Morecroft. Since the death of my older brother I have become Viscount Axeley."

For a full minute, Persephone could think of nothing to say. It was fantastic, and yet, seeing Dr. Rowe, recalling all her observations about him—his manners, his air—it made perfect sense. She had thought him far more genteel than the doctors she had known throughout her life. She didn't imagine he could actually be noble. "Well," she said. "Well." And after a moment, "Can you not tell that to Mr. Tresillian? Or Sophia?"

"And say what? That I came amongst them under false pretenses? No, if this travesty of a wedding is to be stopped, it must be done without that. I would not want to appear to be trying to buy Sophia's affection. Miss Wilkins, you are Sophia's friend. Can you not prevail upon her to consider crying off?"

"I don't see how that could come about unless she could present her father with an alternative that's at least as appealing. Really, I think it is not so dishonorable for you to have decided not to puff off your consequence here. One could see it as rather the opposite."

He shook his head and looked down at the floor as if its plain flagstones were the most interesting objects he had seen that day. "There is another reason why I cannot suddenly reveal my family background."

What on earth could this reason be? Clearly he was still holding something back. "You needn't tell me. But be assured, anything you do tell me I will certainly keep to myself."

"You are a kind woman, Miss Wilkins. I believe I can trust you. I would ask you to keep to yourself everything I have told you this evening as well as what I will now explain."

"Of course, as I said. I am no gossip."

Dr. Rowe sat once more and drank half the Madeira in his glass before speaking again. "I mentioned my brother, Andrew. We were close. He knew of my dream of pursuing a career in medicine and helped me to achieve it—unbeknownst to our father."

"I think it can be rare to have such a brother, one willing to support you in your ambitions in that way. But how could you keep it from your father? And why?"

"Why? Being a physician is not a suitable profession for someone of our class, according to my father. I once suggested it and all he did was laugh, assuming I couldn't possibly be serious."

Persephone well knew what it was like to have a father who did not value her ambitions. "And so?"

"We told my parents that I was going off to manage a small estate up north, one that would constitute my second-son inheritance. The details are not important, but the deception worked. I thought it would continue for some time, but I fear that with Andrew's death I shall soon be unable to sustain it much longer."

"What happened?" Persephone reached a hand out toward Rowe instinctively, as if he was a child who needed comfort. When she realized what she'd done, she turned her gesture into a vague wave toward the chair Rowe had vacated a few moments earlier.

"Six months ago—not long after I'd achieved my licentiate—I'd gone home for a visit and went on the hunt with Andrew. He took a drop fence and misjudged the slope. His horse stumbled and he was thrown and broke his neck."

His words hung in the air. Outside an owl hooted. When the fire settled and sent a spray of sparks into the room, Persephone said, "I am so terribly sorry for your loss. I lost my sister, but long ago."

He whipped his head up and stared at her hard. "Grief is one thing. The other is related to the consequence of that event. Matters have become a bit tangled. I found an excuse to supposedly return to the estate in Northumberland, but my father wasn't happy about it. The steward up in Northumberland knows all and has been sending letters from me—that I send to him from wherever I am. That worked well when I was merely the spare. Now that I am the heir, I am being pressed to return to Bedfordshire. I am not ready to become the scion in training for a noble position. Of what use would that be? But I fear I will have to relinquish my career soon. I had not planned to fall in love, I assure you."

Persephone couldn't help but see the similarities between Sophia and Dr. Rowe. Whatever disagreements they had about medical care, they were cut of the same cloth. "It all seems rather impossible then," she said. "I don't see Sophia simply changing her mind—or making the world and her father believe that was all there was to her decision to end the betrothal. There would have to be a powerful reason."

"I don't expect to find an answer to this difficulty today. I don't know how much time I have, though. Once my father actually locates me, I will have to leave. I have no doubt he will manage to do so. If that happens and this situation is not put to rights I will never see Sophia again. In any event, my father would likely not look favorably on a match with her. Her father is in trade. What do you think of that ironic little twist!"

Ironic indeed. "I cannot believe anyone who knew Sophia could possibly disapprove of her." She said this to comfort Rowe, but yet she doubted it would matter to the earl. She knew that true individual worth was never of as much important as breeding to the aristocracy.

He smiled. "I would brave any disapproval from my father. I am of age, so he cannot forbid me. But that still doesn't solve anything."

"I truly want to help you, but I don't see how I can," Persephone said.

"You have helped me by listening. It's a relief to share my secret."

"I still think you should tell Sophia."

Rowe drilled his gaze into her as though he were trying to glimpse inside her head. "And what of you and James? If we can think of a way to right this wrong, it will benefit all of us."

Persephone couldn't help blushing. "I assure you, I have no pretensions to Mr. Pentarrant's affections."

"I don't believe there's any pretense involved. However, I see that you have decided to deny your own feelings, and if that is what will enable you to come through this with your heart intact, so be it."

Dr. Rowe held out his hand. Instead of shaking hers, he lifted it and kissed her knuckles lightly before giving her a very elegant bow. "Until we next meet, Miss Wilkins."

She saw him to the door, then climbed up to her bedroom. As she washed and brushed her hair, Persephone marveled at all she had heard that evening. He was a viscount. It made complete sense in retrospect. He was also a very talented and dedicated physician. What a travesty that the two identities couldn't coexist in one gentleman. And what a pair he and Sophia would make.

Persephone rubbed her hand where he had kissed it. She couldn't help imagining a different touch there, different lips. But she had no right to such imaginings. Even if he was not betrothed to Sophia, he had made no declaration to her. And yet… Oh it was all such a hopeless tangle! And she—who prided herself on being able to find her way through any situation—could think of nothing that would make everything come to rights. Not just then.

CHAPTER 30

It felt all wrong to be standing there swathed in lengths of silks, ribbons, and lace, Sophia thought. They were measuring and planning for her wedding dress and other wedding clothes, including the lingerie she would wear in the marriage bed. The thought made her heart sink. It would be hard enough to get through the betrothal party tomorrow. Sophia suspected that Eustace Pentarrant had been the architect of that plan.

Oh how she wished she and James could be married privately, and soon. Better to get it over with and settle down to the business of a comfortable, monotonous married life with a man for whom she felt no passion. She would have to bear him children. There was no getting around that.

Her ankle was better—it had been no more than a mild sprain. Still, she avoided going about as much as she could. She couldn't bear the felicitations and the sniggers. It seemed that everyone in the community knew of her supposed compromise. If only she could think of a way of getting back at Philippa! What could she have been thinking? Did she have any idea of the real harm she had caused? What was more, it made no sense. Philippa had been throwing her cap at James Pentarrant ever since the end of her second unsuccessful London season. Why would she thrust him into the arms of someone else?

"Ahem, would you turn around please Miss?" It was Mrs. Martin's assistant, pinning her into the rough muslin pattern pieces of her wedding gown. Sophia refused to wear white. It didn't become her. Instead, she insisted on a somewhat somber dusty blue three-quarter spider gauze overdress with a cream satin dress beneath it. Let the busybodies make what they would of it.

She stood in front of the mirror on the six-inch platform feeling like a child's doll, pins stuck everywhere, ribbons of different colors draped over her shoulder. She was supposed to choose the ones she wanted for her hats.

Marrying like this would take away so much of her. So many of her hopes for the future.

"Sophia."

She pulled her attention back into the dressing room of the only dressmaker in Camelford and saw behind her in the mirror the figure of Persephone. Sophia hadn't had the courage to face her yet, half hoping it would be Persephone who took it upon herself to call so she could explain everything. Now, here they were in a public place. Her friend remained silent, her eyes guarded.

"Persephone?" Sophia turned to face her. The assistant still fluttered around her, pinning and unpinning. "Would you leave us please?" she said in a voice that was sharper than she intended. The girl rose, pins like bristles sticking out from between her compressed lips, curtsied, and left them.

"I wanted to extend my felicitations to you, but..." Persephone began, not quite meeting Sophia's eyes.

"I hear your school has some pupils now. Your dream has come true." She wished she hadn't said that. She and Persephone had never spoken of it, but it had been obvious to Sophia for some time that Persephone was very attracted to James if not actually in love. That, she feared, was Persephone's real dream—or perhaps a dream that complemented the other one. "I'm sorry," Sophia said with no explanation.

"I'm sorry too. For you," Persephone said. "I've tried to understand why you gave into the pressure. It seems so unlike you."

Sophia stepped down from the plinth, trailing the half-pinned fabric of what was meant to be a train. "Ow!" she said as one of the pins dug into her side. "Help me get out of this ridiculous fabrication," she said.

Somehow the absurdity of her appearance broke down a barrier between them and Persephone laughed softly. "Come here and don't wiggle or you'll get stuck again."

It took some doing to get her out of the muslin. After a time they accomplished it though, and Sophia, clad only in her shift, corset, and stockings, searched for the walking dress she'd worn to the fitting. Persephone found it behind a modesty screen and helped Sophia back into it.

"Is your fitting finished? It rather appeared that the girl was in the middle of it all when I saw you."

"They'll have to work with what they have so far. I'm not going to stand for any more of this nonsense. Can we go somewhere and talk? Or perhaps you have come to buy a gown yourself to wear to the party. You are coming, are you not? I don't think I could bear if you're not there."

Persephone said, "I had thought of not going. But I don't want to give the gossips any unnecessary fodder. No new dress for me, however. I've just come into Camelford to buy some calico from the draper's to make clothes for teaching, and to see if the stationer has any more copy books."

"What brought you in here then?"

"I thought I might find you—there's a footman outside in

your family's livery. I've wanted to see you. I just wasn't sure you'd welcome a visit from me."

"I so wanted you to come, but..." Sophia had been longing to talk to Persephone. The entire awkward situation had opened what felt like an unbridgeable gulf between them.

Persephone shrugged. "I couldn't have known. To be honest, I wasn't certain that I would welcome a visit from you." She paused, then said, "He's a good man, you know. I have argued with him about some things, but I think his heart is true and he is genuinely honorable."

Sophia knew that. Otherwise he would not have offered for her. "It's what my father wanted for me from the beginning, before you even came here."

"And by all accounts Eustace Pentarrant is delighted with the arrangement."

Mrs. Martin came back into the dressing room and said, "Will that be all Miss Tresillian? Oh, hello Miss Wilkins." She dipped a tiny curtsy in Persephone's direction, clearly more interested in the lady who would probably become her biggest customer. Sophia had let it be known that she had no intention of going to London or even Bodmin for her finery.

"Yes, whatever you make will be satisfactory I'm sure."

She put her arm through Persephone's, intending to leave the shop with her and go to the inn for coffee, when the door opened and Catherine Pentarrant walked in.

The ladies all greeted one another, but Sophia couldn't help noticing Catherine's pallor. What was she doing in Camelford? A glance through the window revealed her barouche—coachman on the box and footman up behind—and her abigail standing outside. At least she'd come in comfort.

"You see me on a quest," Catherine said. "My husband insists I have a new gown for your party, Miss Tresillian, or some new ribbons." She made an effort at a shaky smile.

"It's Sophia. I thought we'd determined that we were beyond the *miss* phase the last time I saw you." Sophia meant it as a jest, but at that very moment, Catherine staggered and looked as though she were about to collapse.

Persephone and Sophia immediately took her arms and supported her to a chair. "You are not well, Catherine," Sophia said. "What possessed you to come into town?"

She tried again to smile and said, "Eustace thinks I'm making too much of a fuss about little Jillian's birth, that I'm using it as an excuse to be lazy." She lifted her shaking hand to tuck a loose strand of hair under her poke bonnet.

Sophia controlled her anger with a great effort, biting her lower lip to stop herself letting loose a tirade against men who dismissed women's complaints when they could have no idea what they went through every month, let alone in childbed. "Has Dr. Rowe come to see you?" she asked.

"He said it was likely just a nervous complaint, that I must get out and be more active and it would soon go away."

Whatever she thought of Nathaniel Rowe's treatments, Sophia did not think he would have said such a thing to a lady who was clearly unwell. "Did you speak to him honestly? Tell him everything about what you are feeling?" Sophia knew too well that ladies shrank from discussing anything to do with childbirth or their courses with anyone, especially men. Very likely Nathaniel was not fully aware of Catherine's distress.

Sophia met Persephone's concerned eyes. They couldn't just leave the lady to conduct her business in town when it seemed as if she might faint at any moment. "Persephone," Sophia said, "Perhaps you will stay with Catherine and help her with her errands. I am afraid I have an appointment and cannot do so myself."

"An appointment?" Persephone said.

Sophia gave her a significant look. "Yes."

"Oh! Yes, you said as much when I came in. Of course I can accompany Mrs. Pentarrant."

"There's no need to fuss!" Catherine said, but Sophia could see the relief in her eyes knowing that she wouldn't be left alone.

Sophia said to Persephone, "We'll finish our conversation, yes?" her voice rising to a pleading note at the end.

"Of course," Persephone replied, then said to Catherine. "Do you have pressing business in town today? Let me help you with it, then we will go back to your home together."

Sophia took Persephone's arm and whispered in her ear, "Stay at Tarrant Hall until I come, then I shall take you home. Or back here to collect your gig?"

"I walked," Persephone said.

Sophia hurried away, hoping she would find Nathaniel Rowe at his lodgings and not out on a call to tend to a patient. This was too important to wait. At least, that's what she told herself.

"Stay where you are!" she commanded the footman who clearly intended to follow her. "I won't be long."

The fellow, who had been hired too recently to know that Miss Sophia was subject to rather unwise behavior, simply did as he was told.

She had only been there once before, but the location of Nathaniel Rowe's lodgings was stamped on her memory. Hardly aware of how she got there, Sophia soon found herself knocking peremptorily on the door.

She was about to knock again when the landlady opened it, a sour grimace on her puffy face. "There's no need to raise the dead with yer knockin'!" she said before she registered who was standing on her doorstep. "Oh, I beg yer pardon, Miss Tresillian." She bent her knees in the semblance of a curtsy.

"Is Dr. Rowe here? I must see him immediately."

As she finished saying this, the doctor himself stepped halfway out the door that led to his study at the back of the hallway, his eyebrows drawn together in a scowl.

Without waiting to be invited, Sophia pushed past the landlady and marched up to Rowe. They faced each other in tense stillness for a moment before Rowe stepped suddenly aside and gestured for her to enter the room.

He cleared some papers off a chair so she could sit, but she was too agitated to do so and paced back and forth in front of him as she spoke. "I have just come from Mrs. Martin's, where I met Catherine Pentarrant. She said you attended her recently?"

Nathaniel stared at her, his eyes full of questions he wasn't asking. "Eustace called me in a few days ago at Mrs. Pentarrant's insistence. But when I got there to examine her she said there wasn't really anything wrong, that she was just a little tired and not sleeping well."

"Hah!" Sophia said, unreasonable anger boiling up inside her. "Did you ask her to tell you more? To describe to you her exact ills? No. Of course not. Society doctors do not ask the difficult questions of delicately nurtured females."

Dr. Rowe folded his arms across his chest and said, "You cannot make such a judgement if you were not there. In any case, it is none of your affair how I choose to help my patients."

"Not my affair? When someone I care about all but faints at my feet a few weeks after childbirth?"

Rowe let his arms drop and took two steps closer to Sophia. "What? When was this? Where?"

"Moments ago. At the dressmaker's. Catherine has clearly not recovered from her ordeal as yet. Somehow her body has not replenished itself in the usual way. I expect some of that is because she has been pushing herself—or has been pushed—to reenter society as if nothing has happened.

And I don't doubt to take up her wifely duties before she should."

Nathaniel raked his fingers through his hair. "You must appreciate the difficulty of my situation in such cases. She said nothing to me that would have suggested she was not in perfect health."

"You must have examined her."

He said nothing for a moment. "As much as she permitted me."

"Was Mr. Pentarrant in the room?"

Nathaniel said nothing.

Of course he was, Sophia thought, but Rowe was too polite, too cautious to encourage Catherine to say something her husband might not want to hear. She said, "I myself did not examine her, of course, other than noting her extreme pallor and weakness. I fear Mrs. Pentarrant is still bleeding, and should be taking fortifying draughts, not tinctures to help her sleep."

NATHANIEL'S WORLD TILTED ON ITS AXIS A BIT AS HE LISTENED to Sophia and watched her flashing eyes and suffused cheeks. What was this magnificent creature doing betrothed to someone else? He and she were somehow akin, connected in a way that could not be denied.

In fact, the invisible connection was drawing them closer and closer together at that moment. Before he knew it, Nathaniel found himself inches away from Sophia's face as she continued to inveigh about the failures of male doctors to treat women's complaints as they should.

He didn't quite know what came over him, but he could stand it no longer. He reached out for her, grasping her around the waist and stopping her words with a fierce kiss. She stiffened at first, then melted into him, her lips soft and warm. He could feel her heart pounding against his, as if those two organs were attempting to break through their bodies and unite.

After a long, breathless moment, Sophia ended the kiss. She put her hands on his shoulders and then moved them down to his chest. Nathaniel expected her to push him away, but she didn't. Instead, she curled her fingers around his lapels and gazed at the top button of his waistcoat.

"This cannot be," Sophia whispered, at last meeting his eyes. Hers were filling with tears.

Nathaniel bent to kiss them away, but she resisted him. "I'm sorry," he said. "Not sorry I kissed you, but sorry for the way things are. And I'm confused."

At this, she cocked her head to the side. "Surely you know why I had to accept him."

"I know why he had to offer. I don't know why you said yes."

Sophia took a quick step away. "It's complicated. You must simply trust that I had no choice."

"Do you have feelings for him?" he asked, suddenly alive to that possibility. Pentarrant was a handsome man of property. Sophia did not know him, Nathaniel Rowe, as anything other than a country doctor.

"No!" she said. "That is, I respect him. He will be kind, I'm certain." Her voice cracked a little on this last word.

He would be kind, but he would not kiss her the way I have just done. And then he felt guilty, presumptuous. "Is kindness enough to sustain a marriage for your entire life?"

She whirled around, pure distress on her face, her hands clutched together at her waist. "It has to be!" Her anguished words tore at his heart. She drew herself up and said, "But enough. You must go to Tarrant Hall and insist on seeing Catherine Pentarrant."

It took Nathaniel a moment to recall what it was that

Sophia had told him. That kiss had obliterated everything that came before it. "Yes. I will confess to you that I didn't like the cast of Mrs. Pentarrant's complexion when I was there. I suppose I can use that as an excuse to impose my presence on her again."

Sophia once more approached him and grasped his arms, not in a loving way, but with fervent urgency. "Eustace Pentarrant is away for the day. Perhaps without his presence you will be able to perform a more thorough examination and prescribe something for her, even if it is just rest. She needs your help, Dr. Rowe." She said this last with resolve.

"I will prepare to go right away." How he wished he could take Sophia home in his gig! But of course, she must have come to Camelford in her own carriage.

And they must forget this episode had ever happened.

Sophia curtsied quickly and fled from his study before he could murmur his own goodbyes. He would cherish the exquisite pain of feeling of her beautiful lips on his, knowing they never would be so again.

CHAPTER 31

It was clear to Persephone that Catherine Pentarrant was in no frame to spend the afternoon shopping in Camelford. Once Mrs. Martin had given her a cup of tea and she revived a little, Persephone bundled her into her carriage and accompanied her back to Tarrant Hall.

Persephone hadn't been in such a luxurious barouche since she lived at Atherleigh Manor. In fact, this carriage was still more beautifully fitted out, with burgundy velvet squabs, ornate brass fittings, and a crest on the door. As to what the crest represented, Persephone did not know, since the Pentarrants possessed no title. The carriage was drawn by four magnificent matched bays—very high bred—and a liveried footman stood on the back strap. All that was missing was a postilion. The equipage must have cost well over a thousand guineas. Was the family so very wealthy?

With a team to pull them swiftly along the road, it did not take long to reach Tarrant Hall. When they arrived, Catherine drew herself up and walked steadily to the door, held open for them by the butler. "Thank you, Tonkin.

Would you ask Mrs. Cheeping to send tea up to my drawing room?"

Catherine's transformation from a frail woman who could barely stand upright to the majestic lady in command of her domain was remarkable. Persephone saw it for what it was however: an act. Nothing led her to believe that Catherine wasn't feeling extremely unwell still, yet she flashed her serene smile on the servants as they took her hat and cloak and did not falter on her way up the stairs.

Catherine's drawing room was in the family wing on the first floor, connected to her bedroom. As soon as Persephone followed her in and closed the door behind her, Catherine staggered again. She allowed Persephone to settle her on a delicate rose silk-covered divan.

"You must think me a poor creature!" she said, her voice a little shaky.

"Not at all! You have been through a great deal, and only two weeks ago at that. Surely you should rest and marshal your strength."

Catherine raised a carefully plucked eyebrow and said, "Didn't you know that we ladies are supposed to perform our duties with no apparent difficulty? It was so with the boys. I only realize now how fortunate I was then."

Persephone was aware that there were sons, but she knew nothing about them. "Where are your boys?"

"At Eton."

Away at school? Catherine did not look old enough to have children who were ready for that.

"I see your expression. Yes, they are a bit young. John Eustace is ten years old and Grayson is eight. Eustace insisted they go away last year. He wanted to throw them together with boys of the right stamp, he said. And then I was with child again." She said it with a weary sigh just as a light knock on the door announced the arrival of a tray of tea and biscuits.

She pointed to a table and made to rise, but Persephone said, "Let me! I'm accustomed to making the tea."

"Thank you, Miss Wilkins."

"Persephone, I insist. How do you like it? I would suggest you allow me to make it milky and sweet. I find it most refreshing that way."

"As you wish," Catherine said, closing her eyes.

They sat quietly over tea, the only sounds the gentle ticking of the French clock on the mantel and the soft clatter of spoons on porcelain. Persephone wondered if she should offer to read aloud, and whether Sophia would arrive soon with Dr. Rowe.

"I am told that you plan to open a school for the quarry children," Catherine said, surprising Persephone, who thought because her eyes were still closed that she had perhaps nodded off.

"Yes. In fact, I already have a couple of pupils. It's not much, but it's a start."

"Do you really think educating those uncouth raga-muffins could do the slightest bit of good?"

Persephone swallowed the acid retort she wanted to make, realizing that Catherine was probably merely echoing her husband's opinion. "It is my belief that were they able to read and write, they might be a little less uncouth, and be in a better position to contribute to the good of the community in more different ways. Perhaps even become better quarry workers."

Catherine had no opportunity to respond to this, because Tonkin tapped on the door and entered. "Excuse me, Madam. You have a visitor."

Likely the doctor, Persephone thought. But to her

surprise, Lydia Tresize walked into the room. She was the last person Persephone expected to see.

"Catherine!" Lydia said and hastened forward to take the lady's outstretched hands. "I heard in the village that you'd been taken ill, and I thought I'd come and see if there was anything I could do for you."

Persephone's seat over to the side was not in direct view of the drawing room door, and so Lydia did not know she was there until Catherine said, "Are you acquainted with Miss Wilkins?"

Lydia turned a gaze of mixed surprise and consternation to her. Persephone rose and nodded a greeting. "Mrs. Tresize, I am pleased to see you."

"I did not know you were friendly with Mrs. Pentarrant. How do you do." Her voice held a distinct chill.

"Catherine and I are not very well acquainted," Persephone said, "but I happened to be with her when she was taken ill." Lydia stiffened slightly at the sound of Catherine's first name on Persephone's lips, which Persephone had used on purpose. Perhaps that was unworthy of her, she thought. She couldn't deny that Lydia's response to her presence made her want to upset her notion that a former governess was out of place among genteel ladies.

"It was fortunate you were there," Catherine said, her kind tone temporizing Lydia's frostiness.

The drawing room, which was elegantly furnished in apricot and pink silks with green trimmings on gilt-legged chairs and sofas, suddenly felt small, as if there wasn't quite enough air in it for all three of them to breathe. "Perhaps I should go, now that your friend is here," Persephone said to Catherine.

"Must you? I was hoping to get to know you better. I believe James holds you in very high regard."

"I esteem your brother-in-law in return. But I had not

planned to visit this afternoon and have things to do at home. If you will excuse me."

Persephone only just reached the drawing room door when Tonkin opened it again and announced, "Dr. Rowe."

When the doctor entered Persephone could not read his expression. His color was high. In fact, he appeared a bit flustered—not the calm, authoritative professional she had seen him in other similar situations.

More surprising than that, though, was Lydia's reaction to his presence. She opened her eyes wide, took a small step forward, and parted her lips as if to speak. Before she could do so, Dr. Rowe cut her off. "I am so sorry not to have arrived sooner, but I had to hire a job horse to pull my gig. My cob has cast a shoe." He said all this gazing pointedly at Lydia.

They know each other! The realization dawned on Persephone despite the fact that neither of them said so. A quick glance at Catherine showed that she hadn't noticed anything of the kind.

Lydia said to Persephone, "I fear we are in the way here, Miss Wilkins. Perhaps we should both take our leave." She then walked to Catherine and rested a hand on her shoulder. "I shall call on you tomorrow, if I may." After that, she cast a curious glance at Rowe, who barely acknowledged her and turned his attention back to his patient, lifting her wrist and looking at his pocket watch. He studiously avoided meeting either Persephone's or Lydia's eyes.

Tonkin showed both ladies to the door. When they were out on the steps, Persephone gave a slight curtsy to Lydia and said, "Goodbye."

But Lydia reached out a hand to stop her. "Would you permit me to convey you home in my landaulet? Your cottage is a good three miles from here."

This courtesy surprised Persephone, especially since it

was not accompanied by a kind smile. Lydia didn't really want to take her home. "The evening is fine, and I am accustomed to walking," she said. "Please don't trouble yourself."

"That's as may be, but I would very much like to speak with you, and I don't know if another occasion will present itself."

She didn't say it in the manner of someone eager to share confidences, more like a schoolmistress requesting a fractious student to come before her for a dressing down. Persephone could see how Lydia's manner might be intimidating. But not to her. She had endured years of slights and insults from people of her stamp. What could she say to upset her? "Very well. That is most kind."

By then the small carriage had been driven out from the stables by her coachman, who obviously had not had time to partake of the tankard of ale he was no doubt hoping to enjoy while his mistress had a long visit with a friend.

Once they were on their way through the country lanes that threaded the neighborhood, Lydia said, "You perhaps took note of my surprise upon meeting Dr. Rowe in Catherine's house."

"You have not met him before, or had occasion to call him since your return to your father's house?"

"Both I and my father are in robust health and rarely require a physician. But I have some familiarity with him."

Persephone wasn't sure whether to ask the question outright or simply wait for Lydia to offer the information she was clearly so desperate to impart. She opted for silence.

Her patience was rewarded when Lydia said, "You see, although I was not acquainted with Dr. Rowe—we'll continue to call him that for the moment, shall we?—his family is the principal family in Bedfordshire, the location of my late husband's more modest estate."

"If you were not acquainted with him, what leads you to connect him with that family?"

She leaned a little close to Persephone, perhaps to ensure that their conversation could not be heard by the coachman. "I was very well acquainted with his elder brother, who often came to the local assemblies and was quite a favorite with everyone." A shadow of sadness flitted through her eyes. "So very tragic what happened to him. He would have made an exemplary earl. And then his younger brother would have been free to pursue whatever whim he chose."

So, she definitely knew. *Should I tell her I know as well, or pretend ignorance?* "What exactly is your point?"

"You are not surprised, I see. *Dr.* Rowe has confided in you, perhaps. Did you think to add him to your local conquests?"

Persephone stiffened. "I'm sure I don't know what you mean!"

"Well, if what I hear from Miss Vyvyan is true, you had set your cap at James Pentarrant before his betrothal to Miss Tresillian. More to the point, I see that you have managed to captivate my susceptible father."

Ah. So this was her purpose, and no doubt the cause of her barely concealed animosity. Why should she care whether or not her father remarried? Unless, of course, she worried about her inheritance. "Mrs. Tresize, please rest assured that your father and I are hardly likely to become anything more than friendly neighbors. I am grateful for his kindness, but I am also content with my current state." Only a pair of dark blue eyes with a twinkle of humor in them would have the power to make her consider relinquishing that state, and their possessor happened to be engaged to someone else.

"So you say. But I wonder how long it will take you to grow tired of your humble cottage and the dirty urchins who will come to you to learn their letters because they have nothing else to do on a Sunday. Will it take months or only weeks for you to be ripe for accepting any offer that comes your way?"

Persephone heartily wished she had been allowed to walk home. This woman was insufferable! How dare she say such things to her. To anyone! And what could possibly have given her the idea that the squire had any intentions toward her? They hardly knew each other. She longed to say the most biting things, but put a guard on her tongue. It wouldn't due to make enemies in such a small community. Perhaps Lydia Tresize still mourned her late husband and was angry at the world for taking him away from her. More likely was that Philippa—her good friend—had had a hand in provoking Lydia's unfounded animosity.

Persephone took a steadying breath and said, "What do you intend to do about Dr. Rowe?"

"What do *you* intend? A viscount and heir to an earldom would be quite a catch."

Persephone stared open-mouthed at Lydia. "I wish you would believe that I am not on the catch for a husband! In any case, I am some years older than Dr. Rowe, and I assure you, he has no interest at all in me."

Lydia pursed her lips. "So you say. But come, let us not dispute. You asked what I intend to do about my knowledge of Dr. Rowe. I think, for the moment, I will say nothing. It's clear he wants to prove something, the Lord knows why. Perhaps he feels guilty about his brother."

"Guilty about his brother? What do you mean?"

"You don't know?"

Persephone shook her head.

"They were on the hunt together when Andrew—Lord Axeley—had his fatal fall. Those who saw it whisper that

Rowe egged him on to take a jump that his horse couldn't manage."

Could that be true? How would she know? She wasn't there herself. It must be vicious gossip. If so, Lydia Tresize was no better than Philippa Vyvyan. Why should she feel it necessary to say such a terrible thing?

"So I see he didn't tell you that!" Lydia said, a distinct note of triumph in her voice.

Persephone longed to tell Lydia exactly what she thought of her. But to what purpose? "I find it is best not to listen to gossip, especially when one is far removed from the actual event. It appears we are at my cottage. I thank you for taking me up in your carriage, and I wish you a goodnight."

The coachman drew the horses up and Persephone leapt down without waiting for any help or saying another word to Lydia. A frosty, "Good night" sounded at her back just before the horses started up and the carriage wheels crunched over the stony packed dirt.

Poor Nathaniel! she thought. Is this what people thought? Of course there was no question of it being true. Was there? No. He was at heart a doctor. Harming someone, especially someone he loved, would be anathema to him.

More to the point, if Lydia knew about Nathaniel, how soon would word spread? And what would Sophia think? Or perhaps Lydia Tresize planned to wait until after the marriage to reveal Rowe's secret, thus creating the most possible pain and confusion for everyone involved.

Persephone would never understand why people—so often women—found it necessary to be so cruel. She supposed such things happened in all classes. But just then, she was ashamed to think she belonged in a world where Philippa and Lydia existed, and marched resolutely to her front door, eager to scrape all traces of that world off her shoes.

CHAPTER 32

Persephone's blood was as close to boiling as it ever got when she walked into her cottage. "Hannah!" she called. "I'm in very great need of a cup of tea." She really wanted something stronger, but knew that it would not help her to become calmer. Besides, she always had a headache the next morning if she drank brandy.

Hannah hurried out of the kitchen and put her finger to her lips.

"What is it?" Persephone said, curiosity taking the edge out of her voice.

"Let me take your hat and pelisse, ma'am," Hannah said jerking her head in the direction of the kitchen. When she was close enough to receive Persephone's outer garments from her she murmured, "You have a guest. He's in the kitchen."

"A guest?" Persephone whispered. Who could this be? The last thing she needed was any more company. She had hoped to retire to the quiet solitude of her bedchamber, perhaps to read or write a letter. But apparently that was not to be. She drew herself up and gestured to Hannah to lead her on.

When she entered the kitchen a gentleman rose from one of the chairs by the fire and put out his hand as he walked forward to greet her.

The squire! She barely suppressed an ironic smile and said, "Squire Carlyon, how delightful—and unexpected to see you." She put as much warmth into her greeting as she could. Having just received what amounted to a dressing down from his daughter, this required her to call upon all her resources of manners and address.

"Forgive me, Miss Wilkins. I sometimes ride this way of an afternoon, and I thought, why not stop in and pay my respects to you? Your excellent housekeeper said she expected you back at any moment, that you had gone into Camelford to do some shopping."

"Begging yer pardon, ma'am, but you said you was only going to be out for an hour or so."

Persephone told herself she must have a chat with Hannah about whom to admit when she was not at home, but she gave her a reassuring smile. "As I had intended. But I met a few friends and ended up visiting with Catherine Pentarrant."

"Oh?" the squire said. "I believe my Lydia intended to call on her today. They are old friends, as I suppose you know. They attended school together in London. Did you happen to meet her while you were there?"

What should she tell him? After only a moment's hesitation Persephone said, "I did indeed. In fact, Mrs. Tresize was so kind as to convey me home in her carriage. She has just now gone away. I expect by this time she's too far to call back though."

The squire waved a hand dismissively and said, "It was you I most particularly wanted to speak with, if you have a moment?" He turned to smile in Hannah's direction. "And if you will allow me to have some private words with your mistress."

The last thing Persephone wanted was for Hannah to leave her alone with the squire. Something told her she was about to experience an awkward scene. There was nothing for it, however. "You may leave, Hannah. I'll ring if we need you." She and Hannah exchanged a speaking glance.

Once Hannah was gone Persephone sat down, but Carlyon remained standing. She asked him somewhat awkwardly, "Is there some matter you wish to discuss with me, Squire?"

"I wanted to inquire whether you will be in attendance at the grand betrothal ball Mr. Eustace Pentarrant is holding for his brother and Sophia Tresillian Tomorrow."

Ah yes, the ball. Persephone's invitation had been delivered the day before, a knife made of gilt-edged paper that lodged between her ribs as soon as she read it. She had planned to stay away, wanting to spare herself that humiliation. But now, after Sophia's plea to her in Camelford, she felt she had no choice but to attend. This event must be difficult for Sophia as well, and she deserved the support of her friend. "Of course I shall be there."

"Then I hope you will do me the honor of saving the first dance for me."

This was what he had sent Hannah out of the room to ask? Surely Carlyon was beyond the age of dancing or certainly of feeling moved to reserve dances in advance. "Why, yes, if you insist, but I did not think I would dance. I'm not a young girl anymore!" She gave a little laugh meant to lighten the atmosphere, but instead it sounded dry and cynical.

"You are not a young girl, but you are a very attractive woman, Miss Wilkins," the squire said, gazing down at her in a way that held something more than friendly regard and brought heat to Persephone's cheeks.

With what Lydia had said to her still fresh in her mind, Persephone said, "Really, Squire, I think you're paying me Spanish coin!"

"I'm not," he said, and held out his hand to her.

She couldn't ignore it, so she placed hers in his and rose in response to his gentle tug. Carlyon placed his other hand over hers, engulfing it in a strong clasp, and drew her closer. Persephone wanted to hang back but to do so would be rude. She feared what was coming. Perhaps Lydia had been right, had seen something in her father's behavior to make her think he had designs on Persephone.

"I'm not an impulsive man, Miss Wilkins, so this is as surprising to me as I see by your expression it is to you."

"Squire, I—"

"Please, hear me out. I have been a widower these ten years. My daughter has come home to keep house for me, but she is young and I have no doubt will soon be married again." At that he shifted his gaze to examine the kitchen, scanning it thoroughly as though taking its measure. "I imagine this cottage is not the kind of home you are accustomed to. I am familiar with your circumstances and situation with the Ambleton family. I can offer you something a great deal more comfortable than this, more suited to your degree and talents. I imagine you would grace any establishment of which you were mistress."

Persephone's heart was tumbling, her mind flying through thoughts and words—what could she say to him? Was he going to propose? How could she stop him? "You are too hasty, Squire. I am content with my situation, humble though it is."

He reached for her other hand and squeezed them both.

"Indeed, I believe you are a woman of strong enough character to achieve contentment wherever you find yourself. I see that in you. What I am offering you is something that, I hope, would go beyond that to actual happiness."

"What exactly are you offering me?" Persephone asked, suddenly wondering if he intended to offer her a carte blanche. Surely not!

Those fears were put to rest but others aroused when he knelt down before her. "Miss Wilkins—Persephone, if I may—would you do me the honor of becoming my wife?"

"Squire!" she all but shrieked and then said, "I'm sorry. It's just..." His wife! How could she, when her heart was not engaged? She did not love him. She did not know him! And yet, many women—especially those who might be considered to be at their last prayers at the age of over thirty—would leap at such an offer. It was a kind offer. She was a nobody. Of good enough family, but nothing of distinction, whereas he was the squire, the master of the hunt, and gentry from many generations back. When she could at last command her voice, again she said, "You are too kind, Squire, and I am truly honored by your proposal." She gently drew her hands out of his and walked a little away from him. "This has come as a great surprise, I'm sure you understand."

He hoisted himself up and dusted off his knees. "Of course. We have not known each other long. But we are both at the time of life when it would be unwise to overlook an opportunity for companionship. For more than that. Do you not want children? Surely this scheme of yours to start a school is nothing more than a means of satisfying your motherly instincts."

Is that what he thought? That she was a lonely spinster trying to justify her existence? That she was so desperate for children she would have them vicariously through her school? She felt the stirrings of anger in her breast, and fought to suppress them. He likely had no idea he'd said something offensive. And after all, perhaps there was some truth in it. Although she did not believe that marriage and children was always the pinnacle of a woman's expectations, she was finding it difficult to see exactly what her place in the world should be. As to falling in love and living happily ever after—at her age the idea was laughable.

Yet that is exactly what had happened. The falling in love part, anyway. She had in truth fallen in love with James Pentarrant—wholly and completely, without wanting to, without trying to, without any expectation of doing so.

And in a few weeks that solid, dependable, kind, disturbingly attractive man would marry someone else. He would marry the girl he'd been destined for before Persephone moved to Delabole. He would be unhappy, her heart told her. But he might end by being content. Sophia is an intelligent, beautiful young lady. They might deal well together.

Could she marry the squire and settle for a useful life filled with friendship but not love? Perhaps that was what she truly deserved, not to experience that stirring of passion that arose in her at the sight of James Pentarrant.

The squire had continued to gaze at her fixedly as she tried to think of something to say to him. She smiled as warmly as she could. "As I said, I thank you. But I cannot give you an answer, not now. This is too sudden, as I'm sure you must appreciate."

He held out his hand again. She couldn't ignore it, and so placed hers in his meaty grasp. "Of course you may have a little time to think it over. It's an important decision. But I can't help feeling we are meant to form this comfortable alliance."

The squire bowed over her hand and planted a light kiss on her knuckles. Persephone had the urge to snatch her hand away and rub it off on her skirt as soon as he was no longer looking at her, but she didn't.

Hannah walked back in, clearly bursting to know what had transpired.

"Oh Hannah, I have had a day you would not believe." She sat down and leaned on her hand.

"Did squire offer for ye?"

Persephone's head jerked up and she said, "What made you say that?"

Hannah shrugged. "There's not but one reason I can think on as would make a single gentleman desire private speech with such as you, young and pretty as you are."

"Pretty? Young?" That was too much. "I simply don't see it. And you might as well know, since no doubt you'd find out tomorrow through whatever connections you have that he did indeed offer for me."

"Did ye accept him?"

"I didn't give him an answer. It's all so sudden, and I just don't know."

Hannah boldly took the chair opposite Persephone and reached for her hand. "I see what's occurred wi' you and Miss Tresillian and Mr. James. It's a right old mess, but I don't see no way out of it. If I was you, I'd marry squire. This life isna fer the likes of you." She swept her arm around in a gesture that encompassed the entire room. "Ye're too good fer it. Mr. James knowed it, and it's a cryin' shame what happened, but it's best to pick up the pieces and put yer life together as fitty as you can. There now, Miss."

Hannah held out a cambric square and dabbed at Persephone's cheeks which, to her own surprise, were wet with tears. She smiled through them and took the handkerchief. "I'm no watering pot. I shall be well, Hannah."

After a welcome cup of sweet tea and one of Hannah's biscuits, Persephone made her way slowly up the steep stairs to her bedroom. Try as she might, she could not picture herself as mistress of Carlyon Grange. But perhaps, she thought, after a night's sleep, she might feel differently.

CHAPTER 33

Sophia raced out of the building that contained Dr. Rowe's lodgings so fast that she hardly knew where she was. She took two wrong turns—difficult in so small a town as Camelford—before she finally arrived at the livery stable to reclaim her horse and gig. And then, when the stableboy brought Galahad and the gig around, she stared at it uncomprehending until he said, "Miss?" and she let him help her into it.

Fortunately, Galahad was well acquainted with the route from Camelford to Tresillian Manor, and they arrived home without mishap. It was no thanks to her, she thought. Her mind was so disordered and confused that she couldn't keep two thoughts in it and kept going over and over what she and Nathaniel had said to each other, what they'd done.

That kiss.

Every time she thought of it her face burned and she swore her heart would beat its way out of her chest. What had possessed her to go to him in his lodgings, where he was bound to be alone? She should have known. She should have known that it wouldn't be enough for her to simply alert him to Catherine Pentarrant's genuine indisposition. She must secretly have wanted exactly what happened. They had not been entirely alone since the last time she visited him there, and certainly not since her betrothal to James.

And that kiss.

She could never have imagined what it would be like. All the novels she read, all the whispered confidences between friends—none of it prepared her for the rush of sensations that went from her lips down into her very core. She should have pushed Nathaniel away, but she didn't. Instead she returned his kiss with all the pent up passion she'd been trying to bury in her heart. Now the guard was off, she was thoroughly pixie led. Perhaps that is what happened out on the moor, in the mist. All she wanted was to stay with Nathaniel in that humble apartment, away from the world, in a magical bubble where reality didn't exist. She wanted to kiss him again, to feel his arms around her and lose herself in his smoldering eyes.

Wicked girl! But why wicked? Could love be wicked? Surely the only wicked thing was turning one's back on the truth. In the face of what she now fully understood, how could she think of marrying James Pentarrant? Must she truly sentence herself to a lifetime of unhappiness because of someone's mistaken interpretation of something that had happened when she was injured and ill?

No. Her heart told her she could not. It couldn't be. Surely her father would see that. He must. It was no small thing, one's future. And it wasn't just her future. It was James's and Persephone's—and Nathaniel's.

Nathaniel. She'd never uttered his name aloud, yet there it was, stamped on her heart. Did he feel the same as she did? Had he murmured her name to himself in the still of the night? He must love her as much as she loved him. He would never have kissed her like that if he didn't. Would he?

Doubts began to nibble at her. Perhaps he would think her fast, a hoyden. Perhaps he was accustomed to kissing ladies that way—a thought that made her burn with sudden jealousy. If that was so, she would prefer to remain single than marry where her heart was not engaged, where she had no hope of ever being kissed like that again.

So ran Sophia's thoughts as Adler fussed around her in her bedchamber, helping her out of her day dress and into an evening gown of cerulean silk trimmed with scallops of ivory Mechlen lace. While her abigail brushed her golden hair until it gleamed and arranged it in becoming curls, Sophia stared at herself unseeing in the dressing table mirror. Who was that girl looking back at her? What did she really want? She didn't know that for certain, but she was now utterly sure about what she did not want. She did not want her life to be over before it began, to be forced into the role of wife and elide into the static society of Camelford.

There was so much more waiting for her in the years to come, even if she couldn't say exactly what. She was meant to be more than a wife and mother. Her knowledge could contribute materially to the health of the women in the community. She cared deeply about her fellow creatures and was committed to all she'd learned through her own study and Mattie Davy's mentorship. Only now, she didn't want to do it alone. She wanted to be connected soul to soul with someone who understood. She wanted to experience true passion, to live over and over again the feeling that had passed through her like a shooting star when Nathaniel kissed her. The thought of not having that possibility opened a chasm in her heart wider than the quarry itself. What did it matter that he was only a country physician? It might matter to her father, true, but she would have to persuade him that her happiness was more important than considerations of social rank. More, that her very life depended on being with Dr. Nathaniel Rowe forever.

"Would Miss like to where the sapphire ear bobs? Or the pearls?"

Adler's voice broke into her thoughts and she looked around at her elegant apartment as if she'd been transported there magically from the other side of the world. "I think the pearls."

Time to come back to earth from whatever heavenly region she had glimpsed that afternoon. Soon dinner would be announced. I shall tell father, she thought, this very evening. He was doing better. He seemed to have revived considerably in recent days and his old energy appeared to be returning.

Sophia took a deep breath and accepted the spangled fan and shawl of Norwich silk Adler handed to her. All the way down to the dining room she rehearsed her speech to her father, growing more and more anxious with every step, worrying that she wouldn't be able to put her conviction into words.

But when Hosking opened the drawing room door to admit her, two voices reached her ears. Her father was not alone. She didn't know they were to have a guest at dinner.

Pasting on her most practiced smile, Sophia walked in with her hand out to greet Eustace Pentarrant.

"You look charmingly," Eustace said, taking her hand and lifting it to his lips after sweeping his appreciative gaze over her from her head to her hem.

"As do you," Sophia said, knowing it wasn't the response a gently bred lady was supposed to give to such a comment. If she were to behave properly she should blush and lower her eyelids and become a little tongue tied.

I am never tongue tied, she thought, and smiled. "To what do we owe this pleasure?" she asked.

He colored up a little and said, "Eustace and I had some business to discuss, and so I invited him to stay to dinner. Might as well get to know your prospective brother-in-law!"

"Of course. We will be seeing him tomorrow evening as well, however." Sophia soon realized that she would be unable to discuss anything with her father before that fateful event. This evening was out of the question now, and he spent his days closeted with his man of business or his steward, or riding out around his property, now that he again felt more himself. In any case, even if she did manage to tell him what was in her heart, it would be too late to call off the grand ball Eustace had planned to celebrate the alliance of his brother with an heiress.

Sophia also thought she ought to inform James first of all. Perhaps she would ride over to his house in the morning. Now that they were "officially" engaged, no one would take much exception to their being alone together.

But the next morning, events continued to thwart her plans. By the time she reached Pentarrent Lodge, the servant —for he hardly looked like a butler—informed her that his master had already left for the quarry.

"Do you expect him back soon?" Sophia asked.

"No ma'am," the servant said. "He's like to stay out all day until the last minute before he must dress for t' party at Hall."

That would never do. She thanked the fellow and rode slowly home. She would have to think of something else. And then she realized how close to Persephone's cottage she was. Indeed, less than a mile lay between the two houses. She turned Penny in that direction. She would tell Persephone and ask her to advise her on how to go about untangling the hopeless mess that Philippa Vyvyan had caused.

Thank heavens for her wise, kind friend.

. . .

But it seemed to Sophia that no matter what she did, the gods would conspire against her that morning. She arrived at Persephone's cottage to find Philippa Vyvyan's smart landaulet outside, the horses tied to the post, her coachman nowhere to be seen. Her only hope was that Philippa would be leaving soon and she could have a private word with Persephone.

She rode Penny to the barn that served as a stable. Bobby, the lad of all work, came trotting out and took the reins from her. Penny was hardly winded and not sweating at all—Sophia had ridden to her destinations at a contemplative pace—and the mare still itched for more exercise. She supposed Bobby was capable of managing the feisty roan, judging by the smile on his face as his eye roamed over the horse's excellent points.

"Has Miss Vyvyan been here long?" Sophia asked.

"No, Miss," Bobby said. "She just come in her carriage not ten minutes afore."

Damn! Sophia was so vexed she nearly uttered the curse aloud. She wanted to simply remount and head back to the manor, avoid seeing Philippa altogether, but the lady's shrill voice sailed out from the open window.

"I say! It's the celebrated Miss Tresillian. I would think you'd be at home preparing for this evening's festivities, making yourself beautiful."

As she walked up to the front door—now held open by Hannah—Sophia said, "Oh, it only takes a few minutes for that." It was a nasty quip, but honestly, Philippa was insufferable.

In a few moments she was sitting with Persephone and Philippa at the large table in the cottage's roomy kitchen. It had become yet more comfortable and home-like since she'd last been there—new curtains at the windows, cushioned chairs near the hearth, a hooked rug. It suited Persephone, she thought. But so would a home like Pentarrent Lodge, with its air of having been lived in and loved in for centuries. And James had certainly not seemed eager to leave it for the grander, more luxurious Tresillian Manor as her father wished, so would no doubt be happy to be able to stay in his family's ancient residence.

"What brings you so far from your home, Philippa?" Sophia asked as Hannah placed a cup of tea in front of her.

"I came to offer to collect Persephone in my carriage for this evening's ball," Philippa said.

Sophia suspected that Persephone had been planning not to go at all, given what she expected of the evening. Philippa would have made it impossible for her to make that choice. No doubt the busybody was well aware of that and looking forward to Persephone's discomfiture. But there was yet something Sophia could do to rescue Persephone from the necessity of hearing Philippa's poisonous prattle to and from Tarrant Hall. "Have you forgotten?" she said, raising her eyebrows at her friend, "We had already agreed that my father and I would convey you there in our carriage."

The fleeting look of relief in Persephone's eyes reassured Sophia that she had guessed correctly. "Yes, of course. Stupid not to recall."

"The guest of honor stopping to take on passengers? It's most irregular," Philippa said with a little titter.

Sophia smiled blandly at her. "We don't hold ourselves up so high that we wouldn't offer to help a neighbor when it is clearly necessary. Besides, you would have to go well out of your way to fetch Persephone, whereas for us it is directly on our route."

Defeated, Philippa simply lifted her teacup to her lips. Not daunted for long, she said, "I understand from my dear friend Lydia Tresize that the two of you helped Catherine when she became unwell in Camelford. It was fortunate you were there. She told me that she found Persephone at Tarrant Hall when she arrived, but you, Sophia, were otherwhere. Perhaps you went to fetch the doctor? Our estimable Dr. Rowe, that is." She put her finger next to her nose and pinched her lips together as if holding in some special knowledge that was bursting to come out.

Sophia struggled not to blush as she remembered exactly what she had been doing at the time Philippa referred to. Still, none of those involved—Catherine, Persephone, or Lydia—would have any reason to know about what had passed between her and Nathaniel. So why was Philippa making such a face? What tantalizing secret did she think she possessed that somehow had to do with Rowe? She would not ask. She had long ago vowed never to be caught in one of Philippa's gossip traps. In her eagerness to seem the bearer of privileged information she so often got things completely wrong and caused endless trouble.

"I came simply to let you know that we would call for you at seven," Sophia said to Persephone. She tried to convey that it wasn't at all the reason she was there, that she had something else important to tell her, but with Philippa listening, she dared not be too obvious.

For an excruciating half hour, Sophia listened to Philippa's incessant stream of malicious nothings, wishing every moment that she would take herself off. Poor Persephone!

At last, Sophia could bear it no longer and rose. "I think we have kept Persephone from her chores long enough, don't you?"

"And," Persephone said, "Unlike Sophia, I need all the time I can find to beautify myself for such a splendid occasion." The ring of irony was not lost on Sophia.

As if suddenly noticing the time, Philippa clapped her

hands together. "I say! Of course. We will be seeing each other again this evening in any case."

If only, Sophia thought, Philippa's horses would throw shoes, or her coachman come down with the ague—anything to prevent her from being at Tarrant Hall later.

But, as she knew, fate had decided to be unkind to her that day, and none of that would happen.

Bobby helped her into the saddle while Philippa's coachman—who had likely wandered off to smoke a pipe—saw Philippa into her carriage.

"See you this evening!" Sophia called over her shoulder to Persephone, who stood in the doorway waving and smiling bravely.

CHAPTER 34

Work. Only work could distract James from the endless circle his mind insisted on plodding around as he felt his future being taken out of his hands. For the past two weeks, he had ventured early to the quarry and stayed until the light was gone and most of the workers had returned home. He used the preparations for blasting to reveal the new rock face as an excuse to decline every invitation, including from Tresillian. Apparently, Sophia's father had been gaining strength, heartened by the realization of his hopes and plans for his daughter, and professed himself eager to get to know his prospective son-in-law.

It did not surprise James that no such wish had been expressed by Sophia. He wondered if they might eventually find solace in their mutual disappointment. At least he could escape to the noisy, dusty world of the quarry whenever he wanted. Sophia would be forced to fill a role in Camelford society that it was clear she had no desire to fill.

James's wish to escape to work was aided by the fact that Eustace wanted the new terrace to be dug out as soon as possible. His brother didn't seem to realize, as James did, that if the upper terraces weren't widened and made free of debris before any excavation began to deepen the quarry—at the same time taking care to channel the ground water away—no one working on the new terrace would be safe. It was his responsibility to make sure there were no tragic accidents. Not again.

At the end of every day James's muscles screamed with painful fatigue. But he welcomed the pain. The work was dangerous and required his complete concentration. He welcomed that too. Anything to stop him thinking, to stop him imagining Persephone Wilkins's soft, intelligent eyes, alight with laughter or flashing with indignation; her unconsciously graceful movements; the way she had of knitting her brow in concentration as she thought over some vexing question. Try as he might, he couldn't picture Sophia Tresillian in her place. The girl was a beauty, yes, but so young, so temperamentally unsuited to him.

Of course, Eustace didn't see it. If he did, he didn't care. All he cared about was the alliance that would secure the quarry's future—at least for a while—and the new terrace. The day after James had rescued Sophia from the moor, Eustace gave him two weeks to prepare for blasting. Those two weeks were now elapsed, and by James's reckoning, they were still at least another two weeks away from when it would be safe to place the explosives. What had taken the extra time was the fact that the quantity of rubble deposited above the proposed new face as the delvers guided the slate blocks to the terrace beds turned out to be much greater than James had anticipated.

Eustace's answer when he told him this was to tell him just to make everyone work faster and longer hours or put more men onto the job, but that wasn't possible. They had as many workers as the space allowed in safety on the narrow benches, and most were opting to stay and work well past the normal six in the evening stopping time. Besides, rushing —well, rushing something like this was a recipe for disaster.

The morning of the engagement ball James persuaded Eustace to come to the quarry so he could show him what he meant and persuade him to let the process take whatever time it took.

"Has Bray shown you the progress, and explained that we aren't yet ready to start the new terrace?" James asked as Eustace climbed up the final ladder to the rim and brushed slate dust off his pantaloons.

"I hardly call this progress. You've known for weeks that we needed to dig more."

Bray climbed up and stood next to Eustace. "I've showed him that rich seam, or the top of it leastways. It's waitin' fer us. No reason we can't get started."

James bit his tongue. Bray knew better than that. How dare he pander to Eustace's uninformed counsel! "All the same, we will not begin the work, not until I say we're ready. I am the quarry captain."

"And I am the head of the family and principal shareholder," Eustace said.

That was the truth. Could Eustace not see that none of that mattered here? The quarry was the boss. The conditions in the pit would dictate how quickly they could proceed. But Eustace didn't understand. He had always been content to let James run the actual works. It was pointless to try to make him see it. He would believe whatever suited him best.

"Come, brother! Let us not quarrel on this of all days. You need to be presentable for the big celebration this evening."

James looked down at his smirched and dusty clothes, his scraped-up hands. "Don't worry. I'll bathe." But he should leave soon if he was to arrive at the party on time. To do otherwise would be disrespectful to Sophia.

He stayed to watch Eustace march off in his now-scuffed hessians to climb into the barouche that awaited him just beyond the limit of the quarry. The gold braid of the coachman's and footman's livery glinted in the sun. So much waste, James thought. No amount of finery would ever make Eustace the grand personage he wished to be.

It was in a contemplative mood that James made his way back to the Lodge to prepare for the evening. On his way, he passed by the fallow field where his groom often let the horses out to pasture on fine days. That day, his own hack, Arrow, shared the field with the chestnut mare. James sighed, remembering the day he bought her on a rash impulse after seeing the glow in Miss Wilkins's eyes when the mare entered the auction ring.

Since then, matters had gone completely out of his control. What was he to do with her? Perhaps he should simply sell her, now that a future with Persephone Wilkins was impossible. He didn't have the heart to give her to Sophia, who was an excellent rider but had her own spirited roan. It simply seemed tragic not to find a way to make sure Persephone had this beautiful beast for her own. Yet such gifts to a lady who was neither a relation nor a fiancée were improper.

Yet what should propriety have to do with it? Persephone was a grown woman. She had been in and of the world. If she did not want to accept such a gift from him, she need only refuse it. But he would not pretend he'd never wanted her to have the chestnut. The question was how to make this gift without giving her an easy way to refuse it.

He had an idea. It was bold, but the best he could think of

in the moment. He went into the lodge to prepare for that evening's party. Before he left, he would instruct his groom about his plan. After that evening little else would matter anyway, and no one but he and Persephone need know where the chestnut came from.

CHAPTER 35

I should have stayed away, Rowe thought, soon after he arrived at Tarrant Hall on the evening of June first. What had caught his eye was Sophia seated next to her father. He couldn't set his eyes on her even from across the room without recalling the sweet feeling of her lips pressed to his, her body wrapped in his embrace. He wanted her, he desired her with his whole heart and soul. But he could not have her. James Pentarrant was to have that honor. Nathaniel derived some comfort from the fact that he was a man worthy of respect.

When her eyes finally met his, her face lit up with warmth. He'd half expected her to be furious with him for having kissed her so ruthlessly the other day, but there was no sign of that in her expression. Could it be that she truly did love him as he loved her? He was certain that she did not disdain his regard. What use was that certainty, though, when it gave him such exquisite pain? They could not be together. She was lost to him.

"She is lovely, is she not? My brother is a fortunate man." Eustace Pentarrant had come over to Nathaniel to stand a little behind him, forcing him to turn away from Sophia.

"Yes," he said. "Yes he is."

"The match may have come about rather quickly in the end, but it was some time in the making. Her father and I had long ago agreed that an alliance between our family and the Tresillians would be most desirable."

Nathaniel said, "Is that all she is to you? A bargaining piece in an alliance?"

Eustace lifted one corner of his mouth in a cynical half smile. "That's all any marriage is at bottom." He let his hand fall heavily on Nathaniel's shoulder. "I daresay we can find someone who will be the best helpmeet for you in your work. Someone practical yet still acceptable to your family. Not afraid of hard work. Miss Wilkins would be ideal, I should think. She's well enough born."

Shaking Eustace's hand off his shoulder Nathaniel said, "I am quite capable of knowing my own heart and deciding my future in a way that will constitute my own happiness, thank you. And my family's opinions do not enter into the matter."

Eustace pursed his lips, a sly glint in his eye. "Do they not? Still, I advise you not to set the schoolteacher aside. She's quite lovely when she's not frowning or dressed in any of her dowdy clothes. Best get in there before the squire cuts you out. Or is it you yourself who thinks she is not quite up to your weight?" Eustace nudged him and winked. "Then again, the Tresillians are tainted by trade, which I imagine wouldn't do at all in your family."

"What?" He knows, Nathaniel thought, furious. How could he? Damn him!

At that moment, Persephone passed by on the arm of Squire Carlyon. She flicked her eyes to him, opening them wide as if sending him a message. Did she want him to rescue her? But why? In default of James Pentarrant, the handsome, affluent squire would be a good choice for Miss Wilkins. He was a little old, but not so that it would really matter. Nathaniel wondered idly whether Persephone would accept the squire if he offered for her. As to Eustace's suggestion that she would do for him—it was patently absurd. They were mere friends. He liked Persephone, but cherished no warmer feelings for her and he was certain it was the same for her with regard to him.

Still, how was he going to bear it when Sophia was wed? Perhaps he would give up this pretense of being a country doctor and go home to his father, let him train him up to take his place at the head of the family, go to London for another season and suffer all the matchmaking mamas to fling their daughters at him. But that was unfair. What else could a lady do but find a suitable husband? As Sophia had pointed out to him almost the first time they met, ladies did not have the option of training to take up an honorable profession.

Honorable. How honorable had he been not to say who he really was when he came among these people? At that moment he wasn't sure why he'd done anything, what had led him to this place at this time.

Be that as it may, here he was. And he must learn to bear it.

SQUIRE CARLYON HADN'T ATTENDED THE ROSCARROCK BALL. He generally did not participate in the local society events. Although untitled, his was the oldest family in the district, and he held himself somewhat aloof from those who were newly arrived and engaged in trade rather than working the land.

So why was he here, James wondered? He might not have

noticed his presence except that to his amazement he'd seen him deep in conversation with Persephone Wilkins. The squire did not act like a politely disinterested acquaintance, but someone genuinely interested in her. How did she know him? For how long had they been acquainted? What circumstances might have thrown them into each other's path?

The sight threw James off balance. It was so wholly unexpected. The squire's expression spoke of more than distant friendship. James knew he should just let it pass, but he couldn't. He had to know what the squire's intentions were with regard to Persephone, and hers toward him. Who might know? Eustace? Or Catherine? Before he could seek out either of them to inquire if they knew anything about a friendship between Carlyon and Persephone, Miss Philippa Vyvyan tapped her fan on his arm.

"You naughty man!" she said, a wicked little smile on her lips. "Everyone's been looking for you."

"By everyone do you mean Eustace?" James said without bothering to greet her politely. This lady had much to answer for.

She tittered. "No, of course not! I was speaking of Sophia. Your fiancée has been besieged by so many gentlemen I don't doubt that her dance card is already full. You should have arrived early if you hoped to stand up with her at all. And Miss Wilkins, too. I recall you danced with her several times at the Roscarrock ball. At that time, however, you were not affianced. I see the squire has been speaking with her. Frankly, I find his interest in a dowdy governess inexplicable."

James said nothing, only glaring down into her eyes.

She had the decency to blush, then spread her fan and waved it vigorously in front of her face. "You are, of course, entitled to your own opinion."

"Do you know something about Miss Wilkins and the

squire? You seem so well informed about everyone in Camelford," James said through gritted teeth.

Rather than taking this as the insult James meant it to be, Miss Vyvyan stood a little straighter and her smile widened. "Why, yes! My good friend Mrs. Tresize—the squire's widowed daughter, you know—has confided to me that she is somewhat anxious that her father is considering a very unfortunate alliance, one that is well beneath him." She leaned toward James and raised her fan to hide her mouth, whispering, "You have probably guessed that I mean Miss Wilkins. How unsuitable that would be!"

The squire? Offer for Persephone? Surely it could have not come to that already. "But he is a great deal older than Miss Wilkins."

Philippa tsked. "When you are on the shelf as she is, it doesn't matter how much older your husband is. It is far better than being a spinster," she said on a sigh.

"Will you excuse me, Miss Vyvyan? I see my brother and I must speak to him."

James gave her a curt bow and strode off before she could say anything else. He had no intention of seeking out Eustace. Hardly knowing why, he decided he must talk to Persephone. He would wait for the squire to be distracted by some other acquaintance and then go to her. He must do this now, before the dancing started and she became occupied with her many partners, as she had been at the Roscarrock ball. He stewed and fretted inwardly, watching the guests still arriving and forming and reforming little conversation groups. Still the squire monopolized her. Did she want him to? And what right had he himself to interfere in her life? He had no right, yet he could not let her make such a mistake. Surely he wasn't being selfish. He was not the sort of man to think that if he couldn't have her she must not belong to anyone else. Was he?

The image of Rowena flashed through his mind in all her wild loveliness. He recalled all too vividly the stab of pain he felt upon hearing that she had not only rejected him, but chose to remove herself far away and into another man's household. He swore never to live through such a nightmare again. But this case was not the same. He never offered for Persephone. They had never declared any intentions to each other. It was his actions alone that drove her away and rendered any possibility of intimacy between them the merest chimera. *I have no right.* So why did he feel so compelled to speak to her? Perhaps it was because he knew Persephone would suffocate in Squire Carlyon's world. The starched up fellow would certainly curtail any of her ambitions to teach. He would mold her into a role that James was certain would make her unhappy. She would take her place as mistress of Carlyon Grange, manage the household, and entertain the local worthies. He would no doubt want to have more children. A son. James forced himself to picture Persephone in that role, and failed.

No matter how hard he tried, the image that came to his mind was Persephone standing at his side at Penterrent Lodge.

At last, the squire's daughter claimed him and led him away to talk to Catherine. Just as James took a step toward Persephone, Eustace arrived at his side.

"Where have you been?" Eustace asked, a smile on his lips but venom in his voice.

"Doing my job. I was at the quarry most of the day until I was forced to leave so I could prepare for this farce."

Eustace glared at him. "I see you mooning over that interfering schoolteacher. Don't think I'm so naive. All I can say is that thank heavens you're in no position to make another ill-advised alliance. Since you're both of age, no one could prevent you."

James, who had barely attended to his brother, now snapped his head around to look at him. "What are you referring to?"

"Oh come now, Jamie! You don't seriously think that ambitious little Rowena would have willingly set you aside without some inducement."

James clutched Eustace's lapel. "What did you do? Or was it father?"

Eustace peeled James's fingers off his lapel and flicked a languid hand down it to remove invisible creases. "It was a long time ago, brother. Let's leave it at that, shall we?" He then greeted a bejeweled matron who had just arrived. "Ah! Lady Batchelder! How wonderful to see you."

Of course Eustace just walked away. As he walked away from anything difficult or unpleasant. His revelation was infuriating but somehow not surprising. Why did he not know of this before? He always suspected something, but something kept him from inquiring too closely. At that age, newly taking on the responsibilities of adulthood, perhaps he had been too insecure of himself, or not wanting to believe that those who supposedly cared for him would do something they knew would make him unhappy. How stupid he had been! Was Rowena persuaded? Or threatened? The late Archibald Pentarrant held complete control over the lives of the quarry workers. It would not have shocked James to learn that he'd made it impossible rather than undesirable for Rowena to stay true to him.

And now, Archibald was about to have his way again, from beyond the grave, through the instrument of his eldest son. The gossip about Miss Tresillian and himself could not have spread so convincingly without Eustace's help, he was certain.

Well, without knowing precisely how he would bring it

about, James determined that Eustace would not be able to take his future away from him again.

James resolutely crossed the saloon to talk to Persephone.

SOPHIA HAD NO CLEAR RECOLLECTION OF AGREEING TO anything, but she glanced down at her dance card and saw every slot filled—and James Pentarrant's name was not there. He had arrived a little late and remained talking to Eustace rather than joining in any of the festivities. Talking—more like arguing. Was he, too, planning an attempt to get out of the betrothal? But he couldn't. Men didn't cry off. It wasn't done. They could be sued for breach of promise. Why that didn't apply when ladies changed their minds Sophia had no idea. In any case, he disappeared soon after that.

Courage, she thought. She knew she was about to do something that would earn her condemnation in the eyes of society and distress her father deeply. She didn't care what the busybodies like Philippa Vyvyan would have to say, but her father was another matter. She could only hope he was strong enough to weather the coming storm, and that his concern for her happiness would reconcile him to her choice.

As to what would happen after the deed was done, well, the look in Nathaniel's eyes had said it all. It banished any doubts she had that he felt as she did. He was not trifling with her. She wished she'd had an opportunity to tell him what she intended, not leave him in a state of hopeless dejection—for she couldn't help seeing it in his eyes, even from across the room. Where was he now? What if he'd gone away? Perhaps that wouldn't be such a terrible thing for that evening at least. It might not be very politic to reveal their attachment on the same evening she jilted Pentarrant.

That was the important thing, what she needed to focus on. If only she could have done it before the party! But circumstances had conspired against her.

Her papa said there would be a toast before the dancing began. She would be expected to be the center of attention along with James. Everyone would be quiet. That was the right moment—before the toast, of course.

But James—she had to find a way to tell him first. This must not come as a surprise to him, however much as he might welcome it. He must be seen to agree with her, to be willing to relinquish his claim on her. He would, of course. Of that she had no doubt.

"If you will excuse me for a moment," she said to the young man who had come up to talk to her—and whose name she was having a hard time remembering. He bowed to her but she hurried off too quickly to acknowledge it.

A casual survey of the saloon did not reveal James. Eustace was there, at the center of a group that included her father, of course. Eustace kept glancing around distractedly, and his fixed smile did nothing to hide the vexation in his eyes at his brother's absence.

The other person who had disappeared from the company, Sophia suddenly realized, was Persephone. Perhaps she, too, had fled, unequal to the trial of seeing the betrothal of the man she loved celebrated so publicly.

Sophia ran to the ballroom—still empty as the dancing wouldn't begin for a while yet—and through the other saloons on that floor. James wouldn't have gone upstairs to the family wing, she thought, so she ran down to the ground floor where she knew she would find a breakfast parlor, the drawing room that had been given over to hats and cloaks, and the library.

Standing in the entrance hall, she turned in a circle, listening. A moment later she heard voices: hushed, urgent, coming from behind a closed door that she thought was likely the library. She crept closer. A male and a female voice, and they were arguing.

"You can't marry him!" It was James Pentarrant.

"You have no right to say that," said Persephone in a shaking voice. "You are a married man in all ways but one."

"Persephone!"

A pause.

"No!" she cried. "That is unworthy of you. This cannot be."

Sophia could stand it no longer, rapped quickly on the door then threw it open.

James had his arms around Persephone and her hands were on his chest, pushing him away but without conviction. They saw her at the same moment and broke apart as if someone had poured a bucket of cold water on them.

"Forgive me!" Sophia said and raced forward, taking a hand of each of them. "I am glad I found you both here. "Persephone, you must not marry anyone but James."

"But!—"

"And James, by the end of this evening you will be free to marry whomever you wish, and I sincerely believe that would be Persephone."

"How?—"

"I am going to make it right. I don't care how much it distresses anyone or upsets their plans. It was wicked of me not to face my father's displeasure from the outset and decline your honorable offer, James."

By now the two of them were staring at her open-mouthed. "You can't mean it, Sophia. Think of your father!" Persephone took Sophia's hand in both of hers. "I am not angry with you. You behaved as you thought you ought."

"You should be angry! I was weak and foolish. I allowed myself to care too much what people thought of me."

James shook his head. "It's too late. The banns, the contract."

"But we are not married yet, and will never be so."

"What are you planning to do?" Persephone asked, sinking into an armchair.

James let go of Sophia's hand and went to Persephone, standing by her and resting a hand on her shoulder. Both of them kept their astonished, confused eyes on Sophia.

She said, "Come with me. We will go upstairs. I think Eustace has been looking for you, James, and I know my father will be wondering where I am. The dancing is soon to begin but first there will be a toast. I shall announce my decision then. It will be much easier for me if both of you are by my side." She clasped her hands together. "Please?"

Before they could answer, a voice behind Sophia said, "What is this? Could it be?"

Nathaniel! Sophia whirled around and ran to him, stopping just short of throwing herself into his arms. "Yes, yes, my love!" she said. "James and I will not marry. I shall announce it now. And you must come with us. Quickly!"

She went back to James and Persephone and pulled them forward. They did not resist.

~

JAMES CLASPED PERSEPHONE'S HAND IN A STRONG GRIP AS THE four of them ran up the stairs to the saloon where a crush of guests was milling about. They burst in before the footmen were finished opening the doors. Would she go through with it? Did Sophia Tresillian have the strength of character to do this very hard thing?

Within moments, every eye was trained upon them, people craning around to get a better view of this odd interruption to the festivities. Sophia didn't look at any of them, but marched straight up to her father, the others following close behind.

Eustace rose and picked up his champagne glass, tapping it with a silver spoon to quiet the already much less noisy room. "I believe this is the moment we have been awaiting, when Mr. Tresillian and I will share the joy of toasting the betrothal of—"

"No, Mr. Pentarrant."

Sophia's clear, confident utterance provoked a murmur among the guests that grew into a roar. James stole a look at Tresillian's face. He appeared more shocked than anything, but it didn't seem that he would collapse. Until the hubbub quieted, Sophia would not be able to continue her announcement.

Eustace leaned toward James and said in a harsh whisper, "What is this nonsense!"

"I believe the lady—"

Before James could finish what he was going to say, another disturbance arose. Tonkin's normally calm and composed voice had risen to a near shout. "You cannot go in there, sir! You are not properly attired!"

But the door to the saloon flew open and a young man hardly more than a boy—disheveled, dirty, covered in slate dust so that his hair appeared gray—stumbled in.

"Robert!" James said and ran to catch hold of him before he collapsed on the floor at the feet of an overdressed matron. "What is it? Tell me man!"

Panting, hardly able to speak, Robert Penwarden—a young splitter—gasped out, "The quarry, Mr. Pentarrant. There's been a fall. You must come."

James saw that the lad's dusty face was lined with tear tracks. "Who, Robert? Who's hurt?"

Robert's lower lip quivered, but he managed to squeak out the name, "Jago. And others besides."

"No!"

James hadn't noticed that Persephone had followed him almost immediately and now stood by him, clutching the sleeve of his evening coat.

"Rowe! We'll need you!" James said and turned to Persephone. "You cannot do anything. Wait here."

"I will not!" she said. "I'll do whatever you say, only let me come!"

A crowd had gathered around Robert, who had recovered a bit. "I'll run ahead and say you're on your way," he said.

"No, Rowe will take you in his gig. There's no time to waste."

"How will you get there?" Persephone asked.

Without answering her James called out to Eustace over the growing hubbub, "Your best horse! Send down to have him saddled for me!" When Eustace failed to move or say anything, James barked at Tonkin, "Do it!" and the butler scurried away.

My God, James thought. How could I have let this happen again?

Ever desirous of being in the midst of scandal, Miss Vyvyan bustled over and placed herself directly in front of James. "You cannot ride in your evening clothes!"

James peered down his finely chiseled nose at her, scorn dripping from his words. "I can do whatever I wish. Kindly step away."

Just before he passed through the doors of the saloon, James looked back to see Eustace sunk into a chair, his face white. *He did this,* James thought, and he would believe it even without any absolute proof. "Eustace! You must come!"

Eustace shook his head. Then his wife stepped up to him and pulled on his arm, forcing him to stand, and pushed him in James's direction.

Good girl, Catherine, James thought, and dashed out to leap onto the horse a groom held in readiness for him at the front door.

PERSEPHONE DID NOT TRY TO FOLLOW JAMES BUT SPRANG INTO action. At first, the milling and talking guests impeded her, but she pushed her way through to Nathaniel, who still stood near Mr. Tresillian and Eustace and said, "You and Sophia must go in your gig, if you have it here. It has room for two I believe. Do you have your medical bag?"

"Yes," he said to Pentarrant, and then so Sophia said, "My love, you must—"

"Don't you dare tell me to stay behind!" she said, her eyes wide and hard as chips of sapphire. "I can help. I know more than you realize."

"That's settled," Persephone said, not giving Nathaniel an opportunity to argue with Sophia. "I must go too. Eustace," she said, "We can take James's curricle." Eustace was about to protest, but Catherine had a firm hold on his arm and a determined look on her face. "You can drive, I assume, Eustace" Persephone said.

"Yes, yes, I suppose I must."

"What about me, ma'am?" Robert said, who had come to join them after being revived with a tankard of ale by a fast-thinking footman.

"You can stand up behind in the curricle," Eustace said.

Persephone was about to hasten away to put these plans into immediate action when an iron hand clasped her upper arm. She turned, ready to struggle with whoever it was who dared to accost her in that way, and found herself facing Squire Carlyon.

"A rock fall is no place for a lady," he said, staring sternly down at her. "You will not be permitted to behave in so impulsive and reckless a way when we are wed."

Gone was the jovial, benevolent lord of the manor. Persephone was a little shocked. Would he have been a tyrannical husband?

"Besides, it isn't safe." Carlyon's expression softened. Perhaps his gruffness came from fear. She could not fault him for his genuine concern for her safety.

She put her hand over his and gently loosened his grip. "I realize that. But perhaps I don't want to be safe. I thank you for the honor of your proposal, but I cannot marry you. I'm sorry to have to tell you in this sudden way, but I have not a moment to lose. I must go and help James."

"James?" the squire said, a crease between his brows.

"Yes," Persephone said. She almost said, *the man I love. The man I shall marry if he asks me.*

The squire shook his head. His attention was immediately claimed by his daughter and Philippa Vyvyan, who rushed over to him and said, "Squire Carlyon! We must go and try to help. Order your carriage right now."

Persephone, somewhat surprised that Philippa would be so considerate of others, took the opportunity to escape and ran out and down the stairs to the front door where the curricle was already waiting.

As she climbed up to sit next to Eustace Pentarrant, Persephone's stomach clenched. Jago. Was he hurt? Or worse? And James had galloped off to put things right—and that no doubt meant putting himself in danger. He was that man. He would do everything he could to save the quarriers. She trembled with anxiety, but took deep breaths to calm herself. She mustn't arrive behaving like a hysterical female.

In her distress, she'd almost forgotten that mere moments before that she declined an honorable offer of marriage, one that would have conferred status far beyond any she ever thought possible and given her the kind of security that was the envy of many young women. But after what had passed between her and James, and knowing that Sophia was ending the engagement with him, she could not have done otherwise. It didn't even matter that James had not actually made her an offer.

Eustace set James's smart bays off at a brisk trot on the winding lane from Tarrant Hall. As soon as they turned onto the wider road, Persephone, seething with frustration, said, "Can we go any faster?"

Eustace looked back at Robert, who was on the back strap clinging to the rail. "Hang on boy," he said "I'm about to spring 'em."

Persephone barely had time to grasp the rail herself before Eustace cracked the whip over the horses' flanks and they took off at a gallop.

CHAPTER 36

For the rest of the short journey to the Delabole quarry, Eustace uttered not a word to Persephone. If he had, in any case she could not have attended to it. Her mind was engulfed with fear and dread about what they would find when they reached the quarry. She didn't know the details, but both James's reaction and Eustace's disordered countenance betrayed that whatever had happened could very likely be laid at Eustace's feet. This was no time for recriminations, though. All that mattered was the safety of the workers. Jago. A scrappy little boy, intelligent and eager, who had worked his way into her heart alongside James without her even realizing, was in great peril.

After what seemed like an agonizing length of time but was likely not more than fifteen or twenty minutes, the horses slowed and strained as they ascended the final hill before the quarry. The change in the rhythm of the pounding hooves woke Persephone up to what was around her as from a disturbing dream. Her ears were on the prick for the usual sounds of quarry work. But of course, nothing would be as usual because of the rock fall. Heart banging in her chest,

Persephone expected to hear shouting and crying and chaos braced herself.

But something much more alarming than voices raised in panic or screams of pain struck Persephone's ears when Eustace drew the horses up to a walk.

Silence. Or as near silence as mattered.

No more sharp ting of metal on stone or grating squeal of ropes and chains in pulleys. No heavy thumps of massive blocks of slate shearing off from the side of the quarry onto the terraces beneath them. Instead, other noises surfaced against a backdrop of quiet tension: The brittle scraping of small, settling stones. Hurrying footsteps and tense, murmured exchanges.

The sun was very low in the sky and had started its colorful dying throes against the patchy clouds, a blazing display that reached the level of the quarry where thick stone dust swirled, garishly lit by shafts of golden orange sunlight.

"Where is James? Why can't I see anything?" Persephone whispered. Eustace, whose pallid face was set in a grim scowl, did not answer her.

A peculiar smell lingered as well, reminding Persephone of the acrid aftermath of a gunshot. She reached for her handkerchief to wipe her watering eyes.

Eustace drove around to the north of the rim where the offices and the horse whims were located before he pulled the sweating pair to a halt. The nearby workhorses, standing still in their harnesses on their well-trod circles, nickered softly to the newcomers, and the matched bays shook their heads and snorted.

To the deadened sound was now added a dearth of human presence. Where was everyone? Only a handful of men stood about, not doing anything but looking down with brows furrowed, shaking their heads now and again, speaking in lowered voices. She caught a few phrases, "Down at the new bench," "Boy's trapped, it seems," "Shudna blasted yet." Each murmured comment drove a spike into Persephone's heart. She must do something!

After she had gathered her wits enough to act, Persephone jumped down from the curricle and ran to the stairs that led to the first terrace.

"Don't ma'am!" a quarryman called in an urgent, hoarse whisper, and before she could put a foot on one of the stone steps, a rough hand grabbed her upper arm. "Beg pardon, but it's not safe. Not fer you nor no one b'low."

At that moment a breeze blew in off the sea and cleared enough of the dust out of the way that Persephone could make out some evidence of the fall. At first she was relieved. The damage didn't seem to have affected the entire quarry. It seemed to be concentrated in one place at about the fourth or fifth terrace below her in the very center of the crater. The rim itself at that point appeared only slightly chipped away. Yet when Persephone looked more closely, she could see that with each terrace deeper, the damage became more dramatic. A gash as if a huge beast had bitten chunks out of the quarry wall started at the third terrace with a tentative nibble then became more and more ravenous with each subsequent level until it devoured a significant portion of what had been a neatly excavated series of five terraces. What had once been orderly paths wide enough for horses and carts at the top and for several men abreast and huge slabs of slate even on the main terraces were either nonexistent or buried in rubble down below. Splinters of wood were all that was left of a lattice of ladders that allowed for quick access between levels.

Even more eerie was that the walls of the quarry, once an organized hive of activity, appeared suspended in time. Workers must have stopped where they had been when the fall occurred. Persephone was ready to tear out her hair in helpless frustration. Why didn't they rush to safety? Get out of the quarry? It was only when she watched one man pick his way gingerly a few steps along a path and lose his footing on loose stones, sending them skittering down the sides, that she began to understand. The man steadied himself, but did not try to move again. How could they do anything, with the entire fabric of the quarry so unstable that any movement by anyone within it risked initiating another rock fall, or unbalancing precarious piles of rubble?

But James would know what to do. He had to. "Where is Mr. Pentarrant?" Persephone asked the man who still gripped her arm.

"Mr. Eustace, he just come. Over there." He jerked his head in the direction of the offices.

"I mean Mr. James Pentarrant."

"He's down b'low. Fifth terrace. They've got a rope around him, so's he don't come all a bits himself."

So far below! Was he with Jago? "How will he get everyone out?"

The fellow, his face gray with slate dust and his eyes red-rimmed, let go of her arm and scratched his head. "I wouldna like to say. Mr. James, he'll have to see who's trapped and what's stable, and then decide. It mun be slow like."

This was unbearable. Persephone didn't know how she'd expected she could help, but she certainly didn't think she would be relegated to no more than a spectator, idly watching the dance of life and death below, waiting for an outcome that was completely beyond her power to affect. "Is there no way to get down? To be of help?"

The quarryman shrugged, rubbed his chin ruminatively, then jerked his head toward the west side of the quarry. "It's a sight safer over there."

Persephone followed his eyes and saw a group of the quarry women clustered by the rim on that side. Someone had built a fire and it appeared they were boiling water. A few of them made their way down a path she hadn't notice on her previous visits that was adjacent to the worked terraces. It was only wide enough for people to pass single file. "Thank you!" she said, yanked herself free of his grip, then skirted around the buildings and equipment to reach the women, anxious to be doing something, anything.

Perhaps they would know something of James or of Jago. Of course he would be in the thick of it, risking his own skin for the sake of the workers. The thought terrified her. What if something happened to him? What if he were killed? The happiness that had seemed within her reach less than an hour ago now receded into murky distance.

"Persephone!" A familiar voice called out from the midst of the quietly busy women.

Sophia! Persephone had almost forgotten that she would be here too, her mind had been so occupied worrying about James and Jago.

"Thank heavens. I need you," Sophia said as Persephone raced over.

Sophia knelt on the ground surrounded by small piles of lint and bandages and a few pots of salve. "I had no time to get all my supplies," she said, waving her hand over the assortment around her. "Nathaniel didn't want to stop and wait. These are just what I take with me everywhere. He has some others in his medical bag."

Sophia's glorious ivory silk gown was now dirty and torn beyond what might have occurred by accident. Persephone watched, horrified and fascinated, as the heiress gripped her hem and tore the fabric along the grain, making neat strips that she then handed to the young girls to coil for use as bandages. She began to do the same to her own ball dress, thankful that she'd worn a long shift beneath her stays.

"Where is Nathaniel? What about James? Tell me everything you know," Persephone said, breathless. "What happened? How many are hurt, or..."

"Try to calm yourself, my dear. What's needed are sober heads and capable hands." She gripped one of Persephone's as she said this. "Which I well know yours are."

"You're right." Her hands shook as she continued to rip her gown. "How did it happen?"

"I don't know it all, only what I've been able to gather from overhearing some of the men talk. Apparently the overseer, a Mr. Bree? Or something—"

"Bray," Persephone said her voice tight with anger.

"Mr. Bray, then, insisted on blasting for the new terrace even though James had said not to, that it wasn't safe yet. Bray said Mr. Eustace ordered him to do it anyway."

Bray. Persephone wished he would stand before her just so she could knock him down. She knew the instant she saw him that he was evil.

Sophia paused and took a deep breath, which she expelled in a long sigh. "It apparently happened exactly as James predicted. The supports on the immediate upper levels were dislodged by the blast, and once one thing started to go, everything around it followed. Fortunately, most of the men were out of the way because of the blasting, and some had gone home earlier, but the repercussions sent shocks outward and men who thought they were completely safe slid down hundreds of feet."

Sophia painted a grim picture, which Persephone could imagine all too easily. "And Jago?" Her voice came out in a choked whisper. A vision of him with his hands bloodied from picking up sharp slate fragments swam before her eyes.

"We don't know yet. Apparently, he'd been sent down to help place the fuses."

"He's just a boy! Surely that's a man's job?"

Sophia shook her head. "I only know what I've been told. It seems Bray wanted to punish him for something."

If she could get her hands around Pasco Bray's neck, Persephone thought, she would willingly squeeze the life out of him. "I can't just wait. I have to find James and Jago if I can," Persephone said and rose, straightening her skirts.

Sophia looked up at her. "You must do as you wish. I have plenty of help here." She smiled around at the women and girls, busy getting blankets ready, rolling bandages, and boiling water.

Persephone had no idea if she was being utterly insane, but she followed a woman heading toward the rim with a basket full of bandages, and resolutely started down the path after her. It was narrower and steeper than it had appeared from afar, and putting a foot wrong could send her sliding down to the bottom of the pit, fathoms below. It would do no good to add her own injury to the situation, so she steadied herself and forced herself not to look down.

The lower they delved, the denser the stone dust became, and Persephone's eyes stung and her throat ached. She fished her handkerchief out of her pocket and clamped it over her nose and mouth with one hand, keeping the other on the packed dirt and stone wall next to her. She riveted her eyes to the woman's back and stepped just as she did, in exactly the same places, no faster, and together they made their careful way down to what was left of the fifth terrace.

This terrace was only deep enough to accommodate a few people at a time—more a bench than a terrace. Nonetheless, what Persephone couldn't have seen this far down through the dense stone dust from up on the rim was that about a dozen men sat and lay sprawled on that stable but narrow strip of ground, holding their heads, clutching gashed limbs, and quietly moaning. A few women were already there, winding bandages around injuries they could see, comforting those who lay prone with their eyes closed. The woman Persephone had followed silently went to work, heading for a man gripping his forearm where blood was dripping out of a big gash.

"Persephone!"

A hoarse whisper from beyond the injured men caught her attention. "Nathaniel!" She whispered in response.

The sight of his calm, determined face eased her panic a little. They picked their way slowly toward each other until they were close enough to talk quietly. "Sophia is above, making bandages and organizing the women," Persephone said. "Where's James? Tell me he's all right! And what about…"

Nathaniel took hold of her arm and looked her steadily in the eyes. "He's doing what he can. Mostly he's preventing the injured from becoming more so by keeping them still. He's got a rope tethered to him. They lowered him down from one of the winches that's still holding. It was the only way to get to the worst of the damage."

So like him. "He's in danger! Why can't I see him from anywhere?" She peered past Rowe, but all that met her gaze was a wall of rocks of different sizes, stacked as if a giant had thrown them there for sport. She made herself ask, dreading the answer, "Has he found Jago?"

"The boy? Yes. He's badly hurt and trapped."

"Then he must free him! Right away!"

Nathaniel shook his head. "It has to be done with great circumspection. The large boulder that's on his leg must not be moved until the smaller rocks above it have been removed. Otherwise, they will fall and not only trap him more, but possibly kill him outright."

Persephone swallowed hard. This was excruciating. Yet to do nothing but fret was intolerable. Activity, that's what she needed. "Tell me how I can help you here," she said.

"Mostly you could just find out how badly hurt these men are. Any who are incoherent could have dangerous head injuries, but I can do nothing for them until we get them back up to the rim, which won't happen until stable supports are replaced. If I know which ones they are, though, I can make sure they're first to go up. Oh, and watch for falling rocks. You'll hear them first. Press against the wall and put your arms over your head if that happens."

She nodded and turned away—partly to commence doing as he bid her, partly to hide the tears that had at last begun to make their way down her cheeks.

CHAPTER 37

James had never done anything like this before. The previous rock fall, although fatal to the three boys, was smaller and limited to one side of the quarry, and by the time he arrived, it was too late to help them. What in God's name had Bray done to cause such massive destruction? James knew that just then, so soon after it happened, the damage appeared worse than they would find it to be. But that did not lessen the immediate danger. He must proceed slowly if he wasn't to lose all possibility of releasing Jago Penwarden from where he was pinned, right at the bottom of the quarry on the edge of the proposed new terrace, surrounded by an unstable berm of loose slate fragments.

The immediate hazard was that the ground water seeping from the new digging near the shallow lake in the center of the quarry would find its way into the cavity where Jago lay, unable to alter his position and escape being drowned even in only a little water. In less than an hour, it had seeped several inches closer to the trapped boy. Before anything else, he would have to get some loose stones and try to direct the water into a channel away from Jago.

He called up quietly to the two men above him. "Get the terrace where the worst damage starts shored up, then work your way down, terrace by terrace, until you reach this one. Work quickly but carefully. We only need a narrow strip, enough so that the boy can be hoisted up without destabilizing everything again." Even as he said this, one of the ledges above shed stone fragments, thankfully missing everyone below.

The men—the most experienced quarrymen who were not injured—began, like mountain goats, climbing up the ruined wall, somehow finding the few stones and declivities that would support their weight.

James tugged on the rope that held him suspended a little above the level of the ground. On that signal, the men far above him let him down inch by inch until he could stand at the base of the quarry. He gave two sharp tugs to tell them to hold him there. He'd seen Jago's booted foot sticking out beneath a boulder too big to move. It wasn't resting entirely on his leg, but had it pinned there, so the leg was likely broken rather than crushed. He couldn't see any blood from where he was.

"Jago?" he said, not shouting, but speaking clearly and sharply. "Jago Penwarden?"

No answer. The boy might be unconscious. If so, the job would be trickier, because if he came to suddenly, he might jerk and bring the smaller stones above him down on his head. The boy wasn't dead. James had seen his foot move slightly. At least, he hoped that was what it meant. If not, then the job would be one of restoring his remains to his family—something James had vowed he would never be in a position to do again.

"Jago?" he said once more, a little more loudly.

This time, a quiet moan answered him.

"Jago, listen carefully. We will get you out. But you mustn't move a muscle. Be patient. It will take some time, but everyone is doing their utmost to bring you to safety." James's heart pounded. This Jago wasn't just an unknown urchin. He was someone who was dear to Persephone. Not that it would have made any difference to how he acted in such a circumstance, but that fact added a strain of urgency that might not have been there for him. "Do you hear me, Jago? Can you say something so I know you understand?"

After another soft moan, a weak voice said, "Y-yes."

"Good. Now you don't have to say anything else. Just let me do my job."

With steady hands, James tested the pile of rubble above the large boulder, starting at the top and finding the stones that were loose enough and small enough for him to remove without shifting anything below or above them. It was slow work. Before long, his hands were raw and bleeding. But the pile of small stones at his feet gradually grew. As soon as he had enough of them, James placed them so that they would form a barrier to the encroaching ground water, channeling it off to the east. The trouble was that the ground was already so saturated that it would be impossible to stop it altogether. The best he could hope for was slowing it.

As he worked, the light in the quarry, which was already tenebrous, faded to darkness. It took some time, but soon torches were lit, starting at the rim then being handed down terrace by terrace until they reached the one above him. These shed just enough light for him to continue seeing what he was doing.

James was not a devout man, but every prayer he'd ever learned as a child came to his mind as he worked steadily. It was a way to keep his thoughts from circling back to his anger at Eustace and Pasco Bray. Such feelings were out of place right then.

One stone. Two. Three. Four. A hole opened and let in enough light for James to see through to where the boy lay. A gash on his cheek oozed blood, and one arm was twisted in an odd direction. But nothing rested on his chest or abdomen. Perhaps he had escaped without internal injuries, which were the ones that most often had fatal results. Another stone. And another. And another.

It might have been an hour later, or four. James could not say. The sky above—what he could see in patches revealed when the dust cleared—was pocked with stars. By now, he stood nearly ankle deep in water, and it had begun to seep into the cavity where Jago lay. The large boulder was still in its place. But if more water found its way beneath it, would it settle and crush the boy? They would have to act quickly.

He tugged twice on the rope, and the unseen workers above hauled him up to the level of the terrace immediately above. There, he could see that work putting a massive wooden beam into place with rocks behind it was well underway.

"How is it up there?" He asked.

"Sir, your hands!" It was young Robert, Jago's brother, who had insisted on being a part of the rescue team. He pointed to the lacerations on James's palms, which streamed with blood.

"Never mind that. How long until we can get a hoisting tray down here? Where is Rowe? We'll need his help making sure we don't injure Jago any more than necessary to get him free."

Suddenly James felt the physical exhaustion he'd been

ignoring ever since he arrived at the quarry, and his arms began to shake. *Not long now,* he thought making a supreme effort to conquer his fatigue.

He didn't know how long he waited there, every now and again picking his feet up to free them from the sucking mud. But when he was next aware of anything, two men were being lowered down beside him, and together with another man in the terrace above they were maneuvering a cast-iron flat wagon, suspended from drawing chains connected to the largest crane on the rim. One of the men was the man James knew to be the strongest in the quarry, Barstow. He'd win every wrestling match he entered, and was known for miles around. He held two heavy iron bars. As soon as he was on his feet, he handed one of them to James.

The other was Nathaniel Rowe. Still in his evening silk breeches and stockings, brocade waistcoat and linen shirt. He grinned at the expression on James's face. "Bandages and a splint," he said, nodding toward his armload. "I'll stay out of the way until I'm needed."

Barstow squeezed his large self between the huge boulder and the rocky wall behind it. As soon as he signaled that he had succeeded in positioning his bar so that it wouldn't slip and hurt Jago, he indicated that James should do as he'd done about two feet away from him, down by Jago's feet. Braced against the wall of the quarry, they would likely have enough strength to lever the boulder up. But it would be tricky, because rather than sloping away from the boy, the ground tilted a little toward him. It was also possible that moving the boulder might clear the path for a rush of ground water. Thankfully the seepage was slow at the moment.

"Are ye ready, Mr. James?" Barstow said.

"Of course," James said, shaking himself out of the exhausted daze he'd fallen into as he watched Barstow work.

"We'll have to do it gradual like. Shoving the bars under

just a little. Might be Jago can inch hisself out of the way if we ease the boulder off him."

"Yes," James said. So many things could go wrong. "So, are you ready, Jago?"

The boy's eyes had been half closed, but the reflection of the torch on the terrace above danced in his now wide and frightened eyes. James realized the lad had spent enough time around the quarry to understand that if something happened and they lost control of the boulder, he could be crushed to death.

"You have my word you'll get out of here," James said. He meant it. Even if he had to throw his own body in the way of the massive rock to shield him.

Each of them took hold of the end of their bars. "On the count of three, sir," Barstow said. "One, two, *three!*"

Both of them put every ounce of strength into lifting the boulder up high enough to make it possible for Jago to get out, the stout iron bars bending slightly. Through gritted teeth, James said, "Can you wiggle yourself out?"

Jago moved, but emitted a sharp cry that echoed around the quarry, sending small stones skidding down from the still unstable berms.

"Good lad to try." James said, and met Barstow's gaze. "We'll have to send the boulder quite away."

"Do ye have enough strength left, Mr. James? If it falls back, he's done for."

True enough. And he'd have another lad's life on his conscience. But he wouldn't let that happen. "Yes. Let's do it, on my count this time."

Each of them braced their feet against the rock behind them and tightened their grips on the bars. James counted slowly, breathing with each word. "One...two...THREE!"

Faces purple with strain, James and Barstow levered the slab up on its end. For a moment it seemed as though it would teeter backwards, but James threw his full weight into pushing the bar, and in one slow, graceful movement, the boulder that had held Jago captive for what must have been eight hours by now tumbled over the slightly raised edge and rolled innocently a foot or two before becoming stuck in the groundwater-soaked mud.

James and Barstow stepped clear and collapsed. At that point, Rowe sprang into action. He soothed the frightened Jago, wrapped his twisted arm close to his body and put a splint beneath his broken leg. Then he and Barstow lifted him onto the wagon as gently as they could. The pain made Jago swoon.

"Probably best he's unconscious. We'll revive him at the top," Nathaniel said. "By the way, you should know that Persephone's here. She's been tending to the wounded."

Yes, James thought. It wasn't that he hadn't already made up his mind, but all that had happened that evening made him even more determined. They would be married. She would stand at his side for the rest of their time on this earth. She would make a quarry captain's wife to be proud of. More than that, to cherish, to love, to adore.

He pulled his attention back to the moment. Two sharp tugs on the ropes and the boy—who couldn't have weighed more than a few stone—was gradually hauled up on his iron bed, from one narrow terrace to another, until a cheer arose far above James.

When he heard it, he closed his eyes and wept. *Thank God,* he murmured.

Persephone saw the flat iron slab being winched down to the bottom of the quarry and knew that Jago would be on it when she next saw it, alive or not. She scurried off the terrace where only a few men remained to be tended and made her way back up to the rim as quickly as she could, then ran around to the horse whims at the center. She joined the crowd of quarriers watching, holding their breath, as the horses walked their endless circles and pulled the bed back up to the rim in agonizing slowness.

They wouldn't let her close enough to be able to look down into the quarry to see if Jago lay on the bed. Up it came, the squeal of the chains sharpening. All she could do was wring her hands and pray. When she tasted blood in her mouth she realized she'd bit her lower lip until it bled.

At last the iron bed crested the rim and five strong men ran forward to guide it to the ground, then lifted Jago off and placed him on a door that had been sacrificed to serve as a litter. With no heed to anyone around her, Persephone ran forward to Jago. His leg was splinted, his arm strapped to his chest, and a wound on his face covered roughly with sticking plaster. She knelt down by him and took his uninjured hand. "Jago. It's Miss Wilkins," she said, squeezing his hand gently.

Jago's eyes flickered open and a fugitive smile lit his face before he swooned away. She stroked his hand.

"He'll be all right."

Persephone looked up. It was Nathaniel, who apparently had been pulled up immediately after Jago. "James?" she said. Nathaniel pointed toward the rim.

There he was, loosing himself from the protective ropes that had worn right through his evening shirt. "James!" Persephone leapt to her feet and ran to him. Without a word, he folded her in his arms and she buried her face on his shoulder as sobs of relief shook her.

CHAPTER 38

The boy was badly hurt, but would survive, Nathaniel thought. A few of the men carried the litter to his house, where his mother had been well supplied by Sophia with salves and tisanes and Nathaniel had provided a phial of syrup of poppies to keep him quiet and soothe his pain.

By the time the rescuers had all reached the grass and the other injured persons attended to and removed from the pit it was close to dawn. Torches were burning low, and strain showed on everyone's faces. But Nathaniel had never been happier in his life. He looked around him at the odd assortment of people left in front of the quarry offices. Eustace Pentarrant, haggard and pale, paced up and down. Apparently his role had been to see that torches were lit and food and ale brought for the workers. Not enough, Nathaniel thought, to soothe his conscience, but something. James, bruised and abraded from his hazardous work with the rocks to rescue Jago, sat on an upturned bucket, gazing adoringly down into the face of an exhausted but happy Persephone, who perched on the grass by his side.

Some yards away, the squire looked on with a frown. Then his daughter and Philippa Vyvyan came over from where they had been busy directing the servants and footmen from Tresillian Manor and Carlyon Grange to clear up the crockery and tankards. Not a scrap of food was left, of course. Miss Vyvyan might be a meddling fool, still, she had risen to do what she could in this emergency.

And he and Sophia—they had set aside their disagreements and coordinated their work together, each of them taking on what was most within their power. Sophia, he discovered, had a natural ability to organize others. She'd helped turn the willing but somewhat chaotic group of quarry women into an efficient on-site infirmary to handle the injured as they gradually came up from wherever they landed after the fall.

Sophia. His Sophia. How could he ever have considered allowing her to slip through his fingers?

"What are you thinking about, Nathaniel?" Sophia, who'd been standing by his side surveying the scene, took his hand.

He pulled her around to face him. "I was thinking that even though we seem to have sorted ourselves out, we never actually made the announcement."

"Which announcement exactly?" Sophia said, a little gleam in her eyes.

He put his arm around her waist and pulled her to him. "Why, that you are going to marry me and James will marry Persephone."

"Is that so, Dr. Rowe? I don't believe you have actually offered for me."

At that, Nathaniel let her go and got down on one knee before her. "Miss Tresillian, I would very much like you to be my wife. But there is something you must know first."

Before he could continue, Philippa Vyvyan, who along with Lydia had busied herself providing food and drink to the diligent quarry workers, had wandered over close to them and interrupted him. "Sophia, don't be fooled by Dr. Rowe. Or should I say, His Lordship?"

Damn the woman! Nathaniel thought. What was she doing here?

"What do you mean, Philippa?" Sophia sounded more confused than vexed.

"He has come among us under false pretenses. He is not what he seems."

Nathaniel wanted to wipe Miss Vyvyan's self-satisfied smile off her face. What did she think she knew? If she had somehow learned of his true identity it would seem as though he'd intentionally withheld this from Sophia—which, in a sense, he had, but he wanted to tell her in his own way. "Let me explain," he said, standing again and taking both of Sophia's hands in his.

"You mean, there is some truth in what Philippa says?" In the wavering torchlight, Sophia's eyes sparkled—and not in a friendly way.

"I should say so!" Philippa said. "He is not Nathaniel Rowe. He is Nathaniel Rowe-Wisbeach, Viscount Axeley, of Bedfordshire. Lydia recognized him."

At this, Mrs. Tresize joined her friend and glared disapprovingly at him.

"As I said, Sophia, I want to explain, if you will just let me tell you," Nathaniel said.

At that, Sophia pulled herself up to her full height, which made her see nearly eye-to-eye with him, opened her mouth to say something, and then closed it again.

"So you see, Sophia, you have removed one obstacle only to face another." Philippa was positively reveling in being the one to deliver the shocking news. "There is no chance that your union will be acceptable to his father, the earl. You are from trade, after all. Lydia wrote to her friends in Bedfordshire telling them that the viscount is here."

If Nathaniel hadn't taken an oath not to harm others, he would gladly have wrung Miss Vyvyan's neck. His father would find out, and no doubt come to drag him home. "Please, Sophia! I didn't mean to lie. I mean, I didn't lie. And it's not true, what she says."

"You just didn't tell the truth! A fine distinction," she said, in a voice loud enough to attract the attention of everyone who remained there. That included her father. "And which part of what Philippa said isn't true?"

Nathaniel looked helplessly at Tresillian as he came into the pool of torchlight that illuminated the small knot of people from the party, all now showing varying degrees of dirt and dishevelment. "Sir, I had every intention of confessing all to you before I asked for your permission to offer for your daughter."

"Confessing?" Tresillian said. His face was haggard. The evening had been a strain on him, even though he'd been much better of late. Nathaniel would call on him tomorrow in his professional capacity as well as on personal business.

At that point, Lydia Tresize spoke up. "It was the talk of the county. The Honorable Nathaniel took his elder brother out on the hunt and bullied him into taking a rasper his horse couldn't handle. He was thrown and broke his neck, making Nathaniel the heir."

What? And this is what everyone thought? True, he was there on that day, but Andrew wasn't anywhere near him. How could such a vile rumor have been started? It sickened him. He loved his brother. And the last thing he ever wanted was to step into his shoes.

Nathaniel's feelings had been buffeted about from one extreme to another that day—from utter despair to elation to fear to relief—and now he was too exhausted to figure out what he felt anymore. "I don't even know where to begin to untangle all of this."

"Is Mrs. Tresize speaking the truth?" Sophia's voice rose dangerously.

"In some respects, yes," Nathaniel said, knowing he was digging himself into a deeper and deeper hole. "I'm just too tired to explain it all."

"Nathaniel." Sophia's troubled eyes searched his.

"I can't, not here. When you know all, you may judge for yourself."

"Come, Sophie," Tresillian said, holding his hand out for his daughter.

With hesitant steps, she went to him, taking one final look over her shoulder at Nathaniel before the footman helped her into her father's carriage. The coachman—who, along with all the other servants present, had done his bit to help the injured—lit the carriage lamps, mounted to the box, and gave the horses the office to go.

Nathaniel shook his head at Miss Vyvyan. "I don't understand you. Why must you do your utmost to spoil things for other people? You don't know the entire story. Nor do you, Mrs. Tresize, whatever you heard of servants' gossip in Bedfordshire. And now my father will doubtless make an unnecessary journey."

James and Persephone walked up and stood next to him, the three of them facing the squire, his daughter, and Philippa, line facing line in a standoff.

"I know the whole story," Persephone said, "And it reflects no discredit on Lord Axeley." She said to Nathaniel, "Come. It is nearly dawn. We are at the end of our nerves this night, and should all return home." She curtsied to the squire. "I owe you a better explanation of my own decision as well, Squire, and will write to you."

. . .

EUSTACE, WHO HAD WISELY STAYED OUT OF THE WAY, BRAVED James's ire and offered to take Persephone to her cottage in the curricle.

He looks deathly, Persephone thought as the predawn light washed any color from his face. *Good. Who but he should feel it?* "I shall walk," she said. "The sun is almost up, and my cottage is so close."

The two brothers faced each other in silence, and all around them activity stopped. James's jaw worked ominously. Persephone touched his arm and murmured, "There is no point. Not right now. Time enough for all that."

James slowly turned his eyes away from Eustace and met Persephone's searching gaze. One of the quarry workers brought James's borrowed horse up to him. "I'll walk you home," he said, throwing the reins over the horse's head and looping them on his elbow. He offered the other elbow to Persephone. She took it gladly, not just because she wanted to feel his solid presence, but because she was so exhausted she genuinely needed the support.

Both of them were too drained to talk at first. Persephone couldn't imagine what would pass between the brothers when the dust settled. In the meantime she hoped Eustace would have recognized his culpability.

They were halfway to the cottage when they finally broke their silence.

"You were wonderful—" "I wanted to tell you—"

They laughed. Persephone's heart was so full, her mind churning with things she wanted to say, that she just began to talk. "Do you suppose Sophia meant what she said? We had to rush away before she could make her announcement. And then, Philippa's thunderclap."

"Can you picture her marrying anyone other than Nathaniel?" James asked, squeezing her hand against his side.

"No, but what Philippa said this evening. I confess that I

knew it all. I didn't think it would ever matter, because Sophia had given up hope of marrying Nathaniel." She stopped walking. "You don't think less of him for his subterfuge, do you? I think he sincerely wants to help people. So ironic that his privilege should prove a hindrance to following his inclination and exercising his talent. I only hope Sophia can forgive him for what was, after all, an innocent deception."

"But is it true that he engineered his brother's accident?"

"Of course not!" Persephone said. "That's idle gossip. Mrs. Tresize did not move in the same circles in Bedfordshire. She was only repeating servants' tittle-tattle. Nathaniel was devoted to his brother."

"In that case, when he explains all, I'm certain she will accept him. She must. And I think his rank will have a beneficial effect upon old Mr. Tresillian. He nearly gave his daughter away to a mere quarry captain."

"A captain with a noble heart, though," she said, searching his eyes. The sun chose that precise moment to rise above the eastern horizon and bathe James's face in golden light.

He stole his hand around Persephone's waist and pulled her closer. She snaked her arms up and around his neck, and he bent to kiss her lips, softly at first, and then more deeply. She shivered and pressed herself against the length of his body. No one had ever kissed her like that, not in all her one and thirty years. Whatever he ultimately intended, she would cherish that kiss forever.

The gelding snorted and stamped a foot. "I think he wants us to keep going," James said with a laugh, releasing Persephone so they could continue toward her cottage.

Persephone's heart raced, and yet she had never walked home so slowly before. Normally she was eager to get to the comfort and safety of her own cozy hearth. Now it seemed as if comfort and safety were only to be had so long as James Pentarrant was next to her.

Too soon the cottage came into sight. A wisp of smoke curled out of the chimney. Hannah must have known what happened, had possibly been there herself at some point, and anticipated Persephone's needs so returned home to boil water for tea.

"Will you come in and rest a moment?" Persephone said.

"I will, but first, let's go to your barn."

Persephone assumed he wanted to tie the gelding up safely, and so acquiesced.

As they approached, Miss Pie's familiar nicker greeted them, followed immediately by a long whinny. Persephone gasped. "That's not Miss Pie!" She dropped James's arm and dashed forward to open the barn door.

The space was not large enough for any loose boxes, but there were two adequate stalls and room for tack. Miss Pie occupied the stall nearest the door. The other one had lain empty ever since Persephone moved in. She had a fantasy that she would one day fill it with a spirited riding horse. A horse like that beautiful chestnut she saw at the auction and again running free in a field.

A horse like the one that now stood in her barn.

"I don't understand!" She whirled around to face James, who had looped his mount's reins over a hitching post and walked up to join her.

"I bought her that day. I always intended her for you. Then this mess happened with Sophia, and I wasn't certain what to do with her."

"Sophia could have ridden her," Persephone said, a little doubtfully.

He shook his head. "She was yours from the moment you saw her. I had decided I would find a way to give her to you."

Had he really felt that so long ago? Before he truly knew

her? "But she's much too dear a present for me to accept from a gentleman!" The smile she couldn't prevent gave the lie to her words.

He shrugged. "But not too dear to accept from your betrothed."

Suddenly Persephone could hardly breathe. She had persuaded herself, despite all that had passed between them in the previous twenty hours, that James would need time to recover from the shock of everything that occurred, in his personal and professional life. She had permitted the kiss, deciding that if necessary she could mark it down to the heightened emotions of the day.

It seemed that she was wrong.

The next moment, James was down on one knee, clutching both her hands in his. "I know I look like a common laborer, and I've pushed you into a corner, but Miss Wilkins—Persephone—will you consent to be my wife? I don't promise you riches, or a life in the center of society, or—"

She put her finger against his lips to stop him. "Yes, you ridiculous man! Of course I'll marry you!"

Before she could draw breath, Persephone found herself once more engulfed in James's strong embrace, being kissed with more passion than she had ever hoped to experience in her life. When they at last paused to catch their breath, Persephone said, "We'd better go inside and have some tea. I'm not sure my knees can hold me upright any longer."

"No? I can help with that."

In one swift movement, James swept Persephone off her feet and carried her to her door, where Hannah waited with a huge smile on her face.

"Yes, Hannah," Persephone said. "I think there will be some changes ahead."

CHAPTER 39

Sophia was so exhausted by everything that happened that she did not leave her bedchamber for three days. Not merely physical exhaustion, but the maelstrom of emotions that tormented her kept her tossing and turning in bed. She thought she might have a fever, but on the third morning, she felt herself again. She had no idea what had happened outside of her isolated realm, and knew that it was past time to face it all.

She emerged from her bedchamber at last well after noon on the fourth day after the rock fall, the memory of dreams of falling rocks and bloody limbs, of Philippa Vyvyan's triumphant face, and of Nathaniel's sad eyes still tormenting her. One thing Sophia knew for certain about Nathaniel: She would not marry him if it meant relinquishing her purpose in life and becoming a vapid society hostess. Lydia said she'd written to the earl, his father. Now he would know everything and come to bring Nathaniel back to Bedfordshire, where he belongs. It would be the end of his dream, too. Whatever she might think of his deception, Sophia recognized Nathaniel's passion for medicine, his true desire to heal his fellow creatures, and loved him for it.

It was a beautiful fantasy, while it lasted. A fantasy that seemed real in the face of that terrible disaster. The two of them working side by side to improve the health of the community—she for the everyday complaints of the women, he for the more serious illnesses. Sophia allowed herself a moment of daydreaming, gazing out of the long windows in the drawing room to the manicured gardens of Tresillian Manor. *Just there,* she thought, her eye drawn to the patch of lawn she'd identified as sunny enough to turn into her own herb and medicinals garden. She would start tomorrow.

A light knock on the door was followed by Hosking's entrance. He cleared his throat. "A caller, Miss," he said, holding out a silver tray on which lay a single card.

Nathaniel? Was she ready to see him? She took the card. After staring at it for a moment, she tapped the edge of it against her palm and gazed into the middle distance. "Is my father at home?" she asked.

"Yes, Miss. He's in the library."

"Would you ask him to come in here please, and after he does, bring our visitor in."

"Very good, Miss."

Hosking bowed and withdrew. A moment later, her father entered the drawing room, a worried frown on his face. "Are you well, Sophie? I was quite worried, you know."

"Yes, I am completely fine. Better now. Clearer. I wanted to show you this, and ensure you were here when our visitor comes in." She handed him the calling card.

He read it over several times, even though all it contained was a name. "What can this mean?"

"We shall find out at any moment."

As soon as the words were out of her mouth, Hosking

opened the door again and announced, "The Earl of Morecroft."

Sophia sank down in a curtsy of the precise depth required to acknowledge Nathaniel's father's rank, but no deeper. Her father, who had not attended an exclusive seminary in Bath, strode forward and put out his hand. "You see my daughter Sophia. I'm Tresillian. How d'ye do."

Sophia could see the man's resemblance to his son despite the fact that the earl's dark blond hair was threaded with gray and his brown eyes somewhat red rimmed. But he had the same profile and athletic build. He'd arrived in impeccable morning dress and carried himself as one who was fully aware of his consequence.

No one spoke for a moment. Finally Sophia said, "Won't you be seated, My Lord?" and gestured toward an armchair.

He bowed slightly. "In a moment. I would stand to say what I came to say."

"Would you mind if my father sat? He is not in perfect health and tires easily. We have had a harrowing time, which no doubt your son has told you about."

"He did indeed. It was one of the many astonishing things he told me when I arrived from Bedfordshire late last night." He nodded to Tresillian, who cast a grateful glance at Sophia and sat on a sofa in front of the long windows.

"Now, sir," Sophia said, "If you will proceed." She steeled herself to hear the worst. To be told that Nathaniel would be leaving Camelford to return to his father's estate, giving up his practice of medicine. *I can bear it,* Sophia thought, lifting her chin.

"My son related to me the extraordinary facts of his medical training and licensing, and his journey to Cornwall to establish his practice here. I confess, neither I nor my wife had any idea of his ambitions in this regard. No doubt we would have discouraged him. He was fortunate in having the support of his late brother." The earl paused and cleared his throat.

Of course he's still grieving, Sophia thought, and her icy resolve melted just a little.

"He also told me he had met and fallen in love with the most extraordinary lady. One whose spirit and wit he had never hoped to encounter. He described your valiant efforts at the quarry, Miss Tresillian. He tried to describe your beauty as well, but I now see he made poor work of it.

"The viscount made no attempt to deceive me about your humble origins, Tresillian. And I confess, we had hopes that Nathaniel would choose a lady of his own order to wed, thereby continuing the impeccable breeding of the Morecroft line. But it seems he has made a different choice. He is of age and may marry as he chooses. But I have some misgivings about the suitability of the match."

At this, Sophia took two steps closer to the earl. Did Nathaniel have the same misgivings, at heart? "I, too, have misgivings, My Lord, but only since discovering your son's true identity. Before that, I saw nothing more than a sincere, loving, dedicated young gentleman whom I would be proud to call my husband. You speak of breeding as if your family were a line of race horses. I am all too familiar with that way of thinking from my years in Miss Crandall's seminary in Bath. I made a vow to myself that I would never be treated as an inferior in a marriage because of it.

"And I assure you, I was not taught to address in this forthright way someone so much my superior in rank as you are, My Lord. But all that so-called education could not erase my character. This, as you see me, is my character." She spread her arms wide. "And I am as proud of my breeding as any princess of the blood royal could be." She walked over to stand by her father and rest her hand on his shoulder, which he covered with his own.

The earl was silent for a moment as he looked at the two of them, an inscrutable expression on his face. Then, as Sophia watched in amazement, his face relaxed and he slowly smiled—a smile that transformed him and made his eyes come to life just as Nathaniel's had. *He must have been so handsome,* Sophia thought, and couldn't help smiling herself.

Morecroft spoke again. "I said I had some misgivings about the match. You, Miss Tresillian, have just reassured me that my son has made a wise choice. I may never be fully reconciled to his marrying into trade—apologies, Tresillian —but I could hardly imagine a more fitting partner for him in his chosen life."

He walked forward to Sophia with both his hands out, taking hers in a firm grasp. "If you have no objections, my son has empowered me to ask your father's permission to pay his addresses."

A heartbeat later, earl or no earl, Sophia flung her arms around Morecroft's neck.

EPILOGUE

June, 1816

Persephone and James held hands as they climbed up the steps of Tresillian Manor to visit Nathaniel, Sophia, and their new baby son, Peregrine. It was early to pay such a visit—the baby was only two days old, and Sophia had not yet left her bedchamber—but the note from Nathaniel to Penterrent Lodge had insisted. *Queen Sophia demands your presence to welcome the Honorable Peregrine Rowe-Wisbeach into the world.*

How like Sophia, Persephone thought, to want to reenter the world as quickly as possible so she could get back to work. Did she realize how much that tiny bundle would demand of her? Persephone doubted it, but Sophia was not one to be daunted by anything.

Hosking greeted them with an uncharacteristically broad smile, and said, "That's three generations I've seen born in this family." Persephone swore she saw the glitter of tears in the corners of his old, watery eyes.

He wasted no time, however, in ushering them up to Sophia's bedchamber, where they found Nathaniel seated in a chair by her side, clutching one of her hands, and a nursemaid standing beside a cradle.

"So, my dear friend, how did you weather the delivery? I hear you had a bit of a time," Persephone said, taking the chair on the opposite side of the bed while James wandered over to stare down into the cradle.

Before Sophia could answer, Nathaniel broke in with, "She did, but that didn't stop her ordering everyone around as if I was the one giving birth and she was the midwife!"

They all laughed and fell to sharing the usual commonplaces about new babies, neighbors and friends, the quarry, and business.

"Tell me, Persephone, how many students do you now have in your school?" Sophia asked.

"Fifteen! I'm afraid the building will soon be too small for us."

Not long after Persephone and James were married at Penterrent Lodge by special license the previous June, he told Persephone that the unused structure she'd noted on one of her first visits to the quarry was meant to be a schoolhouse, although he hadn't had the time or inclination to carry the idea to completion. Now it was Persephone's domain, and she held classes there every Sunday afternoon for any of the quarry children—and one or two of the older workers—who cared to come and learn how to read and write and do sums.

But that wasn't the only newly apportioned building on the quarry grounds. James had given Nathaniel and Sophia an abandoned horse shed to convert to an infirmary. Sophia did all the ordering and stocking of tinctures, salves, and bandages—anything that might be needed to treat the common injuries and illnesses of the quarry workers—and held monthly clinics for the women, so they could discuss their particular ailments and concerns out of the hearing of husbands and children. One of her first patients had been The Honorable Catherine. Sophia recognized that her loss of blood when she delivered her daughter had weakened her excessively, and that the bleeding so often prescribed by medical practitioners who didn't know what else to do was more harmful than otherwise. Sophia put her on a restorative diet to strengthen her blood, and within a few weeks she was back to her usual self.

The local gentry thought it altogether odd, this arrangement. That a viscount would be permitted to continue practicing medicine like any humble country doctor was unheard of, let alone that a viscountess would be permitted to not only mix with the scaff and raff, but to tend to their needs. They could not have known that it was all part of an agreement Nathaniel had reached with his father: He would return to the estate—with his wife and any children—three times a year, and make a month-long appearance in London during the season. Since he was safely married and needn't fear the machinations of ambitious mamas, Nathaniel acquiesced. One day he would have to relinquish his life in Cornwall and accept his position as earl. But his father was healthy, so that time was long in the future, he hoped.

The other part of that agreement was that he and Sophia could also be married by special license, quietly, at Tresillian Manor. Sophia thought it would be more fitting than a grand wedding so soon after having jilted her previous fiancé. And they didn't want to wait a moment longer than necessary.

"How long, do you think, until we can all go for a ride?" Persephone asked Nathaniel with a mischievous twinkle at Sophia. She referred to their habitual outings every week: James on Arrow; herself on the chestnut mare she named Grace; Nathaniel on the handsome hack he'd had sent from Bedfordshire; and Sophia on the ever lively Pennyroyal.

"At least two months!" "Only a week or two!" Nathaniel and Sophia spoke at the same time and they all laughed.

"In that case, I say a month, if all is well." She gave Nathaniel a reassuring wink then rose and went to join James by the sleeping infant's cradle.

"Are you envious?" James whispered.

Persephone shook her head. "I'll take my life however the Almighty sees fit to give it to me. Besides, you're enough to handle all by yourself!"

He put his arm around her waist and gave it a squeeze.

That was all she needed, and it was something she used to think she could live without. How wrong she had been. There may never be children, but she would always be the loving aunt to Sophia's progeny, and of course Antonella's and Belinda's. She and James had visited them at Atherleigh and the two men had become friends as well. James was fascinated with the hawking, and Atherleigh expressed an interest in seeing the quarry—perhaps becoming an investor.

Persephone fleetingly wondered what her father would have thought of it all. The world was moving too fast for the likes of him, she mused. Napoleon defeated at Waterloo. Great strides being made in steam power beyond even what Trevithick imagined. A new safety lamp would make it easier to see in mines and quarries without hazardous naked flames. And vaccinations that might prevent terrible diseases were gaining acceptance at all levels of society.

We live in a remarkable age, Persephone thought. And young Peregrine would—God willing—live to see many more marvels come to be.

But Persephone was happy with what *was*, in that instant, in that place. Life could never be better than this. Not just personally, but in the community, the quarry. Eustace had retired from any direct management of the works, putting everything into James's hands, and Bray had been pensioned off. A younger and more humane quarryman now managed the boys who scurried around collecting the helling stone. None of them felt the sting of the switch anymore.

She smiled up into James's face. "Let's go home. I need to plan tomorrow's lessons."

"As you wish," he said, and tapped her nose with his index finger. "How will you survive without your students when you go to London?"

Persephone laughed. "I'll be fully occupied with a former student then, I imagine!" She had long promised Belinda a visit, and Lady Lewiston expressed a wish to see her as well. It would be the first time she had left her husband's side since their marriage. But he vowed to overcome his aversion to the metropolis and join her as soon as he could be spared from the quarry. "Perhaps I should delay my visit until Nathaniel and Sophia make their next appearance during the season?" The season. How odd that would be!

"What are you two plotting and planning over there?" Sophia said.

"Oh, nothing much. Just making sure the future lives up to its promise." Persephone snuggled herself closer to James, tucking her head beneath his chin. She could not imagine anyone being happier than she was. Not the wealthiest nabob nor most powerful royal prince. She had learned that what mattered was not earthly possessions or rank. What mattered was this, she thought, placing her hand over James's heart. It was his greatest gift to her. His love. His heart. His generous, compassionate, noble heart.

ALSO BY SUSANNE DUNLAP

I hope you enjoyed *The Teacher's Noble Heart.* This is the fifth book in my series of *Double-Dilemma Romances.* While all five books can be read as stand-alones, you'll meet characters in them that have been introduced before.

Start the series: *The Dressmaker's Secret Earl*

Here's a peek at Chapter 1:

Tired, travel-weary, determined Augusta Hastings descended from a grueling ride on the London stage clutching all she could carry of her possessions in a single valise in one hand—and in the other a slip of paper that she hoped would lead her to her future. She had just given her rumpled skirts a straightening twitch when a man's voice screamed from behind her, "Out of the way, damn you!"

Two galloping horses pulling a high-perch phaeton bore down on her so fast she hardly had a moment to think. She leapt to the side just in time to avoid being run over, and—*splat!* Heart plummeting, she looked down. As she feared, she'd landed plop in the middle of an an ankle-deep, foul-smelling puddle, and the moisture was fast wicking up her best pelisse on its way to her knees. "Oh, blast your —" Augusta stopped herself before uttering the vilest curse she could think of. Which, being well born and gently bred, would not have been very vile. Not enough, anyway, to express her utter dismay at being mud-spattered and drenched when it was imperative that she look well-dressed and highly presentable.

Not the way to appear when entering on a career in fashion.

Before she could gather her wits enough to decide what to do next, a curricle wheeled around the corner nearly as fast as the phaeton had moments earlier. Augusta prepared to shrink even farther back against the brick wall of the coaching inn. This time, though, the much more skilled driver pulled his spanking pair of chestnuts to a halt in front of her. Instead of simply driving on, he touched the handle of his whip to the brim of his hat and said with a chuckle, "Did that rascal Lewiston nearly flatten you? He didn't mean it."

He was laughing at her. How dare he! She drew herself up, craned her neck and shielded her eyes from the bright sun behind the gentleman. A man of fashion, clearly, but the expression above the expertly tied neck cloth and many-caped drab driving coat was kind rather than haughty. A smile lifted the corners of his mouth, and he looked her over with a shake of his head. "Gudgeon!" he said.

"Sir! I—"

"Not you! The marquess!"

She pressed her lips together and lifted one eyebrow. After all, she couldn't deny the absurdity of her situation.

"But truly, have you suffered any lasting injury?" he asked.

"As you see, I am unharmed."

The gentleman's gray eyes softened, searching hers. This sudden shift caught her unawares, and she found herself struggling against the urge to cry. No one had looked at her that way since the last time she'd seen James over a year ago, resplendent in his dragoon's uniform.

"I see you're traveling, ma'am," the gentleman said, suddenly all crisp politeness, nodding at the valise dangling from her hand. "Have you just arrived on the stage? May I direct you to your lodgings? Or better still, convey you there? Plenty of room for you, and we could squeeze in a chaperone if need be."

A bell of warning clanged in Augusta's mind. She must look like a bedraggled waif, ripe for plucking and ruining, all alone without a chaperone in sight—and she was exhausted. The constant sounding of the yard of tin at numerous toll gates, the rocking of the stage coach on rutted roads, and being squeezed in among five other passengers had made it difficult to get so much as a wink of sleep. She said, with a sigh and a note of reluctance, "I thank you, no. I am traveling alone."

"Ah. You are wary of trusting a stranger. Quite right. But truly, I would be very happy to help you on your way and lend you my paltry protection. My friend has done you a wicked turn." The spark of amusement leapt back into his eyes. "He's doing his best to become a top sawyer!"

She couldn't help smiling at this and saying, "Those poor horses! But I beg you not to trouble yourself." Then she remembered the paper she held crushed in her hand. She'd read it over at least a hundred times, hoping it would reveal a morsel of information that might help her find her way in London, but to no avail. "However, if you would be so kind, you could render me assistance by informing me which way I must go to reach Madame Noelle's establishment in Curzon Street."

"Hah!" he said, his face brightening, "I know it well. I've shepherded my sister to that door more times than I can count. It's too far to walk from here and you'll find a hackney very uncomfortable. You might as well let me take you there. It's the least I can do to atone for my friend's folly."

He reached down with one gloved hand, gazing at her with a look of entreaty. "Well, don't leave me stopped in the middle of Piccadilly," he said with a quick glance over his shoulder, where several carriages and barrows had stalled behind him, their drivers leaving Augusta in no doubt of their feelings on the matter. "I'm a much better driver than the marquess, I promise."

Before she had a chance to decline the offer, the gentleman bent nearly in half so he could grasp her hand and held it too firmly for her to get out of his grip. He smoothly lifted her as she took a step onto the board, drawing her up and into the open carriage with a little too much force. As a result, Augusta landed heavily on his lap and nearly lost hold of her valise. Laughter erupted among the curious bystanders, and a little boy pointed at her and said, "Look Mama! She nearly took a toss!"

Mortified, Augusta slid herself to the seat next to the gentleman as far as she could without tumbling down into the road. What must he think of her? She straightened her back and lifted her chin, stowing the leather valise firmly between her feet. "I do beg your pardon, My Lord," she said, deciding to over rather than underestimate his rank.

"Please do not trouble yourself. As you see, I am unharmed."

A choked laugh escaped her as she recognized his teasing echo of her own words. "I am relieved to hear it!" she said.

"Now that we have established that we have both survived the hazards of London carriage travel, allow me to introduce myself," the gentleman said, bowing slightly in her direction. "George Lanyon, Earl of Bridlington, your servant. Whom do I have the pleasure of escorting? I assume you've come to order your gowns for the season?"

"Augusta Hastings, My Lord," she answered. "And I am not here as a customer of Madame Noelle but as an employee. I am a seamstress." And as a seamstress, she hoped, it was entirely expected that she would travel sans chaperone.

"Hastings—any relation to the Earl, or any of the Grantleys?"

A quick flush spread up from her neck. "Of course not! I mean, no," she stammered.

This time Lord Bridlington's appraising gaze was unmistakable. Thankfully, he was forced to look away in order to maneuver his horses through a crush of crossing traffic. That accomplished, he said, "I am sorry. From your voice and your carriage, and under the mud on your ensemble, I assumed you to be a gentlewoman."

I am a gentlewoman, more's the pity. A gentlewoman with no desire to acknowledge it. A gentlewoman with ambitions more suited to a bourgeoise, and education appropriate to a bluestocking. A gentlewoman well aware that she should not be alone in a smart curricle with a man she does not know. "I would be grateful if you would set me down a short distance from Madame Noelle's. She has never met me, and I don't want to give her the wrong impression."

"Of course," he said.

They progressed in uncomfortable silence for a while. Augusta could hardly bring herself to look around at this hurly burly city she was hoping to make her home, afraid of accidentally meeting Lord Bridlington's disturbing eyes.

He pulled up the horses after they had traveled about a mile. "The address you seek is just there."

Augusta expected he would jump down and help her out of the carriage, but he remained seated. Perhaps the revelation of her assumed station in life had made him think he needn't treat her with further courtesy. So like a member of the *ton!* She supposed she must accustom herself to different manners in this world she was entering where, because she labored for a wage she would be beneath consideration. Yet Bridlington's expression told a different story. It was no less kind than it had been at the first. Definitely a contradiction.

Well, if he couldn't be courteous, at least she could. She stood and put out her hand for him to shake. "I can't thank you enough, Lord Bridlington. You see, I've never been in London before."

"And look how we've welcomed you!" He shook his head and took her hand just as the horses gave a little start of impatience and the carriage rocked.

Augusta was thrown off balance and had to brace her other hand on Bridlington's shoulder to avoid once more falling into him. For a moment, they were close enough that she could see the faint lines that led from the corners of his eyes, which deepened as a smile spread across his face.

And then he frowned, and his gaze shifted from her eyes to her mouth. Before she could guess what had caused this sudden alteration, he lifted his hand and touched the corner of her lips with his index finger, wiping gently. "There," he said, and held up his glove for inspection.

A dab of mud stained it. Augusta's cheeks flamed. "Oh Sir!"

He laughed and helped her stand upright and regain her balance. "I hope you will find the metropolis more to your liking once you've found your footing."

Again, he was laughing at her. But she couldn't help laughing at herself, too. Lord Bridlington held onto her until she'd climbed down to the flagway. Augusta drew her hand out of his with a little reluctance. It had felt for a moment like an anchor, something solid in her recently tumultuous life. She curtsied without meeting his eyes, then hurried toward the elegantly painted sign up ahead that indicated she had at last arrived to face the future she had chosen for herself.

****

Book 2: The Soprano's Daring Duke

A gifted soprano and a princess with a dangerous secret step onto the glittering stage of Regency society. Caught between music, scandal, and unexpected passion, two women find that love—like opera—demands everything.

Book 3: Miss Pauline's Perfect Present

An unsigned letter, an impossible order, and a looming deadline force Pauline Dawkins to rely on the one man she thought she could never trust. Together, they discover the magic of Christmas love in this holiday novella.

Book 4: The Falconer's Lost Baron

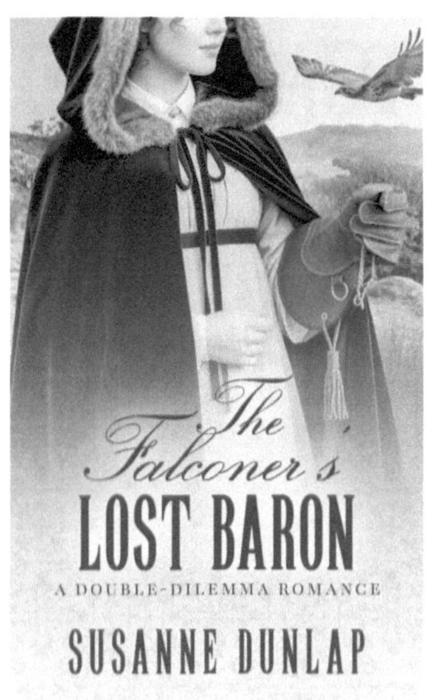

Antonella believes she is Lady Belinda's twin—until a devastating revelation strips away her identity and her place in society. Cast adrift, she clings to the only constant she's ever known: her passion for birds. But when rescuing an injured goshawk brings her face-to-face with Lord Atherleigh, Antonella must decide if love can bloom from ruin.

Join my newsletter and receive a free prequel novella!

Get *Miss Winthrop's Vanishing Viscount* free when you sign up for my newsletter. Simply scan the QR code below!

BE THE FIRST TO READ THE FINAL INSTALLMENT!

The final book in the Double-Dilemma Romance series will be out this summer. We'll return to London during the season of 1817, and characters from the previous five books will have roles to play in the story.

Be among the first to know when it's available! Join my newsletter!

HISTORICAL NOTE

Anyone who loves the Poldark TV series or who has read Winston Graham's fabulous books knows that Cornwall was one of the chief locations of copper and tin mines in the eighteenth and nineteenth centuries. What is less well known is the history of slate, another natural resource from Cornwall.

The recorded history of the Delabole slate quarry goes back to the fifteenth century, with evidence of possible earlier excavations. There are no specific records of exactly what the quarry and its surrounding buildings looked like in 1815. The quarry itself was likely not quite as big or deep as it is today, and there was no central village right nearby, more loosely organized collections of dwellings in small hamlets (Meadrose, Pengelly, and Rockhead as shown on an early Ordnance Survey map). The village of Delabole didn't really exist until later in the 19th century.

While there were certainly accidents and rock falls throughout its history, the accidents I put in this story are completely fictional—although plausible based on historical information.

Whatever the physical realities, life definitely revolved around the quarry. At the time, Delabole was the largest man-made crater in the world, and must have been awe-inspiring to someone seeing it for the first time.

The quarry still exists and is worked sporadically, mostly for heritage projects. It is largely a historical artifact.

Despite having done a lot of walking in Cornwall and Devon guided by the wonderful Ordinance Survey maps, I've never actually been to Delabole, so I had to rely on documents and images for this story. I intend to visit the quarry the next time I'm in England!

ACKNOWLEDGMENTS

Thanks are due once again to my intrepid beta readers, Margaret and Kayli, and to my patient book coach, Julie. And again, I thank Susan Babcock for her careful proofreading, which helps me put my books out into the world with confidence. It most definitely takes a village!

www.ingramcontent.com/pod-product-compliance
Lightning Source LLC
LaVergne TN
LVHW100507110826
845146LV00002B/547

* 9 7 9 8 9 9 3 8 5 2 6 8 3 *